BRUCE KELSEY
21 AUG 97
ID FLS ID

DROWN ALL
THE DOGS

Books by Thomas Adcock

Precinct 19
Sea of Green
*Dark Maze
*Drown All the Dogs

*Published by POCKET BOOKS

DROWN ALL THE DOGS

A Neil Hockaday Mystery

THOMAS ADCOCK

POCKET BOOKS

New York   London   Toronto   Sydney   Tokyo   Singapore

This book is a work of fiction. Names, characters, places, and incidents either are products of the author's imagination or are used fictitiously. Any resemblance to actual events or locales or persons, living or dead, is entirely coincidental.

POCKET BOOKS, a division of Simon & Schuster Inc.
1230 Avenue of the Americas, New York, NY 10020

Adcock, Thomas Larry, 1947–
    Drown all the dogs : a Neil Hockaday mystery / Thomas Adcock.
        p. cm.
    ISBN 0-671-77041-1
    I. Title.
    PS3551.D397D76   1994
    813'.54—dc20   93-30416
                                                        CIP

First Pocket Books hardcover printing February 1994

10 9 8 7 6 5 4 3 2

POCKET and colophon are registered trademarks of
Simon & Schuster Inc.

Printed in the U.S.A.

For my Aunt Jean and Uncle Fred Bradshaw

Acknowledgments

Thanks is given here for great help from the living and the dead, and from the shadows between these worlds. Among the first of this influential group are my friend Jeffrey Essman, the actor and writer, who is perhaps not a lapsed Catholic; my friend and dear editor, Jane Chelius, who one day on a train ride along the Atlantic coast of Spain encouraged me to write from the heart; and my wife, Kim Sykes, who is no less than the hope of me. The poet William Butler Yeats, who often worried that his verses might inspire the darker angels of man, died in 1939. Excerpts from his "Remorse for Intemperate Speech" and "A Full Moon in March" (published in *Collected Poems of William Butler Yeats*, Macmillan, New York, 1956) are used herein, with gratitude. The beautiful plays of the late Brendan Behan (1923–64), the borstal boy himself, first taught me to listen to personal ghosts dwelling in Irish shadows. And so I did in writing this.

—*Thomas Adcock*
New York

The fusion of belief and system produces the militant, a warrior fighting for an idea. In the militant, two figures are conjoined: the cleric and the soldier.

—*Octavio Paz*

Prologue

"I HATE IT! PLEASE GOD, I HATE IT."

Having said this, he was at peace with all he had told me this night.

He turned his head toward the wall, as if to feel a morning's warmth at the unseen window.

It was well past midnight, into black Sunday, but the time of day had no meaning for him. A smile played carefully across his face as he lay in his bed, a bed too big for him alone. I put my hand on his. He let it lie there atop his paper skin.

I asked, "What is it you hate?"

He drew a deep breath and his blind blue eyes closed. Then he quoted again, from what his mind still pictured of pages he used to read, time and again: "Out of Ireland have we come; great hatred, little room, maimed at the start ... I carry from my mother's womb a fanatic heart."

There was silence where I should have offered reaction, the kind of embarrassed quietude that tells an old man he has not been understood by a younger man. His useless eyes fluttered open and he said, with some exasperation, "It's the root of this madness I've grown to hate, it's old men at their windows I hate even

1

more." Then he lifted my hand away and said, "Now get you off." That would be all for now, whether or not I understood. He needed rest.

I walked to the door and opened it, but turned to look at him once more before leaving. He sensed this. His head rose slightly over the mound of blankets. He said, "When I'm gone, I want you to remember me."

I said, "Haven't I always?"

CHAPTER 1

IT WAS A GOOD WEEKEND, EXCEPT FOR THE DEAD PRIEST.

It was the weekend when it struck me hard how the past never passes, no matter how we try to bulldoze memory. It was the weekend I finally decided to become a serious character in the story of my life. It was the weekend that began the greatest case of my career.

At first, I did not see greatness; nor even a case, for that matter. But others were alert to the significance of events at hand, and those yet to occur. Ruby, for one. For another, Captain Davy Mogaill, my rabbi. As the captain would put it, "What grander case may a detective crack than the mystery of his own makings?"

This he suggested on a fine Saturday afternoon at Nugent's bar. This piece of wisdom, among others. For my part, I told my rabbi about Ruby, and about the sorry reason we had for flying off to Dublin that Sunday night.

No doubt it was somewhere during this good long boozy conversation of ours when old Father Tim first figured he had it coming.

Back to Friday, when this all started:
It was past five o'clock on an April afternoon that happened to

3

be my birthday, but I am not saying which one. Ruby telephoned to inform me as to how I would want to wear a nice suit and tie that night because of what she wanted, which was dinner at some East Side place with a style to which I am not accustomed. With Ruby, life now contains such announcements.

I said, "Well, I don't know—"

Ruby cut in with, "It's my treat."

To which I quickly responded, "So where do we go and when do we eat?"

She gave me the pricey address of a restaurant I have seen mentioned more than once in charity ball photo captions published in the *Times* and said we should meet there at eight o'clock sharp. Which gave me two hours and forty-five minutes to wind it up for the day at the station house, grab an overdue shave and haircut on the way home, shower and sit around in my shorts for a while with a couple of fingers of Johnnie Walker red, find the claim check to my good suit down the block at the Korean dry cleaner's, and have my shoes with the tassels shined. Then I would need a taxicab, preferably one with a driver who knew without my having to tell him how to get from my earthly place in Hell's Kitchen over across town to the planet of Park Avenue. I was the first to arrive, none too sharply. This was at a quarter past eight.

The restaurant had one of those names that was somebody's idea of terribly chic but which is my idea of just plain terrible. In English, I think the place would be called The Llama with the Ironic Wardrobe. I could see past the dimly lighted command post of the maître d'hôtel how the dining room was crowded up with somebody's idea of the New York smart set: gray eminences holding court for fawning thirtysomething executives in Armani suits, former wives of former potentates, Republicans of color, indicted Wall Streeters, glossy ladies with long legs and short résumés, and a passel of middle-aged white guys wearing aviator bifocals, Bijan suits, and little ponytails.

"*Oui, monsieur?*" The maître d' inspected me with sullen eyes, black as his dinner jacket. Then with a curl of the lip that must have taken him years of practice, he asked, "*Puis-je vous aider?*"

I was not impressed. It happens I know something about France, namely that it is a place where New Yorkers go in search of rudeness; short of traveling overseas, any French restaurant in Manhat-

4

tan will do. Besides which, this guy's accent had way too much of the Grand Concourse where the Champs-Élysées ought to be. And anyhow, I was feeling good and sleek in my charcoal wool worsteds and my rose necktie and my shoes smelling fresh and waxy. I may be the type who pays cash, but I am no peasant.

"I'm looking for a lady," I said. I wanted to add, Knock off the act, Pierre, we both know you take your tips home to the Bronx. But I held this thought. Instead, I said, "Maybe she's already here. I'll just take a look myself."

"Sir, I do not think so!" Pierre was flustered and shocked, the poor thing. He manfully placed himself between me and the archway into the dining room.

I said, "What—?"

He said, "I do not seat unescorted ladies."

"How come? Is this a fag joint?"

Then Ruby's voice from behind, with a laugh in it. "Oh, Hock—behave yourself."

I turned to watch her walk toward me. Outside, from the taxicab, her driver was taking a last look, too. This was the sort of thing I was trying to get used to; Ruby is something to see, and I am not the only man in the city with eyes for the job. She was dressed that night in one of those little black beaded numbers that sparkle in all the right places. There was a bit of gauzy wool fluff nestled around her bare brown shoulders, rhinestones around the décolletage, maroon on her lips and tiny diamonds pinned in her ears.

Miss Ruby Flagg, the actress, knows how to wrap herself up for a good review. And that night of my birthday, she was nicely wrapped indeed. Pierre, on the other hand, was having no part of the festivities.

Appalled by me, he appealed to Ruby. "Mademoiselle—*s'il vous plaît!*"

She told him simply, "Table for Detective Neil Hockaday."

Pierre inspected me again, this time minus the curled lip, maybe out of respect for the courtesy title but probably not. In any case, he consulted his reservations list, taking his sweet time about it before finally saying, "Ah, *oui*. Monsieur Hockaday—for two. *Très bien.*"

We followed him to a corner table. I was surprised how good

this seating was until I realized that Ruby probably did a lot of business here back when she was in the advertising dodge, and that she had no doubt spread lots of money around the place.

Not so long ago, Ruby wore female business suits and flogged a variety of potions that killed an impressive variety of body odors. For this she earned a considerable salary, with bonuses and a brisk expense account. A clever girl, she hoarded a good amount of this "silly money," as she calls it, and invested in Manhattan real estate—specifically, a slanty frame walk-up down on South Street, where she carved out an apartment and a way-Off Broadway theater supported not so much by ticket sales as by rents from the tailor shop and the restaurant down below.

That was a couple of years ago. But everybody from the old days certainly remembered Ruby Flagg. Beginning with our friend the maître d'.

"Thank you, Pierre," she said to him as he held her chair. I was left on my own. When his patent leather shoes went tapping away, I asked Ruby, "His name is really Pierre?"

"I don't know," she said. "But he seems happy when I call him that."

A wine steward dropped by and kissed Ruby's hand. I scowled stupidly. Ruby asked about his wife and his kids and he said the family was just swell. She sent him toddling off after a flowered bottle of Perrier-Jouët. Then she turned to me and said, "You know—you, of all people, shouldn't let the likes of him get to you."

I had stopped scowling by then. I was instead now stupidly smiling at the little cleft in Ruby's chin, and also the charming cleft in the scoop neckline of her evening dress. I said, "You're talking about Pierre?"

"You know what I'm talking about. Allow the man his pretensions why don't you? Where would you be yourself without deception on the job?"

That was an understatement. When I am on duty, it is rarely in a suit, not even the boxy kind from the A&S bargain basement I am sorry to say is favored by most detectives of my acquaintance. And to say my work clothes are plain could be considered felony understatement. Mostly I am dressed in Salvation Army castoffs I have collected over the years, all except for my own good old

6

Yankees baseball cap, circa 1963, and a pair of black PF Flyer hightop sneakers I have had since the days I was married to the formerly lovely Judy McKelvey and we lived in Queens in a cute house with a fence around it and were miserable and I coached a bunch of kids on the neighborhood P.A.L. basketball league. Irregularly shaven and dressed the way I usually am, you would likely not be able to single me out from a crowd of men with nothing to lose and nowhere to go, which is the basic idea of the SCUM patrol—which is for Street Crimes Unit-Manhattan.

This night, on the other hand, I had somewhere to go. In fact, miles to go before we would sleep. I changed the subject with, "Let's talk about the trip."

"Good idea," Ruby agreed.

The steward returned to our table with the champagne, poured out two glasses, set the bottle down in a bucket of ice and left. Ruby raised her glass and said, "To us and to Eire, and to your poor Uncle Liam—and besides all that, a happy birthday to you, my dear Hock."

So we drank to all that. After which I offered a second toast: "And now to Ruby Flagg, sure to be the most exotic woman in the streets of Dún Laoghaire."

Ruby laughed. "The only exotic, you mean."

"You shouldn't be too surprised to see a face or two as dark as yours," I said. "There was the Spanish Armada a few centuries back that left its mark."

"You like black Irish?"

"I like both just fine."

"That's not something most Irishmen would say." She laughed at me again. The way she did it, she made me like it. I stared at her perfect white teeth and her maroon lips and the tip of her pink tongue. I might have drooled.

Ruby asked, "What are you thinking, Irish?"

"I'm thinking of the two of us lying on a beach with sand white as sugar and you're talking to me in French. I look at you and think of things like that."

She rolled her bright hazel eyes and said, "I keep having to remember, you're not like most Irishmen, are you?"

"Neither is Uncle Liam," I said. "If you're worried he won't take to you, don't."

"And how did he take to your wife?"

She had to bring that up? "That was a long time ago," I said. "Was it?"

Now I could not help but think how good it is for the ego for a man such as me, somewhere in the middle of his age, to be the focus of a woman's abstract jealousy. Especially a woman who looked like Ruby.

"Long enough," I said.

"Sorry."

"Forget it."

"All right." Ruby fussed with a starched napkin. "But look, I am sorry about your uncle. It's a shame you're going to take me all the way over to the other side to meet him when he's . . . well, the way he is."

"Dying. You mean to say dying."

Ruby leaned toward me and patted my arm, the way people touch each other at funerals. Here was I, already thinking of such things as a funeral. I barely heard Ruby saying, "I just wish I could be going to meet your uncle under happier circumstances."

The news of Liam had come last week in a letter from Ireland, from one Patrick Snoody, my uncle's self-described "loyal friend." I had never heard of him. Snoody wrote to say that Liam and his weak heart were now confined to bed; he said Liam had "perhaps a year or better" left; he offered the standard Irish condolence, "I'm sorry for your troubles." And now, on Sunday night and under this sad cloud, Ruby and I would fly off to Dublin to show a frail old fellow that life goes on. It was the best I could do.

I said to Ruby, "I am not being morbid. I'm only facing the facts is all. Liam is dying and I think that's the word he'll be using himself."

A waiter came by to flutter over Ruby and ignore me. Eventually, he got around to taking our orders; and eventually, we got through dinner, which was very good and worth nearly all the money that Ruby had to pay for it. Then finally, as we loitered over coffee and port, up again rose that most unappetizing subject of all.

"What was she like?"

"She—?" As if I had to ask.

"You know who."

8

"For crying out loud, it's my birthday."

"So I bring you to this nice place and wish you many happy returns. Now I think it might be nice if you sing for your supper. This is asking too much? You know how to sing, right? After all, you were a choirboy once-upon-a-time, weren't you, Hock?"

Exactly when had I mentioned this? The most frightening thing about women is that they remember everything you tell them.

About the choirboy days, it was true. I was a soprano at Holy Cross Church on West Forty-second Street back when Harry Truman was in the White House, *Sunset Boulevard* was on the movie screens and shifty-eyed Communists were everywhere, working day and night to subvert the American way.

Father Timothy Kelly had been especially concerned about these Communists. He believed the reds were in league with Lucifer, and especially dedicated to the business of corrupting the youth of his parish. Thus, Father Tim hoped to lead us impressionable Hell's Kitchen lads toward the pursuit of our better angels by way of singing the Lord's songs. Father Tim had a particular interest in protecting me against the subversive forces of those days, as it happened I was the nephew of his great and good friend from Dún Laoghaire, my own Uncle Liam.

I had not thought of the boys' choir in a very long while. Nor of Father Tim, I am ashamed to say. Not since Father Tim had left the neighborhood for his professional reward: a room in a home for retired priests, on a leafy street in Riverdale, up in the Bronx. I visited him there once, about a week after he had moved out of sight. Then I telephoned three or four times, just to keep in touch like I promised. Then I became a typical shitheel and put the old fellow out of mind as well.

"When I was a choirboy, I sang to heaven," I said to Ruby. "On my wedding day, they told me marriages are made in heaven. So you'll understand if I don't much see the point of singing nowadays."

Ruby said, "Yes, and nowadays you don't much see the point of marriage. And so you'll be introducing me to your little old Irish uncle as, what—your main squeeze?"

"I wouldn't put it that way."

"How are you going to put it when you're face-to-face with Liam and he can't help notice that I'm there beside you?"

9

"I'm going to tell him we're slow-dancing together."

"Aha! The very words you've said to me, Mr. Charmer. Only now they sound too clever by half."

Absolutely everything they remember!

"What do you want out of me?" I said.

"You talk pretty, Hock, and I like it. But sometimes pretty's not enough." Ruby had been leaning toward me in her chair, and I had been enjoying the warmth of her breath and the heat of her caramel skin. But now she sat back. "When you talk about certain things, you have a way of turning words into walls."

"Certain things?"

"Your father, for instance. Your mother—"

I interrupted. "Pardon me, I thought we were talking about my wife. My *ex*-wife."

"Her, too. We're talking about all those hollow places of yours, where people have dug holes in you. If I dance slow with a man, I want to know where the holes are."

"Why—you don't want to risk falling into his troubles?"

Ruby smiled patiently, like she was a kindly nun and I was the big dumb slow kid in her classroom. "In the case of other men I've known, that's certainly true. But since you're a cop and there's nothing I can do about that, who knows but maybe I'll have to pick you up from time to time. So you see how I'll need to know where the holes are."

I went for a joke, for a wall. "I thought you only liked me for sex."

"I told you I was serious, buster. Meaning this dance of ours isn't entirely about glands. Besides which, I'm sorry to tell you, you'd be awfully alone in the world thinking of yourself as a Great Irish Lover."

I managed, "Remember—I'm not like most Irishmen, am I?"

My vanity was wounded, and Ruby knew it. And knew that I was off balance. So she asked again, "What was she like?"

"She had a great dimple."

"You got married because of a dimple?"

"Would I be the first man who fell in love with a dimple and then made the mistake of marrying the whole girl?"

"That's all you can say?"

"I can say that I'm worried how much I love the cleft in your chin."

"Is that a proposal?"

"For now it's a joke."

"What about your father? Do you want to make a joke out of him, too?"

She had struck me in a hollow place. "I already told you everything I know," I said. "Which is, I don't know much."

My unknown soldier father, of whom my mother, all her life, would only say, *"Your papa went off in a mist, that's all there is to it; it hurts too much to speak of him as if he was ever flesh and blood and bone to me."* Of whom his brother, Liam, on his many visits from Ireland after the war, would add nothing more illuminating than that.

Ruby had of course seen the photograph, maybe the only one there is of my mysterious father—the one that sits on the dresser in my bedroom. Private First Class Aidan Hockaday of the United States Army, in his stiff uniform, with the fear of God tailored into it; a handsome young Irishman who got himself missing in action somewhere in the war against Hitler and Tojo; the sound of him, and the feel of him, and the smell of him missing somewhere in me.

I have the photograph, and a deep sense of the man. I have heard his voice, in the form of his letters from the battlefronts of Europe. These my mother would share with the neighborhood ladies when women gathered in our parlor on Friday nights, to listen to Edward R. Murrow on the Atwater-Kent, to keep the homefront vigil. I was a boy in short pants eavesdropping from the other room as my mother read my father's words; knowing, somehow, that I should commit these letters to fiercest memory, even though I did not understand half what I heard.

But I never dared to write down the words, and so I have lost most of them. The letters are gone; gone with my mother to her grave. Ruby considers this a theft, and so do I.

Now, to Ireland this Sunday night. There to visit my only living relation, my dying Uncle Liam. To have him meet Ruby before he, too, leaves me.

Ruby. There she sat, across from me, through the candlelight.

11

But I was miles away. And yet, I heard her say to me, "Maybe you'll begin to know, with this trip. Do you really want to know?"

How many times, as a boy and as a man, have I risen in the night, believing my father's ghost was perched on the edge of my bed? How many times in my sleep have I reached out to touch this ghost, to hold something in my hand more than a single flash of Aidan Hockaday's life captured in light and shadow on a piece of photographic paper?

"Maybe I need a drink," I said. I flagged a waiter.

"For the record, I disapprove," Ruby said.

Much later, into the half-light of an emerging Saturday morning, I awoke to the ghost on the edge of my bed.

I reached out, clutching the usual air. I strained to hear words I knew the ghost wanted to speak. But nothing. Only the familiar disappointment of wakefulness.

I rubbed sweat from my face and neck with a corner of the sheet. Then I slipped out of bed, leaving Ruby there making her soft sleeping sounds.

I picked up my father's picture from the dresser, and took it with me out into the parlor. I set it on top of the things in my suitcase, which sat partly filled and open on the couch. Over in the kitchen alcove, there was yesterday's coffee in a pot on the stove. I put a flame under it, then went into the bathroom to scrub my face with soap and cold water.

When I was through, I poured out a cup of bitter black coffee and sat down on the couch next to the photograph. Just the two of us, father and son. *Do you really want to know?* If I did, there was one last chance for answers to the questions of Aidan Hockaday; they waited for me, on the other side.

Maybe the photograph would help the cause. I asked it, "Would you like to come along with me to Ireland?"

I decided that the ghost answered, "Why yes, I'd love to go with you, boy." And so I tried wedging the photograph between layers of clothing in the suitcase; then I got the bright idea that I might travel a bit lighter, and without breaking glass enroute, if I removed the photo from its frame.

The metal tabs in back of the frame were brittle, and snapped away entirely when I bent them back. Then I loosened the felt-covered pasteboard and slid out the picture. There was a musty smell, and a small puff of dust, nearly five decades of time and grit under glass.

I held my father's picture for several minutes, staring at it for the first time in my life without the barrier of glass. I touched the features of Aidan Hockaday's face; I touched a nose and lips and a chin that mirrored my own.

Then I placed the photograph facedown among my things in the suitcase. Which was when I noticed the writing.

In an elegant hand, in blue ink protected all these years from fading by the prison of a picture frame, someone had penned a poem:

> *"Drown all the dogs," said the fierce young woman,*
> *"They killed my goose and a cat.*
> *"Drown, drown in the water butt,*
> *"Drown all the dogs," said the fierce young woman.*

CHAPTER 2

HE SAT IN HIS ROOM, IN A CHAIR BY THE WINDOW THAT LOOKED DOWN
on a pretty and peaceful street. The girls who lived in the house
across the way played double-Dutch jump rope; a fat man smoking a cigar walked slowly along with his fat twin dog on a leash;
boys were gathered around the stoop of a house on the corner,
haggling over marbles. Saturday morning's strong sunlight dappled through the new spring green of maples and London planes
lining the block.

With a sigh of expectant regret that sounded a thousand years
old, he turned toward a ringing telephone on the table next to
him. He stared at the flashing light of an answering machine connected to the phone.

When the machine picked up on the sixth ring, there were his
recorded words: *"Father Timothy Kelly here . . . I'm not about just
now . . . Kindly leave your name and telephone number and I'll call you
back as quick as I can . . . Have a blessed day."*

The machine clicked once to receive and record a message.
There was the crackle of static. And with that sound, he knew,
the taint of the past intruding on the present.

Over the past two days, ten such calls had come to him. Ten

14

times he had not picked up the phone. Ten times, he knew who it was who refused to speak up. Yes, Lord, he knew.

But today, the caller spoke: "What is a true patriot?"

Father Timothy Kelly knew the voice. Yes, Lord. He placed a pale, spotted hand over his thumping chest.

The voice was full of the memories of another place: the dark slow waters of the River Liffey moving under O'Connell Street footbridges; February's wind hissing through hedges along clay roads beyond the city; his Wellingtons, mud-spattered, plodding through the dunghill behind the byre, where he and his brothers picked black-gilled mushrooms when there was nothing else for the family dinner . . .

. . . and later, before he had to leave the land of his youth, cloth hoods masking the faces of righteous comrades.

Had he not remembered this voice, and these words, so many times over the years? Had he not dreamed of them only last night?

Again, the caller asked, "What is a true patriot?"

There was no sense anymore in ignoring this. He picked up the telephone receiver, and sighed another thousand-year-old sigh. The machine continued recording.

Father Kelly replied to his past, with the words he had long ago been instructed to say in response to the question posed: "True patriots have guns in their hands and poems in their heads. Nevermore!"

CHAPTER 3

Anybody who is a New York cop, and a shamrock Catholic besides, has good reason for winding up a cynic or a bit of a mystic. Or as in my case, both.

There are probably eight million stories about Irish cops in my naked city. Irish cops—what will they think of next? On this very popular subject, I never read a book nor watched a movie or television show that failed to tell me half the tale. This is because cynicism is easy to come by and easier told, and because writers are a particularly lazy race of man.

A New York cop becomes a cynic along about the tenth time he has to knock down some apartment door to rescue some screaming woman with puffy black eyes and blood gushing out her nose and she takes a snarling swing at him from behind when he tries to put the collar on her old man for what he did to her. A dark mood will protect a cop from heartbreak such as this, the way an asbestos suit protects a fireman from flames. Writers, of course, suck down cynicism with their mother's milk.

But to believe in things mystical, this is the finer side of police work. I myself believe the pure and simple truth is rarely pure and never simple; I believe in the secret work of uneventful days; I believe in questioning coincidence very closely; I believe devoutly in the saints and most other unseen and noiseless forces; I believe in the Holy Ghost, and ghosts who are something less than consecrated souls.

Once, I thought this was all very sound-minded of me to believe in what I do, maybe even intellectual. But thanks to my commanding officer, Inspector Tomasino Neglio, I know now it is only due to a certain imagination I own.

The inspector invited me out for steaks one night a few years back, in honor of my finally joining the detective ranks. After a number of drinks and his fine big show of presenting me with the gold shield, encased in genuine eelskin, I was naturally feeling pretty good and so was Neglio; naturally, we had a number of more drinks. After which, the inspector was moved to reveal to me the real basis of my promotion. "Hock," he said, "you've got an imagination that's very full and active, and just this side of being lunatic. It's what I always look for in a detective."

Often, though, I wonder, Is it entirely my imagination?

There was I, sitting with a ghost on a brightening Saturday morning, long before my customary rising hour, which is the crack of noon. With my eyes wide from strong black coffee and a stern face-washing, like a lunatic I believed I had just conversed with a photograph. To the mystic in me, it was all true enough.

I imagined the root questions of a cop's career: questions of time and distance, the quick and the fallen, right versus wrong. And could it be me alone putting such questions in my head?

No, for there was now something more; more than just the picture of my father. For the first time, there were words, just now discovered, penned to the back of Aidan Hockaday's photograph. Were they answering the questions of my life? Could they begin to help me know? Do you really want to know?

I know that most of us believe in at least some of the Ten Commandments. Or at least we preach them.

We say it is wrong to kill, among other things.

But we kill spiders and pigs and rain forests and burglars and people of unglamorous races, and time and innocence and enemies, and disagreeable ideas and initiative and joy. We kill everything we can get away with killing, except fear.

And so, a New York Irish-Catholic cop such as myself takes some comfort in realizing that God is not so good at being a cop Himself.

CHAPTER 4

THE PRIEST'S LEGS PRICKLED WITH ARTHRITIS, AND HE WEPT, BUT NOT FOR any physical pain. Next to him, on the telephone table, the red answering machine light blinked off and on. One call, received and taped.

He could stand up and walk to the bureau on the opposite wall of the tiny friary chamber and pull open the drawer where he kept a bottle of Jameson's, and that would settle the ache in his old legs. For the tears, he had no cure. He tried to enjoy the scenery below his window, but it was now all a bright and wavy blur; crying had turned his eyes into fuzzy prisms.

He propped silver wire-rimmed glasses up over his head and wiped his eyes with a neatly pressed handkerchief, embroidered in Papal gold thread with the words *Roman Catholic Church of the Holy Cross, New York, N.Y.*, along with his years of active priesthood. His eyes filled again, he wiped them again.

He rose, and stepped over to the bureau to do something about his legs at least. He fumbled in the drawer for the whiskey.

There were footsteps in the hallway, then a hearty knock on the other side of his door. And then the voice of his neighbor. "Are we feeling ready for breakfast now?"

19

"Good morning, Owen," Father Timothy Kelly said, pressing the bottle of Jameson's to his lips, breathing the woody smell of its contents. "I'm poky today. Go on down yourself, I'll be along soon enough."

His neighbor grunted, and moved on. Father Kelly listened to the fading of steps. Then he took a long, shaky pull from the bottle. He had to use his embroidered handkerchief again, this time to wipe his chin of spilt whiskey. Which reminded him of the many drunkards he had counseled in his day. He found a jigger in another bureau drawer, filled it, and returned to his chair and window—to drink like a gentleman, despite it being a drunkard's hour for drinking.

After a minute or two, his chest started banging again, and he wept again. He crossed himself. Had he not always known this sorrow would return? How many times had he counseled the troubled among his own parish, "A man's youth never leaves him, it only returns at inconvenient times"? Was he not counseling himself as well?

He put back half the jigger of whiskey. Then the telephone rang again. He did not pick it up directly. As with all his calls over the last two days, he screened it.

"Father Timothy Kelly here ... I'm not about just now ... Kindly leave your name and number and I'll call you back as quick as I can ... Have a blessed day."

But now there was no sound of static, and no sound of the River Liffey in this caller's voice. The voice was Irish, but New York born. He was greatly relieved.

"It's Saturday morning, Father, and this is—"

He picked up the receiver and said, "Yes, yes—who is it? I'm here."

"It's Neil Hockaday, Father ..."

His chest ached, and he wheezed. He crossed himself.

"Father Tim, are you all right?"

The priest lied. "It's only a spring cold."

"I'm sorry I haven't called before ..."

Father Tim lied again, as lonely people do when asked forgiveness by those who make them so. "Well, I know how that can be."

"I have to see you, Father."

The priest's hands trembled. He said, "It sounds as though you're in a very big hurry, son."

"I am. There's not much time."

"No," the priest sighed, "there isn't."

"So, can I see you?"

"Of course, son . . . only not today." Today, the priest decided, he would go to the movies. How he loved the movies! Never mind that he had spent so many years denouncing them from the pulpit as part of the Communist conspiracy. A priest has as much God-given right to inconsistency as the next man.

"Then, Sunday?"

"All right. Come see me tomorrow."

"I'll be there."

The priest thought for a moment, then said, "Not here. Meet me in the old neighborhood. I'll be taking the late mass."

"At Holy Cross you mean?"

"Yes. I'll be happy to see you after the mass."

Once this meeting had been set, once priest and caller had said their good-byes, Father Kelly decided on a third drink before joining the others downstairs. Whiskey would help him through the job of pretending this was just one more endless weekend among the other tired old priests. Whiskey, and the movies.

Before leaving his chair, he lay down his tear-stained spectacles on the telephone table, along with his handkerchief. The red light on the answering machine flashed for the next thirty-six hours, until the cassette tapes were removed.

CHAPTER 5

I HUNG UP. BUT MY HAND RESTED ON THE TELEPHONE FOR SEVERAL SEC-
onds as I considered how clumsy I had been talking to Father
Tim. But there it was; at last I had made the call, and tomorrow
I would see him.

I took my hand away from the phone and touched Aidan Hockaday's picture again, the photo lying frameless and flat in the
suitcase. I turned it over and read the poem once more, then felt
someone watching me. But not a ghost.

Ruby stood in the bedroom doorway, wearing an old chambray
shirt of mine with one button fastened at her waist and the shirttails dipping down around her knees. "How long have you been
up?" she asked.

"Not long."

She eyed my half-empty coffee cup and asked, "Is that fresh?"

"Reheated from yesterday."

She made a face and walked through the clutter toward the
kitchen alcove, where she started heating water in a teakettle and
grinding coffee beans and otherwise making a lot of noise. "I'll
say it again," she said. "Bachelors live like bears with furniture."

Ruby turned and faced me, probably expecting me to crack wise.

2 2

But what could I say? I do live like a bear. Besides which, I was preoccupied with dialing the phone number of another long-neglected friend. As I heard ringing on the line, I asked Ruby, "What are your plans today?"

"Meaning what, I'm on my own?"

"I need to see somebody. It's important."

The line continued ringing. It was early yet. I had to give him time.

Ruby walked back to me. She saw the empty picture frame on the couch. And the handwritten poem on the back of the photograph.

She picked up the photo, read the poem, and no doubt reached the same conclusion I had: one and one might eventually add up to two, somewhere down some twisting line. She said, "Go take care of business, Hock." And I felt a scribble of guilt that here was poor Ruby also starting to think like a cop.

But what could I say? Besides which, there was finally an answer on the line. A voice birthed in Ireland, full of annoyance for being roused from a fine Saturday morning lie-in: "Hello—?"

Do you really want to know?

The place was dark as ever at midday, full of gray smoke and the sounds of clicking billiard balls and mugs of Guinness and Harp's being poured and drunk. The old mahogany-encased juke still resonated with "Ireland United."

There was the usual hearty band of red-faced boyos debating political topics unexhausted since the days of Cromwell. And the barkeeper was still named Terry Nugent; although Terry Two, as he was now called, but the image of his father before him: round of belly and with a nose full of burst capillaries.

Here to Nugent's bar we had come on this Saturday afternoon. Davy Mogaill and I, for auld lang syne.

And here it was where we had first met, when it happened that the two of us were posted to the Morningside Heights station house. Nugent's was essentially a snug for the tidy Irish enclave of Inwood back then, but it also attracted a large contingent of us Irish cops who worked the precincts of upper Manhattan and the nearby South Bronx. Now the place was a step back in time.

In our younger days, Mogaill and I became a classic pair of cop

23

drinking buddies. I was a rookie in blue, my poor mother had just died from being used up by work, my marriage was in the early and obvious stages of meltdown, and I had a face full of innocent questions. There was Davy, bless him, to oblige my great need of a rabbi. He was ten years my senior and a widower, he had just earned his gold shield, and he was then the wisest cynic I knew.

When I first laid eyes on him, I naturally took Davy Mogaill to be the local barroom poet. His speech had enough of the old country in it to qualify him as an Ancient Order of Hibernia type, and there he was in his cups and quoting Brendan Behan, after all.

He was a broad-backed man of average height, with great stout arms that in the days of the gods might have held up the sky. He had many ambitions and few friends. I was unsurprised that he was a widower. In spite of his being a great talker and drinker, there was that private sadness to him.

With the help of Davy's generous advice, I got through most of the departmental ropes without hanging myself. I also survived the divorce agonies thanks to Davy and his useful wisdom. Later, thanks in part to Davy's connections, I successfully put in for elite duty with the SCUM patrol. And then, in thanks for all he had done for me, I gradually lost touch with Davy, just as I had lost touch with Father Tim. Until now, of course, when I needed them both.

Davy I had actually needed a week ago. I was then closing down my last case, a matter of serial murder involving a poor sod of a carnival artist known by the street name Picasso. And Captain Mogaill was, after all, head of central homicide.

He provided me with important support and assistance, which made this our usual one-sided relationship: Davy helped me, and I let him. But this time I at least had the decency to notice that my rabbi from the past was in great crisis with the present. He was drinking a lot, but not like in the old days, and not in the proper places. He kept a bottle in his desk, like some old newspaperman dead-ended on the police beat. And of the captaincy he had worked so many ambitious years to achieve, he told me, with sour resignation, *"Here I am, the head of homicide in a homicidal town. Which makes me a fool, or maybe some kind of a pimp."*

I thought maybe a few jars and some fond remembrance of the

way it was might buck him up. So we made a vague date for a reunion at Nugent's. Which was conveniently now, on this Saturday when I discovered the curious poetry.

A few hours ago, I had telephoned Davy Mogaill, and he was obliging, as usual. I told him I was traveling to Ireland, and why; I told him about the photograph, and the poem; I told him about Ruby; I told him I had to see him, right that very day.

Had I heard the catch in Mogaill's voice, the same as I heard in Father Tim's? And, did I really want to know?

Terry Two set down jiggers of Black Bush on the bar. He poured one for himself as well, in honor of our return. "A regular pair of prodigal sons," he said we were. Davy took up his jar for a sniff before downing it, the way he always did, the tiny shot glass incongruous in his peasant's paw.

"To Nugent's," I said, raising my glass. Terry Two cheerfully lifted his own, and I added, "To the comfort in seeing how some things never change."

Mogaill quickly set down his drink, making the moment awkward. He looked around the barroom for several seconds, finally fixing his sights on a dour, slight man who had taken a table near the door. He sat alone. His ruddy face was obscured by a tweed cap, a black-and-white beard and smoke curling up from a cigarette. His hands were folded around a mug of Coca-Cola.

Davy turned back to us. He smiled at Nugent, not pleasantly, and asked, "How much are the drinks today, Terry?"

"Three seventy-five," Terry said. "A great bargain."

"How much for the same during the week?"

"Three-fifty."

Mogaill pointed over a shoulder with his thumb, in the direction of the man with the Coca-Cola. "So that's it, and even a better bargain when the little fellow isn't around?"

"That's Finn is all, and he's only collecting the surcharge. It's customary, for the Noraid, you know." Nugent spoke a little faster than usual, and his wide pink face took on a reddish tone. "For the orphans and the widows, you see."

Mogaill turned to me. "Might we drink to truer comfort than unchanging things that result in widows and orphans?" He picked up his glass.

I suggested, "Yesterday was my birthday."

"*Sláinte.*" Mogaill put back his whiskey in agreement, Nugent and I did the same.

I then followed Mogaill's baleful gaze over toward Finn again. The little man now stared back at us through his cigarette haze. Terry Two set us up with refreshers on the house, in honor of my birthday. But clearly, he had had his fill of us prodigals. He said to Mogaill, "What am I going to do about Finn and his friends? Call the cops?" He did not wait for an answer. He moved off to attend to his other customers.

Mogaill asked me, "Remember Finn and his gang?"

"I remember the surcharge on weekend drinks, and I remember it was the teetotalers always collecting the proceeds."

"Aye, and where they sent those funds?"

"I suppose the money never reached innocent hands."

"No, it was always for marching feet. Bloody IRA feet." Mogaill picked up the gift drink, sniffed at it, drank it down. "Marching feet never changed a bloody thing, my friend. They only produced more marching feet."

I thought, Speaking of marching feet . . .

I had wrapped my father's soldier picture in plastic and slipped it between pages of the *Daily News,* which I had taken along to read on the subway. I now spread the paper open on the bar, to where the photograph was, faceup. I flipped it over to the poetry side and said, "Here's what I want you to see."

Mogaill turned the photograph back over. "This would be your father?" he asked.

"Yes. Aidan Hockaday."

"He's a good-looking man, Neil."

"Thanks, but it's the poem I brought for you."

I flipped the photograph. Mogaill looked at the blue inked words. He said, "Sorry, but I haven't got my specs."

I reached into my jacket and gave him mine, bifocals that Ruby had talked me into buying as an early birthday present to myself. Some birthday. Mogaill reluctantly put them on, and read aloud, " 'Drown all the dogs, said the fierce young woman. 'They killed my goose and a cat. Drown, drown in the water butt . . . Drown all the dogs,' said the fierce young woman." He took off the glasses, handed them back, and said nothing.

"So, what is it?" I asked.

"Mystic doggerel."

"Yes, but do you recognize it?"

"No."

Seldom have I known Davy Mogaill to be stingy with words, especially not with a few drinks inside him. But now here he was, in Nugent's bar, of all places, silent as a clam.

"Another jar?" I suggested.

"Good."

I caught Terry Two's eye and motioned for another round. Mogaill closed the newspaper over the photograph, and said quietly, "Put it away now, you'll not want to be splashing it."

"No."

Then again, an awkward moment as Mogaill slipped into private sadness. He looked away from me, straight ahead at the long mirror up behind the liquor bottles on the business side of the bar. I looked at the mirror, too, and saw in it the distant reflection of Finn. He had left the table by the door, and now stood off behind us, with his flinty gray eyes on our backs, and close enough to hear us when we spoke.

"What do you suppose he wants?" I asked.

"Let's have us an answer," Mogaill said.

Davy got down off his barstool and stepped over to Finn. The two men talked, but I heard nothing of their conversation; nor did I see anything besides Davy's wide back. After a minute or so, Finn was apparently persuaded to leave the premises. All eyes trailed after Finn, with nobody the sorrier to watch him go, not the least of whom was Terry Two.

Davy returned to his barstool, seeming his old expansive self; but all the same, holding something back. He called over Nugent and negotiated yet two more drinks, at the rate of three-fifty each. When the whiskey came, Davy sipped at his, pensively. Then, with a quick nod toward the door, he said, "Out with the bad, in with the good, eh?"

Presuming it useless to ask straight-out what, exactly, had just happened to improve the atmosphere, I tried the oblique approach. "It's been a long time away from here, and from so many old micks all in the same place at one time," I said. "I don't know that I follow the politics anymore."

"What makes you think you ever did? What does a right-born American know about politics?"

"That he can be educated on the subject by any right-born Irishman such as yourself."

Mogaill laughed, but not happily. He said, "There are no politics in America, only elections."

I thought a moment, then said, "But there are so many politicians. The newspapers are quoting them every day."

"Aye, because politicians are full of certainties. And haven't you noticed by now that newspapers are more interested in certainties than in the truth? And how they're certainly not interested in the truth about politicians themselves?"

"Which is?"

"There's polite politicians, then there's Finn and his gang, but they're all the same: great snorting hogs forever in pursuit of power, which makes them violent fools. Of course, this is doubly so of Irish politicians, since Ireland has never held any power in the world. Hell, my American friend, Ireland hasn't once produced a battleship."

"Only battlers, and an army of poets."

"Poetry now. There's the real hope of the Irish race, since everybody knows the gag about our luck, hey? The trouble with hope is that it only pays off when there's some sense in back of it. And you know what brother Behan has said about sense and us folks."

"What?"

"If it rained soup from heaven, the Irish would all be rushing out from their houses with forks."

Mogaill laughed again, no more happily. I ordered us more drinks, and decided the time was right to shift our conversation into the direct mode.

"What sense do you make of poetry hidden behind the picture of an Irish soldier?" I asked.

"It's not my place to be making sense of this, Detective Hockaday." Mogaill's words were slurry, but carefully chosen. "The case is yours, I fear. And what grander case may a detective crack than the mystery of his own makings?"

We said nothing for a while. I, for one, considered all the brooding I had to do during the long dark hours of flight to Ireland, to the place where my Uncle Liam would die; where I might see the very last of my father's flesh, besides my own. *Do you really want to know?* So much to brood about: politics, secret poetry, a soldier lost in the mist, my rabbi and my priest and the mist of hesitancy in their voices. And Ruby.

I finally said, "Did you ever think of maybe finding another woman for your life, Davy?"

"How you do prick the ears and thirst the tongue!" Mogaill said. Then he called for more drinks. My head was already swirling, but I did not decline; I could think no more, but this did little to slow my talk, nor that of the barroom poet. Mogaill said, "I'm as regular as the next man in my nightly dreams of women, and I've learned one powerfully important thing that most of us never learn of our opposite creature."

"Which would be what?"

"The allurement women hold for us men, my friend, is the allurement that Cape Hatteras holds out to sailors. Women are enormously dangerous, thus they are enormously fascinating."

"There's a woman I'm seeing . . ."

"Do tell."

And so I did. So much, and for so long that daylight left Nugent's time-streaked windows, replaced by shadows and dusk, then the forgiveness of the night.

Forgiveness.

"Got to be going," I finally said.

"So soon?" said Mogaill, his eyes hazed by alcohol.

"Tomorrow, there's a priest I'm seeing."

"God bless you, Neil. Who would be this priest?"

"Father Tim Kelly, from Holy Cross parish in Hell's Kitchen. An old family friend. Maybe he'll make something of my father's picture, and the poem."

I left, drunk, for the subway. And Davy was suddenly on his feet.

I remember Davy at the bar, asking Terry Two for the change of a dollar, for the telephone. And him wishing me safe home that night, and bon voyage for tomorrow; warning, "Sorry to say, Hock, there'll be no easy sleep under your Irish roof."

And I remember stumbling home to Ruby's sweet disapproval,

and telling her, as we lay in bed, she in my grateful arms, "Davy talks pretty like me; prettier, to tell the truth, and he turns his words into walls even higher than my own."

I thought, as I shut my eyes to the swirling ceiling, Do I have the right to claim forgiveness for trespassing in the private sadnesses of my friends?

CHAPTER 6

LATE IN THE AFTERNOON OF SUNDAY, I TOOK MY SPOT IN THE LAST PEW and waited for it all to end. The droning mass, and also maybe my hangover. My stomach felt like somebody had spent the morning walking all over it with stilts. My head felt somehow wet and leaky inside, as if my brain was a broken inkwell. I gave a passing thought to laying off booze, at least until takeoff from JFK.

Father Tim was far up in front, about a half dozen rows back from a plump, monotone monsignor who was providing half the crowd a fine nap with his homily. The bald crown of Father Tim's silver-rimmed head was lit by a shaft of saintly light, softened and colored by its passage through a stained glass tableau of Christ's crucifixion at Calvary.

I was thankful for Father Tim's choice of this final mass. No way could I have met him earlier, not in my condition. I was even more thankful when the organist struck up a rousing recessional and the altar boys snuffed candles and trundled off with great bouquets of ferns and lilies and the late show was finally over. I myself am not the showy kind of Catholic; I say leave the big impressions to the Boss.

The sanctuary of Holy Cross Church quickly emptied of wor-

31

shipers. All but Father Tim, who remained to meet me; while waiting for me to appear, he lighted a votive taper to the statue of St. Jude, west of the pulpit among the stations of the cross. I walked up a side aisle toward him. He did not turn at my sound. Poor old guy, I thought, he must be going deaf. It occurred to me then that middle age was maybe not so bad, considering what comes next. I started to call his name. I stopped when I saw his eyes crinkle shut in solemnity, a rosary bead draped through his red-knuckled hands.

I stood still and crossed myself, then laced my fingers in front of me and bowed my head. And listened as Father Tim recited a novena.

"St. Jude, Apostle of Christ and helper in despairing cases, hear my prayers and petitions. In all my needs and desires, may I only seek what is pleasing to God, and what is best for my salvation." Father Tim paused for a breath, then went on. "These, my petitions, I submit to thee, asking you to obtain them for me, if they are for the good of my soul. I am resigned to God's Holy Will in all things, knowing that He will leave no sincere prayer unanswered . . . though it may be in a way unexpected by me."

He opened his eyes and stared at the painted limestone statue, then up at the dust-speckled bands of sunlight fading rapidly in the stained glass window. From the corridors and cloakrooms surrounding the sanctuary there were familiar sounds: heavy doors moving on old hinges, light-switch buttons snapping off, oak floors creaking. Father Tim dropped his rosary into a side pocket of his black suitcoat.

"Father Tim?" I said, stepping toward him, expecting his customary grizzly-bear embrace.

"Hello, Neil." Father Tim kept his arms stiffly at his sides, and looked at me blankly, as if it were hours rather than years since we had last seen one another.

"You look good," I said. The truth was, he looked twice as terrible as I felt. His face was puffy, and pale as lard. His once trim waist now bulged. He had a rash on his neck that I could see clear up over his Roman collar. His knees shook inside his baggy black trousers like two kids on a high school dance floor. "Listen to your lies, and here in the house of God on the Lord's own day!" Father Tim smiled, and forced a tinny laugh that made his nose hiss.

I closed the space between us and wrapped an arm around his shoulders, like I was his great-auntie and fearing that today was the last time I would touch him. I remembered his shoulders being so much bigger and harder once-upon-a-time. I smelled whiskey on him, and damn me but I fondly pictured a lowball of Johnnie Walker red over some shaved ice.

"Thanks for coming back to the old neighborhood here to meet me, Father," I said, vaguely wondering why he suggested such.

He gave my back some dutiful, fluttery pats, then broke free of my clutch. He pushed up one of his frayed coat sleeves and squinted at a gold Rolex underneath, his retirement gift from the Hell's Kitchen CYO. "What's this big ugly thing say?" he asked, raising his wrist for me to see the gaudy dial. "I forgot and left my cheaters up at home."

I thought, Where have I heard that before? I said, "Coming onto half past five."

"What time's your flight, Neil?"

"Eight . . . and how did you know about that?"

Father Tim wiped his mouth, like maybe he wanted a nip so bad he thought he might taste whiskey on the back of his hand. "Well, look, I have recently been on the horn over there to Patrick Snoody, you know . . . about poor Liam and all," he said. "Snoody, he mentioned how you're soon on your way to Dún Laoghaire."

"Did he now?"

"He did. He said you and some woman would soon be there. Who's the woman?"

"Who's this Snoody?"

"A friend."

"So he says. How come I never heard of him?"

"Your uncle has many friends on the other side. You can't have heard of them all, see." Father Tim squinted again at his Rolex, for what it was worth. He muttered, "There's precious little time for a proper chat, Neil. Kindly don't be sounding so much like the cop with me today."

"Let's go someplace for a jar," I said.

"Coffee'll do."

We left the church and walked slowly along Forty-second Street over to Pete Pitsikoulis's All-Night Eats & World's Best Coffee, which is how the orange neon sign reads. We had to stop for a minute halfway up the block so that Father Tim could rest up his heart, as he put it. "Satan made off with my strength, leaving me cursed with this decrepitude," he complained, leaning against a mailbox and wheezing like a freight train. "It seems only yesterday when I was chasing you little shits from the choir all 'round the churchyard, eh?"

We made it to Pete's, finally, and settled into a window booth. Wanda the waitress sponged the Formica tabletop, wiped it dry, then splattered it generously when she set down our ice water, two cups of coffee, a sugar bowl and creamer. "Enjoy it, you's couple of big spenders," she said, turning and then waddling off. I sopped up the spillage with paper napkins.

Father Tim spooned three mounds of sugar into his cup, and stirred in plenty of cream. I left mine black, which made Father Tim twist up his face with disgust. I asked, "What's the matter?"

"You're drinking Protestant coffee now? How can you stand it?"

"I live, I let live."

"Oh, I see. How very liberal, Mr. I-think-I'll-just-be-taking-along-some-woman-on-a-jet-airplane-trip-without-benefit-of-holy-matrimony."

"The lady's name is Ruby Flagg, we're both over twenty-one, and you and I aren't here to talk about that." I took a long, slow sip of black coffee. Father Tim looked away, shuddering. I asked, "What's with the praying to St. Jude?"

"I'm despairing of my health."

"Maybe so, but it seemed like something more."

"I want to be in the pink."

"Sure you do, but isn't going to St. Jude a little drastic?"

Father Tim looked very tired then; his eyes wandered, unfocused, unable to see beyond his screen of painful thought. He said, mechanically, "Well, there's St. John for matters of general health . . ."

"Whoever."

"That'd be whomever."

"Skip the grammar lesson," I said brusquely, in hopes of reducing Father Tim to the obvious. "Tell me what's eating you."

3 4

"Let's remember it was you who called me."

"I wonder if you know why." I reached into my jacket, pulled out Aidan Hockaday's soldier portrait, and held it up between us. "See this?"

Father Tim glanced at it, then dropped his head and sipped his creamed, sweetened coffee. He said, "I see that you're showing me some picture. I don't see what of."

"You ought to, you've seen it a million times before. Think back to when I was still singing soprano for you, and you still had your health. And you'd come visit my mother and me—and your friend Liam, too, whenever he came to town. Especially then . . ."

I paused, realizing that I sounded more like a cop than a friend; realizing, too, how this did not bother me. I said to the priest's bald, bowed head, "Think of the photograph that was always on top of the radio in our parlor. Remember, Father? And isn't it that photograph that's troubling you now?"

Father Tim said nothing. For endless seconds he did not even look up. When he at last did, his face was as blank and closed as it had been in the church, after his novena to St. Jude.

"I went to the movies yesterday, Neil," he said, with a faraway and long ago sound to his words. "We've got a first-rate revival house up in Riverdale, you know. I went there. They were showing John Huston's *Beat the Devil*, from 1954."

"Some title for a priest to be seeing."

"Oh, but it's a wonderful picture. There's Bogart in it, and Gina Lollobrigida, and Robert Morley, and Peter Lorre. Truman Capote wrote the screenplay, not many people remember that. He wrote this great line about time that Lorre delivers. It goes, 'Time—what is time? The Swiss manufacture it, the French hoard it, the Italians squander it . . . The Americans say it's money.'" Father Tim sighed. "And would you like to know what I think time is, Neil?" I shrugged. At the moment, this did not seem important.

"Time is a vandal," said the troubled priest.

And now I gave him the blank look. And said, "There's a poem on the back of the photograph, Father. Would you like for me to read it?"

"No!" Father Tim's eyes welled with tears, and he placed a

hand over his heart. I was only adding to his troubles, whatever they were.

"I'm sorry, Father . . ."

But was I?

"You see how come they went and retired old Tim Kelly," he said, daubing his face with a napkin. He rose stiffly from his side of the booth. His black vest had bunched up over his soft belly, and he smoothed it down, then buttoned his coat over it, and struggled to put some dignity back into his voice. "I'll now be returning to the home for us used-up priests. And if you don't mind my thanks, Neil, the coffee's on you."

"Wait." I stood up, and put money on the table. "How are you getting back to Riverdale?"

"Subway, same as I come down. I've made a big success of the poverty vow."

We walked out to the street, Father Tim unsteady on my arm. Then in a surprising rush, he wished me well on the trip, and with Ruby, too, of whom he said, "It's better a man's with a woman, best he's married to her, son." But of his old friend Liam, he said nothing.

I flagged a taxicab at Tenth Avenue and, over his mild protests, put Father Tim inside. I gave the driver thirty dollars, and he squawked about having to go all the way up to the Bronx with the likely prospect of dead-heading it back to Midtown. So I showed him my shield and my NYPD bracelets and reminded him about my very generous advance payment, as well as the public conveyance laws of the City of New York. He stopped squawking.

Father Tim rolled down a back window and told the driver, "Hold on a second, son." Then he went to his pocket, the one with the rosary in it, and pulled up a medallion about the size of a silver dollar. He gave this to me.

"You'll find Ireland's so full of unluck and storming rain that Jesus Christ Himself would need an umbrella," he said. He touched the medallion in the palm of my hand. "Always keep this in your pocket while you're on the other side, Neil. And for the sake of your life with Ruby Flagg, remember it's there when you need it."

He rolled up the window, staring at me with wet eyes. He said something I could not hear, and crossed himself. Then he tapped the driver's shoulder and the taxicab drove away.

I stood there, frozen in reflection of all that Davy Mogaill and Father Tim Kelly had told me that weekend, and all they had not. And the mood of my reflection was a betrayal, for I thought, Can you ever really know about your friends?

CHAPTER 7

"TAKE A RIGHT AT FORTY-FOURTH STREET."

"How come?"

"Never mind, do it."

"What happened to the Bronx?"

"That's not where we're going."

"Okay, no sweat off my nuts. So where to?"

"Double back around to Holy Cross Church on Forty-second."

"You forget something there, padre?"

"Just take me there. You can keep the whole thirty bucks."

"No problem."

Father Timothy Kelly stepped out of the taxicab in front of Holy Cross, and walked up to the black wrought iron gate that encircled the wide stoop. He leaned against a post for a minute or two, to rest up his heart. A teenage girl with a swollen stomach stopped on her way up the stairs.

"Are you all right?" she asked the resting priest.

"Bless you, darlin', I'm well enough," Father Tim said. He gave her belly a suspicious look.

The girl went on ahead into the church. In another minute, Father Tim took the eight steps up to the big blue doors himself, pulled one of them open, and entered the dimly lit sanctuary for the second time that Sunday.

He crossed himself, then sat down in a pew. The girl sat a few rows up from him, deep in prayer. The tower bells struck a quarter past six o'clock. Father Tim dozed off for a time.

When he woke, he looked over toward the confessional near the statue of St. Jude. He noticed the tiny cross over the curtained doors had lit up, meaning that a confessor was inside, making his peace with a priest. He waited.

A tall brown-skinned man left the confessional, and the little cross went dark. Then the girl rose from her pew, and walked slowly to where she could be absolved of her sins, if not of her baby. When she finished, she sat down again and prayed. Three more made confessions by the time the tower bells rang out the eighth hour of the Sabbath night. Then, when he was certain that Neil and Ruby would be in the air, Father Tim headed for the confessional.

He pulled open the purple curtain. Purple, the color of penitence. He drew the curtain closed behind him, then lowered himself to the kneeler, which activated the cross light outside. Inside, in the waxy-smelling darkness, he faced the grille between himself and the unseen parish priest, and said, "Bless me, Father, for I have sinned. My last confession was this Wednesday past. Since then, I have lied."

"How many lies?" asked the unseen priest.

"It's the same lie to others as to myself, it's always the one big lie."

"Have you made an examination of your conscience?"

"Indeed I have."

"For your sin, you may say ten Hail Marys."

"Thank you, Father."

"I'll hear your act of contrition now."

"O my God, I am heartily sorry for having offended Thee, and I detest all of my sins, because of Thy just punishment—the loss of heaven, and the pain of hell. But most of all because they offend Thee, my God, who art all good and deserving of all my love. I firmly resolve, with the help of Thy grace, to confess my sins, to do penance, and to amend my life ... Amen."

"Go now in peace and absolution, my son."

Father Tim rose from the kneeler. His knees ached, his chest pounded. He stood in the confessional doorway, frozen there, his left hand clutching at the half-drawn purple curtain. Two men and a teenage boy in nearby pews watched him as he said ten times in rapid succession, "Hail Mary, full of grace! The Lord is with thee; blessed art thou among women, and blessed is the fruit of thy womb, Jesus . . . Holy Mary, Mother of God, pray for us sinners, now and at the hour of our death . . . Amen."

Then, with his right hand, Father Tim raised a Mauser WTP .25 caliber automatic vest-pocket pistol to his mouth, shoved it in, and fired.

CHAPTER 8

THE STEWARDESS WORE A CRISP GREEN UNIFORM, WITH THE NAME
Deirdre stamped on a silver, wing-tipped brooch pinned over her left
breast. "If you don't mind my saying so," she said, "you look familiar."

She was young, slim waisted, and russet haired, with moss-
colored eyes and an accent not unlike my Uncle Liam's. I enjoyed
looking at the splash of freckles across the bridge of her nose, and
also down around her slender kneecaps; for a heartbeat or two, I
imagined the freckles that lay between.

"I don't mind," I said.

At that wistful moment, with the warm sensation of my own
rushing blood and the first light of Europe's dawn breaking midway over the Atlantic, Ruby lifted her head from my shoulder,
shaking off a nap. She noticed young Deirdre beaming her own
brand of sunshine my way, and it somehow felt to me that Ruby
minded this very much indeed.

"Don't I know you from somewhere?" Deirdre asked.

"Sorry, no," I answered.

Ruby turned to me and said, "Do try to remember, dear."

Deirdre, oblivious to Ruby, said, "Oh, but I've seen you, I have.
I wouldn't forget you, sir."

41

"You wouldn't?" I said.

Ruby said, "Don't get too excited, Hock. She called you sir."

Deirdre said, "You're in television, is that it?"

I told Deirdre it was not.

"The movies?"

"No."

"Well, you're not likely a musician."

"Not likely."

"But you are famous, aren't you?"

"Not really."

Deirdre was disappointed. I hated to see her that way, so I suggested, "You might have seen my picture in the newspapers, back in New York."

"You're so helpful," said Ruby.

Deirdre thought for a moment. "Aye, that's it! The *Post* is where I know you. You're the policeman! The one what dealt with the mad killer."

"I'm the one."

"A brave man you are."

"He is indeed," Ruby said, a little steam building.

Deirdre answered Ruby, "I admire brave men. Don't you, ma'am?"

I said to Ruby, "She called you ma'am."

"I'm so happy that's settled," Deirdre said. "I'll now be getting back on the job." She smiled at us both, a little differently at me than at Ruby; she tilted her head prettily and said "Ta," then breezed up the aisle toward the service galley. There would soon be soda bread with Kerrygold butter and marmalade and watery orange juice to deal out.

Ruby wagged a finger in my face and said, "Let's you and I get this straight: look around all you please, but I see you with another woman and I kill you."

"It's so nice to be the object of your desire."

"I am not kidding."

"What about vice versa?"

"That's fair."

"Okay. But what we have here is a murder pact."

"What's wrong with that? Weren't you married once?"

"I didn't kill my wife."

"You never thought about it?"

"Let's just say I went to confession a lot."

A crafty dance played over Ruby's lips. She had wormed us around to that topic of conversation again. And she wasted no time getting right down to it.

"Tell me something awful about her."

"About who?"

"You mean whom."

"Whatever."

"Tell me about that Judy person. Give me some dirt and I'll leave it alone all the way to Dublin."

"You realize this is sick?" But Ruby only shrugged and said, "I don't care." And I realized there was no way out. "All right," I said, "there was the time we divided up the property. What was left of it once the Queens County Civil Court gave her my house and my life insurance, and even my little dog Buster . . ."

"So, tell me."

"So I'm looking around at all these earthly possessions, and there wasn't much I really cared about besides the books, which was okay by Judy. The Cuisinart, though—that I wanted. I don't know why."

"But you didn't get it?"

"I got half."

"Half? How do you split up a Cuisinart?"

"She took the blades, I got the rest."

Ruby thought this over, and when the full ramifications had sunk in, she said, with great perception, "That's very scary."

"That's very Judy."

Deirdre and her freckled kneecaps happened by. I flagged them and ordered a drink. Ruby, pointing out the cabin window to the brightening sky, said, "Don't you think it's a little early?" I thought about real time and said, "Not in New York it isn't."

And then when I was finally sipping Johnnie Walker red from a plastic cup full of ice, I got us off the disagreeable subject of Judy McKelvey by switching over to the troubling subject of Aidan Hockaday. I told Ruby about the conversation with Davy Mogaill up at the bar in Inwood, and the one with Father Tim after the mass that afternoon at Holy Cross.

It seemed strange now, at thirty-thousand feet over the ocean in a jet airplane, to recount disquieting moments back in New York: the forbidding presence of Finn at Nugent's; Mogaill's oblique political references, and his warning; Father Tim's praying to St. Jude, and his tears, and another warning, his in the form of a medallion; and, unless I was only imagining it, the reluctant way in which both old friends dealt with my father's photograph.

"Sounds cryptic to me," Ruby said.

"I was hoping I wasn't the only one who thought so."

"The medallion, let me see it."

I felt for the right side flap of my secondhand Harris tweed jacket, the one I had decided at the last minute was just the thing for arrival in Ireland. With little more thought, I had slipped Father Tim's medallion into the pocket. I pulled it out now and passed it to Ruby. She put on her reading glasses, the thick ones she always said made her look froggy, and inspected the medallion front and back. Then she looked up at me and asked, "Have you studied this thing?"

"Not actually." I asked myself, Why not? And I could think of no explanation for my reluctance. I wondered, Could Davy Mogaill and Father Tim explain theirs?

"Fine thing for a priest to be having." Ruby gave a contemptuous sniff and returned the medallion, handling it as if it were something just fallen off a leper. "Take a good close look, Hock."

There was a design stamped on one side of the brass piece: an axe tied up with a bundle of rods, beneath which were the letters H.O.S. That much I could see without the aid of my bifocals, which I then squinted through to make out a very worn, italicized script engraved on the reverse:

> When nations are empty up there at the top,
> When order has weakened or faction is strong,
> Time for us all to pick out a good tune,
> Take to the roads and go marching along.

"What do you think it means?" I asked.

"I'd say this priest friend of yours has a dark side to his personal moon," Ruby said.

"Like a lot of other priests."

"Sure, but how many of them are Fascists these days?"

"Fascist? What are you talking?"

"Let's have that thing again," Ruby said. I gave the medallion back to her. She showed me the side with the picture, and asked, "You have any idea what this is?"

"The design? No."

"It's the *fasces*. That's Italian."

"Meaning?"

"In ancient Rome, all the various magistrates liked to advertise how they were hotshots in the empire," Ruby explained. "So whenever they went out in the streets with the common herd, they'd have packs of slaves along with them to wave the *fasces*. The symbol of privilege and authority back then. The peasants made way."

I thought about that for a second, then said, "I wonder if there's anything new under the sun. Nowadays, all the politicians run around with these entourages of camera crews, and guys wearing sunglasses and little earphones and navy blue Secret Service suits."

"Which is supposed to mean they're hot stuff. Same thing. A gimmick is a gimmick, down through the ages."

"But what's any of that got to do with Father Tim?"

Ruby sighed and looked at me like I was wearing a round haircut. "So then later on," she said, "there was an Italian guy who looked like a pro wrestler called Benito Mussolini. He needed a logo for a political outfit he started up after World War I. So ... the Fascist party, from *fasces*. Anyway, you might have heard that the party was popular with a lot of pious types."

"Yeah, I heard. But Father Tim? I really don't think ..." My voice trailed off because I had no respect for my thoughts. Nor for a picture from my boyhood that suddenly played through my mind, like an unfamiliar yet unforgotten tune: Father Tim in my mother's house, sitting with my Uncle Liam, the two men listening to Joe McCarthy on the Atwater-Kent and getting all lathered up about America going straight to Commie hell in a handbasket. I shook my head, and said, "I think he's really harmless."

"Well, probably. Poor old guy living up in the Bronx all alone like he does, with only somebody's cast-off war souvenirs to keep him company, never hearing regular from his friends." While I felt guilty, Ruby turned over the medallion. She read the script

4 5

again, and said, "Maybe Il Duce, the bald-headed creep, wrote this charming verse himself. Before he went into politics he was a journalist, you know."

"I'll keep that in mind from now on when I read the newspapers."

"Good idea." Ruby took off her glasses. I relieved her of the brass medallion. She said, "You're not actually going to keep that old damn thing. What for?"

"You never know."

I drifted back in my seat then and slept the rest of the flight to Dublin. I dreamed of war: of tyrants in ridiculous hats motoring down grand boulevards lined with men and women wearing grim faces, holding tight to children wise enough to laugh; of ignorant boy armies striding through fields of mud and clay, many falling in the slop, never to rise; of smiling young soldiers in picture frames; of aristocrats telling lies to journalists, and politicians believing what they read.

And in these sorry dreams, I heard my father's ghost voice; his words penned in a letter to my mother, written from wherever in the war he was, words I had once heard read aloud, and which I committed to fiercest memory:

"The world's gone cockeyed and a moral truth doesn't have a tinker's chance against the Devil without vast armies; and God's very own sweet army doesn't have a chance without spies and betrayals and secret codes and treacheries and propaganda and the very thickest plots and all manner of deception and cruelty required to preserve a man's civilization . . ."

CHAPTER 9

Mogaill sat in the pew near the statue of St. Jude, smoking a cigar and wondering what the world was coming to. He needed a good, thick odor of tobacco. In all his years of working homicide, he had never got used to the skanky smell of a corpse.

Thirty feet away was the late Father Timothy Kelly, surrounded by a forensics squad from the Midtown-North PDU. The dead priest was sprawled facedown on the floor outside the confessional. Red and gray fluids seeped from a dime-sized exit wound at the back of his bald head. His trousers were wet, and getting wetter as death drained his body.

An officer with a camera photographed the body from all conceivable angles. Another used a knife to scrape out a spent bullet from the back wall of the oak confessional. Tiny red blood spatters against the purple confessional curtain were calibrated for density and directional thrust. Fingerprint powder, white and sticky, was everywhere. Everybody was making notes, everybody smoked, nobody seemed particularly excited.

Up at the front of the church was Father Twohy, the unfortunate young priest who had heard Father Kelly's last confession; who had then, for the first time in his career, administered the last rites of the Roman Catholic church. He stood by a chair next to the altar now, wiping an ashen and horrified face with a damp handkerchief. In the choir loft behind him were a dozen keening nuns, black and screechy as a flock of crows. Uniformed officers had cleared the sanctuary of the few parishioners. One of them, a frecklefaced pregnant girl, remembered seeing a bald-headed priest pull up in a taxicab just before she walked up to the church.

"He looked all out of breath or something, and I was real surprised to see him in the pews like a regular person with something really heavy on his mind."

The precinct detectives had also interrogated Father Twohy. Not too many questions were asked; cops tend to respect the morbid privacy of suicide. And Father Twohy's few answers revealed nothing about the dead priest's troubled world. "I don't know what to think! I heard this shot, I jumped off the bench in my side of the confessional, I opened the curtain and there he was—a priest, with a pistol in his mouth, falling. Then I saw it was old Father Tim. He's retired, he lives up in Riverdale . . ."

Open and shut. Mogaill had been told as much on his unexpected arrival, which was about twenty minutes after Midtown-North got the call to come running over to Holy Cross. "If you want, go and talk to the little mother and to Father Twohy yourself," one of the interrogating detectives suggested, "but I don't think they've got anymore spill than they already gave us." Mogaill said that was probably true, but he nevertheless took down names.

Lieutenant Ray Ellis, a unit commander of Mogaill's long acquaintance, was the supervisor on the crime scene. He was short, bald, sloppy and thickset, and wore a brown cop suit and black shoes with rippled crepe soles. He also wore the impersonal expression of a department lifer; distrust of his fellow man was etched in his face like the scowl on a bulldog. It was Ellis who had further horrified Father Twohy by passing out the cigars right there in the sanctuary.

Ellis broke away from the ring of cops performing cleanup duties around the mess of Father Tim's body. He walked over to Mogaill. "Forensics says no question the padre ate his gun, so there's no percentage in dusting for prints on this, Captain," he

48

said, handing a small pistol to Mogaill. "Get a load of this antique."

"Thank you, Lieutenant." The suicide weapon fit easily in the palm of Mogaill's hand. He stared at a .25 caliber automatic with a short, blued barrel, about four inches in overall length, still warm from one shot fired out of its six-round magazine. The checkered grips were made of hard rubber, which were aged and brittle, but unworn. Mogaill looked up at Ellis, and said, "An oldie but a goody, hey?"

"It's been more than a couple of years since I seen a beaut like that," Ellis said. "Back in the fifties, there was lots of them little Mausers showing up, on account of guys in the service taking them off Germans to bring back home."

"How do you figure a priest comes by one?" Mogaill asked, hefting the pistol. It weighed little more than a fat wallet.

"I guess before he was saving souls for Jesus he was maybe in the war? Maybe he stripped down a dead kraut like everybody else who wanted a swell souvenir?"

"No, I shouldn't think so," Mogaill said, shaking his head. "He's too old to have been a soldier then. Besides which, he's Irish. And in the war that we're speaking of, true Irishmen served nobody's army."

"Sounds like there's something personal behind that, Captain." Ellis's distrust, as well as his reliably suspicious view of humanity, extended equally to civilians and colleagues. "You know the padre, or what?"

"I know of him."

"Friends and countrymen, like that?"

"Us harps stick together."

"So I heard," the lieutenant said. Mogaill gave him back the Mauser. Ellis pulled a plastic evidence bag from a pocket and put the pistol inside. "By the way, Mogaill, I'm wondering something about that."

"Are you now?"

"I called up to where the padre lived, this old priests' home in Riverdale. They tell me one of you harps who stick together was the last who seen him alive, before he went and took off in a plane to Dublin."

"That'd be Detective Hockaday you're talking about?"

Lieutenant Ellis nodded his bulldog head slowly. His eyes flattened.

"When he was a wee kid, Hockaday was a choirboy here at Holy Cross and the priest was in charge of the choir," Mogaill explained. "There was something more, too, I think. Father Kelly's a friend of the Hockaday family—was a friend. Looks to me like Father was having himself some terrible time of it. Maybe he wanted to talk over his troubles with an old friend."

"Yeah, maybe so," Ellis said, scratching an ear. "But unless you're an old friend, too, I wonder how come you're Johnny-on-the-spot here? As you can see plain, this ain't homicide. So what's your interest? And anyhow, don't a division captain get Sundays off?"

Mogaill said nothing for a few seconds. He puffed on his cigar and glanced over toward the altar, at Father Twohy still in a state of shock and the chorus line of moaning nuns. Then he turned back to Lieutenant Ellis, and said only, " 'Tis a hell of a way to be keeping the Sabbath, hey?"

Again he circled the block in the unmarked Plymouth. And still it was there: a dark sedan idling at the corner like a panther half asleep, the green illumination of dashboard lights and the orange dot of a lit cigarette reflected in the windshield.

This time as he drove by, he memorized the license plate number, for whatever that might be worth. Nothing, probably. Then he pulled up in front of the big red-brick friary and double-parked. He stepped out of the Plymouth and started up the sloping walkway to the entrance. Halfway there, a yellow floodlight over the doorway caught him in its sweeping glow, big as life. He turned, and looked down toward the corner. The dark sedan pulled away from the curb, passed by slowly, then disappeared.

He continued up the walkway.

An old priest answered the door before he was able to land the first knock. The priest was thin and white haired, with eyes as gray and dead as the East River. He was a head taller than Mogaill and had to look down to speak to his visitor. "You're the policeman who telephoned?" the priest asked in a reedy voice, faintly accented from an Irish youth.

"That's me," Mogaill said, flashing a shield. The priest examined it closely. Besides reading New York Police Department, Mogaill's gold shield contained his name, rank, serial number and division. The priest said, reverently, "Captain D. Mogaill, central homicide, just as you told me."

"You'd be the priest who answered the phone? Father . . . ?"

"Father Owen Curley."

"Yes. Might I come inside, Father?"

"I'm so sorry. Yes, of course."

Mogaill entered a foyer dimly lit by a chandelier, several bulbs of which were missing. The papered walls were peeling. The floor groaned under a stained rug. There was a soapy, old man smell to the place. A cat trapped a cockroach along the baseboard of a wall and pawed it to death.

"Where are all the others tonight?" Mogaill asked, stepping past Father Curley into a salon off the foyer. This room was brighter, and full of cane-bottomed rockers, cracked leather club chairs, and reading lamps. There was a fireplace and a television console and a round, oak table piled neatly with unread copies of *The Catholic Messenger*. Father Curley answered, "Why, in the chapel. Offering invocations for the soul of our poor Brother Tim."

"Of course."

"Your news was a shock to us all."

"We'd best not disturb the prayers then."

"No."

Mogaill returned to the foyer. He walked to a paneled staircase and stopped, resting a hand on a newel post and looking up into the darkness of the first landing. He said to Father Curley, behind him, "So you were telling me on the phone, Father Kelly was out of sorts this morning?"

"Very much so," said Father Curley. "It's not like him to put off his breakfast like he did. Good food was Brother Tim's favorite of God's many bounties."

"You mentioned, too, that your room was next door to his?"

"That's right. We've been neighbors for quite a few years."

"You want to show me his room now?"

"Of course, yes." Father Curley pressed the button of a switch plate on the foyer wall and lighted the stairs. He stepped ahead of Mogaill and led the way up the first flight, pausing at the landing to ask, "From what you told me, it appears poor Brother Tim took

5 1

his own life. But, since you're here from the central homicide division
. . . well, do you honestly think this might be a case of murder?"

"It's times like this when I honestly don't know what to think."

"But a man of your experience . . . surely you have an opinion."

"In my opinion, people aren't altogether human."

"I'll have you know, Brother Tim was a good friend and a
fine priest," Father Curley said. He added, icily, "And a good
human being."

"Even so, you leave good silk out in the rain, it shrinks."

"Captain Mogaill, you are a Catholic, are you not?"

Mogaill thought, So that's it. He said, "Better a good Catholic should
be murdered in cold blood than commit the cardinal sin of suicide?"

The priest muttered in Latin and crossed himself. "Perhaps we
should simply get this business behind us, Captain." Father Curley
continued up the next flight and Mogaill then followed him, wordlessly. They walked halfway down the second-floor corridor to Father
Kelly's door. Father Curley pushed on it, and said, "In here."

It was a tidy room, functional and unadorned, with all the
warmth and personality of an airport hotel. The colorless walls
contained nothing besides a crucifix. There was a sagging twin
bed covered in chenille, a bureau, a small closet, a chair and table
by the window. Twelve flashing lights on a telephone answering
machine were the only signs of life.

It took Mogaill less than two minutes to search through Father
Timothy Kelly's belongings, the accumulations of a man who had
lived so many years; a priest who owned unthinkable memories,
and an old gun that had finally made them go away.

He was not surprised to find the bottle of Jameson's hidden in
a bureau drawer beneath some socks. Nor was he surprised that
Father Curley feigned astonishment at such discovery. Davy Mogaill understood a man who would hide himself in drink; he understood, as well, that a charade is only good when there are
friends who claim they never knew.

In his brief but thorough search, Mogaill found only one item
of any possible significance. He slipped this into a pocket. Then
he bade a good night to the priest with the dead gray eyes.

Davy Mogaill was not anxious to get home. He never was.
The house in Queens where he had once lived with his wife

had grown cold, as cold and lifeless as the room he had just searched. When Brenda died, he wanted to sell the place and take a small apartment in Manhattan. But then, where would he put her things? So he had remained with Brenda's belongings, all neatly stored in rooms he seldom entered, in a house with the heart and joy cut out of it. And in these years alone, Davy Mogaill rose through the ranks, eventually becoming a captain.

Before leaving the Bronx, Mogaill drove the unmarked Plymouth to a diner on Broadway at Two-hundred-fortieth Street. He expected to be followed, and he was. The dark sedan waited, just across the way. He took a booth where he could see out the window to the street and keep track of the driver's burning cigarette.

A waitress, no more than Brenda's age when he married her, came over to his booth. Like his Brenda, this girl had hair the color of October's pale red leaves in the Galty mountains, and a ready smile that took a wistful Mogaill home to County Kildare. She set down a glass of water, handed him a menu, and said, "Would you like a few minutes?"

Mogaill choked when he tried to answer. He took a sip of water.

"Are you all right?" the waitress asked.

"You scared me."

"I what—?"

"Dear girl, you remind me of my wife."

"I'm seventeen years old, mister."

"I didn't mean anything—"

"Good."

"My wife is dead."

"I'm sorry."

"She was from the other side."

"The other what—?"

"Ireland."

"Oh."

"We had only two years together. And that's nowhere near enough time, is it?"

"I don't know what to say."

Neither did he. The girl stood there awkwardly with her autumn mountain hair, her smile lost. Mogaill stared out the diner window. He could see the panther shape of the sedan, the burning cigarette inside, rising from unseen hand to unseen lips, then dropping from sight.

He opened his menu, glanced at it quickly, and said to the girl, "My apologies, miss. I've been crowded by memories lately, the kind that do not lie softly in mind."

"Oh."

"I'll have the fish and chips."

The girl wrote this down on a pad, glad to be off and away to the kitchen with the order. Ten minutes later, Davy Mogaill's lonesome dinner was delivered by a busboy, who complained about the waitress suddenly deciding to take her break.

Mogaill ate half his meal, put down enough money on the table to pay for it twice, then left the diner. He did not bother looking at the dark sedan. He figured it would follow him, which it did.

On the way home, he tuned the car radio to an all-news station, the kind of station where you know a story is big when they pad it up with adjectives and metaphors and it comes at you from an echo chamber. Mogaill was almost to the Queens side of the Triborough Bridge when the announcer, who might have been somewhere in the Swiss Alps, reported the "shocking Sabbath suicide of Father Timothy Kelly, beloved but troubled priest who put a gun to his head after confessing his secret horrors to another priest—smack in the middle of the sanctuary of Manhattan's Holy Cross Church, the Lord's house of hope in Hell's Kitchen, the tough West Side neighborhood where blood and bullets have never been strangers . . ."

Along with that load came a sound bite from a quavering Father Twohy: "I am deeply saddened by today's tragedy . . . We here at Holy Cross will pray for his soul . . . Of course, I am not at liberty to discuss the nature of Father Kelly's confession." Followed by a quote from Lieutenant Ray Ellis: "This sure ain't about who done it, that's as obvious as boils on a fat guy's neck . . . The padre, he decided to check out, big time . . . Leaving us the question, what the hell for?"

Mogaill switched off the radio.

The clock on the dash read half past ten as Mogaill turned his car into the street where he lived. He calculated that Neil Hockaday and Ruby Flagg would land at Dublin airport in about four more hours.

Mogaill swung the Plymouth up into the narrow driveway leading to the tuck-under garage of his row house, pressed the remote control that opened the pleated door and slowly eased in. He checked his rearview mirror. The dark sedan cruised by.

Before leaving the car, Mogaill reached inside his suitcoat and unholstered a .38 police special. He stepped out into the drive, right arm and revolver cocked for action. The sedan was out of sight, the sounds were innocent: neighborhood cats, the rush of traffic from over on Metropolitan Avenue, the complaint of rusty hinges as he lowered the garage door. He walked up the short stoop, once lined with pots full of Brenda's marigolds and geraniums, and let himself into the house with his keys.

Mogaill was home again in his house of unshared memories. He stood for a moment in the foyer of Brenda's house; he thought of it that way, he had not been comfortable living in it alone all these years. And the idea he had begun to form at the Bronx diner was complete to him now: soon, I'll be free of this, and other Irish memories that do not lie softly in mind.

He reholstered the .38 and loosened the fat Windsor knot in his tie. Before taking off his coat and tossing it over a chair, he went into a side pocket for the cassette tape he had taken from the late Father Kelly's answering machine, a Panasonic model much like the one he owned.

He poured himself a tumbler full of Black Bush and took this with him to the desk in his parlor. He fitted the priest's cassette into his own Panasonic, and pressed rewind. Then he sat down, sipped whiskey and eavesdropped. There were three voices on the tape, all of which Mogaill recognized:

What is a true patriot?
True patriots have guns in their hands and poems in their heads.
Nevermore!
It's Saturday morning, Father, and this is—

Mogaill finished the whiskey. He would need more for the long night's wait. He got up and poured out another Black Bush, and returned with the bottle to his desk.

5 5

He picked up the telephone and dialed the operator. "International connections, please." He waited, then said, to a woman's voice, "This is Captain Davy Mogaill of the New York Police Department. I'll be needing someone in Ireland—with the Aer Lingus desk at Dublin airport. Can you do that for me, dear?" He hung up the phone, and waited for the operator's callback.

Fifteen minutes later, Mogaill spoke with a clerk at Aer Lingus. He identified himself, and asked, "Could you have someone page Detective Neil Hockaday on arrival? Flight nine-zero-eight from New York. I'll be wanting the detective to return my call."

The clerk took down the information, and gave his assurance that the message would be passed to Detective Hockaday. Mogaill thanked him and rang off.

He then organized the things he would need later, and laid them out in the bathroom. Then he went from room to room of Brenda's house, laying down wire that connected to a black box concealed beneath his favorite chair.

There he settled in to wait. And to drink, and wonder all over again what the world was coming to.

At midnight, his doorbell rang.

CHAPTER 10

RUBY NUDGED MY SHOULDER, AND SAID, "HOCK, LOOK—THERE IT IS!"

I woke from sweaty dreams of war and ghosts, lying aristocrats and slow-witted journalists. My face and neck were as clammy as a butcher's handshake.

She nudged me again, and pointed out the cabin window. There below us, on the Atlantic horizon, was the Irish landfall: a great gray line of surging waves; pounded stone coastal walls topped in green; white sea mists, plumed like geysers between jagged cliffs; sunlight arced through ocean spray in bands of blue, yellow, and red.

"My God, it's beautiful," Ruby said.

And of course, it was. My whole life I had waited to savor this first sight of Ireland; always, I had believed in the simple charm of returning through time, of seeing what my ancestors saw, walking where they walked, knowing what they knew. Now the time had come. But not so simply as I had long believed. There were the recent dreams and the voices in my head, all warning that immigrants' abandoned sorrows lay waiting discovery by the likes of me.

There'll be no easy sleep ... Time is a vandal ...

I shrugged, and said, "Beautiful, and terrible, too."
Ruby turned from the window. "What's with you?"
"Irish eyes don't always smile."
"Yours should, after all the drinks you had. And the nap."
"It wasn't restful."
"What, you had a nightmare?"
"Nightmares only scare you."
"You're dreaming about your father again?"
"You know about that?"
"It's not so hard to know."
"I can hear his voice. I know, that sounds nuts."
"So it's a little nuts. What does he say?"
"I'm not always sure." I took another long look at the rugged
Irish coastline, growing nearer. Ruby looked, too. Beyond the cliffs
were brown bogs, villages and foggy pastures.
Ruby said, "Maybe he's telling you that things down there on
the ground don't square with the picture postcard we're seeing
up here."
"Like what?"
"I saw a movie once about an Irish farmer. He didn't think the
old sod was beautiful at all. He said the Irish land's so hard it
makes the Devil weep."
The plane nosed downward slightly, and the whine of the jet
engines changed pitch as we now left the sea behind us. We began
a long, gradual descent toward Dublin on the eastern coast, not
so far away. I checked my watch. In less than an hour, I would
be with my ancestors. *Do you really want to know?*

"You ordered a car?" Ruby asked.
"No," I told her.
"Then who's the guy over there with your name on one of those
little signs?"
We had just left customs. Which is to say, Ruby had just won
release. My own fair and trustworthy face had been whisked
through the line by the brown-clad agents. Ruby, since she is not
a member of my own gene pool, was detained for the kind of
luggage inspection reserved for suspected terrorists and drug cou-
riers. Back home we would have made a stink about it; as foreign-
ers, we were meek as moles. But we should have complained. I

have since decided that when in Rome, it is not necessarily a virtue to do as the Romans do. So call me an ugly American.

Anyhow, we were in the main terminal of Dublin airport, where it is doubtful any of my ancestors ever walked; certainly none of them was ever greeted by a man in driver's livery. And yet there he was in the taxi corridor, patiently shifting the weight of his solid body from one foot to the other, a fellow about twenty-five years old dressed in a chauffeur's cap and a four-button coat. He had one of those big doorman's umbrellas hooked over an arm, and held between his capable hands was a neatly lettered cardboard sign that read HOCKADAY.

I said to Ruby, "Unless I have relatives on the flight, he's all ours."

"Good, he'll make up for the Klansmen back there in customs."

We headed toward the chauffeur, pushing along our bags on a cart. He spotted us about halfway and gave me a snappy salute, which I returned. He looked not at all surprised to be meeting an American couple of our contrasting hues.

"Hi," I said as we reached him, "I'm Neil Hockaday."

"Top o'day to you, sir," he said, taking my hand and pumping it. He tipped his cap to Ruby. "The same to you, colleen. I'd be Francis Boylan—Francie is what they call me."

"And I'd be Ruby Flagg," Ruby said, blithely. She put her lips to my ear, and whispered, "I love the *colleen*."

"My uncle sent you?" I asked.

"In a manner of speaking," Boylan said. He smiled at me, the way an undertaker does when somebody asks the price of a coffin. "Mr. Patrick Snoody, he's the one wanted you well met this morning."

Because I was tired from the flight, I suppose, I forgot all about the most elemental rule of the detective business and asked Boylan a question to which I did not already know the answer. "My Uncle Liam never in his life mentioned this Snoody to me," I said. "Just who is he?" Boylan only gave me one of his funereal grins.

Then Ruby gave me a look she no doubt learned from her head-waiter friend, Pierre, back in New York. She said to me, "I'll bet you never gave a thought to how we'd get from here to your uncle's, did you, Lover?" When I shrugged, she turned to Boylan and said, "Thank you, Francie. We'll rely on the kindness of strangers."

Boylan said, "Shall we be off to Dún Laoghaire then, Miss Ruby?"

"Yes, we shall," Ruby said.

"How far is it?" I asked Boylan, with a small grumble.

"I should think two hours, including a wee tour-about."

"Tour?"

"Mr. Snoody, he suggests I show you a bit of Dublin along the way. Just follow me." Boylan took charge of our baggage cart, we trailed after him down the corridor toward the car.

"Could you tell me how my Uncle Liam is feeling?"

"I expect he's in no immediate danger," Boylan said.

We were nearly to a wide double door of glass that led to the passenger arrival drive when we heard a loud commotion from behind. I turned around and saw one of the customs agents galloping in our direction. He was shouting in a thin, nasally voice, "Mr. Hockaday . . . Mr. Hockaday—!"

I waited. Ruby was none too happy to see this one again, the very agent who had riffled through her clothes. I noticed that Boylan seemed to lose some of his cheer, too, although he said nothing. Ruby complained, "Again with the Klan?"

"Begging your pardon, sir," said the agent, gallop ended. His face was wet and flushed. He took a deep breath. "In all the excitement of inspecting your companion's belongings—"

I interrupted him. "Rummaging through a lady's unmentionables, this excites you?"

Ruby laughed. So did a dozen or so passersby who happened to hear the exchange. They stopped, expecting further entertainment.

"See you now—fair play!" the agent protested. "It was rummaging in the line of duty."

There was another round of laughter, this one very hearty. The agent's face grew stricken, and redder still. In an attempt to recover his dignity, he drew himself to military attention. He was a man in uniform, after all. The trouble was, it covered his lumpy body like the puckered skin of a baked potato. For all his effort, he only looked ridiculous. A voice in the crowd taunted, "He can't help it, he's a nancy-boy is what!"

He was now well deflated. But he manfully ignored the jeering, and appealed to me, "Sir, I never touched your lady's knickers but when the law required."

The poor sod was hopeless. I said, "You came charging after me in an airport to talk about knickers?"

I barely heard him over the belly laughs. He handed me a folded-up bit of paper and said, "In the excitement, I forgot. They asked me to give you this message, sir. And, I might say—never did I realize you was the police."

He tipped his hat to Ruby apologetically, then strode away, the back of his neck bright with embarrassment. Someone shouted after him, "Ta now, Nancy."

I unfolded the paper. Ruby said, "What is it, Hock?"

"It's Davy Mogaill. I'm supposed to call him, at his home number."

"The captain from central homicide? Your drinking buddy?"

"That's him," I said, ignoring Ruby's little dig. Could I expect her to understand a cop's rabbi? I looked around for a public telephone. There were none in the corridor.

Ruby crossed her arms in front of her and scowled. "What are you going to do now, turn around and go back home?"

"How do I know?"

"You mean you would?"

"I'd better go call."

Ruby sighed. "I'll wait here with Francie."

I went back into the terminal, located a telephone, and dialed the international operator. Mogaill would have to take it collect.

After ten rings, the operator said, "I'm afraid your party isn't about, sir. Would you like to try again?"

"Let it ring some more, will you?"

"A little."

Six more rings. I looked at my watch. Nine A.M. in Ireland, which meant four A.M. in New York.

"Sir, you really must try your call some other time."

"It's good you've come now, in the spring," Francie Boylan told us over his shoulder as he drove the Citroën south from the airport to the city. "Spring's the finest of our year, and today we've a fine, rare sun to help us see the sights."

The sights just now were cute farms dotting the highway approach to Dublin. The scenery fascinated Ruby. I was even less interested in a rustic panorama than usual.

Farms I have seen before, on occasions when well-meaning friends have included me in trips to Jersey and Pennsylvania and places like that. Farms have black and white cows, things growing out of the ground and blowing in the breeze, raw-boned men puttering along on tractors. And red barns, with advertisements for Mail Pouch chewing tobacco painted on the sides. So this was very familiar to me, except that in Ireland the barns are decorated with ads for Kerrygold butter, a lot of the roofs are slate and there are rocks and heather cluttering up everything.

Ruby rolled down a backseat window, which only let in a blast of farm-ripened breeze. She took a great swallow of the stuff, and said, "You can really breathe out here, can't you?"

Up in front, Francie Boylan coughed. And this somewhat improved my estimation of his character.

"I've never understood what people see in the country," I said. "There's nothing to read and very little sin. Also there is no decent Szechuan takeout."

"I wish you'd get your mind off New York," Ruby said.

"Sorry, I can't help wondering about Davy and why he would want me to call him right away from the airport—and why he's not around to answer his phone."

"It's probably no big emergency."

"Maybe it doesn't have to be."

"Twenty bucks says he went to that bar where he got you all drunked up Saturday, he got himself swacked again all by himself, and he thought it would be a good laugh to leave you a message in Dublin. Then he stumbled home and forgot all about it. Right now, he's passed out and can't hear the phone."

"Could be," I said. Which was a lie. I believed none of Ruby's easy suspicions. Davy Mogaill has long been a boozer, but never the easy sort. "I'm able to get drunk all on my own, by the way."

Ruby, with the exasperation of a long-suffering cop wife in her tone, said, "Call him up later tonight if you want. But please, Hock, try to remember where we are, and why we're here. Then ask yourself what it's got to do with Davy Mogaill."

There was an answer to that somewhere. But all that came to me were a few of Davy Mogaill's very recent words: *Might we drink to truer comfort than unchanging things that result in widows and orphans?*

Boylan grew chatty again. He said to Ruby, "If you love the look of the land 'round here, colleen, you'll fancy it further down the line to Dún Laoghaire as well. Down there, the air's not only sweet from working earth, but from the sea breeze, too. My own father Joe's from country down around there. It's him who loved the springtime so . . ."

Francie Boylan paused, as if to burst into some wet-eyed song with a lot of "Tora loo" to it. Instead, he said, "Would you like to know what Pap says of spring?"

Ruby did. I did not.

"Joe Boylan, he says spring's when the milk tastes like onions."

"How's that?" Ruby asked. I was sorry she did.

Francie Boylan took a deep breath, then spoke as if reciting drilled lessons from a classroom: "It's because cows put early out to pasture eat on the onion grass, which sprouts just after the pussy willows, but before the forsythia . . . That would be along about the same time as the skunk cabbage coming in . . ."

And I had to endure about a half hour more of bucolic travelogue until the landscape turned thankfully urban. Which comes suddenly in Ireland, even at the edge of its capital. With no suburban sprawl of announcement, there lay Dublin before us: city of a half million, just beyond the fields. Shipyards and docks, huddled buildings, flax mills, trolley cars, and the sweet steam of breweries and distilleries. Ruby rolled up her window.

We drove first through working-class ghettoes that skirted the city, row upon row of smudged red-brick houses all strung together, low and slanting. Skinny children with dirt in their faces and scabbed knees played in these poor streets; games of bally-cally and Annie-over, as I myself had played in the streets of Hell's Kitchen, in another time and Irish place. Then the broad commercial high streets of succeedingly better districts, with housewives in head scarves setting off to market with their mesh bags, and gray-haired pensioners ambling along with their blackthorn sticks looking for the likes of themselves for another long day's gossip. And finally, in the diamond of Dublin—O'Connell Street itself.

"*Baile Áthe Cliath*—that's Dublin, in the Gaelic," Boylan said to us, now that our eyes were accustomed to the city and we seemed in the mood for sound as well as sights. "There's plenty of us never gave up using the glorious name."

"The old-timers?" I asked.

"Aye, and certain younger ones with respect for all the blood's been spilled in these here streets."

"During the Easter Rebellion?" Ruby asked.

"That and other times, and long ago," Boylan said. He brought the car to a stop at a red light, and pointed out the window toward an ancient public house. Three boys in their teens, wearing leather jackets and construction boots loitered and smoked outside the door. "Have a look at where Black Monday began, back in the year of 1209. That's when gangs of lads such as them standing right there now set out to massacre the ones lording it over us in our own *Baile Áthe Cliath.*"

"Who might that have been?" I asked, as if I did not know.

"The English!" Boylan spat.

"You're a young man, Francie, but somehow you've got an old man's grudging memory."

"And not a pretty one, neither."

"How do you come by it?"

"We got our way of remembering all the evil the English done. Ever hear tell of a *shanachie?*"

I said I had not.

"The *shanachie's* a storyteller. His pap before him was the same, and his pap's old man before that. Back it goes in a *shanachie* family, through all the hundreds of years of English bastards committing their crimes against us."

Ruby said, "But now you have it in the history books."

Francie Boylan shook his head at this innocence, and said, "That's depending on who's doing the writing and who's doing the publishing, colleen. Freedom of the press belongs to them rich enough to own a press. A poor Irishman has only his God-given tongue. Nae, there's no better way of understanding the horrors than listening to the *shanachie* telling it true to your face."

"You've grown up with *shanachies'* stories, Francie?" I asked.

"I've heard my share of tales."

I surprised myself by saying, "Maybe you could tell us one?"

Boylan pulled off to the side of the street without a word, expertly wedging the Citroën between two smaller cars. Across the way from where we now sat was a massive, official building, with stone columns at the top of marbled stairs and people flooding in and out its great doors. Boylan cut the motor and secured the brake, then turned round in his seat to face us.

"Why are we stopped?" I asked.

"So's I'll be telling the tale proper like, Mr. Hockaday."

"All right."

Once again, Francie Boylan drew deep from his breath, and deeper still from memory: "It was six months into the great hunger caused by the potato blight, and half the Irish nation was homeless, and most was starving. Those in the villages, too proud to die in the streets for all to see, would crawl up into the bog caves and dig scalps in the wet ground, there to wait for sweet death in lonesome dignity. In the diseased fields, children with their bloated bellies and ribby little chests lay dead and scattered like a battle's losing soldiers, their lips green from chewing grass at the end. Families, what was left of them, lay about all day in their rags and fevered stink, clinging together, moaning from the pain of scurvy and dropsy, bodies filled with sores.

"And all this while, the English landlords serving up more and more evictions in all the counties where the croppies, the tenants, could nae afford to pay, what with the business of starving to attend.

"In County Galway, in the village of Ballinglass, on the thirteenth of March of 1846, an English bitch by the name Mrs. Gerrard called in a detachment of the Forty-ninth Infantry of the Royal British Army, commanded by Captain Brown, as well as the local English constabulary, and ordered some three hundred croppies to leave their houses—so's the land could be cleared of the people who had made it their lives, and turned more profitable as grazing ground for cattle.

"The English troops worked with a ferocity that gladdened Lucifer's heart. They demolished every wretched thing; they set fire to thatched roofs, and tore off them made of slate and pounded the slate down to slivers; they pulled down the walls, they crushed a family's possessions under horses' hooves. The women ran about mad and wailing, and them that was not yet booted aside by mounted soldiers barricaded their doorposts, screaming like banshees. Any bare-handed man fool enough to attack a soldier or constable met his maker, quick as an English sword could arrange the introduction. The children cried themselves dry.

"And that night, in the hopeless dark and wind, the people slept in the ruins, only to be driven out at dawn—and the very foundations of the tumbled houses then torn from the ground, and burnt and pulverized, and no neighbor allowed to take in these damned and despised left in the ashes.

"Turned from every door, the people dug their scalps—burrows of two or three feet deep, covering themselves against the cold with sticks and turf. The ones better off had scalpeens, merely a bigger burrow, sometimes inside the smoky ruins of a tumbled house.

"But in the days and weeks that followed, not even this misery could satisfy the shameless bitch and her soldiers. Even these poor folk huddled in their holes, oft' times hanging on to a dead one for days, were hunted down and evicted.

"Word of this particular outrage could not be kept silent, reaching even into the Parliament at London, where some few shook their well-fed barbarian heads at the news of us dying and suffering so—but where most held honest and true to the grotesquery of their self-interest. On the twenty-third of March in that year of 1846, Lord Brougham defended Mrs. Gerrard and all her evil ilk, by saying: 'Undoubtedly, it is the landlord's right to do as he pleases. The tenants must be taught by the strong arm of the law that they have no power to oppose or resist. Property would be valueless, and capital would no longer be invested in cultivation of the land if it were not acknowledged that it is the landlord's undoubted, indefeasible and most sacred right to deal with his property as he wishes.' "

Francie Boylan paused then, finished with his oral script. He added to it his own conclusion, "And so it is left not to books of history, but to these stories told face-to-face, to keep alive this lesson, among so many others at Irish expense: the landlord is no lord of the land, he is the scum of the earth."

Ruby asked quietly, "And you, Francie—you're a *shanachie?*"

"I've heard tales from my pap, and from my grandfa'r, too, but I've remembered precious few to tell myself," Boylan said. He shook his head in self-reproach. "It's the truth I'm a disappointment to the family tradition, yet I do enjoy believing I serve the cause in my own way."

"The cause?" I asked.

"Aye—the cause of memory, Mr. Hockaday." Boylan smiled his undertaker's smile. "Including all the nightmares."

Boylan then turned toward the great pillared edifice across the way. "That would be the General Post Office," he said, absently, "where the uprising began on that fine Easter Sunday of 1916." He gazed intently at the swarm of people on the wide marble steps, his eyes moving over the crowd, as if seeking out someone in particular.

And I was overcome by a sensation as deeply instinctual to a cop as hair rising up off the back of an edgy cat; an instinct I was told way back at police academy I would likely develop, and which I would be wise to trust. I knew in this flashpoint, and without a scrap of logic, that it was no time to be turning my back. Impending violence may have no more immediate logic than this; no more logic than the sudden, profound regret I knew in being without any of the usual weapons I carry.

Francie Boylan was suddenly done with staring at the post office steps. He said, abruptly, "It's come time." Then he switched on the ignition, gunned the engine, and pulled the Citroën away from the curb.

With shoulders squared and his sights purposefully ahead of him now, Boylan drove us slowly up O'Connell. The street whose gutters had so long known the running of Irish blood; where in certain doorways still, as I had seen only moments ago, were the brooding faces of a new generation of Irishmen unwakened from history's nightmares.

And there at the wheel in front of me sat the young Francie Boylan with his old man's memory. He was not in the least distracted by the men at my back: the ones clattering down from the Post Office, now charging toward us.

CHAPTER 11

THERE WERE THREE OF THEM.

Solid-built men in tweed caps and dark flapping suits. Faster on foot than the slow-moving Citroën in the choke of O'Connell Street traffic; gaining on us, grimly, like pursuing bogeymen in quagmire dreams, each of them with a menacing hand tucked in his coat.

Now their emergent faces. Red and relentless, encased in women's nylon hose, rendering their features flat, meaningless, surreal.

Drivers panicked, and angered. Tires screeched, horns honked. Shrieks of warning cut through the traffic hum.

But still, our driver's senses did not stray.

And the breathless bogeymen drew close enough to kill.

They pulled guns from coats. Long-barreled revolvers that might have been .44s, like my own big, ugly Charter Arms Bulldog. Which regrettably was locked in a closet back in New York.

They were now only steps away. I saw flat eyes behind the nylon, and the murder in them. And did I hear Francie Boylan's curt, forbidding words again? "It's time now."

Ruby screamed.

"Hock—!" I put a muzzling hand at the back of her neck and shoved her roughly to the floor. "Stay there!" I ordered.

Boylan, startled, swung around for a look at this minor commotion. And what a look was now revealed in his face.

Francie Boylan was no longer the earnest chauffeur, nor the compelling *shanachie;* certainly not a stoic functionary in whatever deadly mission was under way. He was all arrogance now, like the sulking toughs loitering in the doorway of old Black Monday's pub, waiting for his chance at taking a blow for all the real and imagined slights to an Irishman's honor.

But it was me who struck first, not him. I filled Francie Boylan's troubled face with my fist. His nose broke, bursting red. "You son of a bitch!" I shouted at him.

Boylan cupped his blooded nose and fumbled the steering wheel, and the Citroën veered. Outside, I heard the assassins growl.

I crouched at the back window, clutching the door handle. Fists and gun barrels pounded the outside of the car, as if to force us to a stop. I pulled the handle and jerked open the door, shoving it quick and hard into the knees of the closest gunman. He was knocked to the street, screaming as a wheel crushed one of his limbs.

Up front, Boylan struggled with his wound and the spinning wheel, screaming back at me, "You bloody American bastard! You bloody, fookin' bastard you—!"

I pulled the door shut, then jerked it open again. And broadsided another one. He fell, and in the sliver of space between the door and the body of the car I saw a masked head crack against the pavement.

The third assassin opened fire. Two bullets ripped through the door I held, just above my head, searing through the leather of the front passenger seat, slamming into the dash.

A third shot. Boylan screamed, "You fookin'—!" And this became Francie Boylan's final life utterance.

With a corpse at the wheel, the Citroën careened out of control. Our chauffeur was only so much more nameless blood spent in O'Connell Street.

The car shot forward, spinning as blindly as a billiard ball cued off the mark. We caromed off a line of other cars and trucks for several eternal seconds, until everything came finally to a jolting halt, then quiet; the silence was more shocking than all preceding sounds of ripping steel and shattering glass.

The stillness was broken as a crowd of people left the sidewalks, surging tentatively through the twist of cars toward our Citroën, at the epicenter of the wreckage. From the floor came Ruby's frightened voice: "Hock, be careful!" I knelt down and leaned across the seat, touched her shoulder, then poked my head up for a look to the street.

The crowd was milled all around us now. Somewhere, back beyond the line of damaged vehicles, were two gunmen downed in the street. The third man, the shooter, was no doubt gone with the wind.

I touched Ruby again, and said, "All clear. Are you all right?"

"I guess so." Ruby had made a protective ball of herself during the siege. Knees bent, hands and arms looped over her head. She rose now from this huddle. She touched scrapes on her forehead, and a wrist. That was my fault. She looked me over, and said, "You're white as paste and shaking, do you know it?"

This was true. "A drink will do us both," I said.

For once, Ruby agreed.

I then took close notice of the wide-eyed people packed around the Citroën. They were not so much looking back at me, nor at Ruby unfolding herself and sitting up. It was the mess of Francie Boylan that held their attention, and had them gasping, and looking like they needed drinks far more than either of us.

What was left of Boylan's head was splattered against the driver's window, like the remains of a melon heaved against a wall. His ear had been blown away, replaced by an oozing hole roughly the size and shape of a coffee cup. Clearly, this was a wound caused by hollow-point dumdums, the preferred ammunition of an assassin engaged in a close-up job of work. Just as clearly, here were bullets far more common in New York than Dublin.

Ruby finally set eyes on Boylan. She covered her mouth, then quickly turned her head, and said, "My God, Hock—what is this, what's happening?"

I knew the answer, but could not yet say it. I stared at the sea of Irish faces instead—horrified, sickened faces beyond car windows blown to shards by bullets.

And for one fugitive moment, it seemed as if I was asleep.

Asleep in a bullet-riddled Citroën; in O'Connell Street, no less, with the press of its awful history. Not asleep at home, not exactly in that familiar, restless state when I can hear my father's ghost. But asleep just the same, as if my head was submerged in water; as if I was suddenly distanced from the raucous world above me, and freed from the rush and confusion of O'Connell Street, its noises secondary to secret sounds below the surface of what I could merely see.

In this momentary sleep, I imagined other Irish voices, floating somewhere in time through the pubs and the parlors of Dublin. Quiet, revealing voices that made sense of Ruby's natural question. I listened, as if to sleeping friends of my own father's ghost.

Ruby asked, again, "What's happening here—?"

"Bloody politics," I answered.

Eamonn Keegan, chief of the Dublin Garda, was a dapper fat man born to the great oak desk that divides his office into two unequal realms: the baroque expanse of himself, and the Oriental rugs and mahogany and red leather that warm Keegan's side of things, versus two puny chairs on a patch of bare wood floor where Ruby and I sat as hardly more than a pair of rowdy convicts dragged by the scruffs of our necks to an audience with the warden.

That was not quite how we had arrived at the chief's office, now fully two hours ago. But it was the true sentiment of our police escort from the murder scene in O'Connell Street.

A fleet of uniformed Dublin cops showed up there first, with their black wool jackets and trousers, leather Sam Brown belts with holstered .38s, and visored caps with black-and-white checkerboard bands. Theirs were among the more suspicious faces peering at me, right as I said, "Bloody politics." After which they hauled Ruby and me out of the Citroën and trundled us off to a police wagon with no windows. This was for initial questioning by somebody in a bad suit and hemorrhoids called Constable Mulcahy.

We sat on a dimpled steel bench inside the police wagon, with Mulcahy on the one opposite, flanked by two uniforms fondling big rubber saps they might have been happy to use. Since I do not own one, I am forever leaving home without an American

Express card. However, I am at all times obliged to carry the NYPD gold shield. This I hustled out of my pocket like it was a crucifix and Ruby and I were faced off against three vampires.

Mulcahy sniffed at the shield, rotated his suffering buttocks on the cold bench, and wanted to know, "What sort of trouble are you bringing us all the way from New York now?"

When somebody asks me a loaded question, and sneers like Mulcahy had just sneered, I find it useful to reply with something disarming. That way, I sometimes dig out the reason behind the prejudice. Besides which, there is little percentage in any other style of response. So I wriggled my own hips in imitation of Mulcahy's discomfort, and asked, "What do you do for that?" Mulcahy's face shook, and he said, "What—my arse?"

The uniforms laughed like they were a couple of kids who had just broken wind in a church pew. Ruby rolled her eyes, and whispered, "Oh, Hock!"

I said to Mulcahy, "When I was working the Bronx—this was way back, when I was a rookie assigned to precinct prowl duty—I had to ride around in squad cars all day and night. I can see I don't have to tell you about the occupational hazard of that. But maybe you'd like to know, I came across the surefire cure."

"Never mind any of that!" Mulcahy snapped. "It's murder we got here and now."

"When you can't stop scratching your after-side? Damn straight it's murder . . ."

I waited for Mulcahy to bark again, but he said nothing. Instead, he again shifted his afflicted buttocks.

So I continued, "What happened was, one night I'm just like you—grilling a perp, squirming in my seat, wishing to God I could go someplace for a good long scratch. Now, the perp is this Bronx drug dealer called Sweet Dick, who notices my predicament and says to me, 'You want to lose that ol' bad itch, man?' I say sure I do. And Sweet Dick says, 'Well, you come on over to my crib and I fix you up good . . .' "

I paused. Mulcahy said, "Well—?"

"So we go over to Sweet Dick's place. He takes a little jar of Vaseline down off a kitchen shelf and says, 'No peeking now, man—trade secret, you know.' He goes off to the next room by himself. In a couple of minutes, he comes back and gives me the jar, and says, 'To thine ownself be kind, just rub this on your skinny behind.' Which to Sweet Dick is the funniest thing anybody's ever said. You should have heard him laugh."

"Did you use the stuff?" Mulcahy asked, anxiously. "Did it work?"

"Sure, I used it. Never had one more problem with the itch. Not until I ran out of the stuff and had to go find Sweet Dick again. Trouble was, I found him dead. Which in New York can happen."

"Never mind that. What was in the stuff?"

"Well, I eventually had to go to the police lab for a chemical analysis . . ."

"What the deuce was in it, man?"

"Petroleum jelly and cocaine."

The uniforms sniggered some more.

Mulcahy's eyes narrowed, and he said, "I'm marking you down as uncooperative."

"Noted."

He looked at both of us, sneered again, and said, "Maybe we've just got us a couple of real political types here, what?"

Ruby spoke up at this. "I won't speak for the gentleman, but I'm certainly no politician," she said. "Constable, do you know why a politician has one more brain cell than a horse?"

"No. Why?"

"So he doesn't crap in the street during parades."

"That corks it!" Mulcahy said. He stood up, furious at us both for spoiling his interrogation, more furious yet at the fire in his seat. He moved a hand discreetly back behind himself. "We'll now be taking you down to Keegan himself for formal questions about your bloody politics."

Which, as I said, was fully two hours ago.

We had spent most of this time minus our passports in a small closed room with a couch and two side chairs, a table with ashtrays and lukewarm tea in a flowered ceramic pot and the Dublin newspapers. And a mirror along the top half of one wall.

"I recognize a two-way viewing and holding room when I see one," I whispered to Ruby. "They've probably got the room wired for sound, too. We should talk about anything but politics."

"Better we should talk about nothing, period—until we see a

lawyer, or at least somebody at the American Embassy," Ruby said. "So I'm going to shut up now. Later, I'm going to scream. I suggest you do the same."

Good advice, I agreed. After all, we were a couple of shady foreign characters by the lights of whomever was observing us from the other side of the mirror. So we mostly drank tea and caught up on the news and stayed cool. And therefore looked guilty as hell of something, as I have always assumed of the calm, cool and collected types I myself have sweated in such rooms.

Eventually, we were shown into Keegan's office. That was ten minutes ago, with us sitting all the while in the puny chairs and him ignoring us while he scanned a short stack of papers an aide had spread out on his desk.

Chief Keegan now clipped down the tip of a cigar and lit up. He did not offer me one. The sweet aroma of Cuban tobacco mixed nicely with the other smells in the room: old books lining the shelves behind Keegan, bay rhum gleaming on his jowls, lanolin slicking down his thinning black hair.

He looked up and across his desk at Ruby, and said, "Madam, what exactly is the nature of your association with Mr. Hockaday?"

"*Detective* Hockaday."

Keegan smiled at her, but not to be friendly to a tourist. My guess was he would have liked to slap the insolence off her face. "As you say," he said to Ruby.

"Hock and I, we're slow-dancing together," Ruby said.

The chief riffled through papers, shaking his great, glistening head. His eyes narrowed between pudgy, hooded lids, and he said to Ruby, "That's a very amusing answer, madam. Here I thought perhaps Constable Mulcahy was exaggerating, but I now see for myself how you're the uncooperative type."

Then Keegan turned to me. "Let's try you, Hockaday. Have you any clue as to what happened today in O'Connell Street?"

"That's a professional question?"

"Maybe so."

"What makes you think I've got a professional answer?"

Keegan leaned back in his chair, puffing his cigar. "There's been time enough for us to make certain inquiries—Detective."

"That's real nice," Ruby said.

"She means it's nice you're calling me Detective," I said to Keegan. "She doesn't think it's nice the way we've been treated here. Neither do I."

Keegan waved a hand and said, dismissively, "You know how these things are."

"Where I come from, there's a local custom called professional courtesy. That means we don't go around figuring some out-of-town cop who happens to witness a shooting on some crowded street is the one who pulled the trigger—which means we don't confiscate his passport and then sit him down for two hours in a little room with a phony mirror."

"So that's the way we're making you feel now? I'd hate to think the Garda could be responsible for straining Irish-American relations." Keegan, yawning, picked our passports out from the papers on his desk and handed them to us. "Speaking on behalf of all Dublin, my apologies to you and the lady. You're quite free to leave, you know—right this minute if you fancy."

"You forget, you asked me a question."

"True. But tell me, did I receive the professional courtesy of an answer?" Keegan now displayed the malignant smile.

I did not take the smile kindly, and said, "What's the joke, Chief?"

"There'll be no jokes coming from this side of the desk, Hockaday."

"Except for the gag about your treating us here like a couple of murder suspects."

"*Murder*, you say?" Keegan pulled forward, consulted his papers again. "But look here—according to Constable Mulcahy's report, you said it was something more than murder. Something about politics, was it now?"

Ruby nudged me, and said, "Maybe we ought to go."

Davy Mogaill's words were in my head: "*What does a right-born American know about politics?*" So I said to Keegan, "Maybe we'd better just trust the Dublin Garda to sort it all out."

"Trust—now there's a quality lacking in our brave new world," Keegan said. "And yet I cannot forget me sweet father always telling me, Never put trust in the inevitability of a glorious morning sun or your mother-in-law's smile." He paused, fixed me with a stare, and asked, "How about your own father, Hockaday? What's he tell you?"

I have given the same answer to questions about my father many times over the years. The words are always the same. They have always served as the numb explanation for the fact of my life, until I heard myself saying them now: "My father was a soldier, he died in the war and I never knew him."

"Is that so?" Keegan said, with no particular trust in this simple fact.

I changed the subject. "Let's move this along, Keegan. Everybody in O'Connell Street saw the same thing we did: three armed men running down from the Post Office steps. I took down two of them, the third one got away after nailing our driver. Now then—who the hell was it after us, and who the hell is Francie Boylan?"

Keegan's eyes danced and he began laughing, loud and merry, like a boy watching a chair collapse under a fat lady. No doubt he was laughing because I had just broken any halfway competent detective's first rule for asking questions in a hostile situation; which is, keep your mouth shut unless you know the answer. That much of the amusement I could readily understand. But there was more behind Keegan's laughter, and to understand it all would wind up consuming the balance of a sentimental journey to my ancestral land.

"The answers to your questions, Detective Hockaday—why, they'll add up to so much more than simple murder, wouldn't they now? And wouldn't you agree how this is all so much more complicated than one of your American whodunit novels?" Keegan was good at this, and he was enjoying himself; now it was me wanting to knock the insolence off his face.

"Hock, it's time to go," Ruby said.

"The lady's so right," Keegan said.

Again, I asked the artless question. "What's his politics?"

"Whose politics would you be wanting to know?"

"Boylan's."

"Francie Boylan," Keegan said, folding his hands, "is our living and dying Irish history."

"Meaning—?"

"Boylan was a fanatic. As Father always told me: fanaticism is protected by ignorance and is, therefore, irrefutable. And what about your father, Hockaday?"

"You asked me that before. And I told you, he died in the war."

"That you did."

"Our work here is done," I said, rising. Ruby stood up and took my arm. We headed for the door.

"Only one thing more," Keegan said.

I turned and looked at him, saying nothing. He was smiling again.

"I nearly forgot," Keegan said. "When I was on the line to New York, chatting with your Inspector Neglio, he asked me to pass along a bit of unfortunate news."

"What news?"

"It's about a friend of yours, the inspector says. A priest, name of Timothy Kelly . . ." Keegan paused to study my reaction to this, then said, "Poor chap, it seems he's killed himself."

Keegan might well have cold-cocked me. He asked, "Would you like to use the telephone?"

"Thanks, not here," I managed to say.

"No, I shouldn't think so." Keegan stood up from his desk and crossed the floor over to us, boards creaking under the weight of his tread. He offered his hand to me, suddenly as full of fraternal regard for a fellow Irish cop as his remarks only a moment ago were full of ambiguous suspicion. "Sorry for your troubles, Hockaday."

"I have the feeling they've just begun." I did not take Keegan's hand.

"You'll be staying at your uncle's place then, in Dún Laoghaire?"

"Isn't that what it says on my visitor's declaration? You must have read that."

Keegan only smiled.

"If I leave town, maybe I'll let you know," I said.

"The Dublin Garda will appreciate the consideration."

"Which the Garda will get, in direct proportion to the cooperation given to me."

"And what sort of cooperation might an innocent visitor to the Emerald Isle be needing?"

"You show me yours, Chief, and I'll show you mine."

We left him standing there in his snug office, unsmiling.

Outside in the street, and well away from Garda headquarters, Ruby asked, "What in the world just happened in there?"

I reached into my pocket and pulled out the medallion Father Tim gave me the day before in New York. Was it to protect me against such a fate as Francie Boylan met? I held it flat in my hand and looked it over again, at the one side stamped with the initials H.O.S., the other with the *fasces*. I looked at it as if I expected the thing to talk to me. *"Always keep this in your pocket while you're on the other side, Neil. And for the sake of your life with Ruby Flagg, remember it's there when you need it."*

I closed my eyes, remembering the vision of Father Tim in the sanctuary of Holy Cross making his novena to St. Jude, and later in the back of a taxicab with tears in his eyes; seeing in this my failure to heed an old friend's desperate farewell. And my betrayal of him and of Davy Mogaill, too, as I remembered as well asking myself, Can you ever really know about your friends?

When I now failed to answer Ruby, she asked, "You look pained, Hock. What is it?"

. . . Again came the dreamt Irish voices across time, telling me to think not of how poor Father Tim might have died, but how in life he shaped my naïveté. And reminding me of the two earthly things he loved best: politics and the movies, which he used to joke were one in the same. *"Watch and see some day if voters don't start electing men to the highest public office right off the silver screen,"* he used to say. People used to laugh. . . .

"I'm remembering the way I'd go to the movies when I was a kid, never paying attention to the show times," I said. "I'd just walk into the theater whenever, right in the middle of a picture; it didn't matter. I could always stay on past the end, and wait for the next performance—until I caught up with all scenes I'd missed at the beginning."

"We all went to the movies that way," Ruby said. "We were all young once."

"Things are so bright and clear when you're a kid, aren't they?

An afternoon at the movies is the same as forever. There's always time to get the whole story."

"And now that you're not so young?"

"Time is running a race with confusion. No matter how it comes out, something's gaining on me."

"Something should, Hock. I notice whenever you're feeling sorry about your middle-aged self you forget two things."

"What—?"

"There's no magic in being a little boy forever. And you're not alone, you've got me."

"Thank heaven for little girls."

"Do that sometime. Thank heaven. Right now, hadn't you better call New York?"

CHAPTER 12

ANOTHER SIX RINGS.

The sharp sound of a telephone in the stillness of New York's predawn startled Mogaill from his whiskey haze. He dropped his glass to the floor.

Once again, he did not pick up the call.

"What's he going to think of me not answering?" Mogaill asked.

The man with the black-and-white beard and the .45 automatic sitting across from him, smoking a steady stream of Camel straights, stretched himself and said, "Maybe he'll figure you finally drown't yourself in booze."

"And maybe he'll come searching for me."

"They'll not be much to find now, will there?"

"You'd best take proper care of me. Sooner or later, they'll come searching, and they'll not be amused to find one hair of me harmed by the likes of you." Mogaill reached down over the arm of his chair and recovered his glass on the floor, then picked up the liter of Black Bush on the table next to him. He poured another drink, for himself only.

"You've drunk enough by now to fill the Mouth o'Shannon."

"Can't you see, my old friend? It's only my drinking makes you interesting."

"I don't come here to be insulted."

"You're entitled to your opinion, wrong as it is."

"You know what I come for, you hump."

"I do indeed. You've come because you cannot help but what you are, Finn. A very little man with a great big gun."

"We're both of us plenty big enough to shut up a smart mouth!" Finn clacked the cartridge of the automatic.

"And how would killing me advance you, or your betters—or your sinful cause? Think careful now."

"No need to kill you, Davy. When I shoot, I'll be aimin' for your kneecaps, or your elbows, or hips. You'll be spendin' the rest of your days wish't I'd plugged your heart."

"Spoken like a true patriot."

"Aye, a patriot's what I am."

"And would you be claiming yourself a man of principle?"

" 'Tis a dark shame we don't say the same of you no more."

"Nae, the shame's on patriots like you, Finn. You're good at fighting for principles, but not so good at living up to them."

"You'll not slow the struggle usin' your pretty words."

"What a shocking, unpatriotic thing you say. Anybody knows it's words are a true Irishman's best weapons."

Finn jumped from his chair, lunged at Mogaill and whipped his mocking face with the pistol. Mogaill's drink flew from his hand, whiskey and blood dribbled down his chin. In his defense, Mogaill roared with laughter. And Finn, his pistol raised for another blow, could only tremble in confused anger.

"Sit down with your gun now," Mogaill commanded. "Pathetic, isn't it, how a patriot such as you's no match for laughter?"

Finn's arm slowly fell. Mogaill laughed again, and said, "If you owned a tail, I'd see it now curling out between your knees." Finn sat down. With as much authority as he could muster in his voice, which was not much, he said to Mogaill, "Let's us talk of the agreeable thing near to both our hearts."

Mogaill recovered his glass, poured more whiskey into it, and gave it a grand wave. Then he said, "By which you're meaning— the olde sod itself?"

"Aye, Eire."

"As Sean O'Casey wrote, 'The terrible beauty is beginning to lose her good looks.' But then, being a high-ranking member of

81

an ignorant army, you wouldn't be much of a reading man, would you?"

"It's words like that'll do you in when you're facin' the ones less kind and tolerant as me," Finn said, lighting another Camel. "We're friends for years, Davy. Which is why I'm lettin' you live, out of respect for the past—"

"My deepest gratitude to you all," Mogaill said, interrupting.

"But the cause's bigger and older than our friendship. So, never forget, I'm still fightin', along with those you abandoned. And we've no patience for your satire."

"Stop wasting time then, bring on your grim comrades. I'll tell them same as you what I think of your damnable politics. Not that any man jack of you would understand." Mogaill finished his drink. "The way I see it, politics is the pursuit of you trivial types, you little men with your big guns. When you succeed, you become important in the eyes of other trivial men."

"Blast you! I remember the day you was the surest of us all."

"That was then. Today I'm saying there ought to be a kind of politics where a man needn't be certain of every thing, nor every minute. All the good of this life thrives on continual uncertainties provided by God. Did you never hear that, Finn?"

"More pretty words!"

"No decent Irishman owns ears so hard as yours." Mogaill shook his head.

"I ought to blow away a kneecap now."

"First give me a moment, please, I'll be having another jar." Mogaill picked up the bottle. It was empty. "Damn the luck!"

"The sun's coming soon, and with it, the others." Finn clacked the automatic again. "You know what we'll be needing to hear."

"Yes, I do," said Mogaill. His arm dropped over the side of his chair, his hand down to the black box, out of Finn's sight. Then he rose from the chair.

"Where you goin'?" Finn said.

Mogaill rubbed blood on his chin. "To wash me Irish mug for your lovely friends."

Mogaill walked to the bathroom as the telephone began ringing again. Finn followed him, and stood outside the locked door as Mogaill ran water.

CHAPTER 13

"IT'S NOT EVEN DAYBREAK BACK IN NEW YORK," RUBY SAID. "WHERE the hell is he?"

I hung up the phone. "Well, you said he'd be safe and sound at home, didn't you? Innocently passed out drunk."

"That was before our little cruise down O'Connell Street with Francie Boylan, and before Keegan was telling us about your priest's suicide. Now I'm not so sure there's anything Irish that's innocent."

I picked up the telephone again.

"Who're you calling?" Ruby asked.

"Tomasino Neglio. He's not Irish."

I gave the overseas operator Neglio's home number and said it was collect. There was a half-minute of hissing through the trans-Atlantic cable, then Neglio picked up on the second ring. He complained about it to the Dublin operator, but he accepted the charge. By the sound of him, I guessed he had not managed to get back to sleep after Keegan's call.

"Answer me one thing," Neglio said. "How is it you can't just go away for a nice holiday and leave everybody alone, including us back here in New York?"

"So you miss me already?"

I heard him blowing over the surface of hot coffee. "Hock, what gives over there? And for the love of Christ, don't tell me it has anything to do with this Father Kelly smoking himself over here."

"What makes you say that?"

"Little things, like first I hear all over the TV and radio how there's this priest who shoots himself inside a confessional at your old choirboy stamping grounds, Holy Cross—"

"What?"

"That's the way I said it myself when I heard the news. So I call up the PDU at Midtown-North and they give me over to one Lieutenant Ellis, and guess what he tells me? He says you, Hock, are one of the last persons to see old Father Kelly while he's still able to rattle his beads."

My words were slow and weak, and I realized I sounded like a nervous perp hit with a question that cuts straight to the bone. "I paid the cab fare . . . he was going home . . ."

"Not quite," Neglio said. "Right about when your plane was lifting off the runway, Father Kelly was in that confessional giving it one last shot, so to speak."

I decided for the time being to keep quiet about the troubling talk I had had with Father Tim after showing him my father's photograph, and about the odd medallion Father Tim had given me. Which is to say, I decided to make this personal. This despite the fact I was first warned against making cop work personal when I was wearing the Police Academy crewcut. Smart cops back off personal cases like rich people back out of rooms full of relatives. Which maybe says something about how smart I am.

"Did he go quick?" I asked.

"He shoved this antique Mauser in his mouth and it was lights out—one shot, smack into the cortex. From the bullet, he didn't suffer. What led up to the bullet, that's the excruciating question." Neglio paused, then said, "I have to tell you, Hock, I don't think Lieutenant Ellis is going to be so quick about shutting down the book on this one."

"No?"

"Not with Mogaill from central homicide sticking his nose into this suicide for some reason or other. And not when he eventually hears about how you just so happen to be on the scene of a murder in Dublin. You see how it looks?"

"Davy Mogaill—?"

"A pal of yours, isn't he?"

"He was my rabbi." I took a breath. "When I landed here, there was a message waiting for me to call him at home."

"But you didn't reach him, did you?"

"No. How did you know?"

"I couldn't reach him either. Know where I could find him?"

"The message said to call him at home. He's out in Middle Village, Queens, off Metropolitan Avenue."

"I'll send a car to the house. Get back to me. And Hock, take care of yourself."

CHAPTER 14

NOTHING I KNEW OF THE LIFE OF MY UNCLE PREPARED ME FOR THE SIGHT of the house in Dún Laoghaire.

Ruby and I stood with our bags in Ladbroke Street after the taxi left us, gaping at number 10, where Liam Hockaday had resided so long as I knew: the big corner place in a row of Baroque houses and elegant old trees, overlooking the cold blue Dublin Bay and its fleets and ships and ferries that trafficked the Irish Sea. There were five storeys of ivy-covered stone, bay windows of beveled glass in lead panes, wooden pilasters and a square-arched Georgian doorway. For the first time in the two hours since we had left the Dublin Garda, we talked of something besides Father Tim's suicide and the possible whereabouts of Davy Mogaill.

"It's the most beautiful house I've ever seen," Ruby said. "Why didn't you tell me you come from money, Hock?"

"Because nobody ever told me."

I knew, of course, that my bachelor uncle had extra to spare. He sent a weekly check to my mother, drawn on the Bank of Ireland, right up to her end. But this was common practice; even a poor Irishman provided something regular for his brother's widow. That check was greatly needed when I was a boy, but the amount of it never betrayed the grand house where it was written and signed, no more than Uncle Liam's appearance or manner led anybody in New York to imagine he was anything more than what he said he was: a longshoreman, retired, from Dún Laoghaire.

The last time I saw Liam Hockaday was nearly twenty years ago, during the first week of December when my mother died. I thought of him now, standing beside me then at the open grave in St. John's Cemetery, Queens; me in my crisp rookie blues, him in his scuffed brown shoes and tobacco-reeked tweeds and black rain slicker, crossing himself, wet nosed and weeping, dropping red roses into her final resting place, whispering in Gaelic in frosted whiskey breath that danced in the dank gray air.

. . . And who else was there among the tiny party to see her off? Father Tim, who sang a Eucharistic hymn, a cappella, and sprinkled holy water atop the lacquered pine casket. Two anonymous grave diggers in parkas and boots, as accustomed to tears and loss as they were to fog and damp earth. And my solemn-faced rabbi, Davy Mogaill . . .

"Well, come on, let's go," Ruby said, lifting a bag.

"I feel like I ought to be carrying a chicken under my arm," I said.

"How's that?"

"There's an Irish stereotype I've heard about all my life. It's about the shirttail relation who pops up one day here in County Dublin from somewhere out in the countryside, firmly believing that one skinny, freshly strangled chicken in a burlap bundle is fair exchange for the vaguely estimated weeks he'll be eating and sleeping and drinking at your expense."

"Oh, we've got shirttails like that in Louisiana, too. Not one of them's Irish, and some don't bother about the chicken." Ruby started for the house. I picked up two remaining bags and followed her. She said, "Anyhow, we were invited, remember?"

. . . Invited by Patrick Snoody, my uncle's "loyal friend." Who seemed surprised to meet the two of us when he pulled open the big Georgian door following a long chorus of chimes.

"However did you arrive?" he asked, glancing up and down Ladbroke Street over my shoulder. There was only a bicyclist. Snoody shaded his slitted eyes with a hand and watched the bicycle disappear down the hill toward the bay.

"We took the intercity line down the coast, then a taxi from Parnell Square at the piers," Ruby said, pointing in the same direction Snoody was looking.

"Thanks all the same for sending Francie Boylan after us," I said.

Snoody shook his large gray head, and said, "I've heard." He made no effort to stand aside for us. Big as the doorway was, Snoody nearly filled it with his considerable height and girth. He wore a well-cut suit and his speech told me he had been to good schools back when people still valued speech, and this was as imposing as the size of him.

"You don't mind if we come in to see my uncle, do you?" I said.

"Terribly sorry," Snoody said. "What a savage I'm being. Please, do come in."

We were then able to step past him into a rectangular entry hall with a tiled floor and mahogany wainscoting. A curved staircase lay at the far end of the hall, which continued beyond the steps. Arches off either side of the front hall led into a pair of opulent sitting rooms, one dark and small and cluttered, the other sunny and laid out sparely, as if it were ready to be photographed. I could tell the rooms were opulent on account of the cornices and moldings and plaster rosettes on the ceilings, not to mention the paintings all over the place in gilt frames with little lamps over them. Also there was enough marble and onyx around to furnish a nice mausoleum.

Ruby and I set down our bags where Snoody told us to, in front of a desk with a telephone and a stack of mail. Next to this was a tall pegged stand for coats, hats and umbrellas. On the desk was a sketch in a gold filigree frame, supported by an easel. Ruby said, "Look at this, Hock." I said, not very brightly, "Real old, isn't it?"

"Indeed it is," Snoody said. He stood close in back of us, close enough for me to feel the puff of his breath on my neck. How big men like him are able to move so quick and quiet is a wonder to noisy types such as myself. "It was done in chalk, by Giovanni Battista Tiepolo, about 1750," Snoody said. "It's titled *Study of the*

Head of Tiepolo's Son, Lorenzo. Quite famous really, it was used as a figure in a fresco at the palace of the prince-bishops of Würzburg."

"And here it is in my own uncle's house," I said, turning to face Snoody. "This is my uncle's house, isn't it?"

Snoody laughed through his nose, and said, "You're in the right place, Mr. Hockaday." He looked down at our bags. "Well, since Mr. Boylan won't be around anymore," he said airily, as if Francie Boylan had merely quit his job on the household staff, "I'll have cook take your things upstairs. Will you, ah ... will you be wanting separate rooms?"

"I'll be wanting to talk to you about Francie," I said, "but first I want to see my uncle. Where is he?"

"One room, one bed," Ruby said.

"If you'll wait in there," Snoody said, motioning toward the drawing room all ready to become a cover shot. "Cook will prepare your room. I'll fetch Liam. You'll find whiskey and sherry on the table by the chimneypiece. Or if you'd rather tea—"

"No, the booze will do fine," I said. Snoody gave me a sneer nearly as sour as Ruby's. Then he stalked off down the back hallway.

"He doesn't like me, right?" I said to Ruby as we stepped into the drawing room.

I headed straight for the refreshments at the fireplace, *chimneypiece* as Snoody called it. Ruby sank into the cushions of a short peach and green damask couch angling out from the fireplace over a pale blue and cream Oriental rug. She looked ready to fall asleep there.

"Not very much," Ruby said. "Sometimes I feel the same, like now for instance."

"It's not like I'm not officially on duty, you know." I picked up a crystal decanter. I also picked up two glasses and showed them to Ruby.

"This round, you drink alone," she said. I poured my whiskey.

On the wall over the liquor table I noticed another sketch of another guy's head in another chunky frame, this one with a tiny gold plaque attached. I read it off: *"Portrait of a Young Boy, Annibale Carracci, 1591."*

I sat in the twin couch opposite Ruby, sipped a smooth brown single-malt whiskey, the likes of which I have never tasted, and set it down on the low table between us. "Some of this fruity art, I don't know," I said. "What do you think, maybe old Patrick and Liam are a couple of ballerinas?"

Ruby looked at me like I was diseased. "I think you can be a class-A Philistine sometimes, Hock."

"Well . . . Uncle is a lifelong bachelor. I'd bet Snoody is, too."

"You want to try for being a third?"

"I'm thinking out loud."

"There's thinking, and there's jabbering. Only one of these things is done by mouth."

"I'm only trying to figure what it is that's hidden here—"

Noise from the hallway cut me off. There were suddenly two people doing enough hollering for a dozen out there. I recognized Snoody's patrician voice, the second belonged to a woman we could not see from where we sat. She was well past her maiden days and was what my mother used to call bogside Irish, with the thud of *Gawd* in her talk.

"You'll not be makin' me party to the wild depravity of the streets!" the woman shouted.

"I tell you, Cook, you'll take these grips upstairs to the red room!" Snoody bellowed, his rolled *r*'s echoing softly in the hall. "And you'll make damned quick business of it!"

Ruby and I sat very still in our couches, awkwardly amused.

"Moira Catherine Bernadette Booley shan't sing the glories of Gawd on Sunday, then turn 'round t'be servin' Satan Monday! Nae, I'll not be turned wicked, e'en in the horrible face o'your blasphemin' the name o'Gawd! Sooner'd you crown me with boilin' tar!"

"Whatever makes your bloomers roll up, cook old girl!" This surprising vulgarism from Snoody caused Moira the cook to gasp, loudly. To be perfectly clear, Snoody added, "If it's tar you want, it's tar you shall have!"

"Jaysus, Mary and Joseph—Gawd be merciful to your fallen servant!"

There was then the sound of, what—wheels? And Uncle Liam's voice, more cancerous than I recalled: "What's all this cater-wauling now with the two of you?"

"Mr. Liam, he's meanin' for them two in there to fornicate," said Moira. I presumed by them two she was referring to Ruby and me.

"Good Lord, Patrick, you're not offending Cook's pure and Christian sensibilities again?" Liam asked.

I heard Snoody's haughty nose again.

Moira charged, "Aye, he's blasphemin'! And threatenin' a true child o'Gawd besides."

Liam answered, "Dear Moira Catherine, with all the suffering and rot in this corroded vale—really now! What of the crimes of the odd curse, some old fellow's noisy intemperance, or even some unchaste traffic about the jolly bits? Well might you wisely conclude, this is all wee stuff."

"Take the bags upstairs now," Snoody said, calmly.

Moira made a final appeal to Liam: "Did y'get your peep at her in there, sir? Looks like the golliwogg, she does. Mixin' of the blood's against Gawd's holy principles."

"I've always preferred God's people to His principles," Liam said.

Moira gasped.

"Take the bags, Cook," Snoody said. Liam added, "You might as well do as he says, dear Moira Catherine. Then please, take the next hour of your day and pray mightily for our nefarious souls."

There was much huffing about this, and more of Snoody's nose laughter. Then feet clumping on the staircase and luggage bumping ever upward, step by step. Snoody stalked off somewhere. The wheels sounded again. And Uncle Liam entered the drawing room.

He had shrunk some in twenty years' time, as men do, and his skin had spotted. And there was the wheelchair.

I have seen sick old people shape themselves to wheelchairs like infants to their cradles. But not Uncle Liam. There was a small quilt snugged over his knees, to warm the idled legs and keep the blood flowing, but this was his sole concession to immobility. Otherwise, he had not yielded himself to the thing. His back was still defiantly straight, his shoulders thrust back, stomach tucked. At a distance, even in the chair, Liam Hockaday looked perfectly capable of taking up cap, coat and stick for a brisk walk down to Parnell Square. His arms and elbows flailed as he rolled himself toward us, as if the exertion were highly resented.

Up close, there was indeed the wreckage of time in his face. But he hardly looked to be at death's door, as Snoody had advertised. His brown eyes were as bright and sharp as his tongue. He still took obvious care in his grooming. His skin had the good ruddiness of a man who still enjoyed wine and the daily weather.

He might well have read in my own face a rush of anxious questions about his health and wealth. And so maybe this was why Liam started talking to Ruby and me as if the three of us were picking up from only that morning, yesterday at the very latest. "I'm sorry for all the boisterous codswallop," he said, braking his wheelchair to a stop between us.

Ruby and I stood. Liam winked at me, then reached up to embrace Ruby in a brittle hug. She bent forward, and kissed his cheeks. He said to her, "My bonny Ruby Flagg, you're beautiful, and tonight as I'm alone in my bed, I shall cry for being a man born too early to romance you proper."

"Oh . . . ," Ruby said. I have never thought of Ruby as the melting type, but she melted then.

"I've heard no more about you than your name, but we'll get to know one another by-and-by," Liam said. He put his lips to her hand. "Welcome to Ireland."

"Oh . . . !"

I moved to Liam, took him in my arms, kissed his rough cheeks. I asked, "How are you, Uncle?"

"Suffering the usual indignities of a man seven decades here," Liam said. He read pity in my face. Old people in wheelchairs have a right to resent such looks as mine. "This contraption instead of my legs, for instance," he said, sniffing. "Also, an impressive case of constipation. Such knots in my pudding I suffer! And a mighty crink in my neck from looking up at you two. I could go on. But you'd leave me then. So, sit down."

We sat.

Liam said, "I notice you've started on the whiskey, Neil. Too much spirit for me now. You'll be kind enough to fetch me a sherry then?" He turned to Ruby. "And for yourself, bonny?"

"Yes, sherry please," Ruby said. "I enjoy a drink with a charming man, especially in charming surroundings."

I poured.

"Now, let me first say you mustn't be overly heedful of the

house squabblers," Liam said after a small sip of his drink. "Moira's a bit of a bigot and a monumental blister, but graced by God with the talent for cooking. That's a rare woman in this land of potatoes and earnestly boiled beef, as you'll soon come to appreciate. Old Patrick's a defrocked priest, so he's naturally a touch bitter and superior like. But he's been my companion of ten years now, and I've learned to forgive him his mother hen ways."

I shot a look at Ruby, then asked Liam, "Snoody was a priest? What did he do to lose the collar?"

"That was a long, long time ago," Liam said, laughing lightly. "When Snoody was much younger than you, Neil. He was an idealist, believing in the perfectibility of man and such other twaddle. Which might have been tolerated had it not been for an unfortunate habit."

"What was that?" Ruby asked.

"He was given to saying strong things that those above him could remember," Liam said. "This is always most unwise. I suppose you'd like to know just what he said that got him the heave?"

"Yes," Ruby said.

"Yes!" I said.

Liam took another small, slow sip. I felt a pinprick of memory: Uncle Liam sitting in our parlor in Hell's Kitchen, for hours on end with my mother and with Father Tim and the neighbors, telling us wild, funny tales from the other side. And me, never guessing such stories came from anywhere but the house of a man rich only in imagination. Now here we sat in the lavish surroundings of this house, and Ladbroke Street.

"The Lord only knows where priests are delivered of these notions, but our young Father Patrick Snoody got it into his head as how the church must strive to be a blazing force for goodness and light in the world," Liam said.

"Poor Snoody, he quickly found the church lacking in this mission, and this stunned the lad. So he became a viperous critic of the ecclesia, stunned as he further was to discover that the church is only one more society with the ordinary population of cheats, blackguards, mediocrities and Pecksniffs. He once actually sent a letter to a particularly nasty-hearted monsignor, and included the line from Swift that goes, 'We have just enough religion to make us hate, but not enough to make us love one another . . .'"

Liam paused and sipped, then asked, "By the way, have you a fag?"

"Cigarette you mean?" I asked after a moment's confusion.

"Aye, that's it."

"Sorry, no. When I smoke, it's somebody else's cigarettes."

"Well, that's a way of reducing the morbid odds," Liam said. "Patrick and Moira, they're not so very much different as would seem, the recipe for many a battle. Neither smokes, for instance. They won't let me near fags of my own."

"They're concerned for your health," Ruby suggested.

"Overly so," I said. "Snoody wrote me you were dying."

"Did he now? Dying!" Liam freed the brake on his chair, pivoting so he could look at the hallway. He turned to us again, and said, "The mother hen worries that I'm lonesome for my American nephew, and deprived of beautiful American women. He's right. Good fellow, he's got you both here."

"Not without tragedy, Uncle," I said.

"You're speaking of the late Francie Boylan?"

"You know?"

"Aye. He was a good lad, but an idealist, with idealistic friends who spent entirely too much time in angry talking of the troubles."

"The troubles—?" Ruby said.

"We Irish are unfailingly genteel in discussions of the guerrilla war up in Ulster, by which we mean the IRA murderers versus the Brit murderers," Liam explained. "Anyway, as for poor Francie Boylan, loyal soldier to an ancient cause, may he be dead for a year before the Devil hears of it."

"May I ask a blunt question?" Ruby said.

"Americans usually do. Ask away and I'll answer you true, bonny. I would steal from you, but I would never lie."

"How is it you're not excited about any of this? You nor Snoody?"

"We are not so demonstrative as you Americans."

"But your nephew and I could have wound up the same as Francie Boylan, shot dead in O'Connell Street by masked goons. And you're not jumping up and down about it?" Ruby's hands flew to her mouth. "Oh—oh, I'm so sorry."

Liam smiled. "I've done my share of jumping, and look where

9 4

it's got me," he said, patting the chromed steel pushing rims around the wheels of his chair.

"Sorry," Ruby repeated, twisting herself on the couch into a position that looked like it hurt.

She might have pressed Liam further, as I might have myself. But Ruby and I were not up to the challenge. We were numb and weary to the bone, from the shooting and from the long flight over.

"Think no more of it. I'm only a coot who's lived long enough to know how violent death is unpleasant, though not unique. But what is unique is the pleasant moment now and again. In these few years God's left me, I dedicate myself to cultivating the cheerful mood. I command all unpleasantness, no matter how close to home, to fly out of mind at once. So right you are, Miss Ruby, I'm a breezy old goat. 'Tis a form of selfishness peculiar to the aged. Closely related to whistling in a graveyard, don't you see."

Liam finished his sherry. He asked me for another, and I fetched the bottle. He winked at Ruby, then offered me some avuncular counsel, "Lose your darling, Neil, and you're a bleeding fool like myself. I lost a darling of my own, long ago, and now you know the great regret of my life." He took a sip of the fresh sherry. "So tell me, how do you plan doing right by our bonny here?"

"Go on and talk about me, gentlemen," Ruby said. "I'm not even here."

"What she means, Uncle, is we've come for your blessing," I said. How dangerously close I was coming to a real proposal, I thought. Ruby shot me a look that told me she thought the same.

"How old-fashioned, how refreshing. You've got what you've come for, Neil. I fell in love with Ruby at first sight."

"But it's not all we've come for."

"Oh?"

"What he means," Ruby said, "is he's come to fill up his hollow places."

"I don't follow you, bonny," Liam said. There was the slightest quaver in his voice. He turned and looked at me.

"I'm in the pull of memory," I said.

. . . And that I was, remembering the day I first told Ruby how I had all my life dreamed of my father; how dreams, and one photograph, were all I had of him; how anything else I might

9 5

know of the man was taken by my mother to her grave. And how Ruby, staring quietly at me, had said, *"I'm sorry, Hock, but shame on your mother."* And had I not said this same secret thing to myself?

Ruby also said that day, *"Your father should never have been allowed to die that way, with nobody to give you his memory. Nobody survives without memories . . ."*

Liam eyed me suspiciously, as well he should. I wanted to tell him all of it, right then and there: my father's soldier photograph, the cryptic poetry, Father Tim's suicide, Davy Mogaill. I wanted to ask my uncle a hundred questions about himself, starting with his fine house in Ladbroke Street all these years. And if he would not answer quick enough, I would shake the truth out of him.

But Liam's cheery mask had faded, and with it, his strength. It was not now fair to ask him anything.

I could not help but resent this, just as Liam resented his wheelchair. Were we not both hostages? Liam to his chair, I to the silent truth of my father?

I managed to say to my uncle, "I've been dreaming about him, more than I ever have before."

"Who?"

"My father, your brother."

"There's time," Liam said, using his old arms to hoist himself up a few inches from his chair. A leg spasmed. He pounded at it with a fist, then pulled the quilt in his lap farther up toward his waist. These efforts tired him. "We'll talk of Aidan, by-and-by . . ."

"And his mother, Mairead, too?" Ruby said.

Liam, a stricken expression in his face, said, "Yes, and Mairead, too . . ."

"Will you be all right, Uncle?" I asked him.

"I take my lie-down each day about now, that's all. And why don't the two of you run along and rest yourselves? The red room's up on the third floor, to your left off the stair. Moira's no doubt up there praying over your sinful bed."

Ruby and I stood. I stepped behind Liam's wheelchair and took the handles. "Tell me where you want to go, Uncle," I said.

"Be off, you two," he said. "Patrick will come find me here."

As we headed toward the hallway, I remembered the phone on the desk with the eighteenth-century Italian sketch that was such a hit with German royals. I turned and asked, "May I make a telephone call?"

Liam, waving, said, "Yes—sure, sure."

"I'm for a shower and a long nap," Ruby said in the hall.

"Go on up then," I said.

"You won't be long, will you?"

"If I am, come get me."

"What do you mean by that?"

"I mean this doesn't feel good, does it?"

"No," Ruby said.

"Go on."

Ruby climbed the stairs. I dialed the international operator and gave the private number for Inspector Neglio at his office in One Police Plaza. As I waited for the connection, I heard a footstep in the back hall.

I looked. And saw only a shadow, of something.

"Hock—?" Neglio's voice was as clear as if he were in the next room.

"Yeah . . . what do you hear from Mogaill?"

"Bad news."

CHAPTER 15

MY PRESENT LINE OF WORK WAS NOT MY FIRST CAREER CHOICE.

Years ago, when City College was still tuition-free, as politicians had not yet learned they could win votes by mugging the poor, and I was up there taking journalism classes and trying my best to stay out of the draft, I saw myself as a newspaperman. In those days, I was crazy for a Hungarian girl who waited tables in her father's no-nonsense restaurant on Convent Avenue.

I would sit for hours in that dreary spoon nursing coffee and goulash, telling Magda how I dreamed of being a reporter. "It's like a calling," I actually said. I admit, it brought a heat to Magda's face that excited me. "I'm being called to make my living writing The Truth!"

One day the old man heard this. He walked over to where I was sitting with my goulash and where his daughter was floating happily around me. He was as big and solid and cold as a Kelvinator, and he never liked me. He noticed the pink in Magda's neck and face and he did not like that either. The old man knew what to do about it.

"What's it you going to write?" he asked me.

Again, I proclaimed my calling.

"What for you want to write the truth?"

"People need truth."

"Maybe so, but people no want it."

"Gee, I don't know—"

"Don't write truth, kid. You'll die in the gutter. That's the truth."

All the air went out of me. Magda was not so moony anymore, and after a while I stopped coming by. And so I never became a journalist. But I became sadder and wiser, and as I did I noticed how the newspapers only became sadder.

Sometimes I think I would make a great newspaperman today, if I was not so busy being a cop. Which is just as well, because I do not think any newspaper would actually have me.

I imagine myself in some throwback of a newsroom, the kind in the black-and-white movies on late night television. My feet are up on the desk. I am dozing.

Flash! Some guy just murdered his wife of twenty-five years with a ginsu knife he got her for their last anniversary. A bloody, hacked-up job of it. The neighbors are very shocked because the guy and his missus were such a lovely couple and they never missed Sunday mass and all that.

The ladies and gentlemen of the press naturally fall all over themselves rushing over to the house because this is a major paper-seller. The hair helmets from television are there, too, looking into cameras and telling viewers they are "live" at the scene of the crime. As opposed to dead?

And then while all the other reporters are filling up their notebooks with the facts of the matter, I am off in a corner by myself wondering about a guy who once so loved a woman twenty-five years ago that he married her, then one awful day hated her so bad he diced her all over the kitchen linoleum.

The way I see it, this big murder story is no story at all. The real story is what happened during those twenty-five years of these two people being a lovely couple together. Here now would be The Truth. The truth, the whole truth and nothing but the messy and complicated truth so help me God.

Only this does not cut it with the editor, who does not share my enthusiasm for the big picture. He is as big and solid and cold as a Kelvinator, and he does not like me. He says to me, "Just give me the facts, kid. You'll find that's the easiest way of filling up space on the page."

I begrudge no one the warm comfort of an uncomplicated view, least of all simple journalists. Sometimes I wish that I, too, could trust in what I can see and hear, or what can be read in a few column inches of newsprint. Sometimes I wish I was not a cop.

In my time, I have hunted down many murderers. None of it was ever simple. Some killers were meek, small people with faded dreams that corroded their hearts over time, until they burned to show somebody something. They were mostly pathetic, and their crimes were mostly uncelebrated. Others held the city in a thrall of terror until collared, their marks on us validated as much by big black tabloid headlines as by the corpses.

My killers were all tried and convicted in court, where great and costly care was taken to reveal the facts of their crimes, if not their scarred lives. The jury would say what it had to say, the judge would pronounce sentence, then later I would type an *S* for solved after their official case numbers. I would close up their manila folders and file them away, and sometimes forget.

The newspapers would give jumpy readers a soothing coda to the dreadful tale. A story about how the victim's family felt that justice was done. Or how the murderer had bowed his head at the verdict and wept in repentance.

But these were only facts. And facts do not necessarily speak for themselves.

Any good cop knows that. Cops like Davy Mogaill, who would be the first to say that truth is as welcome as the lash; and that the truth may not always set us free.

Certainly not me. I hear a man can die in the gutter from truth.

Far from the gutter, there I stood in the hallway of my Uncle Liam's well-appointed house. Where I had come for The Truth, finally, of my father. Whose name had so clearly troubled absent friends.

The telephone was in my hand, my heart was in my mouth. The priest was dead. And now this with my rabbi, whatever it was.

I was so terribly tired from it all—the flight, the grief of Father Tim's suicide, the murder of Francie Boylan, the strangeness of my uncle's house, now this with Mogaill; I wanted nothing more than to be upstairs, sleeping next to Ruby. Even if that meant hearing voices as I dreamed. Like Aidan Hockaday's ghost, or the last thing Davy Mogaill said to me: *"Sorry to say, Hock, there'll be no easy sleep ..."*

But it was the sound of Neglio coming at me again, which is about as dreamy as a burglar alarm in Canarsie, at least when he is talking to me. Put him in a room full of his uptown Gracie Mansion friends and he sounds different; you would swear Tomasino Neglio never even heard of Knickerbocker Avenue. Now, from faraway Manhattan, he said, "Still there, Hock?"

And I actually said, "I'm here, just give me the facts."

"All right, so far we got one thing for sure," the inspector said. "Davy Mogaill's house out in Queens was wired with a bomb that went off in the tiny hours."

"He's dead?"

"We found a body. Don't worry, not his. But Mogaill's missing."

"I don't understand."

"You think I do? Where were you Saturday, Hock?"

"Where was I? What is this—?"

"Just tell me."

"Saturday I spent time with Mogaill. Up in Inwood, at this bar called Nugent's."

"Ever hear of a guy called Finn? Arty Finn?"

"He's a fixture at Nugent's. Which is a very Irish place in a very Irish neighborhood, so sometimes there's a collection for the Noraid, if you're familiar. Finn's the collector."

"So I hear. He's also the body we found."

"In Mogaill's house?"

"What's left of it. Mogaill and Finn have some big problem together?"

"I don't exactly know. Davy didn't much like him, that I can say. He had a word with Finn at the bar, then Finn took off."

"You talked to Finn yourself, Hock?"

"No."

"Did you see him later that night, or Sunday?"

"No."

"What about Mogaill? You see him Sunday?"

"No, Sunday was my flight."

"Okay, then Saturday at Nugent's. What were you and Davy

talking about starting in the afternoon and winding up in the soft hours?"

"Politics, women, Ireland . . ."

I stopped because Neglio was now sounding too much like Eamonn Keegan for my liking. Too insinuating. Also because I remembered how the two of them had talked by telephone on the subject of Father Tim's suicide, while Ruby and I were cooling our heels in a holding room like we were a couple of perps. I do not take it well when the bosses talk about me behind my back.

They have their reasons, but I know I have mine for clamming up on them when this happens. Nothing personal. I decided that Inspector Neglio did not have to know right that minute about the troubling talks I had had with the missing captain and the dead priest. The talks on the subject of my father, and the cryptic poem written on the back of his photograph.

I asked, "How do you know how long I was at Nugent's?"

"I tend to do a little independent checking around whenever there's funny business involving my cops."

"This is funny?"

"Oh yeah, Hock. Funny like the smell of stale cabbage. *Capice?*"

"Meaning your pal the mayor's not laughing?"

"Let's just say Hizzoner doesn't appreciate the gag like you and me. He only sees how suddenly he's got a captain of central homicide missing after his house is blasted off the block. And how there's some dead paddy extortionist by the name of Arty Finn laying in said demolished house. And how it turns out all this unpleasantness happens right after the paddy captain noses around a Hell's Kitchen church where some retired mick of a padre shows up out of nowhere and fires a bullet into his brain right in the confessional. And how the last guy to see either one of these two is another Irishman, which is you. And what do you do? You hop a plane out of JFK. For guess where?"

"I get the picture."

"Do you? Let's don't forget one more thing: you and Ruby, you're in Ireland a couple hours, and what do you know—you hook up with some IRA goon who gets splattered all over Main Street Dublin."

"So on account of this, you don't take my word, you do your independent checking around?"

102

"No offense."

"None taken," I told Neglio, thinking past the insinuations, which were only natural the way he laid out the facts. Facts! But there was something he said back there that was important, something he had mentioned in the earlier call, too. I asked, "Mogaill was personally investigating Father Tim's suicide? You're sure of that?"

"Unusual, isn't it? Lieutenant Ellis thinks so. I got to agree. Davy's right there on the scene after the padre gives himself the business in Hell's Kitchen. Then he goes way up to Riverdale and talks to one Father Owen Curley, who lives at the old priests' home where your Father Timothy Kelly lived."

"He went there?"

"Searched his room, too."

"Anything else unusual?"

"What do you say to Mogaill leaving the retirement home and driving over to a diner on Broadway and Two-hundred-fortieth Street where he goes very goony on some teenage waitress who reminds him of his dead wife?"

"I'd say you've been doing one hell of a lot of independent checking."

"That's on account of I got an unusual amount of volunteer help."

"Volunteer—?"

"The newspapers and the TV and radio boys, they're on this thing like white socks on rednecks. The goddamn reporters, they think they've got a nice big ugly story about a rogue cop. The mayor and the commissioner, they don't like this kind of bad news."

"I suppose not."

"And I don't like it how I have to put out the word at every precinct shift muster to pick up your rabbi on suspicion. Which is what I have done. This kind of suspicion is not healthy for me."

"No . . ."

"But you and I, Hock, we know there's more to the story here, don't we? Lots more about all this with Mogaill and your priest friend, right?"

Can you ever really know about your friends?

I said nothing. The line was still for a few seconds.

103

"Hock, you still there—?"

"I'm here."

"Yeah, and I got a feeling you're sticking around awhile, too. Don't bother with postcards, but let's you and me stay in touch."

"Whatever you say."

"That's what I say. Also, if it was me with a pretty lady, I'd take her somewhere else besides a place so many of my people would just as soon forget."

I laughed.

"What's so funny?" Neglio asked.

"Smelling stale cabbage was the pretty lady's idea."

Our room was something that could have been right for a New Orleans bordello. Yet another surprise in Uncle Liam's surprising house.

Red flocked paper covered the walls. The window looking out over Ladbroke Street had box curtains with a pattern that made them look like they were in flames. There was a small fireplace and mantelpiece lacquered in maroon, with a couch in front of it full of embroidered pillows. A pair of lamps on the dresser wore pink shades with tassels. The rug looked like a truckload of sweetheart roses had recently had an accident all over it.

Ruby lay peacefully asleep beneath scarlet covers in a bed that came with a canopy of the same blazing color. I wished I could rest as easily.

Our luggage sat open on a settee at the foot of the bed. Ruby's crumpled blouse lay across the other things in her bag, which looked as if she had jumbled through them, probably in search of something to sleep in. My own bag was still neat, but slightly rearranged. I remember packing my father's photograph at the bottom of the bag. Now there it was at the top of the heap, staring at me.

Had Ruby moved it there?

There was a flowered ceramic basin on the dresser, along with a china pitcher full of warm water, pink and maroon towels and perfumed soap. I washed my face, then shucked off my clothes and slipped into bed with Ruby.

She folded herself into me. Her skin and breath and warmth were a comfort, her voice was husky with sleep. She kept her eyes closed. "Did you reach your inspector?" she asked, draping an arm over my chest.

"Yes."

"What about Mogaill?"

"Let's talk about it later, all of it."

"It's that complicated?"

"It's deep. Very deep. Deeper than I ever imagined."

Ruby touched my face, found my eyelids and pulled them closed. "Sleep, baby," she said.

And to sleep I went. And to dreams . . .

There is my father, as usual. In the handsome photograph held by its frame, back in New York. He is brave and young and uniformed.

As in all previous dreams, Aidan Hockaday's head and shoulders never leave that frame. It is the frame that has the legs and the soldier's boots, it is the frame that marches through the battlefields of my dreams.

But that is New York. In this first dream of my father, in an Irish bed, there is a sudden blur, and a changed vision of him.

Aidan Hockaday steps out from my bag at the foot of the bed, free of his frame. He stands beside me.

"How are you getting on, boy?" he asks. He is as young as his picture, younger than me. But his voice is much older than mine.

"I'm getting things mixed up," I tell him. "Stories, dreams, events."

"What's this? A visit from the færies during the night?"

"I don't know. It seems so real."

"Likely it is real, you were visited."

"I don't understand."

"We all know little bits and pieces of things in our lives, boy. But we need the færies—the good and the mischievous—to fit them all together. This is what's happening to you. And oh, but it's a wonderful gift you're receiving."

"It is?"

"My, yes. Everybody dreams, and that is good enough for most. A night's dream may be better than the world by day, but no truer. It's the færies who invite you to the place beyond your dreams. If that's where you care enough to go. Do you care, boy?"

"Yes."

"As well I thought. It's why the færies come to you. What greater gift for a detective who needs to know the true story of his own life? With such a gift, Neil, you've the power of being a *shanachie* one day yourself, a keeper of the truth. You really do want to know, don't you now, boy?"

"The Truth, yes."

. . . Sometime later, I was aware that day had passed to evening. The red room was now black and cold. I was sweating.

Someone was shaking me. It was not Ruby.

CHAPTER 16

"BEGGIN' YOUR PARDON, SIR."

This came in a stern woman's whisper. Muzzy from sleep, I realized I had heard these words repeated several times. And each time, the woman had poked my shoulder as she said them.

"What—?"

"I say, beggin' your pardon. I don't fancy this no more than you. No sir, I never like bein' in the disgustin' sight of sin. I say that, too."

I sat up, rubbing my eyes and mouth. I looked over at Ruby, still slumbering peacefully on her side of the bed. There was some dim light shafting into the room from the doorway. This silhouetted the large woman who was still jabbing me.

Waving an arm at her in the dark, I said, "Would you like to lose that finger, lady?"

She shrunk back a step, whispering coarsely, "Evil, snarlin' fornicator!" Light shone across half her beefy face, and on the gold crucifix hanging from her neck. I recognized, of course, Uncle Liam's God-fearing cook, Moira Catherine Bernadette Booley herself.

"What are you doing here?" I asked her. "What do you want from me?"

"I come to fetch you for master."

"Liam?"

"Aye, you're to come along now."

"Wait outside in the hall," I said. "Unless you want to witness the disgusting sight of my naked, sinful body."

Moira clapped a hand to her mouth in horror. She held up the other hand as a shield and hissed, "Gawd'll smite thee for your mockin' me, and for all your smutty crimes as well!" Then she waddled away from me, backward through the thin light.

I got up and pulled on my clothes. I ran a comb through my hair in the dark and wondered what on earth could be so urgently on Uncle Liam's mind that would have him sending Lady Christer to roust me. Not that Snoody, the embittered nose laugher, would have made the rousting any more agreeable. Ruby stirred in bed. I decided to let her sleep.

Moira was stamping a foot and otherwise seething with impatient disapproval out in the hallway. She greeted me there with a curt command: "Follow me down t'the hole where he's waitin'." Then she proceeded down the staircase and I trailed behind her backside, which moved along like a pair of drunken sailors. She finally delivered me to the smaller and darker of the two sitting rooms on the first floor.

We took a few steps inside the musty-smelling room. There was only the beginning of a blaze in the fireplace and a small lamp on a nearby table that gave light to the room. Newspapers and magazines cascaded over the edges of the table. There was an old cathedral radio there, playing American music that had me asking myself why I did not have sense enough to fly back home where I belonged; especially as Lady Christer said to Uncle Liam, "As you asked, I brung you the transgressin' nephew."

"Thank you, Moira, and God bless you," Liam said, back to us in his wheelchair parked close to the hearth. "Go on back to your kitchen now if you please." Moira shot me a nasty parting glance and bustled off. Liam turned his chair, and said, "Now come here by me, Neil."

I crossed a room that had been neither cleaned nor open to air and sun in a very long time. A bay of windows might have given a pleasant view, but it was blocked by heavy brocade draperies; I wondered if a colony of bats lived in the soiled pleats. There were tall wooden cases swollen with books scattered against the walls, with unsmiling oil portraits of Irish gents in stiff collars and side whiskers hung from brittling strings in between, and furniture that appeared not so much arranged for daily use as warehoused over the years. It was a decrepit parlor, a crypt of dust and shadows and the sour smell of mice. Yet there sat Uncle Liam, looking young and strong enough in the soft firelight to leap out of his chair at me.

He nodded toward the table and said, "Turn up the dial on the wireless." I did as he asked. He looked up at the dark ceiling, closed his eyes, and whispered, "Ah, the wireless . . ."

The Stan Getz Quartet was a few bars into "Sipping at Bell's." Liam said, "I remember how you love the jazz, Neil. Truth to tell, I prefer it myself. Just listen to that tenor saxophone. Isn't it sweeter to life than the pipes and the fiddle and the concertina box and all that unfathomable antiquity of the Irish stuff? Sit down, and listen with me."

I took a seat on a faded maroon horsehair couch opposite my uncle's chair. I figured Liam meant me this seat, as there was a decanter and glasses on a table between us. Liam kept in rhythm to the music with the palms of his hands, tapping lightly against the arms of his chair.

I poured us a finger each of thick brown whiskey, and asked, "You wanted me down here to talk music?"

"A good start it is," Liam said. He picked up his glass and sipped, and looked me up and down, measuring me against whatever was on his mind.

"Maybe we should just cut to the chase."

"Americans!" Liam said, snorting tolerantly. "You're so bloody impatient with the idea of proper conversation. What a curious trait that is. Such a fine young country, yet everybody's in a great rush to get to the bitter end of an otherwise lovely chat. As if you're a nation of old men and old women, all afraid time's going to claim you before you get your say."

"Time is vicious if you take it for granted."

"A point of view subscribed to only by the ambitious, or the ironical."

"Speaking of irony, imagine us two Americans here enjoying your man Boylan's highly informing conversation—until he got himself murdered. Also imagine what I think seeing you in a house like this. You really had to go slumming when you came to see us poor relations in Hell's Kitchen, didn't you, Uncle?"

"I thought there might be certain questions on your mind."

"You thought right."

"I explained about poor Francie Boylan and his unpleasant politics."

"Not quite."

"As for you and your mother, Mairead," Liam said, ignoring the gibe, "did you never know that I made it clear how my brother's widow and little son were welcome to come live with me in this comfort you see?"

"I'm learning fast how many things I still don't know."

"Aye, as bonny says, you've come here to fill up hollow places."

"Will you help me?"

"Sure, and why do you think we two are sitting here together having our quiet drink?"

"Because you sent Moira to drag me out of my sleep?"

Liam laughed gently, then shifted in his chair and took another nip of whiskey. He asked, "Have you got a fag?"

"I already told you, no."

"You could sneak a packet in, you could."

"When you help me, maybe."

"It's good to know you've not put yourself above bribery. This shows me you're the decent sort of policeman."

"You were about to tell me why we're having this heart-to-heart."

"So I was. Tell me, Neil, when's the last time we seen one another?"

"When we buried my mother."

"Quite right. I remember you in the blue uniform, before your becoming a detective. Can you recall the rest of it?"

"It wasn't much of a send-off, there's not so much to remember. Father Tim was there with his blessing, and you dropped roses into the grave ..." And I asked myself, What was the song my Uncle Liam sang?

"And your friend Mogaill," Liam said, interrupting the thought.

"Yes ... there was Davy."

We fell silent for about a minute. Then Liam suddenly said, "I know about Father Tim, please God."

"You know—?"

"Aye, and about Davy Mogaill."

Did he mean that he knew what had happened to Father Tim and Davy Mogaill during these last two days, or was his knowledge deeper? I was about to ask Liam to explain himself when Moira came pounding into the room from the hallway, flush faced and out of breath. "He's a-comin' up the back way now!"

Calmly, Liam told her, "Thank you, Moira. Be a blessed dear now, run upstairs and help bonny with whatever she needs to look beautiful for your good supper."

"She can bloody well fix her feathers without me!" Moira complained.

"It's good to hear you curse, Moira. It shows you're in good health. Be about it upstairs now."

"Oh, Mr. H—!"

"Must I always butter your cat's paws, Moira?" he asked wearily. "Or might you save me some remaining breath of my life by minding that you've got a good thing going in this house."

Moira went clumping upward to the red room, muttering "Gawd bless us 'n save us!"

Liam said to me, quietly, "Quick now, Snoody'll soon be with us. I'm told you're a fine detective, would that be fair to say?"

"I like to think so."

"Right then, I'm telling you now the main reason I pulled you down here all to myself, Neil: I want to put a riddle to you."

"A what—?"

"When you solve it, you'll start seeing answers to questions that have burnt you hollow." Liam's face turned anxious. He looked past me to the empty hallway. "Well then—you do want to hear it?"

"Yes."

"A man without eyes saw plums on a tree. He neither took plums nor left plums. How could this be?"

CHAPTER 17

"Peep o'day, comrade."

"You—!"

"Aye, and glad to be your guest. But look at you now—you're lying spread-eagled in this here bed, and not greeting me with the least sort of proper smile."

"How'd you get'n here?"

"Do you think the likes of you are the only ones knowing about how to persuade a lock when you don't own the key?"

"Stinkin' bastard—!"

"Such talk. But what can I expect, waking you so early? What about a cup of tea now? How'd that be to chip away the temper, make things between us nice and civil like."

"Get that fookin' cannon off me face."

"You're calling this old Mauser of mine a cannon? Let's see how it's wee enough to fit neat in a man's mouth, just like it done in the priest's. Come now, comrade—open up."

"I ain't—!"

"I said, open up! Aye ... that's got it now. And my, but look how it makes the face run red and the eyes big and bright blue as robin's eggs. Tell me if I'm wrong, but I believe this cannon

112

so-called is tickling your tonsils. I said, tell me! What's that you're garbling? Might you be trying to say you can't speak with a wee gun in your gullet? All right then, let's give it a rest."

"Holy Mother, have mercy—!"

"The sniveling's unappealing, but I prefer it over the swearing."

"I'm beggin' you, don't take me out."

"Don't kill you? When you and the boyos were out for the same to me? Would you call that fair play now?"

"He only come to warn you."

"Do you think I don't know you and your bloody Irish games? Don't glink me, man."

"I ain't glinkin'."

"Then what about Father Kelly?"

"I don't know nothin' but what I read'n the New York papers."

"Liar. It was you rang up the priest on the telephone."

"Nae, I never—"

"Your lying's an offense to me and every part-honest man of our guild. I think now's the time for putting you in mind of the poor priest's final seconds. Open up . . . I said, open up! That's the boy. Now, listen close as I'm pulling back the hammer with my thumb, comrade . . .

"Hear the sound of clicking steel revolving in the magazine. 'Tis a horrible sound, is that not true? And dread the bigger sound to come—the one you well know from all the murdering you done to others in your filthy life. The nasty wet sound of your own brains blowing out of your skull . . .

"Click, click, click! Can you hear my index finger rubbing the trigger now? Rubbing it, squeezing it . . . click, click, click! Are you wondering when the big sound's coming now? Pay attention to this vicious moment, comrade! It'll expand and become your well-deserved eternity in hell . . .

"Oh! For pity's sake! Mind your toilet, man!"

"I'm sorry—"

"Well, you should be. Here you go making a mess right in the middle of our proceedings. I wasn't near ready to free your gullet of this here Mauser. What'll we do now?"

"Please, the loo—"

"All right, come on then. Up with you, slow like. That's it. You and me, let's walk along nice as pie. Don't be making any sudden

113

or nervous motions since I'm pressing the Mauser up against your ear now and I'm irritated that I'm one hand short, what with having to cover up my nose on account of your uproaring bowels. Can I trust you now?"

"Yes ..."

"Good. Here we go to get clean again. You'll not be wanting to leave this world soiled the way you are. What do you say to my thoughtfulness?"

"Thank you."

"Don't mention it. Right, now—strip off the mess, and here's the sink, and the soap and water. Take your time, fix yourself decent."

"I need clean things now."

"Not to worry, comrade. Any clothes you wear to hell will only burn away, so we'll not be bothering Old Nick about earthly raiment. Come on, naked as a babe I'm taking you to the roof."

"Please, don't shoot me—!"

"As you like it, then. Let's have a look about your squirrelly den for some other means of sending you off."

"Jaysus, Mary and Joseph, no—!"

"Ah! I have it. Look here at this fine big butcher's knife lying in your kitchen. Why, it's the perfect thing! We'll take it along. Now, let's be to the roof."

"Jaysus—!"

"Enough with your holy jibber, man! Walk along, come on. You're Hearts of Steel, is that not so? Say it for me now as we're moving up the stairs. I said, say it! And proudly put it!"

"Hearts of Steel!"

"Aye, that's it. It's words to die by, all right."

"Please—!"

"Sorry, comrade, you get no mercy from me. Nor even from God, I expect. What you done in your time is so bad it'd raise tears out of Satan. What you done to the padre, and what you done to my Brenda!"

"Nae, that wasn't me who—!"

"Shut up, maggot! You're going to be cut in half now. And when they find you up here, I can tell you this: they might figure I done it, but they're not likely to be interested in proving it. Have you never heard, justice is the sanction of established injustice?"

"I tell you, I wasn't the one! I never called up your Father Kelly, and I never did it to your Brenda!"

"And I told you, you're lying. Glink's my game, comrade. And I been playing it against you and the boyos all these years now, as you see. You're going to die, man—and me, I'm going to howl with delight, like we was only sitting across a glink board over on the other side, and it's me trapping your spoof or pulling off a double barness."

"Mercy! I beg you—!"

"Where's that heart of steel now, comrade?"

"I renounce that—all of it!"

"Nae, you baked your bread for life. Mercy's not in your gift. But pity is. What would you say to that?"

"Your pity then, please . . ."

"I'll consider it. Right now, let's have you back off me a few steps. That's it, back just aways so's I can take a run at you with this here knife. Are you ready now?"

"Pity—!"

"Move back if you must, I'm coming now! That's right, keep moving, moving. Don't be looking back of you. But imagine the glory of walking off one of them dear green bluffs in the west country, clean into the drink. A poetic way for a steel-hearted lad to go, wouldn't you say . . . ?"

"Well, there you go now . . . Fare thee well to one more of you unlovely H.O.S. sons of bitches."

CHAPTER 18

Supper was taken in the smaller of the two dining rooms. The larger one, on the first floor, was probably big enough to support a crowd of dancers if not for an oblong table running down the middle. Ours on the third floor was more intimate, with a capacity for a banquet of merely twenty or so.

I could easily picture a boy growing up in a nice big lace curtain Irish home like this instead of a Hell's Kitchen tenement. Unfortunately, the boy in the picture was not me.

I liked the room very much. The walls were covered in deep green felt and fitted with brass sconces, like library walls of private men's clubs I have seen in New York. There was an ivory-colored marble fireplace with a pair of carved oak flower baskets on the mantel, a single chandelier hanging low over the walnut table, and a mahogany liquor cart with bottles of Burgundy, port, Scotch, and champagne in a bucket of ice.

There was a dumbwaiter built into a corner, and I could not help but picture that boy growing up here spending many a happy day riding it up and down to the tune of Moira's curses. Also there were two more paintings among Uncle Liam's collection of Italian art, which in answer to Ruby's question he identified as

Girolamo Ferrabosco's circa 1640 *Portrait of an Elegant Man* and
Francesco Furini's circa 1630 *St. Sebastian.* While he was telling us
this, Ruby gave me a look that might have said, I don't want to
hear about it.

Snoody was with us. Like black on coal, in fact. He had not left
sight of Liam and me since returning from an errand down in the
village diamond and interrupting our circumspect parlor chat. I
had had no chance to play my uncle's riddle back to Ruby, nor
to discuss with her the strange discomfort I felt about everything
and everybody in my uncle's house.

Liam and I—and Ruby, in a billowy red silk blouse, matching
pants and heels that put her at my own height—were left for only
a few minutes to start on the champagne. This was while Snoody
made like a butler, filling wine goblets and removing plates of
food from the dumbwaiter. He set all this out on lace mats along
one end of the table. From her kitchen down below, Moira was
sending up generous loads of smoked ham, curried new potatoes,
cheese-covered vegetables and warm soda bread.

"Ready now," Snoody announced when he was done arranging
a board for four. He motioned for us to take our places at the table.

I noticed a tired anger in Liam's face as he looked up at Snoody,
and realized this had been Snoody's exact expression whenever
he looked at Uncle. The two of them were like an old and unhap-
pily married couple, exhausted from the triumph of habit over
hate.

Ruby was staring at Liam now, too, and I wondered if she
picked up on the same thing. My bet was that she had.

Liam allowed me to wheel him across the carpeted floor to the
head of the table. Ruby and I sat down to his right. Snoody stood,
lighting candles. He asked Liam, "Would you like me to say
prayer over this evening's meal?"

"Thank you, no, I've got a charming one of my own I've been
saving for the occasion," Liam said, sounding more mischievous
than reverent. "Sit down, Patrick, and get yourself in the properly
humble mood."

Snoody scowled, and sat. We all bowed heads.

And Liam prayed:

"Dear God, tonight as we partake of thy kindest bounty, know
that we'll be eating and drinking to the glorious, pious and immor-

117

tal memories of Thy own Sainted Patrick and our great good brother Brian Boru—who assisted, each in his respective way, in redeeming us Irish folk from toffee-snouted Englishmen and their ilk. We ask a blessing, if you please, on the Holy Father of Rome— and a shit for the Bishop of Canterbury. And to those at this table unwilling to drink to this, may he have a dark night, a lee shore, a rank storm and a leaky vessel to carry him over the River Styx. May the dog Cerberus make a meal of his rump, and Pluto a snuffbox of his skull, and may the Devil jump down his throat with a red hot harrow, and with every pin tear out a gut and blow him with a clean carcass to hell. Amen."

Ruby and I laughed.

But Snoody said dryly, "Such fine holy sentiment for our guests." He snapped open a linen napkin and spread it across his lap. Just in case Liam did not understand his irritation, Snoody said, "There's good reason tonight to sup with a spoon of sorrow. Yet you offer up more curse than prayer. It's only a shame Moira isn't here to have heard it."

"Meaning we must all be solemn by way of showing respect for the memory of poor Francis Boylan?" Liam asked him.

"I do mean that," Snoody said.

"Oh, Patrick—my old sow's teats! You and I been right here together, in this very room and others, the many times that Francie himself has recited this entertaining prayer—and laughed himself silly long afterward. It's partly why I gave it, in his honor, see." Liam turned from Snoody toward me, smiled brightly, and added, "Then partly it's a prayer in keeping with certain other ones gone, or missing."

"Would you be speaking of Father Tim Kelly and Davy Mogaill?" I asked, it suddenly occurring to me that a partisan prayer honoring two men violently killed and another missing was maybe not so funny. Snoody gobbled down a lot of wine and twisted in his seat. Liam's smile turned dead as mutton. I was pleased to see that my abrupt question had stunned some deep, unspoken rhythm to Uncle Liam's house of riddles. Hearing no answer, I put the question another way, "What joke would Davy and Father Tim have got from your prayer, Uncle? The same that Francie Boylan got?"

"Don't go being so bloody tiresome as Snoody here, always

wanting to muck about in solemnity like he was still stiff in his neck with the collar. Let's try remembering I'm an old man who needs his cheerful moods." Snoody's nose laughed derisively. Liam turned from me to Ruby, and asked, "Now speaking of Her Nibs, as Patrick was before his great wheezy snout sprung yet another leak, how'd you get on with Moira when she and her vinegar tongue came to call you awake?"

"She quoted the Bible loudly, and at length, after which I told her that so far as I knew there was not a word in the Gospels in praise of intelligence," Ruby answered him. "She took great offense."

"Well said!" Liam told her.

He was now smiling again, and may well have thought Ruby an easy ally in his determinedly airy table chat. Uncle Liam was, after all, of an age of men who believe women to be dependably soft creatures. But Ruby's generation of women has built a different idea of themselves. When the moment requires, the softest thing about Ruby Flagg is her teeth.

"Thank you," Ruby said. Then she nodded at Snoody, to include him in what she said next to Liam. "Do you want to know what I think about dear simple Moira, gentlemen?"

"Yes . . . ," the two of them said at once, making it sound more like "no."

"It's never entered your male brains that if two women should happen to come together and talk under your roof, one of us might easily see how the other's capable of hiding something from the likes of you behind all her Bible noise? Something about what goes on in this house? Which is to say, gentlemen, the cook's made asses of you."

Liam and Snoody looked as if they had been bitten.

Ruby, in fine representation of her sisterhood, swept me up in a hard glance at this table full of men she had to deal with. Then she asked me, sweetly, "And just what do you think, Detective Hockaday?"

"That we're beginning to cut to the chase," I said. "Thank you, partner."

"See here now—!" Snoody started to say.

Liam cut him off. "Never mind, Patrick. New Yorkers are always in a hurry, and you'll never convince a one of them he's anywhere but on his own turf."

"Or she," Ruby said.

"Quite," Liam said, recovering his smile. "Besides, they've been through a bit now, haven't they?"

"That's a mild way of putting it," I said.

"Yes . . . well, what may I tell you quickly now so that we might get on with Moira's good meal?" Liam asked us.

"Let's start with the legs," I said. "What happened to them?"

"A year ago tomorrow it was, I was shot in the hip in a hunting accident, down in a forest south of the Wicklows," Liam said. "Bloody nuisance, the bullet's still in me and it's seized up most of my pelvic nerves . . . well, except for the ones acting up when my piles itch."

"Can an old man's bum sores actually be the sort of clue you detectives find helpful during an investigation?" Snoody asked.

Ruby took this one. She shot back at Snoody, "What makes you think he's asking questions in a professional capacity?"

Snoody refused to address her. "Tell us, young Hockaday," he said to me, a sneer trilling through his nostrils, "just who is the policeman here."

"That thing your nose does, you should see a doctor."

"I . . . What—?"

"Anyhow, to answer your question, I'm the cop. But I'm not thinking about my occupation anywhere near as much as you seem to be for some reason, Snoody. If it helps keep your shorts dry, I'm way outside my jurisdiction."

"In fact, he's come home here to show off his darling, and he's welcome to stay at home as long as he wants," Ruby said. "Isn't that right, Uncle Liam?"

"Right as rain over Waterford," he answered brightly. A charming man of Liam's generation still had much to learn about estimating a woman like Ruby.

"Then why is this the first time Hock's stepped foot in this house, where he's so welcome as you say?" Ruby asked. "Why didn't he and his mother come here to live with you in this big place?"

"I always sent along support," Liam said, defensively. "Money

120

went regular every month for my brother Aidan's widow, and Neil, too."

"Not nearly as much as you could afford, so we can see."

"But as much as Mairead would ever take from me!" Liam, red-faced and short of breath, pounded the table with a fist.

"Have a caution, won't you?" Snoody said to me. "You'll do no good for yourselves interrogating the man into sickness."

"That's very true," I said. Ruby had done a good job playing bad cop to my good, picking open some family sores in the process. I needed to absorb what I had heard with the help of a full night's sleep. Any further questions to Liam tonight would land easy. Snoody was another matter.

"About your letter," I said to him. "You had my uncle on his deathbed. What's the idea?"

Snoody hissed something. Then he and Liam passed poison frowns back and forth between them. After which, Liam collected himself by coming to Snoody's defense.

"No call to be busting poor Patrick's chops, Neil," Liam said. "I told you he's incorrigible in his mother hen ways. No doubt he got it into his head one day I was all set on my way to croaking, and needing family gathered for the watch. He only meant the best."

"Then you're not sick?" Ruby asked.

"Not especially so," Liam said. He picked up his wineglass, clinked it against Ruby's, smiled, and said, "Bonny, I'm going to appeal to your finer sensibilities . . ."

"Say what you want. I'll decide if it's appealing."

"Oh yes, she's a right peppery darling, Neil," Liam said to me, clucking his lips. Then, to us both, "Here you are now—home, as you rightly say. Can we not try making the most of it? I told you I'm in no grave condition, but I'm also telling you I haven't got so many years left of being so alert and robust as you see me now."

Ruby turned and looked at me, her chocolate eyes relenting. We could have been a mind-reading act. Ruby was telling me she was tired and wanted a restful way to think about all this, and knew I wanted the same. I have seen cops who were longtime partners communicate in this remarkable way. In the police business, this is a sign of "true marriage." Until now, I myself have never experienced this, on or off duty; until now, neither the phenomenon nor the phrase have caused my palms to sweat.

"You were always full of good stories about the people here when I was a kid and you came visiting in New York," I said to Liam. "But I don't remember your ever telling a story about your own brother. Let's hear one tonight."

"A good story—about your father? He was an upstream swimmer." Liam shook his head. "From the day he was born, Aidan changed everything and everybody around him. Now, it's the helpless nature of some people to make a commotion of themselves. That's all right, I guess, as long as they realize they're different—and that most others are happy enough to be docile and obedient. But the trouble is, most people just naturally don't like the upstream swimmers. Most people resent that what's too different from them. For the likes of your father, it's a vexing life then."

"You're saying you can't tell me anything good about my father?"

"Nae, but I am saying I cannot keep the talk of a proper delectability for the supper table."

"He's heard a tough story or two in his time," Ruby said on my behalf. "Where do you think Hock's lived all his life? In a house like this?"

The sound of Liam's and Snoody's skittish laughter would have been right for a cemetery. Liam asked, "Tell me, Neil, did you really and truly come here to dig about in the family's old mash?"

"I did," I said, realizing for the first time this was really, truly so. "And I don't mind smelling stale cabbage."

"Fair play then, I did promise we'd talk of Aidan, and I'm a man of my word. I tell you what I told your bonny, I would steal from you, but I would never lie." Liam looked at Snoody, then at the food on the table, both of which had ceased steaming. "But first, might you pass a hungry old man some lovely potatoes and such so's to build up the story-telling energy?"

We all filled plates then. Liam told us to "tuck in," and so we quickly did away with Moira's supper. I was hungrier than I imagined, and so was Ruby. Uncle pronounced us "fine trenchermen." When we had finished with the food and wine, Snoody went over to the dumbwaiter. Moira had sent up two big pots of tea.

"Put a color of whiskey in mine," Liam said to Snoody as he poured.

When we all were fixed with the tea, colored all around, we settled back in our chairs, our expectant ears tuned to Liam. He hesitated briefly. Then with a great sigh, he reached into a breast pocket of his coat, removed a letter-size ecru envelope fuzzy around the edges with age, and flattened it out on the table in front of him.

And after a long look at me that contained in it the whole heavy load of Celtic history, the beginning of my own family saga flowed from Uncle Liam's lips, easy and musical as a stream.

Yet for all their cool and placid beauty, Irish streams are treacherous, too. They are relentless mountain killers, after all, cutting deep and moving slow through ages-old stone, then plunging into violent waterfall.

CHAPTER 19

"ANY TELLING OF THE STORY OF AIDAN HOCKADAY MUST BEGIN WITH understanding the meaning of the land down County Carlow way. The land where Aidan was born, the land he deserted when he became a man.

"If you think this brutal judgment of my dear younger brother, I confess he only followed my lead, for this is the very premise to my own life's tale. Aye, it's the curse of us—two harps who could not stay true to their right place.

"And you could not in all the world have found a greener nor lovelier place as Carlow. It was all our kin ever knew, since way back to the darkest times when we and every other Irishman were getting about on all fours. God planted us Hockadays in that loam there, it was said, along with his trees and flowers and green grass. The whole clan respected this holy arrangement—up until your father, Aidan, and me, who spit in God's face, so it was also said.

"Glorious the old Carlow soil was. It's still fragrant in my dreams. How I see it in my sleep—soil black and creamy as Guinness stout. Our own wee patch of it nourished generations of us, in spite of the great pestilences the demons of hell delivered to

Ireland, by which I'm saying the English and the landlords and the great famine. Our father's father's father's father broke the rocky crust with his bare hands. All our souls lay buried in that earth; yours, too, Neil. Do you see? The land is close to something sacred.

"So saying all this, why in the world do you suppose I and your father would break faith? My reasons are dreary, as you'll see by comparing them to Aidan's.

"Now, I can tell you almost everything there is to know about your father, for his birth is one of my own first memories. I was seven years at the time ... That's a long stretch between babies in an Irish house, which tells you something about how your grandparents regarded one another ...

"Well, old as I am, I still see clear the day that Aidan finally come to join me. All raging purple and gasping for life, he was—and nae bigger than a titmouse.

"It was the misty time then, late into October, when the winds off the Wicklows hang over the fields and villages like damp woollens. My mother—Finola, may God rest her—lay in the birthing bed all through the night before, moaning and rubbing her big hard belly, and sweating like a spring thaw. I know her suffering intimately, for young and scared as I was, it was me laying there beside her for comfort. All I could think to do in her agony was mumble the only catechism I knew by heart, which I did, over and over until my throat went sore.

"Daddy stayed downstairs on a cot made up in the kitchen. He required an undisturbed sleep for the morning's chores. There was only him with the big strong hands for such work, I at the time being a good three years off from being able to do my part. Besides which, Myles Hockaday was a renowned gentleman, and he was only being considerate by absenting himself in this delicate instance. His breath, you see, had the yeasty stink to it from drinking a new batch of poteen he and his mates had cooked up in the still back of our byre.

"I myself could scarcely stand his stench. Surely it was no fit breath to be wafting over a poor wife ready to burst. And so it fell to a young boy to watch over his mother's labor, night and day. Daddy told me, 'Stay by her, Liam, like you was a good and faithful duckling. But when our mum's belly goes to rumble, leave her quick and come running straightaway to me.'

"Her time come in the lonely gray of morning. Daddy was outside already, he'd just nice be starting to tend to our cow and the pigs. There was an awful bleezer going on, so bad the windows were banging like drunkard's fists, and the wind so stiff it was blowing the sleet sideways. It wasn't the storm that waked me, though. Nae, it was mum's howling from pain—or so I thought until I shook sleep from my eyes and saw different.

"She had kicked the bedclothes off her, and pulled her nightie clear up to her swelled chest. And there she was on that stormy morning, and howling out all the saints' names and struggling to see beyond the top of her belly to some frightful thing between her splayed-open legs.

"Whatever it was made my lovely mum's face go fearful, ugly. I was sore afraid to look, but she made me. 'Quick now, Liam,' she said to me, with the tears streaking down her face as fierce as the sleet outside, 'see down below me gut and tell us if I don't feel it coming out!'

"So I looked. And all I saw at first was a mess of bloody gush covering her womanhood. I turned away, disgusted like. My stomach was all mewly, my head felt like it was floating off my shoulders.

"Mum was screeching, 'What is it, Liam? What is it?' I told her I had to run to Daddy, like he said. But she told me, 'No—there's no time for him. Look down there, tell me exactly what you see!'

"Now, I could hardly believe the sight: a tiny pair of purple haunches, wriggling like a madman. I said to Mum, 'Why, it's baby coming out—rump first!' She screamed, 'Holy Mary, a breach birth!'

"Lord, this frightened me so! No more than a month earlier I'd seen our cow drop a dead calf that breached. I'd no idea the same could happen to humans.

"She began keening the name of Saint Gerard. That's the patron saint of childbirth, you know. I'm still hearing that keening of hers some nights. 'Protect me now in my hour of need, God—in the name of Saint Gerard Majella, blessed with bilocation, prophecy and infused knowledge, your child born to as humble a house as this I'm suffering in . . .'

"Anyway, Mum calmed herself by the saying of this prayer over and over again, and finally she came out of it and told me, 'Liam, be nimble. I need you to grab hold of baby's bum. Use both your hands and be steady about it, pull it gentle out from me so's it'll get the breath of life. You must be very brave and very gentle, and take care you don't go strangling nor suffocating baby.'

"Oh, but I hated to touch the slimy thing in Mum's loins! But I did, and worried all the while how Daddy might take the strap to me later for disobeying him.

"I had no sense of bringing a body to life, but it's what happened. I tugged until the two tiny legs flopped out, and then I tugged some more. And Finola, she grunted like some great gassy beast, pushing and pushing.

"Then, spat from our mother's muck, came this lumpen, gasping head. Happy birthday, brother Aidan . . ."

Uncle Liam had been leaning forward in his wheelchair, his slender hands folded over the envelope, picking at it from time to time. He now sat back, shifting himself. He asked Ruby, "Would you mind pouring me another tea, bonny?"

Ruby poured, dropping in a tincture of whiskey from the bottle Snoody had brought to the table. She asked, "The charming story you told, is it true?"

"But you weren't listening, girl," he said, teasing her. "I would steal from you, but I would never lie."

Snoody's nose whinnied. Liam continued.

"Well, I finally did run to Daddy after helping Mum birth Aidan. First I pulled down Mum's nighty, and gave her plenty of wetted clean linens, then I run screaming to him about what I done.

"The two of us galloped back through the storm into the house, me with muddy bare feet racing ten steps back of Daddy and his sopping Wellies, and on upstairs to mum wiping the goo from Aidan's mouth and nostrils so's he could breathe easy, and singing the babe a little song. Right off, Daddy sees it's a fine new boy, and so he says, 'A good job, Finola—we've got us another spade for the bog.'

"Mum, she looked at him with a slow queer face, queer and

disgusted as my own when I first seen between her woman's legs. Daddy was there, grinning and dripping wet in his farmer's clothes. His breath had not sweetened from a night's sleep, and it was powerful close in the room. She says to him, stern like, 'Nae, Myles, it's a new free day with this birth here. Neither you nor none of your Hockaday ghosts have got the right anymore to be claiming my boys to any further life under this slave's roof!'

"Slave's roof! The slur against the poor castle of a man such as Myles Hockaday! Poor Daddy. How this cut to his peasant's bones, reminding him right there in front of me how he was only forever a docile, obedient sod living with a hateful wife in his rude, drafty tenant house on a wee little rented potato field and its peat bog—with no way out that neither he nor his whole family before him could imagine. All he had was his family's lease to the house and land, which he was honor-bound to glorify, you see. And now here was his wife, coldly mocking even that. *Slave's roof.*

"Whatever pride he felt on that first sight of his second male heir flew away. Instead he took to his heart the worst shot a peasant's wife may fire. His vanity was mortally wounded, forever and ever more.

"So poor stricken Daddy went and sat downstairs by the hearth, flipping bricks of turf onto the fire, one after the other like he was rich as a king. And leaving Mum upstairs with the mess of a new babe, and only me for assistance. Mum, she was perfectly fine on her own, all cooing and larky with Aidan. But there was I, a boy of seven freshly tortured into learning the joke of family virtue. Down by the fire was Daddy, poisoning himself with a brood that'd hang around him like a hairy black dog the rest of his days.

"I'd peek at him down the stair from time to time. Jar after jar of poteen went down my daddy's well-worn gullet. Meanwhile, our poor cow with her udder aching from unrelieved fullness went bleating through the storm and into nightfall. And little me, I grew powerful frightened, for I saw my father cry. It's like the world's ending when your father cries, Neil . . . Ruby. It marks you for life to see such impotence.

"Well, I laid low during the worst of Daddy's tears. Myles Hockaday was a gentleman, sure, but nonetheless he was capable of being mean, and I had the feeling more than once he was about to come strike me, or even Mum or the babe. Just to do something with his hands, mind you, since there was nothing he could do with his life.

"But he finally got hungry, thanks be to God, and this took the raw edge from his rage. He called me downstairs, sat me at the table, and cut us some bread and meat with mustard for a cold supper together. I remember him apologizing for there being no cider nor milk. 'Sorry, you'll be dry packing it tonight, Liam,' he says.

"Then when we were through, he tells me why he's acting the way he is; he tells me the meaning of his distress. It wasn't for years that I understood this was pathetic—how Daddy's telling me, a boy, what his pride would prevent him from ever admitting to another man.

"Daddy takes and hugs me, and confesses: 'Forgive me, son. The shadow of the famine's a heavy burden on all my generation. I grew up hearing the stories from my own mum and pa, and from the *shanachies*, too, of people right here in our own valley laying in ditches when they got put out of their houses. And with green juice running from their mouths when all they had left to eat was weeds. Forgive me, but I was taught never to live a day without the fear of all that coming back. And it's fear that keeps us tenants to the land here, and to this house; it's fear that's killed our dreams of anything more . . .'

"He couldn't go on he was crying so. He left me at the table to go guzzling more of his poteen at the hearth. I heard Mum singing her lullabies upstairs. And little me, I wanted to run. But not to the arms of either one of them.

"By and by, Daddy calls me to sit with him by the hearth. He is swacked to the eyeballs now, which was his customary condition from that day forward. I dreaded to hear him talk. His drunken self-pity was no more becoming than his tears.

"He says, 'I got something to tell you that must always be remembered, boy: it's the English who bring us to all dead ends. There's never been one of them born who believes us Irish to be anything more than a race of donkeys. Hate them English, boy! Drink deep your hate, drink the hate into your nerves and your flesh and your blood . . .'

"Well, I might not have it exact word by word, but it's the sense and pith of what my old man said that hair-raising day everything and everybody changed; the day of your own daddy's birth, Neil. After that, I don't believe Myles Hockaday uttered one more word that caused anybody in Carlow to take note of him.

"He did his work in the bog and the field more or less like always; like a good donkey, with Aidan and me to help the cause when we were old enough. Our daddy taught us the secrets of working the land like his daddy before taught him, but his heart was never in the lessons. He looked queer at us, Aidan especially; he knew that we'd leave him there as the last Hockaday on the soil, never to keep his dreamless faith, nor respect his fear of the shadow. He was dying like.

"Mum, in her spiteful ways over the years, would abet the betrayal by providing certain things for Aidan and me ... That's what daddy called it when he was drinking, his sons' betrayal—to him and to the land, and to the souls of all the Hockadays.

"He'd say she was killing him slow but sure, but Mum would claim it was only her noble desire to liberate us; she'd argue in the night with Daddy, good and loud so's we'd hear, 'Bugger this land you don't even rightly own! My boys shall know finer things than you, Myles Hockaday—things of a real gentleman's world! They'll not grow to be like you, walking around just to save on funeral expenses.'

"Now, he never gave her a thumping, but it seemed in some strange way like it's what she wanted ... No offense to you, bonny Ruby, but a free-tongued woman in the benighted times I'm speaking of was a spiteful creature.

"Anyhow, what she provided us first was the wireless. A very good one, it was, with a band that at night'd pick up voices in the air, like magic, from all the four corners of the earth. We'd only find out years and years later where and how Mum come to get the wireless, mind you—that and all else she got.

"The wireless, she said, was our 'ears to the fine mystery and lovely treachery beyond the mountains, to all the dear sweet turbulent life far from this homely dirt and muck.' And for all the pleasure it gave us, we only owed her the duty to 'listen every night, boys—learn the world's a big place, with many things to do.'

"Oh, but Daddy resented the contraption. Jealous, he was. 'The Devil's voice box,' he called it, though he listened along with us all the same. Mum would say, 'Ain't you feared you'll become a sinner by listening to the wireless?' Daddy'd get all red-faced and say 'No!' Then Mum would laugh at him, and say, 'Too bad, Myles. Sinners are ever so much more interesting men than saints.'

"And this made so much sense to me and Aidan. What do you suppose two Carlow boys would rather do of a long cold evening—read a book of catechisms, or tune into some place in the world where there was jazz music and people laughing?

"Mum knew very well what she was doing. She was intoxicating us. Curiosity drunked us more than whiskey ever done to Daddy. Furthermore, every time the old man's back was turned, and many a time it wasn't, she'd feed us subversive notions.

"She had certain visions of us, and meant us to see the same. We were both of us bright and worthy, she decided, but different as could be; I was her practical one, Aidan possessed a mind in need of soaring.

"To me, she said, 'Liam, it'll serve you well to know it's not work that makes money, it's money that makes money. There's no way you're likely to see this principle put to practice in Carlow here, so I'm seeing to it you go to London and learn, for London's where the money is.'

"Now, my brother loved two things: reading literature, and listening to voices from America over the wireless. Mum said to him, 'It's Dublin where you'll be going for your education in letters, Aidan. To Trinity College, and never you mind it's full of Prods; I know of a priest who'll grant your dispensation. No people put the English tongue to better use than Dubliners. You'll find Dublin a writers' and talkers' heaven, but you mustn't stay longer than need be. New York's the place for you. No people in the world have more need for lettered men than New Yorkers.'

"Well then, she saw us off, the both of us, the funds coming from the mysterious place where she got all her fancy things. We didn't ask questions, we went like shots. First me to London, which Daddy cursed as hell; then Aidan to Dublin, which Daddy thought no more savory a place.

"I cannot tell you much of what happened to your own daddy in Dublin for the next several years, for we lived in two so very different worlds. Aidan's dreamy world of books and Dublin literary cafés and such things, and mine of working in a London bank and taking night classes and generally trying to learn all I could in the great councils of finance.

"I wasn't keen for Aidan's interests, and he no more for mine. I used to think he sounded so much like Daddy when he'd screw up his face and say money was 'nothing but dirty paper.'

"But anyway, there come a day I left London for Dublin myself, to continue in my financial pursuits, which eventually resulted in this house we're enjoying now, among other things. Aidan and I began seeing one another when I got to Dublin . . . maybe not as regularly as two brothers should, but time and separation had changed things between us, see.

"We both got letters from Mum, never from Daddy. She'd be all on about how bad it was becoming between them, back in the place neither one of us called home no more. Only once did we go back there, on account of the scandal that's no doubt bruited about the pubs of Carlow to this day . . ."

Liam paused, as dramatically as any ham at the Abbey Theatre, waiting for either Ruby or me to coax more from him. Snoody had no doubt heard this story many times before, judging by his blank expression. Ruby finally asked him, coolly, "The scandal?"

"Aye, bonny," Liam said. He asked me to pass him the decanter, then he filled his cup with whiskey, spotting it with tea. "Mum and Daddy, as I suppose we might have anticipated, did no go gently unto night . . ."

I asked, "Meaning—?"

"The postman become suspicious when he saw how the box was filling up, and how it appeared nobody was around the old place," Liam said. "So, one day he leaves his bicycle up on the road and goes down to the house for a look-about. There he finds Mum laid out on the kitchen floor, full of wounds from the knife she always used to pare the crust around her pies. And Daddy, he wasn't far away nor in any better condition. Slumped down in front of his chair by the hearth, blood and brain shot out of his head and his shooting hand still wrapped around the old family horse pistol . . ."

For a while, I could not hear what Liam was saying. Maybe this was only for a few seconds, but it seemed at the time so very long. My mind was buzzing and full of moving pictures, racing in front of my eyes at crazy speeds. No sooner was I imagining my father as a young man trying to make his way as a writer, of all things, I was imagining the grandmother and grandfather I never knew—the two of these ferocious squabblers, and the scandal of a murder-suicide.

I am off in a corner by myself wondering about a guy who once so loved a woman twenty-five years ago that he married her, then one awful day hated her so bad he diced her all over the kitchen linoleum. The way I see it, this big murder story is no story at all. The real story is what happened during those twenty-five years ... Here now would be The Truth. The truth, the whole truth and nothing but the messy and complicated truth so help me God.

Then came my uncle back into view, and the pictures slowed. Him with his whiskey and tea, tapping a finger on the envelope in front of him. And moving on through the dreadful family saga, raising a hundred questions for later with every word he said now.

"Well, so before we beat it back to Dublin, Aidan and me stayed in the old house together, long enough to sell the animals and other such tasks of closing down two hardscrabble lives. It was very much on our minds how we were ending the line of Hockadays in Carlow, a long line surely now ending with less than great pride. The funeral, if you could rightly call it that, was short and bitter.

"No church in all Carlow would take Daddy into its cemetery since he was a murderer and, even worse, a suicide. Aidan and me, we decided against separating our two parents, knowing as we did how cruelly Mum must have rode Daddy before he could take no more. No priest agreed to so much as sprinkling a bit of holy water over the coffins, not even when nobody was looking on ...

"... And this includes the randy priest who Mum was carrying on with for all the years she was providing us the fine things, beginning with the wonderful wireless. Thus, our trusty postman informs us.

"The priest's name was Cor. The postman dishes this up like a regular magpie, right during the little service we had at Daddy's sheepeen before we had Mum and him cremated.

"The postman says, 'Myles, he knew all about Cor and his Finola. Never complained, though, mainly on account of how he was kept well provided with whiskey in appreciation of his tolerance. We all come to know it here in this sheepeen. I remember your daddy come to mocking himself as a cuckold, too. He'd say, "My sporting days is over, my little light is out, what used to be my sex appeal is now my water spout." '

"I ask you, Neil, wasn't that a fine thing to be discovering in our bereavement . . . ?

"Well, that night, at home after the burning, when it was just Aidan and me alone together, we talked of Mum and Daddy until the dawn, about the war that was their marriage. We come to grips with the matter of Cor. We drank a mighty lot that night, and cried, too, wondering if Myles was our own true daddy indeed.

"And that started me telling Aidan of the old man's drinking and carrying on that night of his birth . . . how he warned me of the Brits in no uncertain terms.

"Then soon it was me sounding like our wounded, besotted old dad. I myself was moved to telling Aidan what I'd not admitted to any other man—the true reason I'd left London as I did.

"Only I gentled it down a good deal. I said to my brother, 'At the bank, I worked at the teller's desk beside this great oaf bigot, an Englishman. Clever as a box of rocks, this one. He'd greet me every morning with the same: 'Up the long ladder and down the long rope, God bless King Billy and go fuck the pope. Ain't that right, Paddy?'

"Aidan's face grows dark and queer like Daddy's as he's listening to me. I go on, telling him, 'You can't imagine how this grates you, brother dear. After a while, you can bear it no more. You either got to leave, or take one of them out. Me, I left for Dublin.'

"Then we had a final jar to the troubling memory of Mum and Dad. Aidan poured drops from the bottle out onto the floor in respect for the two who gave us life. Then we climb into the beds up in the little room we shared, back all those years ago listening to the wireless as boys waiting for the chance to flee.

"And in the dark, before we drift off, Aidan asks me, 'Liam, do you hate them for how they slurred you?'

" 'Hate the English, you mean?' I said. That's what he meant. And so I said, 'Well ... yes, I confess it, I do.'

"Aidan's quiet then, but all the same I hear him thinking. Finally, he says, 'I do, too. God help me, I hate them all.'

"I think, We never betrayed Daddy after all. And maybe Aidan now hears my thoughts this time. He says, 'Too bad Daddy didn't live long enough to see there's a way now of dealing with the bloody English, for once and for all—' "

Snoody cut him off.

"Hadn't we best carry on with this later?" he said, glowering at me, then Ruby. Then, to Liam, "Really, I must insist."

"Oh you must, must you?" Liam said, twitting him.

The two of them stared at each other for a while like a pair of tomcats about to have a spitting match. Liam sighed loudly, then looked away.

"Well, as mother hen wishes—another time," Liam said to Ruby and me. Snoody quickly got up from the table and stood behind Liam's wheelchair, ready to push.

"Before we call it a night, I want to give you this," Liam said, handing the envelope to me. "Your father took to writing me letters when he finally left Dublin for New York. I haven't got many left, but I found this one and thought you should have it. Like I say, I never did take to the literary side of life. But I do know from his letters, Aidan was a lovely, lovely writer."

"I don't know about you," Ruby said, "but I feel like we've been through one of those ... oh, what was it your uncle called a nasty storm?"

"Bleezer," I said.

"That's it. An awful *bleezer*, with a wind so stiff it blows sleet sideways."

We were back down on the third floor in the red room, settled for the night and dressed in two sets of men's pyjamas and robes that Moira had brought up for us with the fresh towels. Ruby was bustling around the room, unpacking all our things, tucking them away in the wardrobe and the dresser. I sat on the edge of the bed with the envelope in my hands, still unopened.

"Bleezer ...," Ruby said again, thoughtfully. Then she stopped

135

in front of me, pointed to the envelope, and said, "Well, are you ever going to read it?"

"Right now, I don't really know that I'm up to it," I said. "So far today, let's see ... I've learned my grandmother was some priest's squeeze, my drunken grandfather got even with her—permanently, then popped himself out ... Maybe that's enough family history for one day."

"You've heard worse in your time, Detective Hockaday."

"About other people's families, sure."

"You jump in the ocean, you get wet. So what do you expect? Be a person, go ahead—read it." Ruby lunged at me, grabbing for the envelope. "You want me to read it for you—?"

I pulled back. Ruby fell on top of me, laughing. And I was grateful for the moment's diversion from my dark rain cloud of thoughts; so grateful for the feel of Ruby, for the sight of her breasts, brown as caramel beneath the white swaddle of terrycloth robe and the loose pyjamas.

"No!" I said. "I'll read it ... I will."

"What's stopping you? Liam said it's lovely writing."

"Do you trust Liam?" I surprised myself with this question as much as I surprised Ruby.

"That's one hell of a question," she said.

"He's one hell of a talker. Answer me."

"Your uncle's a banker, so we know he'd steal. But lie ...?" Ruby bolted upright in bed, and said, "Sure!"

She was very excited now, as if some of her own clouds had suddenly cleared. She straightened her robe. "You call your uncle a big talker, Hock?" she said. "No, he's a bleezer ... with wind enough to blow the words sideways. Follow me?"

"Well—no."

"Aren't you the one who's always telling me how any half-competent detective ought to approach a case sideways?"

"What are you—?"

"Step on it, Sherlock. Your uncle drops a big storm tonight. What for? To make you feel sorry about the pitiful Hockaday clan? No. He talked up a storm for cover. Follow me now?"

Ruby gave me a second to catch up. When I did, I said, "He's trying to talk past Snoody, you mean?"

"Yes—of course. We know there's something very strained between them, and we know there's something strange going on here. We know there's some secret in this house. Your uncle's trying to get this across to you, Hock. Indirectly, so Snoody won't realize it . . . So what do you think?''

I thought of Liam's words to me, earlier: *When you solve it, you'll start seeing answers to questions that have burnt you hollow.*

I said, ''This afternoon, while you were still asleep and Snoody was off on an errand somewhere, Liam sent Moira up here after me. In the time we had alone together, Liam told me a riddle.''

''Tell it to me.''

''A man without eyes saw plums on a tree. He neither took plums nor left plums. How could this be?''

''Now, let's hear that letter.'' Ruby reached for the envelope.

This time I let her take it. She opened it, and read aloud my father's words, written in a firm hand, in blue ink:

> *Dear brother Liam,*
>
> *In your last, you seemed incredulous as to why I persist in being here—here in this city of right angles and tough, damaged people. Though I hardly needed reminding of it, you nonetheless pointed out that my writing income seldom pays for the groceries, and that I have responsibilities to Mairead and the baby she's now carrying.*
>
> *I've thought long and hard about what sort of answer might satisfy you. What I have concluded is that my answer may only truly satisfy myself, and that you can expect no more. So, here it is:*
>
> *New York is a fabulous lady who gives incredible parties. You're never invited, but you know they're there, and you know that once you get inside, it's going to be great. Every time you're packing finally to leave the city, this lady calls you up and says, ''Hi, I'm having a party, as you well know.'' And so you start unpacking your bag. Then she says, ''I'm not inviting you to the party this year, but I'm keeping you in mind.''*
>
> *Love, Aidan.*

Ruby gave the letter back to me. I looked at the blue ink, and thought of the lines of verse penned on the back of Aidan Hockaday's photograph. But the handwriting in these two things of my father's, the letter and the photo, did not seem to match. I folded the letter and put it back inside the envelope.

Ruby said, "Uncle Liam was right, it's lovely writing. And lovely sentiments about New York. I miss the city something terrible right now."

"So do I."

"Your father should have written books in New York."

"There was the war instead."

"It wasn't that simple."

"No. What we're trying to find is the war within the war."

"Which is to say, the politics. And another riddle."

"It's making my head hurt. Let's go to sleep."

We turned off lights, took off our robes and slipped under the covers together. Ruby shaped herself against me, and whispered, "I want to dream of New York. How about you, Hock?"

"I'll be dreaming like a detective."

"Meaning?"

"A good detective believes in the kind of moment when he can see what people are doing, even when he's not there."

CHAPTER 20

Lieutenant Ellis reached out the narrow window and gripped the cement ledge, careful to keep his hands off any fresh additions to the crust of pigeon dung. He bent at the waist and squeezed his hammy shoulders through the narrow frame, pushing forward into the gray light of a tenement air shaft.

Gritty dust breezed up and down the shaft, along with swarms of flies and yellow jackets. In spite of it, tenants short on money for the corner laundromat strung their hand-washed clothes out on lines. The dust swirled in little wind tunnels every time someone opened a window to haul in clothes, or to dump something that could not wait for a trip down to the garbage cans on the street.

"Smells like a freaking Mexican sewer," Ellis said, wiping his nostrils with a coat sleeve.

He leaned over and looked at the ground, down ten storeys of sooty brick walls and windows caked in grime. There was a gang of cops below, milling around a ten-foot square of broken glass, weeds, syringes, putrefying rubbish and a small nation of rats. The cops wore hip boots, gloves up to their elbows and gauze masks strapped across their mouths and noses. A dead man lay flat on his broken back in the middle of the fetid compost, wearing nothing.

Every few seconds, the air shaft blazed with the strobe lights from two cameras. Down on the ground, a police photographer slogged around the body, snapping the deceased's final portrait. Up on the roof there was a second photographer working the aerial angles. From ten floors up, and in the strong flashes of concentrated light, Ellis could see enough of the dead man's face to know for sure he was no leaper. Which he had already more than half figured anyway.

The lieutenant ducked his bald head back through the window into the apartment and stood up straight, stretching himself. He placed his hands back around his puffy middle and pushed hard, causing his vertebrae to make loud popping sounds. "Christ— finally!" he said, wincing.

"Are you all right, Lieutenant?" The young first-year detective asking the question, and extending his unsolicited helping hand, the one with the college ring attached to it, was named Baker.

Ellis stared at Baker's hand until he took it away, then said, "Take a peek, Detective, tell me what he was thinking about on the way down."

Baker poked his head out the window and looked, again, at the body sprawled below. He had seen it at ground level an hour ago when he first arrived, in response to the lady who called up the station house screaming in Spanish about what she saw when she was taking in the baby's diapers off the clothesline.

It was Lieutenant Ellis who had put Baker on the call, assigning him the uniforms and the forensics unit. But when Baker telephoned his commander with the preliminary on-scene report, Ellis took a personal interest. "I don't want anybody touching nothing in the guy's apartment until I get a look," Ellis had said over the phone, "and that includes forensics."

"Well," Baker said now, confused, "I don't know that you can exactly tell what's on somebody mind when he's—"

"Sure you can," Ellis cut in. "It ain't true what you heard about dead men. They tell all kinds of tales."

"What's this one saying?"

"That he didn't do the brain dive. Every leaper I ever seen looks very calm and collected once he lands. Why not? His problems are all over. The guy down there, the whole lower half of his head is one big scream."

"So you figure it's an accident, or . . . ?"

"It obviously ain't your nice half-gainer into the Lasker pool on a summer afternoon." Ellis relit a cigar that had gone cold after he rested it on the windowsill. "You call up the inspector like I asked?"

"Yes, he told me to say he'd be around in thirty minutes."

"No kidding, Neglio's coming here himself? I'm impressed." But he was not surprised.

He looked past Baker to the furnishings in the small, dreary room: a rumpled bed with stale sheets and a wool blanket that was home and board to a colony of moths, a chair with maroon Naugahyde peeling off of it, a nightstand that held a lamp and the current issue of *Hustler* magazine, a folding table with a portable TV and a half-eaten salami sandwich on it, and not much floorspace for anything else. There was another, even bleaker room on the other side of a wall with no door. This contained a sink and refrigerator, another viewless window to the air shaft, two cupboards full of cockroaches, a hotplate and a stall shower.

The toilet was in a closet out in the hallway next to a pay telephone, both of which the late tenant was obliged to share with others on the floor. At Lieutenant Ellis's suggestion, Baker had posted a couple of uniforms in the hallway. "If you don't," Ellis advised the young detective supervising his first suspicious death crime scene, "the neighbors will make like vultures. Believe me, I know the house." One of the uniforms was questioning the building superintendent, who was sweating heavily.

A suitcase sat open on the floor next to the bed. Some of the things in it, along with what came out of the pockets of a jacket and trousers slung over the Naugahyde chair, were what prompted Ellis to have Inspector Neglio notified. These things were now in the manila envelope that Ellis held under his arm.

"So, somebody maybe pushed him?" Baker asked Ellis.

"What—?"

"No." Detective Baker's face flushed. "A naked guy up on the roof, and somebody happens to come by and shove him. Too weird."

141

"Kid, learn one thing: working PDU out of Hell's Kitchen, you never know. This precinct, it's Manhattan's crème de la weird."

"Yeah, well I guess ..."

"This one, it's going to have some actual logic to it. Watch and see. But for truly weird, take this call that come in last week—also a roof-top incident. Supposedly a bunch of kids was doing drugs, making a lot of noise in the middle of the night and like that. The uniforms get there and find this guy and his wife carrying on with some contraption they'd made out of a big tin can and a couple of pipes so they could inhale the fumes of heated dog doody. Welcome to the neighborhood, Baker."

"So glad to be here."

Lieutenant Ellis laughed and gave Detective Baker's back a fraternal slap. Then he picked up the dead man's jacket and trousers from the chair, tossed them on the floor under the window and sat down with his cigar. He twisted his hips, popping his spine again, and said, "All right, Detective, let's see that super now before Neglio comes around and I suppose we got to start going by the book."

Baker went to the hall. He returned with a small, thin redheaded man about thirty years old in khakis and an unbuttoned flannel shirt. Sweat poured down his face from beneath a blue-and-orange Mets cap. When he spoke, the accent would be Irish. And this, too, would not surprise Lieutenant Ellis.

"Lieutenant Ellis—Mac," Baker said by way of introduction. "That's all the name he's giving us."

"Why ever is that, Mac?"

"You don't need me being involved in any of this."

"Any of what?"

"Whatever, you know ... ," Mac stammered.

"That's the sixty-four-dollar question, ain't it? Whatever. I'm asking you nice to help us, Mac. You got any string I could borrow?"

"String—?"

"It ain't something from outer space, Mac. Don't act like you never heard of string. You got to have some around here. Where is it?"

"My workshop, in the cellar."

"Good. Give me the key."

"There's some law says I got to?"

Ellis turned to Baker, and said, "Take a man down to the cellar with you, blast open Mac's workshop any way you want."

"No! Don't be making a mess," said Mac, handing the key to Baker.

"There's some packaging string, on the shelf on the right-hand side."

"That's real smart, a fine building like this you want to keep up real nice for the white-glove crowd," Ellis said to Mac. Then to Baker, "Make it quick, and while you're down there, find me a nice big brick out in the air shaft, too."

Baker shrugged and left the room.

The super lifted the cap off his head and brushed sweat back into his hair. He asked Ellis, "What are you needing with a brick?"

"You can just think about that for a while," Ellis said, puffing his cigar. "Cut the crapola now, you little mick hump. What's the last name?"

"I tell you, I ain't saying."

"Okay—for now. What's the dead man's name?"

"I don't know."

"He's not the regular tenant, is he?"

"I'm not the nosy type."

"No, I suppose not. But I bet you know the legal tenant's name. What's that?"

"Ask the landlord."

"What's his name?"

"Me, I only talk to some secretary in an office uptown."

"And you're paid off the books, in cash?"

"Hey, every year I file with Sam."

"Sure you do, Mac. Step over to the window there."

"What for?"

"So I can show you what I'm going to do with the brick, since you was nosy enough to ask."

The super stepped to the window, and said, "I don't have to look out, I know what's down there."

"You're sweating pretty bad, Mac. How come?"

"I've got a cold."

"Too bad. Have you got a green card?"

"Come on, man!"

143

"I didn't think so. Too bad, Mac. A man with a green card has rights in this country. A harp like you, you're fair game for the cops and the bad guys, especially in this neighborhood. And we all have our persuasive methods. Know what I mean?"

"What?"

"We'll wait for Detective Baker to come back. You'll see."

Ellis crossed his legs, puffing contentedly. Ten minutes passed without a word. The super sweated, and flinched whenever the strobe lights flashed through the air shaft. He would not look out the window.

Finally, Baker came back with a yellow brick in one hand and a ball of brown twine in the other. "Will this do?" Baker asked, handing them to Ellis.

"Let's see." Ellis took the string and unrolled enough of it to test the strength by giving three sharp yanks. "Sure, it'll do fine."

He stood up, and motioned for Baker to follow him to the window where Mac stood. "Tie up the end of the brick real good and tight with one end of this twine," he told Baker.

When Baker was through, Ellis took the brick and let out about twenty feet of slack line. Then he tossed the brick out the window. The twine held fast. Ellis smiled at the super as he reeled up the brick.

"Yeah, great twine," he said. "Now, Mac—tell us what's down there at the bottom of the air shaft."

"What is this—?"

"He doesn't want to get involved by looking out the window," Ellis said to Baker. "So you'll have to tell Mac here, our friend who unfortunately has got no civil rights, what he's missing."

"The naked and the dead."

"Very good, Detective—and literary, too. That's really getting into the spirit." Ellis turned to the sweating super. "Now, Mac, I'd like you to drop your pants."

"I ain't a nancy-boy."

"What's the number at Immigration, Lieutenant?" Baker asked. "I'll go out and call them now."

Ellis beamed at Baker, as if proud mentor to protégé.

Mac understood, and undid his belt and fly. The khakis dropped to his ankles. "The skivvies, too," Ellis told him. When the briefs fell, Ellis used a penknife to cut twenty feet of twine off the ball

144

and handed the free end to the super. "Tie this end up around your hairy Irish nuts—good and tight," he said, hefting the brick in his hand.

"Oh, come on, man!" the super complained, tossing the twine to the floor. "Are you guys crazy?"

"Yes, very," Baker said, stooping to pick up the twine. Ellis beamed again.

"Look, man—whatever this is, I'm only the little guy," the super whined at Ellis. "Have a heart."

"I'm not hearing you," Ellis said, cupping an ear. "Was that a name you were saying?"

"Okay. It's McGoldrick—Tom McGoldrick. They call me Mac."

"Actually, I don't care about that name anymore. Try again."

"I told you, I only talk to the secretary."

"Okay, Detective Baker—if you please. Lace him up."

McGoldrick gasped, "What—?"

"I give you the opportunity to do it for yourself, Mac. But you want Detective Baker to handle the jewels, it's okay by me. You get hooked up to the brick here, and we'll toss it out the window all the same. Then we'll see if the thrill makes you any more cooperative."

"Jaysus, no—!"

"Ain't it a stone pity you don't have a green card, McGoldrick? You could file brutality charges against us. Go on, Detective—string him."

"I'll tell you!" McGoldrick shouted, flailing his arms at Baker. He bent over to pick up his trousers, but Baker grabbed the back of his shirt and stood him up straight.

"Tell me what?" Ellis asked.

"Honest, I don't know the guy down there," McGoldrick said. "I only saw him once or twice in the last week, coming in or going out. This dump here has different people always coming and going. You know?"

"All of them harps?"

McGoldrick hesitated.

"Don't worry, son," Ellis told him. "I realize you're only the small fish, I'll work it so whatever I get it doesn't trace back to you. Just answer the question."

"There was one guy regular who paid for the place," McGoldrick said, wiping his forehead. "But the other day, he . . . well, he found himself in the obituary column, see?"

"Did I read that under the name of Arty Finn?"

McGoldrick said nothing. Which to Ellis was as good as yes.

There was noise in the hallway, the elevator doors clanking open, cops talking. Then one of the uniformed officers opened the door to the apartment for Inspector Neglio.

"What's this?" Neglio said, pointing to McGoldrick with his khakis and undershorts around his feet. He looked at Ellis, sighed, and said, "Forget I ever asked, Ray."

Ellis waved his cigar at McGoldrick, and said, "Pull them up now and leave us alone, son. And don't worry, you did the right thing."

Neglio looked out the window as the super hurried out. When he was gone, the inspector asked Ellis, "What's the story? No, don't tell me. You find a guy with no papers, so you forget about Miranda and let him know about cop hell instead?"

"Once you ride the bike, you never forget how to pedal, hey Inspector?"

Neglio nodded at Baker, and asked Ellis, "Who's this?"

"Detective Baker," Baker said, extending his hand to the inspector.

"He looks like a chucklehead on the TV news," Ellis said. "But don't mind that, he picks up very fast."

Neglio shook Baker's hand, then said to Ellis, "All right, what's the play here?"

"Maybe you want to ask Neil Hockaday if you can find him. Or his pal Mogaill—if anybody ever finds him."

"Cute doesn't cut it with me, Ray. Not when I have to break an appointment with the mayor. What are you getting at?"

Lieutenant Ellis tossed his cigar on the floor and stamped it. Then he took his manila folder from under his arm and put it in his lap. Before opening it, he looked at Baker, then back to Neglio, and said, "First I got to tell you, Inspector, I don't like this. It ain't going to wind up righteous—when or if we make a collar. And nothing but nothing stinks worse to me than bad cops, including that air shaft."

"Let's not get ahead of things, Lieutenant. First, tell me how you figure Nature Boy came to a bad end."

"Professional bump. The bumper was pretty good, too. Looks to me like he used a set of picks to get through the doors, probably before dawn. He rousts the guy here out of his sleep, takes him up to the roof—naked—and forces him to step off . . . I now repeat what I said about bad cops."

"I'm not sure what you're insinuating here—or why. And since when did you become a whistle-blower, Lieutenant? If you've got anything you want to tell the IAD, my advice is call for an appointment."

"No—you'll do, Inspector. I really think you ought to hear me out. Otherwise, I wouldn't dream of taking up your valuable time."

"Don't press it with me, Ray." Neglio turned up a mono-grammed cuff and checked his watch.

Lieutenant Ellis smiled, running a hand over the smooth manila folder. "Your boy Hockaday, he lives right here in Hell's Kitchen, don't he?"

"Everybody's got his briar patch."

"Sure, but it's Hockaday's that interests me. Half the tenements around here that nobody cares about—including the health depart-ment, as you can see from this one we're in now—they go way back to the Irish gangs of New York, even before the Westies. Follow?"

"I know what a mattress house is, Ray," said Neglio. "Are you giving me the history lesson, or your boy Baker here?"

"Just want to be clear," Ellis said. "This mattress we're in here, it was none other than the late Arty Finn who was keeping it."

"That's what you got out of—?"

"McGoldrick. He's the super, and scared out of his gourd. My guess is because of Finn and his IRA goons."

"So who's the guy down below?"

"Now it gets real interesting." Lieutenant Ellis opened the ma-nila folder. He pulled out a green booklet, and held it out for Neglio to take. "I found a few interesting items that belonged to the stiff. Take a look at this first."

"It's an Irish passport," Neglio said. He read the name of the dead man: "Dennis Farrelly."

"Ain't it interesting how a guy with a nice respectable passport from the Emerald Isle winds up staying in a New York mattress specializing these days in Irishmen you wouldn't want to cross?"

"This Farrelly, he's what—IRA or something?"

"Or something," Ellis said. He reached into the folder again, pulled out a medallion and handed it over to Neglio. "This has got me stumped. Found it in the suitcase. What do you make of it?"

Neglio read off italicized script engraved on one side of the brass medallion:

"When nations are empty up there at the top ... When order has weakened or faction is strong ... Time for us all to pick out a good tune ... Take to the roads and go marching along."

He turned it over, saw the letters H.O.S. and the design of an axe tied in a bundle of rods. "It's political," Neglio said. "I don't know what these initials are, but I've seen the axe logo before. Mussolini and his Fascists used it."

"No kidding?"

"Fascists I don't kid about."

"Honest, I really hate to give you this next thing, Inspector."

Ellis removed one further item from the manila folder. It was a small leather case, the size of a wallet. Neglio took it, half knowing what it was.

"Open it," Ellis said.

Neglio did. There was a police shield inside.

He read the words:

"Dennis Farrelly, Dublin Garda."

CHAPTER 21

"WRAP YOURSELF IN THESE BLOODY DAMN FANTASIES OF IRISH GLORY, lads, and this here'll be the useless end of yourselves—as surely as our poor precious friends here ..."

Saying this, Davy Mogaill nevertheless tipped his glass, spilling whiskey from one body to the other as a gesture of his respect. It fell on the white linen sheets draped over the two dead men, as if they were saints laid out there on the wooden doors taken down for the occasion of the wake.

The doors rested horizontal atop four chairs each, and all circled around were the heavily drinking mourners. To a man, they held vigorous opinions on the life and times of the dearly departed, and none were shy about arguing the smallest point of a differing view.

Uncovered by linen were the dead men's veiny hands folded over their still chests, clutching crucifixes carved from stone—and their big toes, which were bare and tied together to prevent them from wandering through the ages as ghosts instead of joining Jesus and the Holy Mother in heaven. There were racks of candles burning around their covered heads, the only light in the smoky low-ceilinged room. At their feet were new pairs of boots needed for the trek through purgatory. Outside, their beds were smoldering in pit fires dug into the ground, this to ward off unseen troubles with the færies. The smoke and the night fog from outside curled into the doorless sheepeen.

The mourners had eaten huge bowls of mutton stew and many brown loaves of fadge, the bread of potatoes. They had washed this down with rivers of stout and whiskey. Death made for hearty appetites and thirsty throats.

The meal over, they sat about as each man stood in turn between the bodies to have his say, now being Davy Mogaill's time. The mourners were raucous listeners, fueled by the liquor. And they smoked clay pipes, the tobacco dampened with holy water. A plate of snuff was passed around, too, for the purpose of expediting the resurrection of their precious friends. And it was understood through hundreds of years of sheepeen custom that it was perfectly proper at such occasions to argue about any arguable subject, and interrupt at any interruptable moment.

"So look at them here as they are, lads," Mogaill continued, raising his voice against growlers in the crowd. "Recognize at least this one sorry fact of life they've taught us: you see before you proof that learned men, highly intelligent men may still be fools."

"Well said, well said!" crowed a man in a far, darkened corner.

"Nae, 'tis not!" shouted another. Then, laughing and poking elbows into his pals beside him, he said, "Davy Mogaill, I say you're like a noisy great windbag!"

"Here now—I say none of us should be listening to you anyways, Mogaill, for you're one of them that run away!" cried yet another, his angry spittle flying from a toothless mouth. "When it got impossible here, you and yours run off to America. We stayed! By God Almighty, we stayed—and battled the impossible."

"A very great battler you are, sir," Mogaill responded. He jabbed fingers in the air, pointing to all around him. "You men, you're all great battlers, you know I admire what you done. But don't you see by now ... by Christ, don't you see—?"

"Aye—we see you come back here, Mogaill, all high and mighty like from New York, telling us we should just go quiet about the business of burying the sweat and the blood of these two loveliest fighters of us all. And here you be at their wake, calling them fool besides!"

The crowd, slugging down whiskey as the roaring sentiment against Davy Mogaill rose, stamped their feet and waved free fists in the thick air. And somebody shouted, "What right've you to be disparaging a man's sacrifice, being a man unwilling to sacrifice yourself?"

Bristling silence followed. A gauntlet had been thrown down.

Mogaill, eyes glassy with drink and exhaustion, threw back his shoulders. "True, I was unwilling," he said quietly, his calm inspiring the men to hear him out. "But you cannot say I'm one that never sacrificed. Nae, that you cannot! What man will stand up to me, right here and now, to claim he'd be willing to lose what I did . . . ? Oh!" Mogaill choked. "My darling, with her hair like the October leaves of Galty—"

Tears broke. He let them run, unashamed. The men of the sheepeen respected this as the guileless display of dignity it was; not a few of Davy Mogaill's detractors wept along with him over their own personal regrets.

"Don't you see . . . ?" Mogaill's voice was nearly a whisper. "By all that's holy, don't you see it's so bloody damn unamusing to live in a country where everybody acts, where nobody is satisfied with thought?"

A supporter rose from his chair to add, "Davy's right. Here we be at yet another wake, bragging about our manhood, glorifying deeds never done quite as glorious in actual fact as we stand here lying sweetly about them; filling ourselves with whiskey, and what we think is courage. Then somebody comes along to this mushing of ours, he drops in a thought not meant to comfort. And what do we do? We yelp and yelp, like a pack of frightened dogs!"

Mogaill said, "Dogs who cannot think but only snarl—or men? If it's dogs, I'd sooner drown you all . . ."

He was through with what he had to say, and wobbly on his legs besides. Mogaill stepped away from the laid-out bodies. He filled his mug with more whiskey, and his clay pipe with more of the consecrated tobacco. He walked past the first row of men, then the second and the third. On past them all, and out the open space left from the borrowed doors; out where he could gulp down the dark, clean air. His legs gained strength. But tears came again.

Slowly he walked, his feet squishing through a maze of puddles

151

left by the earlier rains. He did not go far, but far enough to still see the shabby outline of the sheepeen as he turned, and beyond it the great graystone manor house on the hill, its smooth walls and colored glass windows glowing in dewy moonlight hanging above clouds of fog.

He stood now at the bank of a crooked stream. There were boulders covered in patches of whitened grass, like the lace shawls on pianos. He found a ledge of rock where he could sit down. He lit his pipe, and said to the wreath of smoke, "Could it be you there, Brenda, floating like a sweet ghost on this dank night?"

But no answer came. Davy Mogaill, who believed himself a fool, cried softly. He lifted his mug to his lips. But the taste for whiskey was gone for this night.

He flung the mug over his shoulder, and it crashed into bits against the rocks. Then he walked back to the sheepeen.

A priest in black vestments, and a cowl that obscured his face, now stood between the two bodies draped on the death planks. He raised his arms slowly up from his sides, extending them at right angles from his shoulders, as if he were hanging on a cross. Each hand held a rosary. The crowd was hushed. From the blackness where the mouth would be, the priest murmured, "Mourn, and then onward, there's no returning . . . he guides ye from the tomb . . . his memory now is a tall pillar, burning before us in the gloom."

The priest nodded to a man sitting in a chair in front of him. The man stood up, wordlessly, to perform as an acolyte. First, he pushed back the cowl to reveal the face of Father Timothy Kelly . . .

Then the acolyte pulled back the linen sheet of one of the dead men, revealing Liam Hockaday. He used his thumbs to seal Liam's eyes. The priest laid a rosary over the shuttered eyes.

The acolyte moved to the next body. He pulled back the sheet.

And there lay Aidan Hockaday, so much older than the photograph owned by his son. The acolyte applied his thumbs. The priest dropped the rosary over Aidan's eyes . . .

But Aidan's corpse rose, slowly from the waist. Aidan sat up, and turned to the terrified men gathered around him. His angry dead voice shouted at them, "Whirl your liquor 'round like blazes, boyos! . . . *Thanam o'n dhoul,* do ye think I'm dead?"

* * *

Ruby shook me. "It's all right, Hock. Tell me what happened."
I sat up in bed. "God, I don't know, I—"

My breath gave out. My heart was running like a mailman with a pack of rottweilers after him. My face and hands were flowing with sweat. I tried to speak.

There was sunlight streaming through the windows over Ladbroke Street, still a strong early light. We had slept through the night.

"No, don't say a word," Ruby said.

She threw back the covers and crossed the rose-patterned rug to the dresser, for the towels and water in the pitcher and glasses. She brought me a drink. I took it down while she wiped my face with the corner of a dampened towel. Ruby wiped her own face, too, and as I collected myself, I saw how frightened she was.

"This is the worst I've seen," she said. "You were dreaming of him again, weren't you?"

I tried answering, but choked.

"Take your time."

I took a breath. "Aidan was in the dream. No, the nightmare. It wasn't like anything else before. It wasn't just my father telling me things this time, it was others, too. Davy Mogaill was there. It was really mostly about him—and the place he was ..."

My heart raced again, as if I was still in the nightmare.

"Where was he, Hock?" Ruby asked. "Where was Mogaill?"

"Here, someplace in Ireland. At a country tavern ... not an actual tavern, really, but someplace where men were drinking. Somewhere near a stream and a place on a hill that looked almost like a castle ..."

I stopped, and took more water. My body shook, as if I had just come in from the cold outdoors.

"And that's when you saw your father?" Ruby asked.

"I saw him, and more."

"In your detective's dream?"

CHAPTER 22

WE DECIDED TO SPLIT UP FOR THE DAY. RUBY DID MOST OF THE DECIDING.

"I want a chance to pump Moira—alone," she said. "She knows something about this house. I can feel it. Can't you?"

"Maybe, yes ..."

"So I want to get her out marketing, something like that. Just the two of us out somewhere so she's free to talk."

"What makes you think she'll crack for you?"

"I explained that to you boys last night—I'll listen to her is why. The lady's a big talker, and she's starved for listeners. And, something else."

"Such as?"

"Something that tells me this house never had to be a lonely one. That's only intuition. So we'll see. Anyway, I'll be listening carefully. It could be the first time anybody's really listened to her. Apart from her Bible crowd—which if it's anything like American thumpers, there isn't an honest ear to be bent—who's poor Moira got?"

"Liam, Snoody—"

"Hah! Your uncle will only tolerate her until she can't cook anymore, or he can't eat anymore, whichever comes first. Then there's that arrogant creep of an ex-priest, Snoody. And you, Hock—you're only in the way."

"Why, because I'm a man?"

"If you were a woman you'd know what a jerk question that is."

"You think women are any better at asking questions?"

She shrugged. "Whatever women do, they have to do it twice as well as men to be thought half as good. Luckily, this is not difficult."

Thus spake Ruby Flagg.

Deciding that I myself needed time and distance from Liam's house, I told her, "Okay then, maybe I'll just strike off on my own to Dublin and poke around in any public records available on Mairead and Aidan Hockaday." Ruby climbed into bed again and buried herself in the covers, yawned and said, "So go, at this hour you'll beat the rush," she said.

I bathed and dressed, and went downstairs. All was quiet, save for the kitchen.

At only a few minutes past six it was still quite early for the house, but Moira, her curly salt-and-pepper hair flattened with a net and her body wrapped form neck to knees in a baker's apron big enough to sail a ship, was already hard at it. Clouds of sweet-smelling steam poured from a double-door oven. At a nearby counter, Moira pounded out piles of dough on two different boards, shaped them with her flour-drenched hands and smoothed them out with a roller. I thought briefly of the nightmare—Liam and my father in the sheepeen, laid out dead on those doors in shrouds white as Moira's flour.

She had a radio on, tuned to one of those charismatics on a tear about perdition and repentance: "He that entereth not by the door into the sheepfold, but climbeth up some other way, the same is a thief and a robber! ... I tell you—repent, or ye shall likewise perish!" This was an Irish voice imitating the standard thumper twang of a Mississippi illiterate with a catfish caught sideways in his mouth. Which embarrassed me, both as a Catholic and an American.

I tripped on a stair step leading down to the kitchen, making a noise that startled Moira. Big as she is, roughly one-eighth the size of a Volvo, she hopped several inches into the air, as if a mouse was running up her leg, and squealed, "Hell's bells and Oriental smells!" She turned and saw me, slapped a floured hand across her impressive bosoms, and greeted me with, "My Gawd—you give me a fright!"

"Sorry, I—"

"You great blasphemin' ox! Can you have no respect for those payin' mind to the holy Gospel?"

"I said I was sorry." Then I put on the lopsided smile I use for brawlers with big mouths and small brains. This always seems to confuse them. I took a few tentative steps toward Moira. "Look here, Ms. Booley, I hope I can soften your opinion of me."

"Don't come near me, sinner man!" The Bible whacker on the radio had started carrying on about sending deliverance with a two-edged sword. Moira picked up a knife that could kill a pig. "Get out of my kitchen!"

Retreating quickly, I said, "That was a beautiful supper you made last night, Ms. Booley."

"Thank you," she snarled.

If I could sound like the thumper, I wondered, would our little kitchen chat be more cordial? "Like I told Ruby," I said, "there was the hand of God in that meal."

Moira lowered the knife a bit. "You told her that?"

"Goodness, yes. I ate every bite. And I'm now the changed man you see before you . . ."

I paused. Moira cocked her head at me, like she was a puzzled cocker spaniel.

"That heavenly food on my tongue started me thinking in a most peculiar way. I am a great sinner, as you say—but I suddenly realized that I am a child of God. And that I am capable of being saved, by the sweet blood of Jesus. You do understand, don't you?"

Moira looked back and forth between the radio and me, the wary hostility in her face giving way to idiotic sweetness. People who are not cops might have laughed at her. I have seen enough people racing around their emotional edges to know that life's jokes are sometimes not so funny.

"Yes, ma'am," I said, "the Lord works in mysterious ways."

"He does. Oh, yes—yes!"

"And it's you I have to thank for showing me His way, Ms. Booley."

"Please now, won't you call me Moira?" There was almost a shyness in her voice now. She put down the pig killer.

"Moira, then." I took a step.

She smiled. An easy thing for most of us, but not for Moira Catherine Bernadette Booley. We smile as infants not because of any goo-gooing efforts to amuse us, but because the expression is a natural arrangement of lips and gums. Life's events become far less amusing as time goes by, but the smile remains a reflex for most of us. Some, like poor Moira standing in front of me with her stiff shy grin and her cow brown eyes about to burst into tears that might mean joy as much as grief, show a kind of bravery by smiling in spite of it all.

"Cup of tea?" she asked, pronouncing it *tay.*

"I'd rather coffee."

"You think my tea's too weak for your breakfast?"

"I don't—"

"Why, a rat'd sink his foot in't."

"How can I resist?"

I was soon sitting at a butcher block table in Moira's fragrant kitchen with a pot of thick black tea in front of me, along with a bowl of sliced bananas and a plate of soda bread straight from the oven, with salty butter and marmalade. If only Ruby could see me getting along so well with Moira. *In the way* indeed. Here now was Moira, fussing over me like I was her long-lost brother.

"How long have you been here with my uncle?" I asked her.

"If you're meanin' as his cook, 'tis only since Mr. Liam took this house."

"You knew him before then?"

"Known him all me life. He was the boy next door, what you call—when we was kids."

"I see." I tried picturing Moira as a girl, but I could not get past the brave sadness of her smile. I asked, "Then you're from County Carlow, too?"

"Aye . . ." Apprehension crept back into her tone.

"And just when did my uncle move here to this grand place?"

Moira looked up, silently going through the years. Her fingers moved as she thought, counting the decades. "Well, it'd be not long after he come back home from London," she said, "all young and educated and looking about like a man does."

"The war would have been on then?"

"Aye, and a good time for a man to be takin' his opportunities."

"Especially in Ireland, which was neutral."

"Aye . . ." There was the apprehension again.

"Well, it's good to see that an Irishman profited from England's troubles."

Moira's face brightened. She might have been more revealing had I prompted her. Then again, she might have closed up on me. I decided I had asked enough direct questions, that I should go easy now, especially about politics. Better for Ruby to go at her sideways on that subject.

"You must enjoy your job here, being at it so long," I said.

"It's nae a job to me. It's me mission bein' with Mr. Liam."

"How wonderful for you."

"Oh, 'tis." Moira used her apron to wipe hands that did not need wiping, and sighed. Maybe she wanted to say more. Instead, she went back to the counter and rolled dough.

"Would there be somewhere in the neighborhood I could catch a bus or a train to Dublin?" I asked, addressing her wide back.

"If you're wanting to go to the city, Snoody'll get a driver for you—"

Moira stopped then, and turned to me. There was fright in her face, more serious than when I startled her by stumbling on the stair. She said, "Nae, you'll not want to risk survivin' another automobile ride!"

"No, I wouldn't." Also I said to myself, It might be a good idea to leave the house as soon as possible, before Snoody or Uncle Liam had anything to do with the day's agenda.

Moira told me where to find the commuter station down in the village, a short walk from the house. I finished eating my soda bread and emptied my cup.

Then before going up to brief Ruby on my encouraging breakfast chat with Moira, I said to her, "My uncle told me a riddle last night, I wonder if you've ever heard it."

"That'd be the one about the man with no eyes and the plums?"

"Yes. Do you know the answer?"

Moira smiled, bravely. And said no more.

The radio thumper was saying, "God be true, but every man a liar . . ."

From Dún Laoghaire station to Dublin's central depot is a journey just short of an hour, which was enough time for me to peruse a newspaper and start up a case book. At the station, I had purchased a bus ticket, the *Irish Guardian,* a spiral-bound journal, and a ballpoint pen from a news agent who was good enough to negotiate the price in American dollars. I would have to change over to Irish pounds later in Dublin, when the banks opened.

Page one of the newspaper found the world in its usual precarious moment. Prosperous nations were variously mired in economic recession, others were in full-blown depression—or civil war. And everywhere, criminals and half-wits claimed to know the pathway out of chaos. These were the leaders of nations, and their followers seemed to be taking them seriously.

I turned to page two. A social item about Trinity College reminded me that this would be the appropriate place to begin a day's research, since I now knew my father had studied there. I folded up the paper to read later. I then noted the Trinity College association in a section of the journal where I had set aside a lot of blank pages for Aidan Hockaday entries, which I had more than a passing hunch would prove somehow central to all others.

For the next quarter hour, as the bus bumped along the harbor route toward Dublin and my hand cramped from the effort to keep the notes legible, I set down in writing the main elements of the case as I saw them. At the core were a few seemingly unrelated occurrences: Father Tim's suicide, Davy Mogaill's disappearance, the murder of Francie Boylan. Surrounding these were scores of messy questions and nasty impressions. And my suspicions; foremost among them, a guess that more was yet to occur.

"Excuse me for disturbing your work . . ."

I looked up from my notebook and across the aisle of the bus to a man about my own age, turned toward me. He wore the suit and hat of an earnest businessman, round wire-rimmed glasses and a small black moustache so neat it looked more like a grease-pencil drawing than clipped whiskers. He had the *Irish Guardian* spread open atop a leather briefcase balanced across his knees.

"I wonder," he asked, "would you be an American?"

"Yes," I said, wishing I had not.

His moustache stretched out thin as a pin over his smile, and he said, "I thought so . . ."

I was expected to respond at this point, I suppose, but instead I returned to my notebook.

"It was your clothes, actually," Moustache said.

I was wearing chinos, a nylon windbreaker with the logo of a New Jersey bowling alley on the back, a cotton jersey, a Yankees cap and PF Flyers. Not too many men somewhere in the middle of their lives wear that sort of thing in Ireland, I suddenly realized. I looked up at Moustache again.

"And your teeth," he said. "Brilliant."

"How's that?"

"Your American teeth—brilliant white."

"I see. Thanks."

"And your name, it would be Hockaday?"

"It would."

"Got it then, I have." He leaned forward and squinted at me through his glasses. "I'm not sure I would have guessed from your picture alone."

"My what—?"

"Why, in here," he said, tapping his newspaper. He looked at my copy of the *Guardian*, folded beside me. "Oh . . . I see. You don't know about it. Sorry then, sir . . . Please, never mind . . ."

Moustache got up, as awkwardly as he had just spoken, and moved to another seat. In the new location, he whispered to a woman sitting next to him and now she craned her neck around to get a load of me, too.

I picked up my copy of the *Guardian* and riffled through it, until I came to a page fully taken up with the story of Francie Boylan's murder. There was a smaller accompanying story, decorated with my own rookie photograph, made on the day I graduated from New York Police Academy. I read this smaller article:

Garda Questions American Detective & Actress in O'Connell Street Massacre

by Oliver Gunston

A pair of visiting Americans from New York City—a police detective by the name Neil Hockaday, and a stage actress by the name Ruby Flagg—figure prominently, and mysteriously, into yesterday's spectacular midmorning slaying of Francis "Francie" Boylan, a longtime local sympathizer of the Ulster-based Irish Republican Army. The Americans were held for an unspecified time for questioning at Dublin Garda headquarters, then released conditionally.

Detective Hockaday and Miss Flagg were passengers in a private car driven by the late Mr. Boylan, a chauffeur by trade. They were unharmed when a gang of masked gunmen attacked the car (see main article, this page). Chief Eamonn Keegan of the Dublin Garda, who personally interviewed the two Americans, would not disclose their destination on the day of the murder, or their itinerary in Ireland. "That would be a confidential matter for our continuing investigation," he told the press.

Nor would Chief Keegan provide any sense of the interrogation, except to say, "We made it known to Detective Hockaday and Miss Flagg that we might wish to discuss this matter with them again, here in Dublin." When asked if he or the government had confiscated their United States passports, Chief Keegan refused comment. He said, however, that the Americans had been "reasonably coöperative."

Contrary to Chief Keegan's unrevealing view was that of Constable Aisling Mulcahy, who was first on the scene at the site of the O'Connell Street slaying. "They was both your typical New Yorkers," he said. "All full of smart-mouthed jokes and not seeming to care a whit for the gravity of a violent murder of an IRA man. In fact, the lady even tried joking about politicians."

Ironically, the celebrated New York police career of Detective Hockaday—or "Hock", as he is known in the popular press there—is highlighted by his involvement in that city's

161

most baffling homicides. According to a prominent American journalist interviewed for this article by trans-Atlantic telephone, Detective Hockaday was, in fact, on holiday after solving one of the grisliest killing sprees in the entire legendary history of New York crime.

Said William T. Slattery of the *New York Post*, "Hock single-handedly cracked a series of murders that had this city completely terrorized, which is saying something. And that wasn't the first time he'd hunted down a crazy killer all by himself. This last one, though, I hear it shook him up real bad. You don't deal with the kind of maniacs and lunatics that Hock does every day without it starting to creep your dreams, you know? So he and his girlfriend, Ruby, took off for a little R&R over there in Ireland, I also hear. But he isn't gone twenty-four hours before a priest friend of his commits suicide right in a church in Hock's own neighborhood, and there's a bomb that goes off in the house where his best friend in the department lives—Captain Davy Mogaill of central homicide, of all things. Then as soon as Hock lands in Dublin—bang, some IRA goon is cut down right in front of him. Some rest, some relaxation."

Detective Hockaday's commanding officer, Inspector Tomasino Neglio, was also reached by telephone. Without elaborating, he acknowledged all that Mr. Slattery said, but termed the violence that seems to have dogged Detective Hockaday "coincidence."

The *Guardian* was unable to speak directly to Neil Hockaday or Ruby Flagg, as no one else contacted was willing or able to disclose their whereabouts in this country.

I tore out that entire page of the *Irish Guardian*, folded it in quarters and filed it in the back of my case book. I also wrote down the name of the reporter, Oliver Gunston, as a possible source to run down in Dublin. He would see me, of course. And if I played it right, I would learn a lot more from him than he would from me.

At the newspaper office, I could also pick up another copy of the *Guardian* and send it back to Slattery, who would be thrilled to have it, since it would likely be the first time anybody called him a "prominent American journalist." Maybe the last. For my-self, I was only happy that Slats had enough sense to wire over some ancient photo of myself to the *Irish Guardian,* assuming he was the source. It would make life in Dublin easier if I could go around relatively unrecognized except for my clothes and my brilliant teeth.

And then, thinking carefully about this publicity, I wrote down one more messy question: Would it be in someone's unkind inter-est here to have me recognized?

CHAPTER 23

"MOIRA?"

"Aye—?"

"May I come in?"

"If you'll want your mornin' tea, I suppose you must. You'll nae have me cartin' pots up and down stairs so early, Miss Fancy Thing." Moira sniffed loudly, and made a great show of taking a kettle of steaming water off the stove and pouring it into a brown teapot. She might be a servant in the house, but this kitchen was her realm, by Gawd. She turned off the radio halfway into the second of the morning's obituary readings. Then, clucking her tongue, she said, "To think we'd want to start the day hearin' which of the neighbors dropped in the night! Such depressin' stuff, that."

"Yes—and what with so few souls sure of leaving for glory these days," Ruby said, stepping down the stair into the kitchen. She had remembered Hock's tip about thumper talk at the earliest opportunity and the warming effect it had on Moira's frost. Much as it cut against her own grain, Ruby now saw the practicality of Hock's advice. Moira's head was tilted, as if in loving study of a sister not seen in decades. And what had it cost Ruby to sink her hook with but a single hackneyed ad-lib?

"Come you," Moira said, smiling her brave smile and motioning for Ruby to take a seat at the butcher block table where Hock had eaten breakfast some two hours before. "I would've thought from your blasphemin' the night before you was nonreligious."

"My lack of religion's got nothing to do with the fact that I'm a believer the same as you, Moira."

"Well, I only thought—"

"Have you ever noticed how many religious people think they are thinking when they are only rearranging their prejudices?"

Poor Moira was now very confused. What passed for conversation in her life were mostly one-sided exchanges between Liam and herself or Snoody and herself, and mostly for the purpose of fulfilling the men's needs. No great thought was required of anyone in such discourse. Moira had supposed this fallowness to be the way of the world beyond the great house in Ladbroke Street. Certainly she knew no different in the few other places she had ever been. But here was this woman—this American, this black woman!—speaking to her as if she had a man's own brain. And what was that she said about prejudices?

Ruby saw the pain of thought in Moira's doughy face. She sat down at the table, glanced at her wristwatch, and said to Moira, "Here it's already after nine. I know Hock's gone off to Dublin, but where are the others?"

"What I got on my hands here is two old men what both ran out of their yeast many years ago. So 'tis a late risin' house."

"Perfect, we'll have the chance to talk—just us girls."

Moira ran a hand over her hair net. A tinge of color crept into her jowls. "My, I ain't been called a girl since the country days when me legs was thin as the rushy grass," she said.

"Lucky you," Ruby said. "My legs were never thin."

"Pish, you're a reedy young thing still." Moira set out cream and sugar, and poured tea into Ruby's cup. She asked, "Would you care for a bit of soda bread? It's fresh this mornin'. And mind, I churn me own butter. There's marmalade, too."

"I'll be pleased to thank you—and God—for another good meal."

Moira, mouth open, fetched bread, butter, marmalade and utensils and set these out. Ruby bowed her head and mumbled a short prayer. When she was through, she smiled, and asked Moira,

"Won't you please get a cup and sit down yourself? We can share this pot."

Had the men ever asked her such a thing? Stunned with gratitude for this simple generosity, Moira did as she was asked. "Thank you, Miss Ruby." Moira sat with her hands folded in her lap while Ruby poured her tea. Then, with eyes lowered in apologetic guilt, she said, "Oh Gawd, I passed a remark the other day, viciously meant for you t'overhear—about the golliwogg. I'm so mortally sorry, Miss Ruby, I—"

"This time, we'll forget it, Moira. Only do me a favor from now on?"

"Aye, anything."

"Lose the *Miss,* okay? No more Miss Fancy Thing, and no more Miss Ruby. Please—just Ruby."

"Ruby, aye."

"Good. Now Moira, tell me—are you happy in this house?"

Moira's eyes looked faraway past Ruby. She said, "I been here me whole life as a woman, Miss . . . Ruby, I mean."

"But you didn't answer. Are you happy?"

Again, there was the great pain of thought in Moira's face. She put fingers on her lips, as if unsure of what words might come out. She said, "Nobody ever asked such a thing of me. I don't know how to say what I'm thinkin'."

"Say it honest."

"If you'll have it plain, then here goes. Happiness ain't what I'm livin' now, 'tis what I remember."

"When you were a girl?"

Moira blushed. "And Liam a boy."

"You were lovers?"

Moira stroked her throat, and Ruby confirmed her intuition. Moira said, "I'm to this day an innocent woman. Do you understand?"

"I meant no offense, I'm sorry."

"Nae, it's me the one who's sorry. Holy Mother preserve me, but I am sorry for bein' innocent."

Ruby reached across the table and touched Moira's hand. Moira scarcely noticed, faraway as she was. Nothing was said between the women for several minutes. They drank tea.

Then Ruby said, "You must still love him very much."

"Must I?"

"You've been here all these years."

"And every day for all these years, I confess I spat in his mornin' tea. Now that is somethin', but I don't call it love, from what I remember of love."

"I'm sorry . . ."

"Aye, but what good does it do? Soon, He Who Rolls—it's what I call him here by meself—he'll be down and callin' out his wants. Rashers and pork sausages and my soda bread, and a soft fried egg . . . and later, a cup of Van Houton's cocoa. That's how the mornin' goes here. And my life as well—day by day, year by year. It ain't likely to change, you see, no matter how sorry anybody is."

"Moira—?"

A man's voice. Ruby and Moira looked up to see Snoody entering the kitchen. He walked with chest thrust forward and hands clutched at jacket lapels, as if he was commander of all he saw.

"You've company this morning," Snoody said to Moira, nodding with a sniff at Ruby. "So this is why you're late with his tea."

"Here I've kept you from taking Liam a delicious pot of morning tea?" Ruby said to Moira with a sly smile. Then Ruby laughed, and so did Moira, as if she had not laughed in years.

"What's this?" Snoody said, his nose wheezing with alarm.

"Sorry, but there's a change today," Ruby said. "You two boys are on your own, I'm taking Moira to breakfast in the village, where somebody will serve her for once."

"I don't understand, Ruby."

"It's easy enough. When you want something, get it yourself. The baking that Moira's started, for instance. Take over, Snoody. Any questions, look it up in a cook book." Ruby stood. "Coming, Moira?"

"Aye, I'll come."

"Look here—!"

"Give him your apron, Moira," Ruby said.

"All right." Moira unswaddled herself and handed over her flour-stained apron.

Snoody held it at arm's length from himself, and said, "I say now, look here—!"

But Moira held up her hand and silenced him. She directed her words at Snoody, but it was Ruby they were really meant for:

167

"A man without eyes saw plums on a tree. He neither took plums nor left plums. How could this be?"

Snoody's hands dropped from his lapels. He started to say something to Moira, then thought better of it. Moira glared at him.

Ruby said, "That's the riddle Liam told Neil."

Snoody said, "When was that . . . ?"

Before she could answer, Moira took Ruby's hand and pulled her across the kitchen, out toward the hallway. "Come quick now," she said, "before himself starts up his growlin'." They left Snoody where he was, searching for the makings of a pot of tea.

Moira took down a coat from a rack in the hallway and slipped it on, along with a kerchief for her head. She offered Ruby one of her own sweaters. If there were two Rubys, the sweater would have fit perfectly. The telephone rang. Moira let it ring, bustling past it with Ruby for the door and into Ladbroke Street.

When they had rounded the corner and were walking downhill toward the village diamond, Moira asked, "Has your fine detective solved the riddle?"

"Not yet," Ruby said.

"Shall I be wicked and give you the answer?"

"Be wicked."

CHAPTER 24

THE DAY HAD GROWN PERFECT FOR SITTING JUST WHERE I WAS. APRIL sunlight dappled yellow through new leaves of old trees and all across the greenswards of the walled campus, a collection of ancient stone halls connected to one another by bricked archways. I was perched at the bottom of the steps to the Trinity College Library, considering for a moment whose feet had trod where I now sat. George Bernard Shaw, William Butler Yeats, James Joyce. And, of course, Brendan Behan. If Davy Mogaill ever surfaced, I would tell him of my sublime loitering.

Professors in caps and turtleneck sweaters beneath tweed coats passed. They carried battered pigskin briefcases and smoked pipes that wreathed their heads in gray smoke. They would glance at me, studiously uncurious about yet another reflective Irish-American tourist writing banal sentiments in his notebook. Students passed, too. In twos and threes, sometimes in boisterous clumps. I was jealous of them all, for their youth and for the good luck of their years learning at a place like this. I consoled myself by noticing that these students, like all the ones I envied at the better schools back home in the States, smelled of dirty laundry.

A gust of wind disturbed the pages of my notebook. I smoothed them out and read over the information I had obtained from the Trinity student yearbooks housed in the library:

> Aidan Hockaday . . . Village of Tullow, County Carlow . . . summa cum laude '35 . . . Gaelic literature, modern Irish literature . . . member, Dublin Men's Society of Letters . . .

Not much for a two-hour effort. What a two hours.

A person might think the librarian of Trinity College had never before met a nice respectable American cop and innocent bystander to a bit of O'Connell Street carnage dragged into his office by a security man to stand before him in chinos, sneakers and Yankees cap. I felt more than slightly reduced. And me being the son of a distinguished scholar and young litterateur, though of some decades past—*and* a minor celebrity in my own right, with my mug shot in there amongst news of bloody murder in that morning's *Irish Guardian* to prove it.

"Good Lord, Clooney, he might have a gun!" the librarian said. The librarian had a great booming voice that badly rattled the security man. His name was O'Dowd and he was just short of retirement age, round from a life abundant in rich food and drink, with a very small head full of red wisps of hair that roiled like ocean waves when he was agitated. He sat in a tall-back chair behind a desk cluttered with books and candy wrappers.

Poor Clooney was the nervous type and well past retirement age. O'Dowd's outburst made him take a lot of air down the wrong pipe, with a spasm of coughs the result.

I pounded Clooney's thin back, and told O'Dowd, "Gear down, I'm not carrying a piece."

"Gear a piece of what—?"

Clooney made some recovery noises and flapped his arms like a wounded bird. He stepped away from me, and said in his defense, "Mr. O'Dowd, sorry sir, but I bring him to you straightaway, the thought of gunplay never once occurin' to me."

"But he's from New York!" O'Dowd fumed at Clooney, hair waving madly. "Look at that baseball cap!" Clooney cringed. O'Dowd said to me, "Isn't that so? You're from New York?"

"That's home," I said. "Where the deer and the antelope take cover."

"He come into the reference department, bold as brass," Clooney continued. "Just wanderin' about the stacks on his own, nosin' here and nosin' there like some daff loon."

"You followed him, very good," O'Dowd said.

"Thank you, sir. As I'm stalkin' him—"

I interrupted. "I usually do carry a gun. Sometimes two or three guns."

Clooney looked like he very much wanted to faint. O'Dowd said to him, "Go on." Clooney looked toward me. I nodded, and he continued.

"As I was sayin', Mr. O'Dowd, I'm stalkin' this one when it suddenly crosses me mind why I'm suspicious . . . beyond the fact of his wanderin' in here, I mean. There's been Americans come in before, thinkin' we're only some bookshop here . . ."

O'Dowd glared at me when Clooney said *American.*

"But this one, sir, he's somehow familiar to me. Then what happens but I remember why! I quick run to fetch me copy of the *Guardian,* and here's what I find." Clooney pulled the newspaper out from the side pocket of his coat and laid it out on O'Dowd's desk, to Oliver Gunston's splashy story and my photograph with the sidebar.

"Aha!" said O'Dowd, raising his head from the newspaper.

"Aha what?" I said.

"Here you are for some nefarious purpose is what."

"Look at the picture, man—I'm in uniform, I'm a cop!"

O'Dowd looked at my Yankees cap instead. Then at the rest of my clothes. He needed convincing. So I went after my NYPD shield in the side pocket of my windbreaker, and said, "I really don't like badging my way into your library here, but—"

"He's going for the gun, Clooney!" O'Dowd boomed. "Do something!"

"Oh my God, oh my God—!"

Clooney made a yipping sound, like a dog being run over by a car, then slowly crumpled to the floor.

"Oh my Lord," O'Dowd said quietly, rubbing his hands. His wispy head looking like it was on fire. "Is he dead?"

I knelt beside Clooney's sprawled body and put a finger to his neck, which was pulsing along satisfactorily. I said, "Go get him a glass of cold water, O'Dowd."

O'Dowd hurried out of the room. I stroked the back of Clooney's clenched neck and shoulders until he came around.

"I need some air," he said, raising himself with his arms.

"Along with a chiropractor and a double Scotch," I suggested. I helped him to his feet. His hands and legs shook, and he headed for the door absentmindedly. "Take a beat now, old fellow. Let's settle you down a minute."

I put him in O'Dowd's chair and found him a piece of candy. He thanked me. Then O'Dowd came crashing back into his office, followed by another man Clooney's age or better, although far more robust, with bright blue eyes and a full beard that was snowy white and well tended.

"That's him, Chancellor—that's him!" O'Dowd said, aiming a finger at me in accusatory triumph. Then he saw Clooney behind his own desk, chewing his own candy. O'Dowd turned to me, and huffed, "Here now, what's this?"

"He's collecting himself after you made him fall, you jerk," I said. "So where's the glass of cold water I asked you to bring? And why don't you comb your hair?"

The chancellor turned, and said to O'Dowd, "What, you knocked old Clooney down?"

O'Dowd laughed lightly, and said, "Now it wasn't quite like that, sir."

With my hand resting on Clooney's trembling shoulder, I said to the chancellor, "O'Dowd thinks it's funny he's so rough on my friend Clooney, but I don't. Do you think it's funny, sir?"

"I'm sure I do not!" The chancellor turned to O'Dowd. "O'Dowd, explain yourself. There's no gunman here as you claim. All I see is this American chap, and old Clooney there in a terrible state."

O'Dowd sputtered, "But that's . . . that's not the point!"

"I'm not a gunman, sir," I said. "Perhaps your man O'Dowd needs a doctor and a long rest?"

"May I say something?" Clooney asked.

"Take it easy, pal," I said to him. Then I picked up the *Irish Guardian* with my picture in it and crossed the room to the two others. O'Dowd shrank from me. I extended my hand to the chancellor, and said, "There's a little confusion here, that's all, sir. Let's try to clear it up, shall we?"

"Peadar Cavanaugh," he said, shaking my hand.

"Chancellor Cavanaugh, my name is Neil Hockaday. I'm visiting here from New York, where I'm a police detective. Here's my identification." I handed Cavanaugh the newspaper, then took the gold shield out of my pocket and showed him that, too.

"Yesterday, as you see by the paper, I was in the vicinity of a murder in O'Connell Street. Then this morning, I came into the library to do a little family research when the intrepid Clooney here recognized me and got slightly excited."

I gave a little salute to Clooney, who returned the gesture. O'Dowd glared at him, and Clooney got out of his chair. I turned back to Cavanaugh, and said, "Clooney invites me in here to see the librarian, next thing I know O'Dowd is hollering about guns."

"I wasn't either *hollering*," O'Dowd protested.

"Yes, you was," Clooney said, taking his advantage now. He sat back down in O'Dowd's chair.

Cavanaugh fingered the edge of his beard, and asked, "Tell me, Mr. Hockaday, what is the nature of your family research?"

"My father was at school here. In the thirties, before the war."

"You're Aidan Hockaday's boy then."

"You knew him?"

Cavanaugh said to O'Dowd and Clooney, "Carry on, gentlemen." Then to me, "Come along, Mr. Hockaday, I'd like a word."

The chancellor turned to leave, and I followed. When I passed O'Dowd, I shaped my hand like a pistol and said, "Bang bang, you're dead." This time Clooney laughed, but not lightly.

A man's youth never leaves him, it only returns at inconvenient times. Walking now through the echoes of Trinity College corridors, in step with the authoritative stride of Chancellor Peadar Cavanaugh, this fugitive thought chased through my mind. I had heard it before. When, and from whom . . . ?

My youth . . . Father Tim.

Not a word passed between Cavanaugh and me. Each of us was enveloped by separate thoughts. Mine were of my youth.

I thought of despised knickers, a despised necktie and Holy Cross School. And the times some scowling nun would catch me at a boy's mischief. Inserting a red strip of cap-gun explosives into a pencil sharpener on her classroom wall, say. Sister would take me by the ear, roughly so I could hear the cartilage pop. Then swiftly and silently she would yank me down some long hallway, black and forbidding as the habit she wore. At the horrible end of this painful march was The Office, sanctum sanctorum of the merciless Father Naughton; him with his wooden paddle laced with tiny holes to insure my swats would come with the fullest aerodynamic sting.

But now, what had I to fear of the past?

Do you really want to know?

We did not go to Chancellor Cavanaugh's office for "a word," as I imagined we might. We passed it by on our quiet long walk through a tangle of corridors finally leading out the back of the library building to the street. Outside, we turned an ivied corner of the high college wall to enter a pub called the Ould Plaid Shawl.

"Halloo, Peadar," the publican said to Cavanaugh as we walked in, his meaty arm raised in greeting. He stared at me, politely curious, waiting for introductions. A half-dozen pensioners were standing at the bar having themselves a fine argument about some arcane point of history, an argument as well worn as their tweeds. They had no interest in us and did not look up. The tables and the booths were empty at this hour, save for a couple of barmaids smoking cigarettes and gossiping and resting up for the lunch crowd.

Cavanaugh did not trouble himself to explain my presence. He breezed us past the geezers, saying stiffly to the publican, "A fine morning to you, Sean. We'll be discussing business for a time if you please. Be a good man and bring us a pot of coffee, white— and whatever my friend will have?"

"Pint of the house ale," I told Sean as I moved past him, feeling somehow as if a nun was clawing at my earlobe.

Cavanaugh had us sit down at a square table in a far, dim corner of the place. There was a candle in a round glass on the table, Guinness coasters made of colored tin and an ashtray crowded with cigarette butts and wooden matches. Cavanaugh pulled a striped Rothman's packet and a Zippo from the side pocket of his black coat.

"Smoke?" he asked me, pushing the packet and lighter across

the table. I said thanks and helped myself. I also lit the candle between us, providing enough light to make a rough study of Peadar Cavanaugh.

The clothes he wore did not belong to the twentieth century. His suitcoat, which he left closed as he sat, was a Victorian four-button model, heavy and shapeless with age. There was a huge purple paisley silk billowing out from the breast pocket; on a younger, less substantial man this would have been effeminate. His necktie, only a shade less funereal than the suit, was largely hidden by his beard, which reached nearly halfway down his chest. Off-setting the dark solemnity of Cavanaugh's suit was his wide ruddy face, ringed by hair as thick and snowy as his beard; and his eyes, the color of cobalt in the smudgy light of the Ould Plaid Shawl.

Were my father's own eyes this shade of blue? And how many times had I caught myself staring at men like Cavanaugh, and projecting my father's black-and-white soldier photograph through time?

"You look so mighty like him," Cavanaugh said. Then I realized he had been studying me, too, and that I figured into his own projections. I took off my Yankees cap, knowing he wanted the fullest view of me. There was the sense of loss now in his voice. "If you were dressed proper, and for the period," he said, "it could be Aidan sitting right there where you are."

"You were close then, you and my father?"

"I was a friend, nobody could honestly call himself close to Aidan. Excepting your mother, of course."

"You knew her, too?"

"Oh my, yes. Mairead was a Fitzgerald, of Bloor Street. Everybody knew the Bloor Street Fitzgeralds."

"And the three of you came here often?"

"Here's where all the great debates of the time were had. Politics was what captivated lots of us then, your mother and dad included."

The publican Sean arrived with coffee and my pint. I reached into my pocket for some money to pay for the round, but remembered I still had to change over my dollars. No matter, Cavanaugh covered.

"Here now, it's me who invited you," he said, laying out a two-

175

pound note. Sean dropped a few heavy coins to the table and picked up the note, then returned to the bar when it was clear to him by Cavanaugh's look that our "business" was private.

I stubbed out the cigarette I was not much interested in smoking anyway, and asked stupidly, "What kind of politics?"

Laughter rolled up from Cavanaugh's solid belly, swelled his chest and then poured out heartily from every part of his bearded face. A Macy's Santa Claus would have been put to shame. He wiped mirthful tears from his eyes, and said, "You might well ask a fish, What kind of ocean? Politics overwhelmed us in the Great Depression, see. One brand poured over another like waves on a beach, and we were a pack of mouthy students spitting out hard and fast opinions as if they took us years to forge."

"Too bad you didn't have Hemingway's *Islands in the Stream* yet," I said.

"What of it?"

"There's a line in the novel spoken by the character Thomas Hudson, from his deathbed: *I was just beginning to learn there toward the end. No one thing is true—it's all true.*"

Cavanaugh lifted snowy eyebrows, then let them fall, and said, "Your father would have appreciated that. He was often saying how literature was something permanent, and politics only a pale and temporary thing."

"You couldn't have thought the Depression was temporary."

"Well now, I do remember the famous economist John Maynard Keynes saying back then how there was only one thing ever before that was quite like the Great Depression. That was the Dark Ages of Europe, which lasted four hundred years." Cavanaugh finished his cigarette, and lit another. "But Keynes being English, he forgot there was something else—the famine times, here in Ireland. How about another pint, lad?"

"Sure," I said. "I'm surprised you've got time on your hands for this."

Cavanaugh raised a hand up over his head and when he caught Sean's eye he made a circling motion to indicate another round. I noticed a handkerchief tucked up one of his Victorian sleeves. He looked back at me, and said, "We've a different idea about time than you Americans."

"I notice that. Two days I've been here, and this is the third

176

mention of the potato famine. That was in the 1840s. People talk about it like it was last month."

"It's the Irish nature. Our only defense against a long history of falling victim to forces we don't understand seems to be talking the bleak times to death."

"That can be a long death."

"Oh, but it's much crueler than that. All our Irish yap prevents history from dying, as it should."

Sean came by with the second round. When he left, I went stupid again, and said, "But history is how we learn—"

Cavanaugh said, as if to a dim student, "We learn from history that we do not learn from history."

"And so it's all just—nothing?"

"No, it's something all right. History is a pack of tricks we play upon the dead. Your father used to say that, it's from Voltaire."

"I believe he was fond of poetry, too."

"That he was."

"Did he write any verse of his own?"

"Not that I remember," Cavanaugh said. "What makes you ask?"

"There's something of his that I found recently, and it's brought me here to Ireland as much as anything else. It's a few lines written down, on the back of a photograph."

"I see." Cavanaugh said this with abrupt disinterest, turning back a cuff to check his wristwatch. Like an impatient American, I thought; like Father Tim, and Davy Mogaill.

"Wouldn't you like to hear the lines?" I asked.

Cavanaugh looked away from me. And I knew I had struck at the heart of something that maybe he wished would die. I recited:

" 'Drown all the dogs,' said the fierce young woman, 'They killed my goose and a cat. Drown, drown in the water butt, drown all the dogs,' said the fierce young woman."

He had no direct response. But then, almost nothing of our meeting in the Ould Plaid Shawl had been direct. Cavanaugh turned back to me. His eyes were runny.

"Go home, boy," he said.

"I want to know."

Looking now as if I had struck him, he said, "You're not like most of the Yanks who come to Ireland. And so I'm sorry for you.

You won't have the luxury of feeling your heart beat slower here, of knowing this as a great place to get yourself repaired. Do you follow me?"

"I don't think so . . ."

"What I'm saying is, I'm bloody sorry for you that you're so much like your dad, may God bless."

Remembering these things that Cavanaugh said before deciding that a chancellor's duties suddenly called, I entered them in my notebook. I then got up from the library steps and walked back inside, where I spent thirty minutes looking through card and computer indexes to Trinity student organizations.

Unsuccessful in finding what I needed, I decided to see O'Dowd again.

"What is it, Mr. Hockaday?" he asked sternly as I was shown into his office a second time, now by a plump and friendly secretary.

"I'm looking for information that's nowhere in your indexes," I said.

"What, exactly?"

"Is there a campus group called the Dublin Men's Society of Letters?"

"Never heard of it, I'm afraid."

"What about years ago—in the thirties, say."

"Before my time, I'm afraid."

"Yes—but in the student yearbook for 1934, the Dublin Men's Society of Letters was listed as one of my father's credits. So it existed, at least in the past."

"Then it should be cross-referenced in the indexes."

"But it's not."

O'Dowd shrugged, and said, "Well, what's past is passed."

I told him, "That's where you're dead wrong—I'm afraid."

CHAPTER 25

"BROADWAY AND TWO-HUNDRED-FORTIETH, THERE'S A DINER. COME alone."

"You're just the guy I been wanting to talk to. But give me a break, it's the freaking Bronx. I got to go up there, my whole night's about shot."

"Don't bother yourself about being a hero then. I'll be merely another perp on the loose. But you should know there's something I'm holding that a certain inspector downtown might like to get his hands on—a certain inspector who can always do right by an old lad pushing retirement such as yourself. But never you mind. I can see your time's much too valuable. I can always just go direct and save you the fuss and trouble."

"Leave us not be busting my chops. What's the deal?"

"Payback."

"Yeah? What's in it for me?"

"Glory, my friend."

"That I already got up the wazoo, on account of I live the fine pure life of a New York cop."

"Like I say, I can go direct."

"Don't let's be shirty. I'm only trying to figure what you mean by *payback*. Now, if it's money—"

"There's Brink's for that, Lieutenant—not you. Sending money by cop is like sending lettuce by rabbit."

"I could take that personal."

"That's right, you could."

"Don't mind my asking, but what in hell do you need me for? And don't give me no more of that glory crapola."

"I always trust a suspicious nature."

He put down the telephone and lay back in bed. There was plenty of time for a nap.

All his life, he had found it difficult to fall asleep. He would toss and turn for hours, even on days he had gone light on the black station house coffee; even when he had his wife beside him, especially then. But ever since Sunday night and Arty Finn's explosive departure from this life, sleep came to Davy Mogaill with the mere shutting of his eyes. As it did now. As he thought, So this now is freedom, my only freedom . . .

Davy Mogaill dreamed of a girl with hair the color of October leaves in the Galty mountains. He had a vision of the day he was married in County Kildare. Himself dressed stiffly in his father's cut-down formal suit, standing up on his young trembly legs near the priest, waiting for the woman he loved to join him at the altar set up in her family homestead; Brenda in her bride's lace and posies, led down the aisle not by her father, a locally famous martyr to the republican cause, but by her scowling brother.

And later, after all the blessings and the wedding jigs and the drinking, his new brother-in-law and the priest and a few of the fiercest boyos from the village surrounding him and slapping his back in boozy congratulations. With his bride looking on so proudly at the men in her life.

Then Brenda's brother at his ear, whispering the family curse as if it were a lullaby, "Understand, you married us all this day, Davy—until death us do part." And his pretty bride's green eyes dancing, and all the men nodding, and their lips frozen in wintry smiles . . .

*   *   *

He awoke with the old aching thought, For the love of Brenda, how many debts have I paid that I never owed?

Mogaill sat up, swinging his legs over the side of the bed. He looked out the window and saw the last foggy light of day give way to an evening of wet, purple haze that promised a coming rain. Lights yellowed the neighboring windows. Traffic noises dimmed. A street full of American families would soon be eating dinner, staring at television and ignoring one another.

Mogaill's stomach roared. He was suddenly hungry.

In the house where he was staying, dinner was served early and he had missed it, not that he cared. Company could be a burden to a man who had lived alone as long as Mogaill had. Downstairs now, the others would be organizing themselves according to dull habits. The usual small stakes poker game would be starting up, the usual blowhards would be carrying on about politics, the usual dyspeptics would be dozing and farting in old tattered chairs. He would miss all this, too, and just as well for the sake of his bouncing blood pressure.

He stood, stretching himself and feeling immensely fatigued despite nearly thirty minutes' heavy sleep, his second such nap of the day. He picked up the shoulder holster slung over a bedside chair and strapped it on, patting the smooth brown leather that encased his .38 police special. Then he slipped on his suitcoat.

Before he left the room, he paused to put back two quick shots of Scotch. Also he checked his pocket again. It was there, all right.

Now he was down the stairs, past the debaters and the poker players and the wind breakers. Then out the door and down the stoop.

Halfway to the corner, where he would eventually flag a taxi, he turned. Someone was calling his name.

"Captain Mogaill! A word—please!"

Mogaill waited, not patiently, until the man trotting up the street with his black coattails flying drew even to him. He waited a few seconds more for him to catch enough breath to speak.

"All right now, what is it?" Mogaill said, glancing at his wristwatch. "I've places to go, people to see."

"House meeting's tonight," said the man in black, holding his side and panting. "I was just coming up to talk to you about . . . the agenda, you know. But out you'd gone from your room."

181

Mogaill groaned.

"Now, I told the others . . . I said I'd have your word for them."

"On how long I'll be staying about?"

"That's it, yes."

"Weary of me already?"

"Oh, well . . . it's not me, you understand. But there's some are scared, that'd be more like it. The others, they've heard talk that—"

Mogaill interrupted, chopping the air with a hand. "Magpies! You should have dryers on your heads all of you."

The man in black wrung his hands and rolled his eyes upward, then said, "For the love of God, tell me what I can say. We've got to know something."

Davy Mogaill, the fugitive head of homicide in a homicidal town, said, "Say a little prayer for me. Very soon, I expect, I'll be leaving you all to your little worries in this sweet cesspool of a life."

Ellis slid into the booth, brushing his brown cop suit. It was splattered with rain that started falling in sheets exactly as he stepped from his car. He said, "So, I'm here and we got Noah's flood coming down. You satisfied?"

Mogaill looked up from his food and smiled at the lieutenant. He pushed aside a nearly empty plate. "I recommend the shepherd's pie," he said.

"Mick food gives me the bloat."

"Since when are you worrying about your figure, Ray? All this time I've known you, you always look the same—like a bagful of doorknobs."

"Ain't this just beauty-ful?" Ellis picked up a paper napkin and mopped rain off his bald head. "You get me up here to this nameless dump—for what? So you and me can rank each other out like we're back in high school with the pimples again?"

The girl who was Brenda's ghost stepped to the booth with her waitress pad. Ellis told her, "Just bring me a Heineken, doll." When she went away, he said to Mogaill, "I seen now why you hang around here. Jesus H. Christ on a stick, is that kid your dead wife's Doppelgänger or what?"

Mogaill, watching the girl walk away, let go of a long sigh with

"Brenda" in the middle of it. Then he turned back to Ellis, and asked, "You come here alone like I said, did you, Ray?"

"Naw, Davy. Everybody's curious about the New York police captain who ran away, so I invited along that putz Geraldo Rivera and a film crew. They're waiting on you outside."

"Inquiring minds want to know, hey?"

"This one's asking himself, Maybe it's the missing Captain Mogaill with the gummy footprints somewheres in a couple of my cases? Want to help me out on that?"

"See? I knew you were suspicious."

"You got no paddle, Davy, and the creek you're up is full of shit. So let's don't tire my ass too much."

"Suspicious, and ever eloquent. But disturbingly impatient."

"C'mon, it's time to give out, you hump. Otherwise I could forget we been such good friends over the years."

The waitress delivered Ellis's beer and poured it into a glass. Mogaill put a ten on the table and said she should keep the change. The girl bit her lip, and said, "Gee, mister, I don't know."

"Go ahead, you only live once," Mogaill told her.

"Such a morbid joke to be telling an innocent sweet-looking kid," Ellis said to Mogaill.

The sweet-looking kid's face flushed with blood and she left the booth in a hurry. But she was not too horrified to grab the ten.

"That mouth of yours," Mogaill said. "You might scare the lass into calling up the sex crimes squad."

"You don't square with me in about two seconds, I'll call myself."

Mogaill ignored the threat. He asked, "Remember what you said on the radio when Father Kelly shot himself?"

"What the—?"

"You said, and I quote, 'This sure ain't about who done it, that's as obvious as boils on a fat guy's neck . . . The padre, he decided to check out, big time . . . Leaving us the question, what the hell for?' That's the kind of probing suspicion I appreciate, Ray. It's altogether too rare in police work."

"There's a couple more choice suspicions I got where you figure into things these days."

"Such as?"

"Like in the first place, what's your nice house in Queens doing with a bomb in it anyhow? And how come this IRA character Arty Finn gets smoked when he drops by? Then how come you pull this disappearing act afterward? You're a very wanted person. On suspicion, you know?"

"Aye, so I see by the newspapers."

"Also I might as well ask you, what's the deal with the Dublin cop by the name of Dennis Farrelly we find naked and dead over in Hell's Kitchen? And did you hear about the nice splashy homicide your pal Hockaday's got himself involved in the first hour he hits the Olde Sod?"

"What makes you think I know about Farrelly?"

"A little birdie told me once you freaking harps stick together."

"Nae, not always, I'm afraid."

"Okay, that's it. My butt's had it."

Ellis shifted in his seat, cracking his back. Then he drained the beer from his glass in four loud swallows. At the same time, Mogaill slipped his left hand into a side pocket of his suitcoat; with his right, he reached inside to his holster.

"It's been real swell seeing you again, Davy, and thanks for the beer," Ellis said, wiping foam off bulldog lips with the back of a hand. "But since I am getting bubkes here, you give me no choice but going according to the book. Which means I'm taking you in on suspicion of murder, Captain. You want to come nice and easy?"

"I don't think so." Mogaill pulled out his .38 and jammed the barrel of it into his right ear. He steadied his arm by resting his elbow on the table. With a pained smile, he said, "If I really must be going, I'd prefer to take myself out."

"Sweet hanging Jesus!" Ellis said in a ragged whisper, hoping heads would not turn. "Let's talk some more, Davy. C'mon, I got all night . . ."

Mogaill cocked back the firing hammer and said nothing.

"C'mon, Davy, you want to put down the piece? What's your point here?"

Mogaill pulled an audiocassette tape from his side pocket and dropped it on the table.

"What's that?" Ellis asked.

"The point. And as you might say, it ain't bubkes."

Ellis picked up the cassette. Mogaill kept the cocked revolver against his head.

"It's what you want to get down to Neglio. Is that it, Davy?"

"Tell him it's from the priest's answering machine. Tell him he should transcribe it and get it off to Hockaday, word-for-word and real quick."

"All right, you got it. Now put down the piece, Davy. Jesus, you're making me tense."

Mogaill did not move.

"Think of that nice waitress who's the spitting image of your wife, Davy. You want to keep coming in here to look at her for old times' sake, don't you? Keep making me tense like you're doing and my pants will start smelling funny, and then Miss Sweet Thing's maybe going to eighty-six you out of this place."

"You remember my Brenda do you?"

"Sure, like it was yesterday."

"Beautiful, wasn't she?"

"Gorgeous. God, we was all so sorry when she went in that house fire over in Ireland."

"I think about her a lot."

"Naturally. Look, Captain, how about dropping the—?"

"Can't you see I'm bloody despondent, Lieutenant? Kindly don't be bothering me about this gun."

"Okay, okay."

"In fact, the last time I saw Hockaday I was thinking about her."

"Brenda?"

"The subject of women came up. I remember exactly what I said to Hock: 'The allurement women hold out for us men, my friend, is the allurement that Cape Hatteras holds out to sailors. Women are enormously dangerous, thus they are enormously fascinating.'"

"Nice, a regular poem almost. But it sure don't make women out to be all sugar and spice."

"You're really quite perceptive, Lieutenant."

CHAPTER 26

Now was a good time to drop in on Oliver Gunston.

I asked a lot of people in the streets a lot of questions, and gradually made my way across the River Liffey footbridge from Trinity College, up O'Connell Street and then through some crooked lanes over to the mall in Grafton Street, and finally to the offices of the *Irish Guardian* at the end of a side lane. I had reached a sleek modern building with a lot of glass and chrome that looked like a chopped-down version of one of those corporate silos on Sixth Avenue back in New York. No traveling New Yorker gets homesick when he beholds this kind of building somewhere else.

There was an old fellow with a gunbelt in the lobby, napping at a desk with a sign on it that read INFORMATION. He was dressed in a mothy gray uniform, a matching leather billed hat with a vaguely official shield on it and the kind of rubbery shoes a postal carrier wears. The hat was a size too big. Instead of poking his chest to wake him, I said, "I want to see Oliver Gunston."

He grunted. Puffy eyelids scrimmed with brittle veins flickered like a toad's, dry lips smacked, dentures clicked. He eyed my Yankees cap doubtfully, and said in a thick voice, "Come again?"

"Gunston. Where do I find him?"

"You'll not be seein' nobody 'til you doff that thing to me," he said, drawing himself to scrawny attention behind his desk. If he meant my cap, I decided it would stay where it was. He said, "Look, you, I'm the man in charge while we're down here."

He did not much care for my silence, which he correctly took to mean I was unimpressed. He snarled, "You're one of them Americans, I see."

"Yeah, one of them."

Who knows why anybody hires rent-a-cops to hang around lobbies bothering the public? When they are not stealing from the store themselves, they are giving access to all the wrong people. Ask the hotel managers in New York who are always surprised when smoothies wearing three-piece suits and packing acetylene blowtorches in their Gucci attachés somehow wind up helping themselves to the house safe. Ask the bad guys, and they will say the world was smarter and a lot more secure when watchful secretaries and alert elevator operators were keeping the lid on.

I took out my NYPD tin, flashed it, and said, "Ring up Oliver Gunston like a good fellow. Okay, Fosdick? The name's Hockaday, like it says here on a real badge."

"Fosdick ain't the name."

"But you're fearless just the same, isn't that right?"

"I do my job."

"That's good." I waved my tin again. "Now call."

Fosdick, of course, was impressed by a badge that could do me no real good in Dublin. He telephoned the news room and a few minutes later I was up three floors of the Irish Guardian Building. An amused young man in rolled-up shirtsleeves, old-fashioned horn-rimmed glasses and a green eyeshade straight out of *The Front Page* met me as I stepped off the elevator.

"Well, well—you'd surely be the American our troll down in the lobby was all on about," he said, extending his hand. I assumed he meant old Fosdick. "I'm Gunston."

I shook his hand, and said, "Hockaday. Nice eyeshade."

"Thank you. Nice Yankees cap."

I liked the man immediately, and I am almost always right when I make a quick judgment like that. He was practically a full generation younger than me, and of course he lived here in Dublin, but somehow I felt that Oliver Gunston and I were two of a kind; that we had shared experiences, or outlooks. Or maybe it was only that I once wanted to be a journalist myself . . . or something.

Gunston said, "Slattery, your countryman—he's been telling me so many charming things about you."

"So I read," I said.

"Aye. Well, come with me."

Gunston led the way through a maze of carpeted corridors and shoulder-high cubicles where men and women who looked more like stockbrokers than newspaper reporters were hunched over glowing video display terminals. Nobody was smoking. Nobody was drinking. Nobody was hollering for a copy boy; in fact, in the whole place, there were only the sounds of Herb Alpert and the Tijuana Brass on Muzak and the soft clacking of computerized keyboards. Like modern public buildings and their lobbies, news rooms have taken a serious turn for the worse.

But the cubicle of Oliver Gunston was a better world, a comfortable one. It contained the standard-issue computer, but the contraption was shoved into a corner on a table by itself and partly shrouded by a tasseled throw. Gunston did his real work on a Royal manual standard typewriter, with crumpled paper overflowing a wastebasket to prove it. His desk was a battered rolltop model with an ashtray containing a cigar butt and a bottom drawer containing a fifth of Irish Mist and some shot glasses.

He sat down at his desk in a carved mahogany chair and poured out two hospitable drinks. I took my place in an overstuffed, time-stained lounger with a lace doily on the back.

"That was my father's chair, which I rescued from the clutches of the rag and bone man," Gunston explained, handing me a whiskey. "My wife won't have it in the house, and so here it reposes."

"It's a good one," I said. I was suddenly homesick for the easy chair in my own parlor in Hell's Kitchen, a green silk brocade Salvation Army number with fringes on the bottom. The salesman told me it once belonged to a downtown whorehouse.

"My father used to read his books and newspapers in that chair every evening when he came home from the shop," Gunston explained. "He worked the kind of job where there was no greater luxury than to finally sit down at the end of a day."

"I know what he means."

"*Meant*," Gunston said. "He died when I was a kid."

"We've got something in common."

"Oh?"

"We both have hollow places," I said.

"So your father's dead." This was no question, the way he put it. It was more a statement of recognition. Gunston knew about the hollow place just like me. We could have been brothers.

"My father was a soldier," I said, as usual. "He went to the States, went off to the war and never came back. I never knew him." This was not enough for Gunston. To him I owed a larger answer. But what? I drank down half the whiskey, and added, "He and my mother lived in Dublin before I was born. My mother's gone now, too."

"And it's why you're here, to learn about them?"

"I sure as hell didn't come all this way to see Francie Boylan get whacked in O'Connell Street. For that kind of thing, I could have stayed home in New York."

"So I hear." Gunston laughed and put back his drink. I did the same. He poured us two more, then put the bottle back in the drawer. "And what have you found out that you never knew before?" he asked.

"Am I being interviewed?"

"I always decide that sort of thing later."

"So you're a thinking journalist?"

"That's not extraordinary," Gunston said, laughing again. "Unusual, but not extraordinary. The truth is, I'm far more keen on stories than I am on newspapers. Can you understand that?"

"Maybe if I was a newspaper reporter instead of a detective."

"Aye, you'd likely see the meaning then. Perhaps like G. K. Chesterton saw it."

"The English novelist who wrote about Father Brown, the priest-detective?"

"Quite right. And did you also know he was once a newspaperman?"

"No."

"He despised the trade something fierce. When he'd had his fill of it, he burned his bridges by writing, 'Journalism consists largely in saying *Lord Jones died* to people who never knew Lord Jones was alive.' You see my meaning now?"

"Yes, I think so. And if you want to help me, Gunston, I think you'll find I'm only a very small part of a story that's going to be much too big for your newspaper."

"Well then, I believe I've been waiting a very long time for you to drop by, Detective Hockaday." Gunston finished off his second drink and rubbed his hands. "Just how may I be of help?"

"You were asking what I'd learned about my parents. We could start there. My father's name was Aidan Hockaday and he was common as tap water, from County Carlow. My mother was well born, here in Dublin—Mairead Fitzgerald, of the—"

Gunston cut in. "Of the Bloor Street Fitzgeralds?"

"That's right."

"What did your father do when he was here in Dublin?"

"He was a student. He graduated summa cum laude from Trinity College, back in thirty-five. And he was a member of something called the Dublin Men's Society of Letters."

"Good, that's something to go on," Gunston said. He wheeled his chair from his desk to the computer. "I'm going to access the morgue," he said, turning toward me after switching on the contraption. "By which I mean the library here at the *Guardian.*"

I told him I knew from morgues, and morgues.

Gunston typed out my father's name on his keyboard and AIDAN HOCKADAY went up in instant orange letters on the gray computer screen. Then the screen responded by offering a choice of command requests. Gunston selected NAME SEARCH. Seconds later, the computer informed us there were exactly two *Guardian* clips on file containing my father's name.

"It's that easy . . . ?"

Oliver Gunston, a man with a hollow place, understood the question. He said, "It is, once you decide your old da's worth knowing. How about it?"

"Let's have it."

"Ready or not, here she goes," Gunston said, accessing ITEM #1. When my parents' engagement announcement flashed on the screen, an inch or so of very small type, Gunston said, "Here we've got the publishing of the banns. Not particularly illuminating, but do you fancy reading it?"

"Go ahead to number two," I said.

When ITEM #2 was punched up, Gunston said, "Now here then,

what's this fine bit of intrigue?" I got up from my chair and read the screen, over Gunston's shoulder:

GAVAN FITZGERALD FOUND HANGED, ONE-TIME CHIEF OF DUBLIN GARDA
—Investigators Suspect 'Peep o'Day Boys'—

by Patsy Converse
[*14 October 1937*]

Lord Gavan Fitzgerald, the prominent barrister and chief of the Dublin Garda during the last three years of the republic's British rule, is the apparent victim of a bold political assassination. His disemboweled body was discovered early yesterday morning, hanged by the heels from a scrub tree in the rubbish alley that runs back of his home in fashionable Bloor Street.

"A real coup de grâce it was," said Detective Kerry Devlin, attached to the Lucan station house. "The killers cut out his heart in his bed, dragged out the body and hanged it, and draped the Union Jack around the body, along with an evil sign, lettered in what we believe to be Lord Fitzgerald's own blood."

The sign read, "We wish to grow peaceful crops, but we must dig our furrows with the sword."

Detective Devlin said further, "It's the work of the Peep o'Day Boys, I'd wager. It's all according to their violent style. We get the anonymous telephone call at dawn telling us about a dead man in a Bloor Street alley, and we find what we find."

The barrister Fitzgerald, a loyalist to the Parliament at Westminster throughout the . . .

"*Lord* Fitzgerald? That's my grandfather. My God, he was lynched . . . !"

191

"And the bloody Union Jack, it was the winding-sheet for his corpse," Gunston said, rubbing his hands again. "Fascinating stuff."

I backed away from the computer screen. Actually, I nearly staggered away. I had to stop reading to catch my breath, which was suddenly hard in coming. Also I had to clear a slight taste of vomit from my throat, which I accomplished by drinking up the rest of my whiskey.

"You never knew this?" Gunston asked.

"Where I was raised, you didn't ask too many questions about where anybody came from, including yourself."

"And here you wind up in a profession where it's questions that sauce your goose?"

"What can I tell you? Irony's like gravity, it's a law." I moved back to the computer, and scanned several more paragraphs. This was mostly background information on Gavan Fitzgerald, and the politics of his time. I could study it later. I asked Gunston, "Can you run me a printout?"

"Aye, and anything else you'll need, in return for my having the bigger story exclusive. This *is* big, isn't it?"

I nodded agreement, and said again, "It's deep . . . deeper than I ever imagined."

I read more, searching for my father's name. There it was, in the final paragraph:

The Lord's good wife, Lady Beatrice, was taken by neighbors to the Sisters of Mercy Hospital, where she is under treatment for nervous shock. Their daughter, Mairead, could not be located, but was known to have sailed for New York, also yesterday morning, from the port of Dún Laoghaire. Accompanying Miss Fitzgerald was her fiancé, Aidan Hockaday.

"Now punch up the other thing," I said, weakly. I felt like walking in the open air, for miles.

"Right." Gunston typed on his keyboard as he said the words, "Dublin Men's Society of Letters."

There was a single item, in a column of social notes, dated May 22, 1936:

LITERARY SOCIETY FÊTES W. B. YEATS

The Trinity College organisation known as the Dublin Men's Society of Letters is pleased to announce an evening fête this Sunday fortnight, open to friends and admirers of William Butler Yeats, the poet and political activist. Mr. Yeats will read from especially selected works. The event is to be held at the Ould Plaid Shawl public house.

Tickets and further information may be sought by contacting the Irish Literature Department of the college, care of Professor Peadar Cavanaugh.

Later, maybe when I was no longer feeling like my head was trapped inside a bell, I would do the notebook work. Just now, I needed that walk. And so I left Gunston a list of references to run through his computer and headed back out to Grafton Street. Fosdick was snoring softly as I passed him in the lobby.

I was glad for the crowd and the noise of the mall. And thankful for the task of locating a bank where I could convert my American dollars to Irish pounds. I craved prosaic distractions the way a thirsty man on a desert craves a cold beer. I needed a break from unending revelations, and from knowing that only more would come before I returned home.

Two days into this Irish sentimental journey, and what had I learned? That one man's politics is another man's murder; dear old Father Tim's idea of a lucky marker turns out to be a Fascist souvenir; my Uncle Liam is stinking rich, bound to a wheelchair and talking in riddles; my mother's side of the family were full-blown aristocrats, with wealth and pedigree; Grandma Finola had a long-standing fling with a priest called Father Cor, which Grandpa Myles put to scandalous rest with murder and suicide; and the Lord High Chief of the Dublin Garda, Gavan Fitzgerald, met his Maker the same as Mussolini, both Fascists hanged.

What next?

I shuddered at the thought, then turned into the first bank I saw. I changed over three hundred dollars' worth of my traveler's checks and decided I should probably drop by to see Chief Eamonn Keegan again, this time under my own steam. Keegan seemed the patrician type. Maybe he would be more willing to chat with me about the murder of Francie Boylan if I told him I was descended from old Lord Fitz.

What would Inspector Neglio say to this bloodline? And Davy Mogaill, wherever he was?

I left the mall and made my way back to O'Connell Street, then over toward the Post Office and up to the Garda headquarters. I paid no particular attention to a half-dozen or so chattering school-girls walking my way, nor to the red-faced nun accompanying them who nodded and said, with the faint whiff of whiskey on her breath, "Top o'day."

CHAPTER 27

"BEFORE WE GO BACK, I SHOULD WRITE IT ALL DOWN. WAIT . . ." RUBY
went through her pockets, searching for a pen without success. "I
should have run upstairs after my purse. I don't even have
money."

"There's a bit in me pocket," Moira said. "Money, that is. Sorry
I don't have nothin' to write with, though."

"I'll owe you." Ruby put her hand in the air. A waiter glided
over and Ruby negotiated the loan of a blunt pencil. With this
and a clean paper napkin, she said, "Okay, Moira, first let's have
the riddle again."

"A man without eyes saw plums on a tree. He neither took
plums nor left plums. How could this be?"

Ruby wrote slowly. Moira said, "Mind you get the words down
exactly as I'm saying them."

"Okay," Ruby said, finishing. "And the answer?"

"Now it's all got to do with plurals, don't you see? The man
had one eye, so he's without *eyes*. There were two plums hanging
on the tree and he took one of them, therefore neither taking nor
leaving *plums*."

"I love it!"

195

"Do you think your shamus might ever get it?"

"It's always possible. I like to tell him he's smarter than he looks."

The cook who had enjoyed every bite of a restaurant breakfast tipped back her head and laughed. Ruby could see now, for the first time and in spite of the years and the weight and the net still matting down her hair, that Moira Catherine Bernadette Booley was desired by men once upon a time. *In country days when me legs was thin as the rushy grass.*

"I'll miss you somethin' horrible when you're off to America again," Moira said. "If only I'd known you long ago, Ruby. Oh, my life . . . !" Moira's brown eyes filled with unembarrassed tears.

"Say it," Ruby told her.

"There'd be a different woman sittin' here before you," Moira said. "That's what I'm meanin'. Never did I dare to be lookin' to someplace I'd not seen, someplace where lights are burnin' all night. Never did I figure I owned the right to a sweet man feelin' obliged to say kind words to me every day. You done that with yourself, Ruby, haven't you? But we were backward in my day, most of us, and we daren't dream such things. Oh, but I wished I'd been a fine rebel girl like you."

"I don't know what to say . . ."

"This Hockaday, he says kind words to you, and knows you won't have it the other way? Am I right?"

"Yes."

"Gawd bless you, Ruby. Your man's like his daddo before him."

"Neil's father? You knew Aidan Hockaday?"

"Aye, and the girl who chose him, too."

Slowly, Ruby began to sense the hidden, mournful texture behind all that Moira had told her; that when Moira talked of certain things, she had, like Hock himself, *a way of turning words into walls.* Ruby asked, "Are you saying you knew Mairead, Neil's mother?"

"A beauty she was. A beauty and a rebel, and the reason I dreamed up the poser about the one-eyed man."

CHAPTER 28

"WOULD YOU BELIEVE A GUY LIKE ME'S GOT A LITERARY SIDE JUST LIKE yourself, Captain?"

Mogaill, experienced as he was in asking sly cop questions, sensed the trap in this. He said nothing. He tightened the grip on the .38 jammed against his head.

"How about now I recite a little something for you?" Ellis suggested. "Something real poetical I come across the other day while I'm on a call about this paddy cop down a Hell's Kitchen air shaft, dead with the dawn."

"It's good you can find something uplifting out of Constable Farrelly's untimely death," Mogaill said.

"Uplifting I don't know. Inspector Neglio, he don't agree neither. Right away, he sees there's some kind of bad politics in back of Farrelly's poem. Real stinking bad politics, Davy. The kind the whole world went and had a war about once."

"Say what you want to say and be done with it."

"Okay. I come across a brass medallion in Farrelly's gear. One side's got this dago Fascist shit branded on it, according to Neglio, and the other side's got this here verse: 'When nations are empty up there at the top ... When order has weakened or faction is strong . . . Time for us all to pick out a good tune . . . Take to the roads and go marching along.' ''

"There's some who'd believe a real patriot wrote that," Mogaill said. "What about you, Ray? Are you a patriot?"

Ellis thought for a moment, then said, "If my country needs me, I'll answer the call. But they better not call me collect."

"We're not so different, you and me."

"Regular allies, that's us. So what do you need to make like a paranoid here with the gun?"

"I see how it's playing against me. You have things all connected I'd bet. The DA could make an indictment out of this as easy as he'd put salami and cheese to bread and call it a sandwich, then it's off with me to a prison full of violent types I sent up myself over the years. I'm not anxious to visit the like. So I am about to blow my brains out, but it doesn't mean I'm crazy."

"That sort of makes sense, Davy. I'll level with you: we got this Irish goon Arty Finn connected to Constable Farrelly on account of I sweat the super and find out Farrelly's crib is being paid the first of every month by none other than Finn. So naturally we see how there's something that don't smell too good here, especially this bad poem I come across on the medallion. Where you come in, Davy . . . well, let's say it ain't very smart politics that you took a powder right after your house goes up with a bomb and Finn goes up with it. Also there's little things that tell me a bumper took out Farrelly, the kind of good bumper nobody ever catches in this town, and I got to wonder if you come in here, too."

"Level with me some more. How are you carrying these two?"

"You mean in the cop court of appeals?"

"Aye."

"The jury's still out, Davy. We're debating the righteous factors."

"Such as?"

"Such as if it's a public service that Finn and Farrelly got whacked, such as your getting in touch like you finally done," Ellis said. He picked up the cassette tape from Father Kelly's telephone answering machine, bouncing it in his thick hand, like he was flipping a coin. "Then there's this here you give me to run down to Neglio. Maybe it's going to save your bacon?"

"When you check the politics."

"So what're we going to find?"

"The voice of a true patriot. But not our kind."

"What kind?"

"The kind that holds a knife at the throat of the world."

Ellis put down the tape, and said, "Give me the gun now, Davy."

CHAPTER 29

REFLECTING ON IT, OF COURSE, I MUST HAVE LOOKED AS MUCH THE MARK as Swedish tourists clomping around New York in sandals and socks. Or the Japanese with their cameras. Or the Germans with wallets bulging in their back pockets.

Me in my sneakers and brilliant white teeth and my Yankees cap. Oh, boy, was I asking for it.

The old nun said, "Top o'day."

I turned to her, touching my cap, and said, "Hi." Nobody but an American says *Hi*.

The girls were all in their uniforms. White blouses, pleated wool skirts of tartan plaid, knee socks, and green cardigan sweaters. A perfectly common sight that time of day in any Dublin street. Nothing to excite anybody but a pederast.

Yet there was something off about it all. When they came close, flocking around me, I saw hardness in these girls' faces. They were familiar to me, faces I see in New York every day and recognize far more quickly; faces older than their time, toughened from living on unearned money.

What happened next occurred well within the pathetically short amount of time it takes the average television commercial to get the average viewer lathered up about something useless or fattening. All I knew for fifteen or twenty seconds was that a gang of girls, eight to ten of them, had me surrounded on a corner of O'Connell Street and they were mumbling something that had me confused and disoriented.

It then struck me that all the green cardigans had slipped down over their hands. Which only after a few more seconds did I realize were roaming unseen all over places where I had pockets. But never once did I feel a thing.

Then out of the corner of an eye, I saw three terrible and deflating things happen in a blur. One freckle-faced girl passed something to the nun, now in back of me, something that looked a lot like my wallet newly stocked with three hundred dollars' worth of Irish pound notes. Another girl, standing outside those surrounding me, reached toward the nun and then sprinted up a side street and out of sight. And finally, I saw my wallet fall to the paving stone like it was a potato peel.

I had now caught on to the big picture, but still my words were those of the tourist mark. I shouted, "Hey—wait a minute!" And much to my surprise, that is exactly what the nun and all the little schoolgirls did, only the nun did not look so holy anymore, nor the girls so little.

"What's your trouble, my son?" the nun asked sweetly.

"You've got the trouble, Sister!" I shouted boldly. My face was now far redder than the nun's had ever been. People on the street passed me by, some oblivious, some smirking. And I could do nothing more than shout at the nun. "You and your little band of thieves—you better all stay right here if you know what's good for you!"

"If it comforts you, son, I'll stay," she said. She now addressed the girls, those remaining after the runner who had made off with my cash. "Girls, we'll be stopping in our own pursuits now to help this poor aggrieved traveler as best we can. We must be good Samaritans in life, don't forget."

The girls mumbled in sweet agreement and put their sweaters back on. I grabbed the sleeve of a man in a suit, and said, "This pack of thieves just stole my wallet!"

He struggled, pulling himself free, and screamed, "You bloody

American fool!'' Then he hurried up the street, stopping at what looked to be a police call box.

"Why, my son, isn't that your wallet right there on the ground?'' the nun said, laying a hand on my clenched arm.

I stooped to retrieve my wallet. While I was down, I heard laughter. When I stood again, there were the thieves' faces surrounding me again, now full of overstated concern. Behind them was an amused crowd of Dublin idlers with nothing better to do than snicker at a tourist's dilemma.

I opened the wallet. Thankfully, my passport was still there. Two weary cops ambled up to the scene of this weary old crime. Although now, I realized, there was no sign of anything amiss. There was only me with my red face and my wallet in hand, and my good Samaritans.

"That's the madman!'' said a man in a suit coming up behind the two cops. "He attacked me—called me a thief!''

"Oh, it wasn't as bad as all that,'' said the nun in my defense. "The American gentleman here seems to have lost something. Do you suppose you could help him, Constables?''

The cops rolled their eyes. One of them took aside the guy in the suit and told him he should run along, and that the American madman would be restrained. The other cop said to the nun, "Piss off, old darlin.' '' The idlers had a good round of laughs.

Then the cop asked me, "All right now, what's your name, where are you from, and what's the story?''

"Neil Hockaday, New York, and this so-called *nun* is running a school of pickpockets.''

"On the last, I am pained to confirm that you're correct,'' the cop said. "Sorry to say, you been robbed by the tinkers, my friend. Our Irish gypsies. Amazing and cleverly disguised they are. And quite talented, too. They'll steal your shoes while you're dancing.''

"Tosh with your slander!'' the nun protested.

"What's your hotel, mister?'' the cop asked me.

"I'm staying with my uncle,'' I said, hoping that a good address might benefit me. "Liam Hockaday, of Ladbroke Street in Dún Laoghaire.''

"I know that place,'' the cop said, duly impressed. Then he had to criticize my clothes. "You come from Ladbroke Street into the city dressed like you are, like a bloody damn larrikin?"

The nun stepped up close to me, squinting up her eyes and breathing her whiskey fumes. With no further pretense to sisterhood, she asked, "Would you be the same Hockaday what was in the newspaper this mornin', the one connected with the murder in O'Connell Street?"

Murmurs swept through the crowd. The two cops' necks went red. This was not going at all the way I intended; try as I might, I could do nothing to get even myself under control.

I decided to ignore the fake nun, and complained instead to the cop, "They stole three hundred dollars of mine!" The way I sounded to myself, I should have been wearing Budweiser shorts and an I-love-NY button back in Times Square and squawking about being clipped by a three-card monte dealer.

The cop took a leather-bound notepad from his belt and a pen from his coat. He said, "Murder? What's that name of yours again?"

"Neil Hockaday," I said.

"Reilly!" he called to his partner. "We'd best take this one in."

"Come on now, men," I said, as Reilly clamped his hand around my elbow, "I'm a police officer myself. Look, I'll show you—"

Somebody in the crowd piped up with, "Run! The American might have a gun!" Nobody moved.

"I was only going for my badge," I said, slowly pulling out the shield from my pants pocket, then showing it to Reilly and the other cop. They each inspected it carefully. "If that's not enough for you, it so happens that my grandfather was once chief of the Dublin Garda."

"Don't know of anybody called Hockaday what was chief," Reilly said.

"His name was Lord Gavan Fitzgerald," I said.

The cops looked at each other, scowling. The crowd murmured. The nun closed in on me again. She said, "Let's hear your mother's name."

"Mairead," I said.

Somehow the old nun's face softened into a mass of lacy wrinkles. She started to say something, but Reilly the cop shoved her aside again.

"Gavan Fitzgerald was a Brit," Reilly said with a spit, as if relieving himself of a mouthful of dishwater.

Somebody in the crowd shouted, "Bugger the Brits!"

The other cop cuffed me, my wrist to his, and said, "You're comin' with us, Fitzgerald."

"It's *Hockaday*!"

The nun trailed along beside me as I was pulled through the jeering crowd. She said, "Listen good and close to me, boy. They call me Sister Sullivan, and I knew your mother well. My camp's up the North Road, out from the city. Ask any tinker you see along the way, they'll know. Only be sure to tell them you're Mairead Fitzgerald's boy. Do you understand me?"

I nodded yes, confused.

The nun said, "You'll be needin' us. These bloody constables, they—"

Reilly shoved her away. "Piss off, we told you!"

Back to the airless room with the bad couch and chairs, the table full of newspapers and ashtrays and thin cold tea. And the two-way mirror. When I wanted to use the loo, a cop had to go with me. I might as well have been put in a cell.

I had been inked and photographed, with and without my cap, for unstated reasons. I was not allowed a telephone call, although the desk sergeant rang up the American Embassy on my behalf. For three hours, I waited, alone. Then finally, company came. He was fat and wheezy with a huge gray moustache full of crumbs. I did not bother to stand up.

"Mr. Hockaday, I presume?" he asked, waddling in with a briefcase that looked like it might have been through the invasion of Normandy in '44. "I'm Brady."

"Are you from the embassy?" I asked.

"Well, your embassy sent me. I'll be your counsel if you like."

"You're a lawyer?"

"Solicitor. Here in Ireland, we're solicitors and barristers."

"Whatever. Can you get me the hell out of here?"

"That depends. What, exactly, did you do to land you here?"

I opened the tea-splattered *Irish Guardian* to the story of Francie

Boylan's murder and my photograph and showed this to Brady. He took the newspaper and studied the stories, shaking his head. I said, "That's what happened to me yesterday. Today, the tinkers robbed me. And now these cops of yours somehow think it's their duty to hold me here, only I don't know why."

"So, you were dipped, were you?" Brady laughed dryly and sat down, flopping his briefcase on the table and the paper on top of it. "How much are you out?"

"Three hundred, American."

"That wasn't all you had, was it?"

"I've got a couple more traveler's checks."

"Thank God."

"Why thank Him?"

"Because money makes God's green earth go 'round, Mr. Hockaday. We all need money, don't we? You need it, I need it . . . You do understand?"

"I understand about chasing ambulances."

"As you Americans say, time is money. Let's not be wasting time."

"Funny, but I was talking with somebody just this morning who told me you Irish have a different idea about time. Or course, it turns out he's a liar."

"I haven't the slightest—"

"I'm sure you don't, so skip it. But tell me, Brady, what do you mean the embassy sent you?"

"The American Embassy is a busy place. Everything's a matter of priority. You can't expect the embassy to dispatch a staff member every time some hapless American is dipped."

"Which is where some chaser like you comes in."

"At your service, Mr. Hockaday."

"That's *Detective* Hockaday. I'm an officer of the New York City Police Department. Like it says right in the *Guardian*."

"Very good . . . Would you happen to have any of those extra traveler's checks actually with you at this time?"

"Is law school difficult, Brady?"

"Exceedingly."

"Then how come there are so many lawyers?"

"Really, Detective Hockaday! Time is money."

"Now that we've got to know each other like this, I think it's

205

time we saw the boss. Be a good solicitor and earn your keep. Go tell the boys behind the mirror I want to see Keegan, and not about some cockamamie tinkers. I want to talk politics, tell them. Think you can handle that?"

Half an hour later and I was out of the airless room, with Brady and a constable on either side of me. We walked down a corridor toward a stairway that I recalled from the day before led up to Eamonn Keegan's office. And though I must have been more exhausted at some other time in my life, I could not remember when.

I would have remained in that room an extra half-hour if I knew I could sleep without dreaming. As it was, I dreamt without sleeping; walking along through that corridor, thinking of myself as the condemned man in one of those grainy prison movies where everything is all sweat and shadows on brick . . .

"So here we go down the dance hall, Louie," the turnkey says to me as I am doing my shuffle-shuffle in paper shoes, and my head is shaved down to the scalp in the back so they can attach the electrodes.

"It's been real swell knowin' you and all the lousy screws," I bravely grunt, cocky to the end. "See you in hell."

"Yeah, see you."

The warden, who is marching ahead of us along with a priest talking Latin, turns now and says with an alligator grin, "Next stop—Old Sparky."

Steel cups rake the iron bars of death row, and this is the final music.

And then the guy at the switch turns out to be none other than Tommy Neglio, who before he throws the juice says to me, again, "You've got an imagination that's very full and active, and just this side of being lunatic. It's what I always look for in a detective . . ."

Which is when Brady informed me, "Lucky enough, it seems Chief Keegan has a message for you. Something from your superior in New York, according to his aide."

"Yeah, that's lucky, all right," I said, imagining how Neglio might not think me diligent about keeping in touch like he had asked.

My mind ran riot about the possible message. Had Davy Mogaill turned up? What troubles did he have?

But I had troubles of my own just then.

I asked Brady, for what it was worth, "What's the percentage of my getting the hell out of here?"

"Not to worry. We'll soon have this all sorted out, and Chief Keegan will see you're no outlaw."

"Some people would point out that I'm a cop."

"Best you let me do the talking, Detective Hockaday."

Not far into the next several minutes of scattered chaos, it was clear that nobody would ever again be talking to Eamonn Keegan.

CHAPTER 30

THAT NIGHT AROUND SEVEN O'CLOCK, I WAS BACK IN MY UNCLE'S SPLEN-
did house in Ladbroke Street considering the dark wisdom exer-
cised by most Irishmen in leaving their ancestral land as soon as
possible. If I was not reasonably certain that by now my name
was wait-listed at every Irish port of departure, I would be out
getting wised up myself.

But there I was in the red room in the pillowed couch by the
fireplace, snugged in a terrycloth robe after a long hot bath,
warmed by a double Scotch, a low blaze of sweet-smelling fruit-
wood branches and an armful of Ruby in black silk. If only
this was all in the peace and quiet of New York City where
I belonged.

"Afraid once you start talking you'll never be able to stop?"
Ruby asked.

"Something like that," I said.

"It's got to happen. Or else you, Hock, are going to blow like
Mount St. Helen. You went out of here this morning to Dublin,
then you dragged yourself back an hour ago looking like a train
wreck . . ."

"And I don't feel much better than that now," I said.

"Okay, so take a deep breath," Ruby said. "And then tell me about the time in between."

"Did you ever have a dream where you float around in the air, up over everything that's happening?"

"We all have that one."

"That's what today was, only my eyes were wide open. I was there, but I kept floating higher and higher until I didn't believe anything anymore. When I see the newspapers in the morning, then I'll know it happened."

"What's *it* . . . ?"

That I could not tell Ruby without first a build-up to the main event.

So I filled her in about Trinity College and the class of '35 student yearbook, my run-in with Clooney and O'Dowd and going to the Ould Plaid Shawl with Peadar Cavanaugh, and Cavanaugh's stiff advice to go home. Then about Oliver Gunston and his computer, and the *Guardian* item from October '37 that introduced me to the lynching of my grandfather, Lord Gavan Fitzgerald, as well as the item from May '36 about the Dublin Men's Society of Letters that proved Cavanaugh a liar. Then about me, a street-weary cop from New York getting himself robbed by a gang of dippers disguised as Dublin schoolgirls. And about "Sister Sullivan" and the invitation to her tinkers' camp. And about me getting hauled off to the Dublin Garda again . . .

"Stop it, you're making me dizzy," Ruby said. I paused, and she pressed both hands to her head. "You had a grandfather who was a cop—who was *lynched*? You were mugged by little girls—then *arrested*? They called the *embassy*—?"

"You should have seen the beauty they sent over to help me," I said. "This chaser by the name of Brady. He looks like W. C. Fields in pinstripes."

"So, you're out on bail—or what? I don't understand."

"Neither do I. Brady went off leaving me twisting in the wind for a half hour, then he comes back and says we've got clearance to go see Chief Keegan, who it so happens has a message for me. From Neglio, I suppose. You remember Keegan . . ."

"What's to forget?" Ruby said. "Big guy in a big office, and he smelled of bay rhum and lanolin."

"Also those good Cuban cigars."

"I liked the way he smelled, but the rest of him bothered me. I didn't much care for the way he dropped the news about Father Tim, or that insinuating way he grilled you about your own dad ..."

"He won't be bothering us anymore."

"How's that?"

That I was now ready to relate.

Just before all hell broke loose in the headquarters of the Dublin Garda, there was I with Brady and the constable helplessly imagining myself as some character in a movie. I was also thinking about the murk of Irish politics at home and abroad that had conspired to bring me to this point. And remembering how Father Tim used to get laughs by claiming politics and the movies were one in the same.

"Don't worry," Brady said again. He was holding my arm, and maybe my tension was contagious because he felt moved to add, "It's always darkest before the dawn."

This bromide did not help. I hate it when people say that because I know very well how light versus dark can really be. Many times I have gathered with cops the night before some huge raid that will ruin the criminal life of some poor unsuspecting perp. Gatherings like this are usually held at one of a dozen Italian places in the Belmont section of the Bronx, where on any given evening there is likely more firepower concentrated beneath dacron polyester suitings than anywhere else in America. We eat and we drink, we reflect with lionhearted amusement on the awful fate of a worthy quarry; we avoid discourse on the potential for the opposite truth. And we all know, deep in our cop bones, that it is always lightest before the dark.

I felt it then, and was not completely surprised when Chief Eamonn Keegan's aide came barreling out from his office like he was on fire. He grabbed hold of the constable on the one side of me and included him in his sprint toward the stairs, yelling something I could not make out in the clattering echoes of the corridor.

Brady and I stood there alone. And from down the stairway below rose the first distant sounds of bells and sirens, then stampeding feet.

"What now?" I asked my learned counsel.

"A jolly good time to leave," Brady said, glancing down the corridor to the alternate stairs.

"You're advising me to walk out, just like that?"

"Aye, if you've any brains, man." Brady moved away from me, toward the other stairway, which did not seem to be the focus of a stampede.

I ducked into Keegan's office and found him slumped forward across his desk. His arms were outspread and his mouth was puffed open, blowing out air and spattered blood like some freshly hooked flounder hauled up on deck and struggling against the stacked odds of his ever swimming again.

I moved over to Keegan, careful to sidestep the steady spray of blood shooting from between his lips like paint from an aerosol can. His skin was still warm to the touch. Also he was still flopping around pretty good, but this was purely on reflex. The two knives in his back, one for each lung, were sunk clear up to the handles.

The plain wooden chairs at the front of Keegan's desk, where Ruby and I had sat during our interrogation of the other day, were now half slimed in red. There was a wad of sticky paper in Keegan's right hand. It slid out easily from his loose fist. I put this away in a pocket.

On the wall behind Keegan's desk, between bookshelves, was an open window. In the corridor behind me came now the urgent sounds of nearby cops. I decided, finally, to take the advice of the lawyer my country's embassy saw fit to provide me. My status as innocent bystander at two homicides in as many days was unlikely to reflect well upon me, especially now in the tender stages of this new one. Before hauling ass out that window, though, I first helped myself to a couple of cigars lying there on the desk I was afraid might go to waste.

I had no problem making a hasty exit, thanks to the fire escape leading from Keegan's window to the courtyard below. Once down on the ground, I followed an alleyway between two wings of the massive Garda headquarters. This led to a tall lace iron gate to the street. The gate was unlocked and untended, oddly enough. I walked through and found myself not far from where I had entered headquarters almost four hours earlier.

An ambulance had pulled up to the entrance, and white-coated men with gurneys and portable blood transfusion equipment rushed into the building. Vans arrived and disgorged reporters and photographers. A barricade line of constables was set up in a large semicircle arcing out around the press and emergency vehicles.

I began walking slowly away from the scene, but turned when a sweet-voiced girl called my name. Then another. I considered making a run for it. Not from the police, but from the sight of two girls in school uniforms trotting my way, green sweaters flapping. Fleeing would bring unwelcome notice, and maybe even a shot in the back, so I waited for them. But this time, I stuck my hand in a pocket and held tight to my wallet.

"Mr. Hockaday—?" the first girl asked. The second one was close behind. And chasing her was—who else?—Brady.

"What do you want now?" I said.

"Here, take it, sir," the tinker girl answered, extending a roll of bills.

"What's this—?"

Brady, now caught up to us, was quick with more advice. "Looks like lovely money to me."

"It's all of it there, sir," the second tinker girl said. "Bless you, we had no way of knowin'."

"What's this?" Brady asked. "Knowing what?"

The tinkers ignored Brady, addressing me, "Sister Sullivan, she clued us in about your mum, and said to wait here 'til you showed yourself again. Don't need your business, friend."

And then they left me, trotting back toward the expanding crowd of onlookers, doubtless with visions of a hundred purses and wallets to their credit before all the commotion died down. As for me, I held in my hand all three hundred dollars' worth of my Irish pound notes. Brady tried manfully to close his amazed mouth, which had dropped open at the sight of the cash.

I turned and continued walking. Brady fell into step, doing what he had to do in the way of staying true to his nature.

"The contingency of one-third is customary in such matters," he said, puffing to match my pace. Had the chaser actually managed to count what I had, I wondered?

"I should pay for that advice of yours?" I said.

"I notice you took it."

"As a convenience, yes. I am now on my way to the American Embassy to explain everything that happened here to somebody slightly less hysterical than one of your Dublin constables. I will also find the moron responsible for sending you over to me, then I'll settle his hash. Then, I am going to drop by whatever Irish courthouse I find appropriate to see about having you disbarred, or whatever you call it over here."

"Of course," Brady said, generously, "we could negotiate a more favorable recompense."

"How about twenty-five bucks and you get lost?"

"Done."

I gave Brady what he claimed was twenty-five dollars' worth of pound notes, he gave me his business card and we went our separate ways. I saw that Brady's route took him toward a pub. I was tempted to follow him there, but figured it safer to do all further drinking for at least the day somewhere beyond Dublin's city limits.

So I flagged a taxi and had the driver take me to the central depot, where I bought a ticket back to Dún Laoghaire. I had fifteen minutes to kill before my train arrived, so I put in the overseas call to Inspector Neglio.

"Where the hell were you when I called before?" he said. There was no *Hello, Hock* to start off the conversation. When his secretary put him on the line, it was a straight-out *Where the hell were you?*

"When was that?"

"It would have been nine or so in the morning to you, middle of the goddamn night for me. The phone there rang twenty times before I got an answer, then I had to talk to some character called Snoody who told me you were gone off somewhere and that Ruby and some *cook* had left him to make breakfast all by himself. Who the hell is Snoody?"

"My Uncle Liam's man."

"His *man?*"

"Like in butler."

"*Butler?*"

"Turns out there's a little money here."

"A Hockaday with money? That's like a fish with a bicycle."

"You want to just tell me what you called about this morning?"

"Not your rabbi. Another cop."

213

"Is Mogaill all right?"

"He isn't dead so far as we know. The other cop is."

"Who—?"

"The name is Dennis Farrelly. Ever hear of him?"

"Why do I have the feeling I'm under interrogation here?"

"Maybe because I've got a feeling that whatever the hell's been going on since that priest of yours offed himself somehow begins with you, Hock—and maybe's going to end with you if you don't watch your butt."

"So who is Farrelly?"

"A question mark we found the other day in Hell's Kitchen, right about three blocks from your place. I went up for a look myself."

"And—?"

"It plays like Farrelly was tipped off the roof, in the dark of morning."

"What's a dead cop I never heard of got to do with anything?"

"He's a Dublin cop. Staying in a mattress paid for by Arty Finn, your IRA friend from Nugent's, the guy killed by the bomb in Mogaill's house. What Farrelly's doing in New York, you tell me."

"Tell you what, Inspector? And what makes you think Arty Finn's my friend?"

"All I know is I'm seeing Irish cop or Irish priest or Irish goon on everything that's making my job a pain these days."

"You and I, we're on the same side here, *paisano*. Read a little history some day. If it makes you feel any better, you'll find out the Irish are a fair people, they never speak well of each other."

"Look, Hock, I'm—"

"Skip it, I can't afford this call. When's the last time you talked to Eamonn Keegan?"

"The Dublin chief? Maybe an hour ago. I left him another message, about Farrelly and what we found on him besides his badge."

"What was that?"

"Some kind of medallion from back in the Second World War, with a Fascist logo on one side and some poetry on the other."

I pulled Father Tim's medallion from my pocket and looked at it. I asked Neglio, "On the side with the logo, the axe tied up with the rods, did you find the letters *H.O.S.?*"

"That's right."

I turned over the medallion. "And the verse reads, 'When nations are empty up there at the top ... When order has weakened or faction is strong ... Time for us all to pick out a good tune ... Take to the roads and go marching along'?"

"Hock, what is this crap anyways?"

I thought of my dream of war on the plane coming over, and of my father's ghost voice warning about a world gone cockeyed. And I said, "It's spies and betrayals and secret codes and treacheries and propaganda, and the very thickest plots and all manner of deception and cruelty required to preserve a man's civilization ..."

But was it only me saying these words?

"That's all?" Neglio said.

"One thing more. I just left Chief Keegan's office. He's been murdered."

Ruby slipped away from me, leaning forward toward the table in front of the couch. She picked up the decanter of single-malt Scotch and the unused glass and said, "On that, I'll have a drink with you." She poured for herself, and also refreshed my own glass.

We watched the fire for a minute or two, sipping. Then Ruby asked, "Well, what do you want to do about it?"

"About what?"

"Spies, betrayals, secret codes, treacheries ... cruelty. The whole nine yards you just rattled off."

"I have to narrow it all down."

"To what?"

"To the ghosts and me."

"You're starting to lose me."

I put back my drink, and said, "I'm lost myself, Ruby. I used to be a regular detective with a pretty good record at cracking regular cases. I used to expect that if I looked, I would see. But I am on a whole different kind of case now. A grand case, like my rabbi said—the mystery of my own makings. And now I'm starting to see without looking."

"You're saying the case is getting away from you? That it's too big?"

"Not that. I mean there's something about *me* I have to figure out before any of the rest of all this makes sense."

"Like Inspector Neglio said?" Ruby suggested. "All this begins and ends with you?"

"Not quite. What I have to do is find out where I belong here."

"Or something here that belongs to you."

"Christ, I wish I could just go home."

"And where would that be?"

"I'll have to sleep on it. Ask me in the morning."

"Okay, but meanwhile there's two questions you can answer for me right now."

"Shoot."

"First—for God's sake, Hock, you stole the cigars off Keegan's desk?"

"They were good Cubans. Fidel would say I liberated them from a state of unuse."

Ruby rolled her eyes. "All right, then what about a little matter of evidence missing from the crime scene."

"The wad of paper," I said. "How could I forget?"

"Let's see it."

I stood up and walked over to a chair near the bed, where my clothes were hanging. I went into a pocket of my chinos, took out the paper, returned to the couch and sat down.

"What possessed you to take that?" Ruby asked as I flattened the paper out in my lap.

"I don't know, I didn't think about it."

"Well . . . maybe it was a case of seeing without looking."

"How do you mean?"

"Maybe you saw—without looking—that there was a possibility this evidence was never going to see the light of day. So you pinched it, on intuition."

"I don't know about—"

"Look—who else gets close enough to a police chief at the Dublin Garda headquarters to kill him but a cop? Who else but a cop was responsible for securing that gate from the alley to the street? So who should be trusted with evidence—a cop?"

"I see what you mean."

"And this is all before you find out about Dennis Farrelly doing whatever he was doing as Arty Finn's guest in New York."

I flattened out the wad of paper. On it was a page from my own family's violent past, which I had only just learned on this remarkable day. Smeared red letters, hurriedly written in what I had no doubt would test as Eamonn Keegan's own blood, read, *We wish to grow peaceful crops, but we must dig our furrows with the sword.*

How I wished I could just go home.

CHAPTER 31

"LIKE YOURSELF, I GOT THIS LITERARY SIDE TO ME," RAY ELLIS SAID. He took a notebook out of his coat pocket, snapped off two rubber bands and thumbed through the pages until he found what he was looking for. "How's about I read you a little rhyme I come across in the late Constable Farrelly's crib?"

Davy Mogaill drank coffee with his left hand and said nothing. The gun in his right hand was still aimed at his head. His left hand was on the table, resting near the answering machine tape.

"So that don't get a rise out of you? Leave me just go ahead and read—"

"Nae—please, allow me: 'When nations are empty up there at the top ... When order has weakened or faction is strong ... Time for us all to pick out a good tune ... Take to the roads and go marching along.'"

"Yeah, that's it, word for word." Ellis closed his notebook with the rubber bands and put it away. "Also you probably know the rhyme's stamped on the back of this special coin Inspector Neglio says is from the Mussolini days."

Mogaill nodded.

"When did you learn these charming lines, Captain?"

"On my wedding day in Ireland."

"Marriage and them garbage politics, they mix?"

"They say all's fair in love and war."

"You ask me, that's a freaking crock."

"Once again I say, you're really quite perceptive."

"Meaning also maybe this here talk we're having, it ain't about exactly *who* whacked Finn and Farrelly but what the hell for?"

"Exactly, Lieutenant."

"So we're talking what—payback, like you mentioned on the phone?"

"Did I?"

"Yeah, I was listening real careful, Davy."

"Were you careful about your listening when Brenda was alive?"

Ellis shrugged, and said, "I heard what everybody else heard."

"And what were these rumors about my late wife?"

"That I ain't saying until you put away the damn gun. There's more guys shot over the subject of broads than all the other reasons for getting shot put together."

Mogaill lowered his gun slowly. "You do understand, Lieutenant, I haven't got a whole lot to live for outside a mortgage and my pension?"

"That I get. Just let's take it gentle on my clock."

"Fair play. Now, about that gossip ...?"

"Everybody seen you and Brenda didn't have your typical marriage. You know, with her being home looking after a mess of little rug runners? You had the nice house out in Queens, with the geranium pots and all. But hell, Davy, half the time she was over on the other side instead of being here with you in New York. We also seen that. I guess it was just everybody's feeling that you and her had one of them, you know—understandings."

"Understandings?" Mogaill's tone was mocking, and so was his smile.

"Well—"

"You're telling me everyone thought these long separations of ours were about sex—or the lack thereof?"

"Give us a break here, Davy. Nobody much gave a rat's fanny about your sex life one way or the other."

"Nor much more about Brenda and me, I'd bet. Americans are

like that. Once the glandular questions about a person are settled, there's little interest in anything else. You've political campaigns here that revolve around nothing but sex, and not very interesting sex at that."

"This is your way of telling me there's some other reason how come Brenda was gone all the time?"

"You're a bachelor. What do you know about holy wedlock?"

"Holy, I doubt it. But I hear there's plenty of lock in wedlock."

"I'm here to tell you, taking a bride is like saying *I do* to the tip of an iceberg."

"Who's talking about sex now—or lack thereof?"

"I'm talking about what there is to a woman like Brenda besides the poor luck of her being born a beauty."

"That ain't good luck?"

"If she was born a plain girl, Brenda might have been absorbed with the business of making herself beautiful. As she was already beautiful, you see, she was absorbed with something else."

"Maybe I'm getting your drift now, Davy."

"Over on the other side, there's a tradition behind politics of the sort that don't get discussed in polite places. Follow me there?"

"Your beautiful Brenda—involved in them garbage politics?"

"Aye, and she was one of the unsuspecting female types. So by this wicked tradition, she won a dirty job. In Brenda's case, they taught her the craft of bomb making."

"Christ, Davy, nobody ever knew . . ."

"That was the whole bloody idea, and you're looking at the biggest fool to it."

"You're drifting away from me now."

"It's a sorry story, but a short one. Many years ago, I took a holiday over to the other side. And what do you know but the loveliest girl in all Kildare takes her shining to me, a fine big New York cop. One thing leads to another, and it's my wedding day. God in heaven, she was beautiful then, Ray."

"I can imagine."

"Unfortunately, imagination's no substitute for experience. Of which I had little. And here I'm not talking sex, understand. I'm speaking of knowing a facade when you see one is all."

"I think I get it," Ellis said, brightening. "What better cover for making IRA bombs than being a tin wife?"

"You see the point now perfectly. That being that so far as Brenda was concerned, our marriage was beside the point."

"I'm sorry as all hell, Davy. Maybe if you'd had a kid ..."

"I loved her enough for that. She could have been charmed seeing a character like me all sappy about his little kid." Mogaill sighed heavily. "But, anyhow, our loving never took that way. If it did, we'd have only been mocking God."

"Man, I never seen a worse Catholic guilt trip than the freaking ride you're on!"

"And you, the most suspicious cop I know."

"You fooled us all, Davy."

"To this very day perhaps. I'd bet you still don't know how solid the facade was built."

"Maybe not. But I'd guess right about here's where Arty Finn and Dennis Farrelly come in. Also maybe the way Brenda went. Let me guess again. It wasn't in no innocent house fire."

"There, I knew I was right to call you."

"Probably. The inspector, he's in a big rush all the time with the mayor and that crowd to come up to the Bronx and hear you out. And your boy Hockaday's sort of long-distance nowadays ... Say, that reminds me. What about Hock in all this?"

"Ask him, Lieutenant."

"I'll do that when I see him. Right now, you can tell me about how Brenda checked out."

"Her own brother's one of the grassers responsible for that."

"So much for you harps sticking together." Ellis thought for a moment. Then, with his voice and his bulldog face brimming over in knowing cynicism, he asked, "Just who would be Brenda's brother?"

"Her maiden name was Finn."

"As in Arty Finn," Ellis said, nodding his head. "And the other one that did her in, that would be—"

"Oh, you're on top of it now. It was Finn and his mate, Dennis Farrelly, who sacrificed my Brenda."

"How do you mean sacrifice?"

"Come now, you can't be as dull as all that, Lieutenant. Bones are thrown to cops the whole world 'round in exchange for ignoring the meat. It's the meat, after all, that keeps us cops employed."

"You're saying that for the greater good of some kind of Irish garbage politics, this Farrelly and your wife's own freaking brother turned her over?"

"Aye, there she was on one of her trips away, the lovely and unsuspecting wife of a New York cop fabricating bombs for boyos of the cause up in Ulster. And all the while, Finn's like a snake in the grass, planning to divert attention from some far more serious mischief by having his mate in the Dublin Garda earn the glory of a bone."

"So what happened?"

"The Garda come 'round for its snoop, and I reckon Brenda was panicky. Her means of concealing the explosive goods back-fired—and her in the effort."

"This they write off as a house fire?"

"No need for further panic. The good folks of Dublin enjoy believing the troubles belong strictly to the north these days. The Garda don't like to be the ones to knock a myth by revealing the likes of a bomb factory in the middle of some ordinary row of Dublin houses."

"Likewise maybe a little bomb workshop here in New York? Say in a neighborhood out in Queens, the kind with geranium pots on the stoop?"

"Many's the time we had a bit of smoke in the house when Brenda got things bollixed up fiddling around with this and that down cellar. She was right clumsy for a terrorist. It's why I reckon she died the way I said."

"So all these years, you kept a little of Brenda's handiwork around the house? And that's what went off the other night, killing her brother?"

"Well, who would have suspected?"

"Not Arty Finn," Ellis said. He pulled out his notebook again and read over a few pages, then asked, "Finn and Farrelly, they're the serious mischief you're talking about?"

"Not them alone. There's a secret and deceitful army of long-standing behind them. Like the Mafia, or cancer."

"This army have a name? Like for instance, H.O.S.?"

"Ah, now we'd be getting to the meat, Lieutenant. Which I must leave to my off-duty friend, Detective Hockaday."

"Some friendship. I don't know why, Davy, but I see how your buddy Hock is somehow connected up with all this freaking Irish

222

intrigue you're laying out in cute little bits and pieces. Also I figure you know there's a certain percentage Hock might wind up coming back here sideways."

The only sound from Mogaill was the drumming of his fingers on the answering machine tape. Ellis put away his notebook.

Finally, Mogaill said, "Here's your glory now, Ray. You make it play like the furnace blew in my place, and my guest Arty Finn gets it while I manage to wander off in a daze for a while. Nobody's likely to care about Farrelly any more than Finn, so you can write him off as a leaper easy enough."

"What makes you think the newspapers will buy that load of bull?"

"The press buys anything and you know it, Ray. Look at them still defending the Warren Commission, for the love of God."

"Say if I put out the line like you want. It gets you paid back, but what'll you throw into the pot?"

"This," Mogaill said, tapping the answering machine tape. "Like I told you, get it transcribed for the inspector. Tell him the caller to Father Tim's answering machine is Dennis Farrelly. Which is information that comes to you from diligently working your snitches. Then be sure to get the message over to Hock. He'll be needing it."

"Davy, that is one piss-poor ante."

Mogaill raised his gun to his head again.

CHAPTER 32

"WHO'S THAT?"

Ruby said to me, the Scotch turning her voice husky, "What? Can't you tell from here?"

"Well, maybe I'd better get up," I said.

"Say, what's all this about your being able to see without looking?" Ruby laughed at me as I rose from the couch unsteadily, the Scotch having its effect on me, too, as well as the day's string of shocks.

I stopped at the bed and held on to a post, waiting for a moment's dizziness to pass. I picked up my Yankees cap from the bed and put it on before heading to the door, where the pounding had renewed from the other side. I shouted a slurry, "I'm coming, I'm coming . . ." and twice stubbed a toe in the folds of the thick rug with the sweetheart roses spilled all over it.

When I opened the door, there stood a tall, stocky man with a well-cut thatch of gray hair. Because he was not wearing a suit, and because the accumulated drinking of the day was now hitting me like breakers at the beach in Far Rockaway, it took me a couple of seconds to realize this was Patrick Snoody. Tonight he was dressed casually, for Snoody anyway. He wore a cashmere V-neck sweater the color of his hair, a silk ascot, navy with tiny red polka dots, and charcoal mohair trousers, severely creased.

"Good evening, sir," Snoody said, his fist raised and ready for more pounding. He dropped his arm, laughed softly through his nose at the sight of my cap, and asked, "What's this, homesick for the old ball game are we?"

"Doesn't anybody wear baseball caps over here? What do you want, Snoody?"

"Terribly sorry, I'm afraid there will be no formal dinner," Snoody said, ignoring my first question. "Your uncle is a bit under the weather and plans to pass the night in his chamber."

"How the hell come? He looked pretty good the last time I saw him. Now he's sick?"

"Just a bit bound up, to tell the truth about the old gentleman."

"Oh yeah, I remember. Knots in his pudding, that's what he calls it."

"Yes," said Snoody, raising an eyebrow. He looked past me into the red room. I followed his gaze over to Ruby, who waved at him with her fingers. Snoody raised his other eyebrow, looked away and said to me, "He sends his apologies."

"Which room is good old Uncle Liam's?" I stepped into the doorway and poked my head past Snoody, scanning up and down the long hallway of the third floor. "One of these doors up here?"

"The old gentleman," Snoody said sternly, "would appreciate being left undisturbed tonight."

"You're not going to tell me which one's my Uncle Liam's room, is that it? Goddamn your Irish bead-rattling ass, is that it?" I know what an argumentative drunk sounds like, and I liked the sound of myself. Also I very much enjoyed the color of red that was taking over Snoody's face and neck. "I ask you one simple thing, Snoody—and you won't tell me?"

"Sir, if you please! See here, I—!"

"Okay, forget it if it's such a big goddamn deal. Where's your room, Snoody? You and me, we'll open a bottle of port and chat later like a couple of regular pals, about all sorts of things. Life, death, fear ... the love of a good woman? Maybe about the old days in the monastery with all your monk pals ... Father Timothy Kelly, say? How about it? Or if you'd rather, we can talk about Francie Boylan and his politics ..."

Snoody's skin tones now pretty much matched everything in the red room, and his arms were shaking hard enough to take leave of his shoulders. Naturally, I decided it was time to hit him with the big one. "Oh, now here's an idea—you can tell me all about the H.O.S."

Poor Snoody sucked in a lot of air, very suddenly, and as it came back up his nose sounded like a distant burglar alarm. He took a beat, holding the door jamb.

When he could move again, he turned on his heel, and said hastily, "Cook will prepare tea and a board for you both. I'll have her bring it 'round in about an hour. A very good night to you, sir."

I watched him escape down the central staircase, knowing he felt my eyes on his clenched back. When he was out of sight, I closed the door and returned to Ruby, lying languidly on the couch, a bare leg dangling off the edge.

The fire needed encouragement. I picked up a poker and stoked up some nice bright flames.

"So look at me, slow-dancing with the sole heir to the Liam Hockaday estate," Ruby said as the fire crackled. "I could get used to this place."

"Better not."

"Why? It sure beats that dump of yours back in Hell's Kitchen."

"It's not my briar patch."

"Oh, pooh!"

"No kidding, Ruby, I'm getting uncomfortable here."

Ruby sat up and her eyes saddened. She said, "The way you say that, you're scaring me, Hock. I thought you just said we'd stay so you could find yourself."

"We don't have to actually stay in this house to figure out its riddles, do we? I have to trust my instinct, and it tells me we should clear out. Tomorrow's not too soon."

"Your uncle's—"

"I'll try seeing him, tonight."

"What I was going to say was, at least the riddle your uncle told you is solved. For what that's worth."

"The one about the blind man?"

"Yes. A man without eyes saw plums on a tree. He neither took plums nor left plums. How could this be?"

"I give up."

"Wait, I wrote it all down." Ruby jumped off the couch and went to a dresser drawer. She came back with a piece of paper. "Okay, pay real close attention to exactly what I say next. Ready?"

"Sure."

"The man had one eye, so he's without *eyes*. There were two plums hanging on the tree and he took one of them, therefore neither taking nor leaving *plums*."

Maybe if I was sober this would have computed the first time. As it was, I had to ask Ruby to run it past me again.

"Come on, Hock, don't you get it?"

"I'm a little drunk, I'm not a moron. Of course I get it. When did you figure it out?"

"Actually, I didn't. Moira told me. She told me several interesting things this morning."

"Oh yeah?"

"For instance, here's another minor riddle solved: Moira and your uncle, they were lovers once upon a time."

"What happened?"

"It was only when they were children, Hock, and all 'innocent' as Moira says. After that, it was not only pure it was one-sided. Poor old Moira, in love with your uncle and all she's known her whole life is serving him. I mean that's *all* she's known of him. You understand?"

"No wonder she went Christian."

"There's more. Hock, she knew your father and mother."

"Do you think she'd talk to me? We didn't exactly hit it off."

"I think you might win her over. It would take some doing, though. She holds back when she gets talking, and *my* instinct tells me the reason for that is named Patrick Snoody. But anyway, from what I told her about you, she seems to think you're very much like your father, and I get the feeling she liked your dad quite a lot. Your mother, I'm not so sure."

"What did she say about her?"

"I wrote that down, too." Ruby looked at the other side of the paper she held. "Okay, here goes about Mairead Fitzgerald Hockaday: 'A beauty she was. A beauty and a rebel, and the reason I dreamed up the poser about the one-eyed man.'"

"A beauty ..."

227

"Hock, is something wrong?"

I thought, Shame on me, for I cannot imagine my mother being beautiful.

I said, "I remember looking at my mother sleeping in the early morning when I'd get up for school at Holy Cross. She'd worked all night, pulling stick at one of the Irish joints in the neighborhood, and so she was much too tired to be up with me. I'd go up and say good-bye to her there in her bed, lying on her back with her hair stringing around her head and her closed eyes like they were ready for pennies. I'd kiss her on the cheek. I don't think she ever knew, she was so damn tired. Her coat would be lying down at the end of the bed. I always liked the way it smelled—like a good time. It smelled of food and liquor and women's perfume. But my mother never ate at restaurants, and she never drank, and she never owned perfume."

"And her brother-in-law, Liam, living here in this place, with all this money," Ruby said, shaking her head. "I just don't get it."

"Liam sent money every week," I said. "I remember that. My mother never complained about any lack of generosity."

"Remember what your uncle said about that the other night?"

"No."

"He was adamant in saying he'd sent all your mother asked for. It's not as if she didn't know about better things. Look where she came from. The mighty Fitzgeralds of Bloor Street."

"They should have seen her. We had one luxury in our house in Hell's Kitchen. That was the radio, an Atwater-Kent. She loved to read, but she could only borrow books from the library, she never bought any. I never saw her wear a dress that didn't come from the dead table at Holy Cross. She'd take me up to the park on holidays, and she'd always want to look at the flowers. I remember her saying that fine homes were full of flowers. We never had flowers at home, when she was alive. There were flowers at her funeral, though. Uncle Liam dropped roses into her grave."

"How did she die, Hock?"

"The same way everybody else in the neighborhood died, worn down by work."

"She died with a lot of secrets, but she can't keep them anymore."

"No."

We had another short drink and watched the fire die. When the embers went to ash, there was knocking at the door again.

"Good, it must be Moira," Ruby said. "I'm starved."

Ruby slipped on a robe and went to the door. I heard Moira's voice, and soon smelled hot food and coffee. I got up myself and started toward the door.

Moira in her apron—smiling nervously I thought—stood behind a small wheeled serving cart. On the cart were covered plates, a carafe of charged water, coffee in two capped glass pots and a bud vase with two yellow roses.

"This is so nice," Ruby was saying to Moira. "It's been quite a day, and we're so hungry."

"If you please, ma'am, I'll be puttin' out your supper on the table inside, over by the fireplace," Moira said.

"*Ma'am?* What happened to just plain Ruby?"

"Shhh!" Moira cautioned.

Then she rolled her eyes in the direction of the staircase just past her shoulder. From a riser a half-step down we saw a glimpse of Snoody's head.

"I see," Ruby said. "Come in, Moira."

Moira rolled the cart across the room to the fireplace, then silently set out the supper things on the table. Ruby followed her.

I moved back into the red room just enough to be out of Snoody's sight, and listened as he crept up the staircase. He stopped outside the door, as if eavesdropping. I could hear his nose.

Finished with our table, Moira returned with the cart to the door. Ruby stopped her there.

"Moira?" she asked.

"Ma'am?" said Moira, turning.

"See you tomorrow?"

"Nae, I doubt it . . ."

Moira motioned with her eyes again, and ran a finger over netted hair. I tried to imagine her as a girl in Carlow, pulling petals off daisies in a spring clover field with the boy next door, Liam. But there was the only Moira I could know, standing in front of me with the great bulk of her wrapped in baker's white, and her feet in the stout black sexless shoes favored by servants and nuns. And somewhere in this sad, riddled house, her girlish love grown to become a master bound to a wheelchair.

"I'm sorry, ma'am, truly."

And so was I.

"So that's what you mean by Moira holding back?" I asked Ruby when we sat down to a supper of poached salmon, asparagus with mustard and dill, boiled potatoes with parsley, soda bread and rice pudding.

"It's the way it was this morning, too," Ruby said. "Snoody waiting in horror at what she might say. You should have seen the hateful look he gave her when she blurted out your uncle's riddle."

"The one she made up?"

"Yes."

"Then we have two additional, greater riddles."

"Please—don't hurt my head anymore tonight," Ruby said, groaning through a forkful of salmon.

"Why did Moira create the blind man riddle in the first place—?"

Ruby slammed down her fork and interrupted, "So he's going to bang my head anyway."

"And could the answer—the lesson about plurals—be the key to all the other secrets here? Is that what Liam meant?"

"Meant by what?"

"After he told me the riddle, he said, 'When you solve it, you'll start seeing answers to questions that have burnt you hollow.' "

Ruby held her head in her hands, and said, "I'm so tired I could cry."

I thought I was tired as well. But after two hours of lying still, I rose from the bed. Ruby had drifted off effortlessly, an ability I greatly admire.

She advised me once, during an especially restless night for me, "Get comfortable, and think of a time you did something so awful you wished you could curl up and die. You'll fall asleep right away. That's how I do it." The prescription never worked for me, though. Maybe for all the awful things I have done in my life I will be condemned to remain alive.

I touched Ruby's warm, smooth face. I envied her there in the bed, curled on her side, her shoulder rising and falling with the easy breaths of a deep sleep, even if it was brought on with a wish for death.

Quietly and without light, I put my clothes back on, minus the cap. I crossed over to the dresser and felt around on top for the basin and the soap and towels. I washed my face. Then I went to the door, half expecting it to be locked, as if we were Snoody's prisoners, and opened it just wide enough to slip out into the hall.

The very old, very big house was making its night sounds. The staircase warped and creaked; a mouse skittered across the oak floorboards in the hallway; the ping of water dripping from an ancient faucet somewhere down below sent echoes up through the stale black air; bats scratched along inside walls on their folded wings, foraging for insects.

I flattened myself against a wall and moved through the darkness, like a burglar, careful to walk nearest a wall, where a floor is less likely to snap underfoot. I stopped at each door, listened, then tried the knob. Nothing was locked. But one after the other, the bedchamber doors opened only to empty rooms and more empty night sounds.

I moved to the staircase, and took a few steps upward, then stopped and thought better of it. Uncle Liam used a wheelchair, but even though there was an elevator in the house, his bedchamber would likely be at ground level. So I reversed course, and headed slowly downstairs.

Near the central hallway at the bottom of the stairs I learned my choice was right. I heard the faint sound of a radio, and followed this into the small, musty-smelling parlor where Liam had had me come to hear his riddle; where he gave me the secret key to filling my hollow place, in haste because Patrick Snoody was said to be coming up the back way.

I whispered into the dark, "Uncle—?"

There was only the indistinct sound of a radio, the old "wireless" as Liam called it. I stepped deeper into the dark parlor, aware of the unsmiling oil portraits of unknown Irish gents staring down at me, and tall cases swollen with books, and unused furniture crammed every whichway, as if all of it was caught in a vast spider's web.

Then I saw the amber light of the radio dial. And smelled the sharp stink of a cigarette. I moved to the light, and heard my name whispered.

"Neil, boy—?"

Billie Holiday was singing "Gloomy Sunday" on the radio, tuned so low that four steps farther off I would not have been able to identify the song. My uncle was lying flat out on his back on the maroon horsehair couch, hands clasped around his belly. His wheelchair was parked nearby. On a low table at his side was an ashtray and a packet of Silk Cuts.

"Where did you get the cigarettes?" I asked him.

"Never mind, I got my sources," he said. "Light me one, and take one for yourself if you know how to shut up about it."

I reached for the packet and matches and lit two. Liam took his and sniffed the smoke before putting it in his lips. He inhaled, coughed, and muttered, "Oh, damn that's good." I sat down at the end of the couch.

Liam said, "I see you're a man what likes his sneak-about in the tiny hours."

"I've got my reasons. One of them being that I'm working on the riddle."

" 'Tis a right terrible tease. I don't know too many what can answer it soon."

"Oh, well—I've figured out the easy part."

"The easy part?"

"One eye, two plums. It's the rest of it that's got me up walking the floor at night."

"I'm not following you too easy now, boy."

"But I think you are."

"Do you?"

"I'm like the man in your riddle, isn't that right, Uncle? I have to keep in mind that only one of my eyes is bad—but that it doesn't mean I'm blind. Also, when I'm looking at a plum tree, say, it's useful to remember that even the simplest things can be more or less than they seem."

Liam hacked some more on his cigarette, and laughed softly as he said, "Aye, that's the lesson for us all. You're much brighter than you look, boy."

"Ruby says so."

"I think it's maybe that baseball cap of yours. Silly thing throws me off, I'm always thinking the circuits must surely be short in a head of your age covered over in the colors of a boy's game."

"If you think baseball is child's play then you don't understand the first thing about America."

"Actually, Neil, I once attended a baseball game, many years ago when you were a wee tad. Your mum left you with a neighbor lady, and I took her up to the Polo Grounds to see the Giants play."

"Did you enjoy the game?"

"Sorry, I don't believe so. 'Tis a purely American sport involving infinite time, chance and redemption. Therefore, the game is unfathomable to the European."

"You understand the game better than you think."

"That, I don't know. But I would dearly love to see New York again."

"Same here."

"Do you hear what's on the wireless?"

Billie had finished singing an up tune, "Let's Call the Whole Thing Off," and had now moved into the moody "Moaning Low." So far as I was concerned, both these numbers were big improvements over the suicidal "Gloomy Sunday," which I did not enjoy hearing in Liam's moldering crypt of a parlor.

"That's a very fine station," I said. "Tonight it's all Holiday, I gather? Last time I was here, I remember they were playing all Stan Getz."

"Lucky we are to have such a fine entertaining program. We hear all the best American music, Neil, we always have."

Liam reached an arm over the radio and tapped it appreciatively. He said, "And I mean that's going way back to when your Grandmother Finola gave your dad and me this very wireless. Like I told you. Here it's all these years later, and still I'm lying in the dark listening to the faraway voices."

"It was like this for you and my father, with the radio in the dark?"

"Exactly like this, Neil. Including the smuggled cigarettes. We had the good low music, and we made up our dreams of what we'd do as men. It kept us awake sometimes until the first light."

"What's keeping you awake tonight, Uncle?"

"I confess the music here's making me think of peachy young

233

ladies, like your own bonny. And the irony of all them smiling American girls in that sad, ugly, dirty, wonderful city of yours. Your daddo, please God—he loved New York so very much."

"Do you often lie here in the dark of night like this?"

"Aye, I'm an old cripple who gets far too much rest."

"What do you dream of the most?"

"My own spent youth. God, what money I'd give to pull up these legs and go dance a fine jig with bonny!"

Liam took a long drag off his Silk Cut and some of the smoke slipped down the wrong pipe. This gave him about a minute's worth of coughing spasms. I mashed out my own cigarette in the ashtray and decided I had had enough of them for a good long while.

"This night, though, I'm lying here especially dreaming of those fine old days when I'd come visit you and your mum in New York," Liam said, recovered. "You were quite the lad, Neil. Always with a good big ear for stories from around these parts. Do you remember listening to the stories told in your parlor?"

"Yes."

"And do you remember your favorite topic, the one that gave you the frightening dreams?"

I thought for a moment of long-ago evenings in the parlor, hearing tales . . . Mother wearing a dress from the dead table, which I was so happy to see she had trimmed with a bit of new ribbon in honor of Liam's visit, and me in my short pants . . . The Atwater-Kent, and the big map of the world with the red pins in it marking off battles of the war in the Allied advance, with my father somewhere out there among the pins, lost . . . Liam and Father Tim telling their endless stories of Ireland, one more elaborate than the other as the whiskey bottles emptied . . . All the many stories of Irish funerals. . . .

The door of a dead man's sheepeen removed from its hinges, resting horizontal atop chairs, the corpse covered in linen, hands folded over his chest with a stone crucifix, his big toes tied together, racks of candles burning around his head, new boots waiting near his bare feet, his bed burning outside in a pit, to ward off troubles with the færies . . . The mourners, bellies hard from eating mutton stew and fadge, drinking and arguing, and smoking clay pipes of tobacco damp with holy water, and taking snuff in hopes of a quick resurrection for the soul of their precious friend.

"Neil—are you there?"

I took my uncle's hands, outstretched in the dark.

"I remember," I said. "The funerals ..."

"Aye, you adored being spooked. I'd see you the next day in the street with the other boys, organizing them all to act out a right Irish funeral. I thought it peculiar at first, but I came 'round to an understanding."

"An understanding of what?"

"There was something that wasn't young about you when you were young, Neil. You wanted to dance and play a regular boy's games, and have your own daddo watching you. But he couldn't because he was gone off to war. So instead you made up games in the New York streets of funerals from the Irish countryside."

I let loose of Liam's hands, remembering this.

The sheepeen, hunkered at the bottom of the hill, with the great graystone manor house on the hill ... The crooked stream, with boulders along the banks covered in patches of whitened grass, like the lace shawls on pianos.

"Once, you told us a story about a funeral that took place in a village where there was a great house on a hill," I said. It sounded, even to me, as if I were a man talking in his sleep. "There was the sheepeen, and beyond it a crooked stream ..."

"Ah, that one! My, but it gave you a proper fright. The tale of a man come back from the dead to haunt his mates." Liam coughed and laughed, darkly in the murk of this room. "I cast it to the memory of back home, in County Carlow."

"In the village of Tullow?"

"Aye ... Tullow."

The mention of the village name caught Liam unawares for some reason I could not then begin to know. I only knew, from the sudden rales in his breathing, that I had somehow shaken him.

Liam said, "I'm growing terrible tired now. Take my hands again, boy."

I took them.

"You must know that Aidan would have dearly loved your Ruby Flagg," he said.

"Thank you, Uncle."

"I'll now be giving you this advice, Neil, as is my duty: do right by your bonny, and never lose her. You'll not wish to wind up in life lying helpless and lonesome on your back, listening to some faraway melody with lyrics that's stabbing your heart with the memory of old love."

Ruby was not asleep when I crept quietly back upstairs and through the door to the red room. In fact, she was not in bed.

And in fact, I was lucky she could tell in the dark that it was me sliding through the door instead of Snoody. Otherwise, my head might have been used to smash a china pitcher.

"Where the hell have you been?" she said, shoving at me as I crossed the room for the bed to take off my clothes once again.

I thought, This I can hear from Neglio. But I said nothing.

Ruby kept shoving, and said, "I'm out of my mind worrying about where you are in this buggy old place."

"Take it easy, will you? I was only downstairs, talking with Liam. I told you I'd look for him tonight, and I waited until you were sound asleep."

"Yeah, you waited, all right! God, Hock!" Ruby picked up a pillow from the bed and slammed me over the head with it. "How could you leave me alone with that Snoody prowling around the way we've seen him?"

"Well, I didn't see him this time out. Can we just go to bed?"

"So you're planning to stick around this time?"

"Promise."

I stripped, and Ruby dropped her robe to the floor. We climbed back into the canopied bed. Facing me, Ruby wrapped a leg and both arms around me. Liam was right. I would not like being alone and stabbed in the heart at the end of my time.

"We should be like this every night, from now on," I said.

"Very romantic."

"Only do me a favor, never hit the one you love."

"Bears do."

"No kidding around, Ruby. I mean it, we should be together."

"That's a proposal?"

"What's your answer?"

"I'll get back to you."

Ruby turned from me, curled up on her side and fell asleep.

While I, overheated and wakeful and envious of Ruby's easy sleep, spent the next hour thinking about men without eyes.

Then, without looking, I could see the two of them drawing near ...

Cold night rain falls soft and thick, pressing down on the day's warmth, steaming the ground. There is not a breath to be drawn in the close and smoky sheepeen. So I am leaning in the doorway, hungry for a breeze that will not come, and gazing out toward the crooked stream. Which I know is there, hidden in all the rolling mist.

They come, as if creatures rising out from the water. A soldier in a blue uniform I do not know, pushing a man in a wheelchair. The two of them, bumping along through dampened stone and turf, drawing closer and closer to the sheepeen.

I hear their talk. As clear as rain over my head and the arguing at my back, in the sheepeen.

"Every man in the place will stand us a round, I bet," says the man in the wheelchair. "Superstitious rabble! They'll think us spirits to be bought off with a jar."

"Ease up on the lads, brother," says the man pushing. "And let loose some money of your own. You'll have no nature in you until you gladly stand the house."

"Just get us there ... get us there."

"Might there be women?"

"You had your bloody share!"

"Will there be music, do you suppose?"

"Oh, bugger the music! It's all so much booziness set to a tune, a farrago of truth and lies appealing to the soft-headed."

"You'll be a sorry old man some day, brother."

"I'll be alive, I will! That's more than you can say."

The man in the blue uniform laughs, all the rest of the way, his laughter forming wet clouds of frosted breath.

I step back inside, and close the door. But I cannot shut out the sight of them, the door no better barrier than a dirty window.

They now stop, just outside. The man in the chair raises his legs straight out from the knees. His chair is shoved hard, again and again, until the door comes battering down to the force of stiff dead legs.

237

The crowd inside falls quiet. In a minute or two, there is a great noise from shuffling feet. Every man is standing, with a cap in his hand for silent waving.

The man in blue lifts his hands from the back of the wheelchair, then raises clenched fists high in the air, and shouts to the stillness, "Whirl your liquor 'round like blazes, boyos!"

He snatches my sleeves and pulls me against him, and I see his eyes are as blue as his shirt, and he says, "*Thanam o'n dhoul*, do ye think I'm dead?"

CHAPTER 33

THIS TIME, I HAD SENSE ENOUGH TO LEAVE BEHIND THE SNEAKERS AND the Yankees cap. Rounding the corner of Ladbroke Street to make my way down to the station, I now looked no more conspicuous in my Harris tweed jacket and suede chukka boots than any man I saw yesterday strolling through the Trinity College campus. For a topper, I had borrowed somebody's tweed cap hanging on a hallway peg, and this I could rake down low over my face if the need called.

Again, Ruby and I decided to split up for the day. This time, I did most of the deciding.

I said to Ruby, rising with the first light of morning, "We're leaving for County Carlow this afternoon. I've got some things to do in Dublin first."

"When did you decide on that, Hock? In your dreams?"

"Yes."

"Then that's where we'll go."

I wanted to look up Gunston again, I told her. Ruby told me she wanted another go at Moira anyway, and she hoped outside the house and out of the range of Snoody's big ears.

That decided and agreed, I dressed sensibly and left the house, this time bypassing Moira's kitchen.

I bought passable coffee and a copy of the *Guardian* at the train station and tried to appear nonchalant as I scanned the news of Eamonn Keegan's assassination under a huge block-lettered streamer. GARDA CHIEF FOUND STABBED TO DEATH! KILLER ESCAPES IN BROAD DAYLIGHT! IRA TERROR SUSPECTED! Fortunately, there was nothing in the story about a New Yorker in a baseball cap on his way to the chief's office right about the same time somebody gave him the business with a pair of long knives before escaping through a window and alleyway to the street.

So far as the various constables and officers quoted in the report were concerned, this "brutal murder" was "obviously the work of the boys from the north" and "clearly proved" the "common knowledge in police circles" that Eamonn Keegan was a "political enemy of the IRA." The story, accompanied by a photograph of the crime scene cropped so as not to be too distasteful for the Irish breakfast table, covered almost a third of page one, jumping to nearly as much space inside. But in all that ink, the story was infuriatingly trite and incomplete. A lot of journalists these days ought to turn in their press cards and take honest work as stenographers.

Is there such a thing as a nonbrutal murder? What, exactly, is obvious about Ulstermen and blades? Or political enemies? And if Eamonn Keegan ran afoul of the IRA—if, in fact, such conspiracy did him in—could it mean that elsewhere in the Dublin Garda there was political sympathy for shadowy terrorists?

My pal Slattery at the *New York Post,* who is nobody's stenographer and everybody's idea of a tabloid crime writer, once advised, "Hock, times change and worms turn, no matter what side of an iron curtain they're on. The Russkis used to have *Pravda,* now it's us. Over in Moscow, they're enjoying the shock of a relatively free press. Here, we should be reading our papers like the Russians did for all those years. You have to always ask yourself, How come they're telling me this? There used to be guys like Izzy Stone asking that for you, making the interesting connections between the official line and the real deal, but nobody's hiring too many Izzy Stones anymore."

Like his American cousin, Oliver Gunston was also turning out to be one of the fine exceptions proving the rule of his tarnished trade. As I leafed through the remaining pages of the *Guardian* while waiting on line to buy my train tickets, I saw that he had managed to get the real deal into print. For attentive readers, there was this article, published between advertisements for trusses and depilatories:

Cashiered Constable Dennis Farrelly
Said to Be a Suicide in New York
by Oliver Gunston

A former constable of the Dublin Garda, discharged from duty two months ago, was found dead yesterday in a New York City slum. Dennis Farrelly, age 44, was declared a probable suicide by the authorities in New York, despite unresolved questions as to the circumstances of his death, and his very reasons for being in the United States.

Mr. Farrelly's body was discovered, completely nude, in the fetid, rubbish-strewn central air shaft of a six-storey tenement house in "Hell's Kitchen", the unofficial name of a colourful Manhattan neighborhood traditionally populated by Irish emigrants. He had apparently taken a small flat in the house, according to Detective Lieutenant Raymond Ellis of the New York Police Department.

In a telephone interview with the *Guardian*, the blunt-speaking Lieut. Ellis suggested, "The guy could have still been distraught about getting canned off the police force over there in Dublin for all anybody knows. His career's shot, so maybe he figures he can start over again in America. Probably he was like a lot of your unemployed foreign persons who think there's still decent wages over here. So when he sees he's a chump, he feels even worse about himself and he takes a leap off the roof in the dark of morning. It happens all the time, I regret to tell your readers. Maybe since he was naked there was also something strange about the guy that you probably don't want to talk about in no family newspaper. Lots of things happen, especially in that bad neighborhood where Farrelly was staying."

Mr. Farrelly was cashiered by the late Chief Eamonn Keegan, who, perhaps coincidentally, was himself murdered yesterday afternoon here in Dublin (see related story, beginning page one). Chief Keegan, in a not altogether popular exercise of his power, sacked Mr. Farrelly for violating the Garda's code of conduct.

Specifically, Mr. Farrelly was accused of fraternizing with a "front group", so-called, of the officially banned Irish Republican Army. He was said to have attended recent meetings of the secretive "Hearts of Steel" political club, an ultrapatriotic right-wing tendency long believed to be defunct. During the Battle of Britain, the club expressed public sympathy for Adolf Hitler's Nazi party, and many of its members were also part of the short-lived Irish Fascist movement popularly known as the Blue Shirts. By the end of World War II, the Dáil's Eireann Committee on Terrorist Organisations had declared the club to be a financial conduit for the IRA, a declaration unrescinded to this day. It was on such basis that Chief Keegan dismissed the Constable Farrelly.

At the time of the sacking, Chief Keegan issued to the press a written statement that said, in part: "Let my action be clear warning to all others of the Dublin Garda that so long as I'm alive I shall not tolerate any manner of association with the IRA." Many constables and officers denounced this statement as a gross libel against their professional and patriotic integrity.

This entire matter was near to being forgotten until yesterday's untimely deaths of both principal players in the minor scandal, Mr. Farrelly and Chief Keegan. As a striking backdrop to these deaths, the former a curious suicide and the latter an outright homicide, there is the additional matter of the horrific assassination two days ago in O'Connell Street of Francis Boylan, a professional chauffeur and well-known IRA sympathizer who was transporting a visiting New York City police detective and his female companion . . .

There were another few paragraphs to the story. But they were pretty much a rehash of the previous Gunston piece, wherein Ruby and I were making a nice innocent trip to Ireland, and then the cock-a-doodle-do quotations from Keegan and Neglio laying everything off on coincidence, including Father Tim and Davy Mogaill's house blasting away.

So I took a moment at this point, as Slattery and all good Russians would, and turned back to the far less revealing story on page one, and asked myself, How come they're telling me this? I also counted up the dead bodies so far (four, and maybe running). By that time I had reached the ticket window.

I paid for my Dún Laoghaire-to-Dublin off-peak round-tripper. Then I walked out to the city-bound platform with a second cup of passable coffee. I then killed my waiting time by using a public telephone to call Gunston at his office.

"I see by the paper this morning you got pretty busy when I left you the other day," I told him. "That's a fine enterprising story."

"Good of you to notice," he said.

"How did you come on it?"

"Well, there's this bare-bones item came in from New York over the Reuters wire, and it seemed in need of some fuller suspicion, shall I put it?"

Gunston said this expansively. Reporters love bragging about their exploits as much as cops. I could just see him and his green eyeshade now, propped back in his mahogany chair with his feet on the rolltop desk, cigar in hand.

"So I rang up your friend Slattery once again, and of course he put me on to Lieutenant Ellis," Gunston said. "Cracking good quotes, don't you think?"

"Cracking."

"The rest of it was a bit of research, then suggesting to the reader that in politics two plus two doesn't add up to three no matter what certain ones holding office would have you believe."

"And then, of course, getting it into print."

"So, you see how it is. Your friendship with Slattery's not for nix."

"I've heard about struggles with the editors if that's what you mean."

"Ah, newspaper editors! They've all the dash and romance and imagination of pigeons, yet they're not so beautiful against the sky."

"Anyhow, I want you to realize—what you got into the paper was very helpful. And what you left out was very appreciated."

"You mean about how it so happens you were detained at Garda headquarters for a second time? And that you're Gavan Fitzgerald's grandson, and how this is all very, very deep?"

"I see you realize real good."

"I've got my fine sources. If you'll stay good to our little bargain I'll even tip some of them your way today."

"Ollie, if I ever figure out my story, you're the biographer."

"Good-o. Now I've been talking about you with a fellow called Dermot Brennan. He'll be grand for filling us in on the finer historical points of the muddy politics we've begun to bare. I'd like for us three to have a talk."

"I'm on my way into the city. I can be at the *Guardian* in, oh, forty-five minutes."

"Best we meet away from here. And we cannot make it nearly so soon. The plan is, we'll have a bite of lunch at noon. Dermot's occupied with his morning lectures. He's on the faculty at Trinity, you know."

"Small world. Too small."

"You're saying that sarcastic like."

"I've got my reasons."

"And sources, too? Mind our bargain, Detective Hockaday."

"I do all right by the helpful press. Ask Slattery."

"I did. He tells me you're a half-honest cop in a town three-quarters on the take."

"I don't mind if you quote him."

"Aye, he said you'd be flattered."

"So—lunch today, Ollie. How about the Ould Plaid Shawl?"

"You know the place—?"

"Here's my train. See you at noon."

So there I was enroute to a morning in Dublin suddenly gone blank. I spent the time on the train working on my case notebook, jotting down the information from Gunston's article, and looking over previous entries for something I could maybe run down before lunch.

A cluster of question marks beside the scribbled name *Joe B.* stared up at me from one of three pages devoted to the Francie Boylan assassination that had kicked off my arrival in Ireland. I decided to look up the bereaved family, namely the father that Francie had mentioned.

The telephone directory at Dublin's central depot listed Joe Boylan to a house in Goff Street. I wrote down a three-digit address, then dialed the accompanying five-digit call number from a pay phone. When a man answered, I hung up. In my business, I have generally found it productive to land unannounced at somebody's home.

Out in O'Connell Street, I flagged a taxi.

"The devil you say!" the hack complained as I told him Joe Boylan's address. He turned around in his driver's seat, and after three or four seconds' worth of assessing his fare, asked, "What's a Yank like you want t'be doin' in grotty old Goff Street?"

"Family," I answered, saying the first thing that came to mind.

"The poor relations got their teats caught up again?"

"Something like that."

"Aye, it's the usual." The hack pulled the taxi out into traffic. I caught him swiping looks at me in his rearview mirror as we rode along, north from Dublin's diamond. "Elsewise, my friend, you're wantin' to lose some teeth in a journey to Goff Street. Have you never seen the district?"

"No."

"Where d'you make home in America?"

"New York."

"Oh, well then, New York bein' a city where your best friend in all the world is the one not hittin' you over the head, I suppose you'll manage in our Goff Street."

"I suppose."

Joe Boylan's house was narrow and sagging and the color of grime, squeezed into a long row of identically ugly houses. Cracks in the window over the street were filled with tin foil and yellowed bits of newspaper. A gray dog with a bony chest scavenged from an open rubbish barrel outside the door. Down at the far end of Goff Street, where the horizon was filled by sulfurous factory haze, boys picked up stones from the gutters and threw them at one another.

Taxis were rare here. "Can't you feel 'em peerin' at you from behind the shades and curtains?" my driver said.

I told him I could. And I imagined what lay behind those shuttered windows, all up and down Goff Street: squawling children, women so tired they looked touched by the hand of death, men with little to do but nurse their resentments.

"How about waiting here for me?" I asked the driver.

"It'd be wise," he said, cutting the taxi engine and lighting a cigarette. "There ain't a trolley line in ten blocks of here."

I knocked at the Boylan door and discovered I was on the mark about the scene inside. A girl of twenty with watery blue eyes, pocked skin and hair the color of a brown paper bag answered. She held a squawler slung across a hip, there was another one screaming from someplace behind her.

"Joe Boylan live here?" I asked.

"And who'd be wantin' t'know?"

"I was with Francie when he died, ma'am. My name's—"

She was shoved aside by a thickset man in a sleeveless undershirt and wool trousers hitched up with braces. He was about the age my father would be, with a blazing red beard and flammable breath. "Get on out with you," he told the girl, cuffing her. She and the baby stumbled toward the back of the dank-smelling house. The baby shrieked.

"I'd be Joe Boylan," he said to me. "State your bleedin' business."

I tried to mask my surprise at the sight of him. Francie had spoken of a man from the Dún Laoghaire countryside, a gentle soul who measured the spring by the taste of onion in cow's milk, between the blooms of pussy willows and forsythia. Here now before me was the waste of a man from a hard street, and drunk before noon.

"Your son Francie was telling me about you before he died."

"Where's it you're from then?"

"New York."

Joe Boylan looked past me to the taxi. He asked, "What's this?"

"I asked him to wait. I only want a few minutes of your time."

"Would you be a policeman?"

"Yes." I showed him my badge.

Boylan tried slamming the door in my face. But I stopped it with my foot, like a salesman. He shook at the latch furiously, and said, "Nae, I don't talk t'your murderin' kind!"

"I'm an American!" I shouted, as if it somehow made sense.

"You're the bastard meant to take them bullets what killed Francie!" Boylan hissed at me. There was shrieking from inside. This time from the girl.

I moved back out of the door, my thoughts as staggered as my step. *Bullets meant for me?*

I said, "Wait . . . What are you talking about?"

Boylan snarled, "You heard me, you Irish-American bastard! Go home t'your stinkin' friends in New York what raise the money for our own simple fools here! Shame on your blood money, you bastard you!"

"I don't understand . . ."

"Joe—!" the girl shouted from behind Boylan. I saw her red-knuckled fingers wrap around one of his hairy wrists, pleadingly. "Oh, Joe, leave it be! Come inside—!"

He broke from her, swinging the door open to the street, roaring at me loud enough for all his neighbors to hear, "This here's the American what should've been shot! Not me Francis! Now comes the bastard here, to call on Francie's widow nice as pie!"

Boylan shambled out the door, with his fists up and flailing. He growled, and took a looping swing at me with his right. I had plenty of time to raise a defense, and Boylan's punch slapped into my open hand. I caught his clumsy left uppercut in the same way.

I pushed him off me, but he wanted more. He lowered his head and charged at me like a bull, spitting and shouting "American bastard you!" I grabbed a handful of his beard and yanked hard enough to send him crashing to the cobblestones.

Francie's widow was as blindly frightened now as the baby, who still clung to her like a chimp. "Jaysus!" she cried. "Oh—Joe!" Up and down the street, people had left their shuttered windows and clustered in open doors for a better view. Likewise, my driver was out of his taxi, gawking like a lawyer at a five-car pileup.

I bent over the downed Boylan, whose face was mashed sideways into the stone grit of the street outside his door. He lay quite still. A drunk is relaxed when he falls, and therefore seldom breaks a bone. And even though blood trickled freely from Boylan's flat nose, he was probably more humiliated by the fall than injured.

"Don't hurt him no more, mister!" the widow said. Tears flowed from her pale eyes. "Joe's all me and the babies got now, don't y'see?"

247

"I didn't come here to hurt anybody," I said to her. I slipped a hand under Boylan's dazed head, lifting it from the stones, and told him, "You've got me all wrong, Boylan."

"Please, mister—he's pourin' blood," the widow said.

"Let's get you inside," I said to Boylan, lifting him to his feet. "The girl will clean you up. Then you and I are going to have a talk."

"Don't be forgettin' me now," the driver said.

I gave the hack a five-pound note and said there was another one coming on top of the fare back to O'Connell Street. This bought his satisfaction and continued patience.

Francie's widow helped me guide her father-in-law's bulk through the front door and onto his back on a lumpy couch in the front parlor, the only furniture in the room besides a chair and a rug and a round table with a bottle and glasses on it. A small boy in diapers wearing a mangy sweater crouched under the table, hands covering his eyes.

I thanked the young widow, and asked her name.

"Catty, short for Catherine," she said, putting her baby down on the rug to crawl.

Boylan grunted and came to life. He reached for the bottle on the table. I said to Catty, "Maybe you could bring some hot water and soap, and a rag?"

She left us and I propped up Boylan into a sitting position on the end of the couch. There was the sound of snapping springs as I moved him.

"I'll pour us two," I said.

"Why not?" said Boylan, the fight gone out of him, even from his voice. "First y'killed me boy, then y'beat me down in the street. Now here y'come into me house like you own the bloody place. You might's well steal yourself a nip o'my own poteen."

"Politics killed your Francie, not me." Any fight left in me was gone, too. It was not difficult to feel pity for the mess of Joe Boylan. "And I won't steal a drink from you. I'll pour one, or I'll pour two. You call it, Boylan."

He waved a paw, and said, "Go on with you, we'll both drink."

Catty came back with a bowl of soapy water and a cloth. She swabbed Boylan's face and nose while I poured out the dark brown poteen. "Aw thanks, girl," he said to her when she was

248

finished. I gave him his drink and sat down in the chair with my own.

The boy came out from beneath the table, toddling my way. He stopped in front of me and stared at my face, confused and sad-eyed.

"Da?" the boy said to me.

"Nae, that's not your da," Boylan told him. He asked Catty, "Can you not take the lads off?"

Catty scooped up the baby from the rug and plopped him on her hip. She stepped over to the older boy and put out a finger; he grasped it obediently, though never taking his eyes off me. Then the three of them, Francie Boylan's achingly young widow and his two fatherless sons, walked slowly from the parlor to the back room.

"I'm sorry for your troubles," I said.

Boylan smiled and tipped his glass back. I had a sip of mine, which was enough. Joe Boylan's poteen had a sour heavy taste, like English beer mixed with a dash of three-in-one oil. I put my glass back down on the table.

"That what you come for?" Boylan asked.

"It's one reason," I said, nodding. And then, knowing something about the world's cops and the world's Goff Streets, too, I added, "How many of the Dublin Garda have stopped by to offer condolences?"

"It ain't likely we'll be havin' the district constable drawin' up his seat to this afternoon's tea."

"Then you see I'm different."

"By Christ, maybe you are." Boylan scratched his beard. "But now why should that be?"

"I say politics killed your son. You know it's the truth. And you say the murderers who did Francie were after me. I should maybe learn a truth of my own. It puts us on the same side, doesn't it?"

"Oh, and ain't it grand of us to be seekers of the bloody truth!" Boylan said, grunting in derision. He finished his drink and held out his empty glass, waving it for another. I poured.

"I am only saying this: what you know could be put together with what I know . . ."

"Then I'll only be askin', to what end? Is there some great and worthy thing t'be found here that's goin' to prevent Francie's two young tads from growin' up cannon fodder like their da? And what about this here street full of cannon fodder? You and your fine friends back in New York, you think you're helpin' these dumb fool lads by your stinkin' damn dollars sent for the Irish Republican Army?"

I thought of Davy Mogaill and the dumb fool lads at Nugent's bar playing "Ireland United" on the juke and drinking up their surcharged whiskies. I then passed along my rabbi's sentiments, "Marching feet never changed a thing, they only produced more marching feet."

"Aye, but just you try tellin' it to these boyos 'round here in Goff Street. Our kind of lads got nothin', they know they'll never have nothin'—and they bleedin' well know they'll always be most of the rest of the world despisin' them, near as much as tinkers. So what d'you truly think they'll be choosin' to do with their feet?"

I told Boylan I would place my betting money with the IRA.

"Then you proved t'me you ain't half the twit you look t'be. Your only trouble is, you ain't yet seen through that uncle of yours what summoned you here. Well, it was poor Francie's trouble as well."

Liam summoned me?

I poured Boylan yet another drink, though his eyelids were dropping off toward drunkard's sleep. And I asked, "How do you mean, *see through* my uncle?"

Boylan spat the name, "Liam Hockaday! Him and that wicked-spirited shadow of his!"

"Patrick Snoody?"

"Aye, and to a fiery hell with them two!" Joe Boylan roared again, his free hand shooting up as a fist. The two boys screamed from the back room, and Catty tried shushing them. Boylan tried standing, but failed. And then looked close to tears.

"I'm sorry for—"

Boylan cut me off, wanting me to hear his fullest accusation. "That devil uncle of yours, he's one of them rotten old dogs of war what's twistin' up the minds of our poor lads like me Francis ... !"

"Francie had something, though," I said. "He carried history, he was a *shanachie*."

"Nae, you ain't gettin' it yet. Francie was clever and learn't the old stories, true enough. But he never was smart enough to see how trainin' a parrot's done for the good of history and for it's evil, too."

"Which is where Liam Hockaday and Patrick Snoody come in?"

"Aye. Them and the whole bunch of the old haters."

"You're saying—?"

This time Boylan succeeded in standing, with a great deal of grunting and the help of his hand braced against the wall. He said, "I'm sayin' it's time you left me house and me sorrows. There's no sense to talkin' more on the old hates, or the new. Just be goin' now, you American bastard you." He added, "Please."

So I left.

And as I walked through Boylan's door to the street and the taxi, I realized my steps fell heavier than when I had come. As if something in me had gained weight, maybe my hollow space. I would have to learn to move with that.

Bullets meant for me?

Liam summoned me?

Old dogs of war?

When we had turned off from Goff Street to the road leading south to the diamond, the hack turned a worried face to me, and said, "I hate to say it, but I swear that brown car back there's followin' us. I seen him before, waitin' up at the corner of Goff 'til we pulled out."

"Don't stop for traffic lights," I said.

CHAPTER 34

AFTER A LONG HOT BATH, RUBY WRAPPED HERSELF UP IN A ROBE AND stood at the window looking out over Ladbroke Street. The morning dew, ice white, still traced grass blades in the shallow yard. Tree branches, heavy with buds, shivered in a wind that swept up the hill from Dún Laoghaire's waterfront.

She chose her clothes accordingly: cream-colored cotton sweater, waist-length jacket of olive green leather, tan corduroy trousers, walking shoes. She also selected a green and yellow silk scarf and tied this loosely around her neck.

Then she removed everything from the closet and bureau drawers and carried them to the bed. She folded and refolded all the clothes—her things and Hock's, too—and stacked them carefully in preparation for the suitcases.

Packing was Ruby's responsibility by default. She had accepted this as a cost of throwing in with a travel slob like Neil Hockaday. Hock was the kind who was perfectly satisfied with any old thing thrown into a D'Agostino shopping bag at the last minute. Ruby took luggage seriously. Socks tucked into the corners of the case, breakables in paper and plastic wrap and cushioned by small soft items, everything pressed and neatly folded, everything kept level.

She and the suitcases would be ready to leave for Carlow this afternoon, by God. Ruby's clothes, and Hock's as well, would look very, very nice on arrival.

Before going downstairs, Ruby took a moment to organize her thoughts about the business of Moira as carefully as she had the suitcases and her day's ensemble. What was it she had yet to learn from Moira? What approach might work best? How much could she expect to pry out of her in the short time available?

Ruby decided to pursue the single essential question of a cloistered, somewhat batty cook's acquaintance with Hock's well-born mother, Mairead Fitzgerald. What was it Moira had said of her? *"A beauty she was. A beauty and a rebel, and the reason I dreamed up the poser about the one-eyed man."* If Ruby could get to the bottom of all that, she had the right to call the morning a good day's work.

She daubed on some maroon lipstick and brushed her eyelids lightly with black liner. She gave herself a final mirror check, pulling the collar of her sweater just so, poking her hair, smoothing the front of her trousers. Then she left the red room and walked down the staircase.

Snoody passed through the hall at the bottom of the stairs on his way into the formal parlor. He turned and looked up at Ruby, but offered no morning greeting. Neither did Ruby.

The radio in Moira's kitchen was tuned to the same demented Mississippi thumper Ruby had heard the day before. It put her in mind of a less than pleasant memory from her girlhood back home in New Orleans: her mother, Violet, dragging her off to the Crescent City Miracle Tabernacle and the Reverend Zebedeh Flowers scaring everybody silly with his screeching and swaying and his big, piercing, bulging eyes fixed directly on Ruby Flagg as he described the eternal tortures of the damned, meaning even little girls who foolishly put off being sanctified in the baptismal font.

Ruby called, "Moira?" But there was no answer.

The thumper wound up his radio sermon with a prayer from the Psalms, "Cleanse Thou me from secret faults!"

Ruby called out again to the still kitchen, "Moira ... Moira?" Again, there was no answer.

A flourish of organ music ended the thumper's spot. Now somebody was reading the day's obituaries.

"Moira?"

253

No answer.

Ruby crossed through the kitchen, past the table where she had sat for tea yesterday with Moira. She opened a door to the back garden, stepped out into the chill and saw nothing but a cat lapping up milk in a dish set out on a patio block. Ruby went back inside.

There was another door, probably leading down to the cellar. Ruby opened it. Beyond the first few risers of a steep wooden staircase, all was blackness. There was a heavy smell of apples and coal.

Ruby felt around the wall for a light-switch plate. She found it and pushed. From below, where the stairs took a right-angled turn, a bare strung bulb popped on.

"Moira—?"

No answer.

Ruby stepped back from the doorway, unsteadily. She turned, and looked behind her. On the table was a half cup of tea, and a cutting board with pie dough and a knife. She went to the table and picked up the knife, then returned to the cellar entrance.

One more time. "Moira—?"

Not even the echo of her own voice in the thick, dusty air. Ruby stepped carefully down the stairs, the dough-streaked baker's knife in a tight overhand grip.

When she made the turn, she met the cook. In soundless shock, Ruby's first thought was to wonder if poor Moira Catherine Bernadette Booley had been a good girl sanctified in the baptismal font.

Moira's huge bell of a body swung gently from a rope doubled around her neck and secured to the low ceiling between two flights of cellar stairs. One arm dangled, the other was dropping slowly away from the rope at her neck. Spit bubbles lined Moira's blue lips. One foot twitched, inches above a life-saving stair. The eyes were reddened from blood and they bulged, like Zebedeh Flowers's bulging eyes.

There was a scurrying sound in the dark of the cellar, below. A rat, Ruby guessed—hoped. She raised the knife.

"Miss Flagg, are you there—?"

Snoody called her name.

Ruby fought against time and panic, and the comparatively dainty fear of a rat. She rushed toward Moira's swinging body, put the knife against the rope and sawed back and forth, back and forth. Moira fell, her lifeless body crumpling along a wall. Then she slid on her dead back, head-first, clattering down the stairs into the smell of apples and coal.

"Miss Flagg—!"

Now Snoody was stamping his way down from the kitchen. Ruby turned and waited, knife raised.

"No!" she shouted up the stairs. "No!"

Snoody stopped where he was. Ruby heard him waiting, nose whistling nervously.

"Miss Flagg—what on earth's going on?"

"You tell me, Snoody." She tried to keep terror from her voice. She slipped the knife under her jacket and looked around the landing wall. There was Snoody facing her, frozen midway on the first flight of stairs down to the cellar, his hands empty. She repeated, "You tell *me!*"

"Miss Flagg, I don't understand you . . ."

"Keep away from me!"

"Not to worry, I shall," Snoody said, moving backward up to the kitchen, his hands against the staircase walls.

"What do you want with me?"

"I only came to tell you, madam, there are policemen here."

"Police—?"

"To see you, and young Mr. Hockaday. Where is Mr. Hockaday? I can't find him."

"Us—?"

"They're waiting. In the hallway, madam. Are you quite all right?"

Police?

A sense of relief washed over Ruby. Then she shook her head. No, she thought, something is wrong.

Snoody said, "Shall I tell them you'll be up directly?"

Of course. What else? "Yes . . . tell them," Ruby said.

Snoody disappeared. Ruby heard him walk through the kitchen. And again, she heard the rat noise below. Moira made no sound.

Ruby moved up the stairs, slowly. She returned the knife to the table, then ran cold water at the sink and rinsed her hands and face. She walked out to the hallway beyond the central staircase, where she saw four men in suits and topcoats, holding their hats in front of them, waiting. Snoody was saying something to them.

"I'm Ruby Flagg," she said to the men in the topcoats. She worried, suddenly, about rope fibers in the knife blade she had left in the kitchen. "You wanted to see me?"

A dark-haired man stepped forward. He produced a Dublin Garda shield, and said, "And would your Mr. Neil Hockaday be about, too?"

"He left, early this morning."

"Left for where, Miss?"

"Dublin."

The policeman was not happy about this. He turned and conferred with the others, then turned back to Ruby and said, "All right, you're to come with us now, Miss."

"Why?"

"Because you're under arrest is why."

CHAPTER 35

THE DRIVER DID ME ONE BETTER BY LOSING THE BROWN CAR ENTIRELY. HE accomplished this by zigzagging his way through a river of traffic, southbound on the North Road, then darting off through a maze of side streets.

"Did you see who was in the car?" I asked him.

I only saw the general shape of a man at the wheel myself. There might have been another man, but I could not be sure.

"Sorry, guv, I only seen the car itself."

We continued through the side streets, and districts not much different from the one we had left.

"How long was he waiting, back there in Goff Street?"

"Don't know, really."

He finally stopped the taxi at a trolley station. "If it was me," he said, "I'd want t'be out of this here taxi, just t'be safe and sure. I'll wait by you here until the trolley comes if y'like."

"You don't trust the Garda, do you?"

"I do not, guv."

"How can you trust me?"

"Your five quid in me pocket's a fine down payment on trust. You might clinch it by handin' over that other fiver you mentioned. Then there's the regular fare, of course. Which is two pounds and four."

I gave him two more fivers and said he should keep the change.

"God bless America," he said.

"That's not what I heard in Goff Street."

"There it's full of hotheads, unlike meself. I am personally aimin' to grow old, not bold."

"You might turn out to be the gentlest man I'll meet today."

"Aye, and potentially the oldest, as I say. No charge for this advice, my American friend: mind well your step."

The trolley came rattling to a stop.

"Can I get to Trinity College on this line?" I asked.

"Aye, tell the conductor to call you for University station."

I stepped out of the taxi and said good-bye to my gentle driver, adding in Gaelic, *"Ní cheolfad a thuille go bhfuighfidh mé deoch."*

"And what's it mean, guv?"

"It's the only Irish I know, taught to me at a fine New York establishment called Nugent's bar by a friend named Davy Mogaill. It translates, I'll sing no more 'til I get a drink."

The driver laughed.

I said, "God bless Eire."

Thirty minutes later I was seated in the Ould Plaid Shawl, rereading Gunston's article, connecting things together in my notebook and having myself a big drink while I waited for my lunch date.

Dermot Brennan was a fifty-year-old professor who looked like a giant Paddington bear. He had a round face, tightly curled brown hair with a frizzy beard to match and button-black eyes. He wore a navy blazer decorated with the ancient Trinity crest, a red-and-white checkered shirt and a yellow bowtie. He even had a Paddington briefcase, one of those attachés with triangular envelope flaps that tied instead of buckled. Professor Brennan's dress and physical appearance was as cheerful as his academic love was morose.

"Irish political history," he explained, as if our pub table was an extension of his lecture hall, "is the dark story of a fatal divide, what the great American scholar Hannah Arendt called the abyss between men of brilliant, facile conceptions and the men of brutal deeds—which no intellectual explanation is able to bridge."

Brennan was nothing if not quick to the point.

"Speaking of politics," he said to me, with a nod toward Gunston, who was opening a spiral-bound reporter's notebook, "our mutual newspaper friend tells me you're Aidan Hockaday's son."

"I'm beginning to think that's not exactly to my advantage."

"Oh? What gave you that idea?"

"Your Trinity librarian, O'Dowd, . . . Your chancellor . . ."

"Peadar Cavanaugh?" Brennan's frizzy eyebrows rose. He took a meerschaum from his breast pocket and emptied out burnt tobacco into an ashtray. "What did he tell you of your father?"

"Nothing direct, except Cavanaugh seems to think I'm somehow an awful lot like my old man, whatever that means."

"Well, you do look powerful like him. I'd say that, all right."

"How would you know?"

"Aidan Hockaday shows up in one of the photographs from my collection, my rogue's gallery, as I call it." Brennan found a tobacco pouch and was now filling the bowl of his meerschaum. Then he lit his pipe. "Of course, I'd be compensating for time. In the photo, your father is a good deal younger than you are now."

I looked at Gunston, who seemed as surprised as I was. "I checked the morgue for pictures, of course," Gunston said. He made a circle with his thumb and forefinger. "Not a one."

"This picture you have, could I see it?" I asked Brennan. "I never knew my father."

"So Gunston also informs me." Brennan opened his briefcase, pulled out a folder and handed it to me. "I've anticipated your interest in this."

The folder contained a black-and-white group photograph, with faces not much bigger than dimes. It was old and cracked, with printing at the right bottom corner. I took out my bifocals, and read, DUBLIN MEN'S SOCIETY OF LETTERS, MAY '36. There were maybe twenty men of college age in the shot, clustered around two middle-aged men, one of them clean-shaven and dressed in a trim-fitting suit and the other in a Victorian four-button coat and flowing beard.

I picked out my father in the student lineup before Brennan could point to him. It could have been my own NYPD rookie mug shot, minus the blue cap with the silver shield and the patent leather brim.

"The picture was made right here in this very pub where we're sitting, gentlemen," Brennan said. "The Ould Plaid Shawl was heavy with politics in the years of the terrible Great Depression . . . and the world war that came of it."

I handed the picture to Gunston, who looked it over appreciatively. "Well now, we're computing," he said. "Here we have none other than Peadar Cavanaugh in his younger version. And himself, William Butler Yeats, the poet-politician. Remember the clip, Hockaday?"

"The notice about the Sunday night fête for Yeats," I answered, "sponsored by my father's campus organization, the one O'Dowd and Cavanaugh claimed never existed."

"We must think charitably on the likes of O'Dowd, and Cavanaugh, too," Brennan said. "In trying to kill an old and inconvenient memory, they're only following their instincts as the decent bureaucrats they've become. By today's lights, you see, the Dublin Men's Society of Letters is a bit of an embarrassment to the college."

Gunston, pen poised over his notebook, asked why.

Brennan looked to him, then to me. He said, "Your dad and his own mentor, Professor Cavanaugh, started up the Society of Letters. There was little time lost in this becoming a radical political movement, as nearly any formal gathering did in those excitable days. The Society's agenda, sorry to say, was the impossible one spoken of by Hannah Arendt."

"A union of college gents and yobbos?" Gunston suggested.

"Something like that."

Brennan paused then, in the self-satisfied way a teacher pauses when he knows he has sparked the curiosity of his class. He puffed on his pipe, very pleased, waiting for either Gunston or me to eagerly pick up on the dialogue.

Gunston handed back the photograph. I said to Brennan, "Professor, I've also got a photo of Aidan Hockaday. It's an intriguing one, not for the picture of him in the uniform of the U.S. Army, but for what I found on the back only a few days ago."

Brennan was now the eager one. "What was that?"

"A poem, about drowning dogs."

Brennan took the pipe from his mouth. "Ah, that would be from Yeats," he said quietly. Then he recited, slowly and with what I took to be great reluctance: " 'Drown all the dogs,' said the fierce young woman, 'They killed my goose and a cat. Drown, drown in the water butt, drown all the dogs,' said the fierce young woman."

Gunston wrote down the words.

"That's it," I said when Brennan was through. "When I recited it myself to Cavanaugh, the old boy broke a few tears, and told me to go home. What do you make of it, Professor?"

"Simply the dark heart of the matter, Detective Hockaday. If you'd like, I'll explain that, as I myself am not a decent bureaucrat. But I warn you of two things. First, mucking about in the Irish past without pain is a lie. And second, what I have to tell you won't be reflecting kindly on any noble image you might wish to maintain of a father you never knew."

The two of them, Gunston and Brennan, waited for me to consider carefully. And meanwhile, there were the barmaids to set out our luncheon of cold meats and pickles, leek soup, brown bread and butter and the house ale.

I thought of my father's army portrait, all I owned of him until I discovered the poem by William Butler Yeats penned to the back of it—for what agonized purpose I might soon know. I thought of his eloquent letter from faraway America to his brother, Liam, written in a hand that did not match the writing on the soldier photo. *New York is a fabulous lady who gives incredible parties . . .*

I thought of the discomfort the photograph and the eerie verse from Yeats had brought to Father Tim and Davy Mogaill, and the strange effect of Aidan Hockaday's mere name on Chief Eamonn Keegan. And then Liam's words, *From the day he was born, Aidan changed everything and everybody around him . . .*

"You're now warned right and proper," Gunston said, dipping a spoon into his soup. "So what'll it be, Hockaday?"

"The truth," I said. *The Truth!* Was this on my say alone, or was the man who sat at the end of my bed putting words into my mouth again?

"The truth's buried somewhere in the tortured politics of Ireland, which is no simple thing as it is in America," Brennan said, addressing me. He had finished half a sandwich and pushed his plate away. He now sipped ale as he spoke. "America enjoys the

illusion of itself as politically complex, especially during your unending presidential elections. But America is merely a one-party
state that has found it useful to have two parties."

"And what is Ireland?" I asked like a good student.

"We're an unending conversation in the shape of a country. The
value of any good conversation is the conflict. Don't you agree?"

"I have the idea the arguments here are rich."

"Aye. In our more civilized moments, we organize the arguments into political parties. Many, many parties. The more to keep
the conversation going, you see. Quite naturally, then, our most
lively and memorable politicians are the writers. It's why they're
the heroes on our Irish pound notes, as opposed to the dead lawyers and such the Americans use to decorate dollars."

"This is leading somewhere, like to gents and yobbos—and
Yeats?"

"Aye, but first understand a bit of the background, at least
during this century. Ireland comes to its independence right as
the world's first going to war, and then afterward we're in for
all the bitterness and treachery and mob piggery that's known
to any country cut loose after its long oppression. Well, no
sooner does the dust clear some but we're right up against it
again with the Great Depression. The most profound social
chaos is what I'm describing to you in this horrible abbreviation,
do you understand?"

I did.

"Everywhere in Europe, the greatest desire of all classes of people is some manner of order—strong, working order—to replace
the disasters of war and depression. There's peppery talk of this
in the finest salons and in the grottiest sheepeens, all the same.
And in every capital of Europe, including Ireland, there were thou-
sands admiring the likes of Benito Mussolini."

"Yeats himself was a notable fan," Gunston explained to me,
setting down his pen. The historical preface was clearly for my
American benefit. "At least for a time. He'd go on holiday to
Rapallo, on the Italian Riviera, then come home to regale his political friends here in Dublin with the wizardry of Il Duce."

"Aye, that's fairly it," said Brennan, smiling at Gunston as if he
were his prize pupil. He turned to me, and said, "Now then, I
trust you read Oliver's fine article in this morning's *Guardian*?"

I said, "The Blue Shirts and the 'Hearts of Steel' club, at the time of the Battle of Britain ..."

Hearts of Steel. I reached into my pocket and took out the brass medallion Father Tim had given me. I looked it over again, then handed it to Brennan. "Speaking of the H.O.S.," I said.

Brennan noted the axe and the *fasces*, and nodded. Then he read off the verse on the back: "When nations are empty up there at the top, when order has weakened or faction is strong, time for us all to pick out a good tune, take to the roads and go marching along."

He passed the medallion to Gunston, who asked where I had got it. I told him of Father Kelly's gift, just before his suicide. Gunston noted this, and returned the medallion to me.

"Would that also be Yeats?" I asked Brennan.

"It would," Brennan said as he relit his pipe. "And written at the same time as the drowning dog bit. He was a great inspiration to the cause—so some people made it their business to say."

"Cause? What are you saying? William Butler Yeats was the father of the Blue Shirts? A Nazi? What—?"

"I'm saying nothing so simple as that. Keep firm in your mind the troubles of the time then, and how it might be that an articulate man of Yeats's ideals might be tripped up by his passions, his words misinterpreted—used. See my meaning?"

"You're leading now to the Dublin Men's Society of Letters?"

"Exactly. I'll get to that footnote directly. But you should first know that what was hardly obscure—then or now—was the basic contempt Yeats held for the Irish government in which he himself served as a senator in the twenties. Oliver, you'll recollect from my class what Yeats called the Cosgrave government?"

So, Gunston *was* a prize student.

Gunston thought for a moment, then answered, "He said the government was 'something warm, damp and soiled, middle-class democracy at its worst.'"

"Just so, Oliver. Very good. Now then, it was also no secret how Yeats and his crowd of intellectuals were beside themselves with dread of Communist rabble overrunning Leinster House. Anybody in political circles knew how in the early months of 1933 it was Yeats who was campaigning strenuously for government by a ruling class devoted to order, intellectual hierarchy, discipline and devotion to culture—what he wrote was to be 'fascism modified by religion.' "

"Please God, may Billy Yeats rest in peace," Gunston said, "but don't it show that you can be an educated man and yet still manage to be a fool?"

Brennan patted Gunston's shoulder, and told him, "Well put, son. The learned man knows his best lesson is remembrance of the severest shortcomings of his school. This causes me no small wonder as to how I've survived a lifetime in academe."

"Back to my father's outfit, the Society of Letters," I said to Brennan. "Whatever it might have been, it wasn't the Communist threat."

"Lord no! It's the IRA was said to have them bogeymen."

"I don't understand."

"With a great lot of thanks to the Catholic Church, the IRA was assumed far and wide to be a creature of the antichrist—Karl Marx. What do you know about Marxism, Detective Hockaday?"

"I myself am a Groucho Marxist."

"Well said to you then, too. The Marxism that grew in this soil back then was always more Irish than Marxist. The same was true with the Irish fascism. You now see how embarrassments come about?"

"I see that. What I don't get are the conflicts. According to Oliver's article, the Society was full of Blue Shirts, who you're now telling me took their inspiration from Yeats and his gentlemanly fascism. Yet the government claims the Society was a front group for the leftist IRA?"

"Left and right don't matter when it comes to the one holy hatred that unites Irishmen of all persuasions," Brennan said. "Surely, being the son of Aidan Hockaday, you know what that is."

"England."

"Precisely. Have you never heard the line—the enemy of my enemy is my friend?"

"I heard that. I also heard about strange bedfellows."

"Aye, and it was a strange bed we were all lying in during the last war. We called ourselves neutral. But there were plenty here thrilled by the Battle of Britain, when it very nearly looked as if our friend Hitler might at long last destroy our mutual enemy. Follow?"

"Yes."

"Now think how it's possible that certain ones were none too innocent in the national thrill."

"Meaning my father?"

"By the looks of it."

CHAPTER 36

WHEN BRENNAN WAS FINISHED RUNNING HIS CASE, AND ALL ITS DIS-graceful meanings, I was convinced by the pain in my heart that I had been told a truth, if not yet The Truth. And that Mogaill was dead right, the truth does not necessarily set men free.

Brennan returned to his lecture hall, after reminding me that I had asked for it, after all. He made me a gift of the photograph. Gunston quickly borrowed it and headed for the office of Chancellor Peadar Cavanaugh, saying it would probably go better for him if I was not along for the confrontation.

Which was all right by me because I could do with a couple of drinks. A barmaid called Mave took care of that.

While I drank, I tried mapping out some way of breaking it to Ruby about the strange bedfellows in my father's story. Also to myself. How do you explain your father's Nazi pals?

The only thing that made sense was the whiskey. Which told me it was time to call it a day in Dublin.

I called over Mave to settle up with her. She cracked a ten-pound note, returning not nearly enough to me.

"You shortchanged me," I said to her.

"Please God, strike me dead for shortin' a Yank!"

"And what's your problem with Americans, Mave?"

"You've got no respect for the proper rules."

"Such as what?"

"Them with money for fine trips to the olde sod, they've got the duty of gettin' a little cheated in a pub now and again."

"You believe the myth about all Americans being rich?"

"Nobody believes myths about Americans more than Americans."

A better man than I would have had Ruby meet him at the Dublin airport for the next available flight to New York. But I, dutifully cheated, left the Ould Plaid Shawl with the bright idea of catching the train back to Dún Laoghaire, collecting Ruby, saying good-bye for a while to Uncle Liam, and making a midafternoon start to County Carlow.

On the way to the central depot, I decided I should probably telephone Ruby. Knowing her, she would want to get a jump on packing up the bags. Snoody answered.

"Let me talk to Ruby," I said.

"I deeply regret to tell you, sir, she's not here."

"She went out again with Moira?"

There was dead air on the line for a second, then Snoody said, "There's been tragedy here this morning. Moira . . . ! Terrible, terrible . . ."

His voice trailed off, and for once Snoody sounded like a human being. Which was reason in itself for my blood pressure to start rising. There had been a tragedy, all right.

"Take a breath, Patrick. Then give it to me straight and fast. Starting with where's Ruby?"

"She's been pinched."

"What—?"

"The policemen were here—Dublin Garda, not our local Civil Guard. And they were looking for you as well, sir. Four of them. I gather you just managed to escape?"

Escape?

"What's the charge against Ruby?"

"Sir, I surely don't wish to think your Miss Ruby had anything to do with . . . with Moira!"

"What's with Moira?"

"She's . . . been hanged. She's dead."

"When—?"

"I don't rightly know, sir. Things are still dreadfully confused."

"Where is Ruby now?"

"I presume she's being questioned, in the city ..."

"Where's my uncle?"

"He's a late riser, you know. He's sitting in the garden now, with his coffee. I've told him nothing."

"All right. But tell me."

"Well, the policemen came to the door, asking for the two of you. I tried to find you, sir, but I hadn't known you'd left the house so early. By the way, did you take my hat?"

"Never mind about the hat for Christ's sake."

"Well then, I went out to the kitchen, guessing that Miss Ruby might be there with Moira. I found them together, all right ..."

"Go on, Patrick."

"I couldn't guess the whole truth at first. There was only Miss Ruby, crouched on the stairway to the cellar, threatening me ..."

"You sure you've got that right?"

"I should know when I'm being threatened."

"Okay, let's skip that part. What happened next?"

"The policemen took her away."

"Hold on a second. Where was Moira hanged?"

"In the cellar."

"Which is where you came on Ruby. So Ruby had to have discovered the body?"

"That could be."

"But she didn't tell the police about Moira?"

"I don't recall she did, now that you mention it."

"What happened after the police and Ruby had gone?"

"I returned to the kitchen, to check the cellar where ... well, where Miss Ruby had threatened me."

"Whatever."

"Poor Moira was arse over teakettle in the gloom at the bottom of the stairs. There was a piece of rope 'round her neck, fresh cut I'd guess. The rest of it was still strung from a ceiling hook."

I checked my watch. "It's nearly two o'clock, Patrick. How in hell have you kept my uncle in the dark about all this? And what are the police doing right now?"

"There are no policemen here."

"You never called?" I said. And I realized, too, that Ruby must not have reported what she saw. *Why?*

"I'll have Moira quietly taken away, in due time."

"You're telling me the body's still there in the cellar?"

"Sir, I—"

I slammed down the telephone. I dialed the operator, who gave me the number of the American Embassy. Then I called for help, my fingers not particularly steady as I pumped unfamiliar coins into the phone.

"My name is Neil Hockaday. I'm an American citizen. I'm in trouble."

"Hold, please."

It could have been a minute or two, although I would have sworn it was an hour, before someone returned to the line. "Your name and place of permanent residence, please?"

"Neil Hockaday, New York."

"City or state?"

"Both."

"Occupation?"

"Police detective."

"Relatives here in Ireland?"

"Look, would you put away the form? I'm in trouble here—and I'm in a hurry."

"Aren't we all? What seems to be the trouble, Mr. Hockaday?"

"The Dublin cops."

"Come again?"

"We're in trouble with the police, I think."

"We—?"

"My . . . companion, Ruby Flagg."

"Someone named Ruby's in trouble with the Garda?"

"They've got her, now they're looking for me."

"Let me get this straight. You're a cop, and you're in trouble with other cops?"

"I'm in the news, for Christ's sake. Do you read the papers?"

"Sir, there's no need to take that tone with—"

I slammed down the telephone again. I took Brady's card from my wallet and called him. There was I, so desperate I was chasing a chaser and thinking maybe my life depended on catching him. I somehow had to keep Brady, of all people, from smelling this desperation.

Brady's "office" was a tired woman with a cigarette voice and the sound of a lot of squawlers around her. "Would it be an emergency job of business?" she wanted to know.

"Well, from the dead woman's point of view, I guess not," I said.

"Oh, my, we'd best allow the solicitor himself to decide that," she said. She told me to ring a second telephone number that turned out to belong to a pub convenient to a hospital and the Dublin Garda headquarters called the Gnarling Cur.

"Oh, but I'm not at all sure I'm right for you," Brady said when he finally answered my page. "You seemed so disappointed the last time you required my services. I know that I myself felt a bit . . . shall we say, cheapened?"

"Listen to me close, Brady, because I haven't got time to dance with you. I am now making my way over to the Garda headquarters. If I don't see your ass waiting for me outside that door, I'm going in to tell the man how you slipped out the other day when Keegan got it. Something tells me the cops are looking for a goat in the case. I'll make sure you qualify."

"Mr. Hockaday, see—!"

"No. Let's see it my way, Brady. I'm in a lot of heat, so I'm capable of spilling anything that might make it cooler for me. If that means burning you, who cares?"

Then to be perfectly consistent, I slammed down the telephone. If nothing else, I needed a witness for going to see Dublin's finest. Brady was the best I could do on short notice and low pay.

I pulled the brim of Snoody's hat down over half my face and headed toward Garda headquarters, using the side streets that paralleled O'Connell. Ten minutes later I rounded the corner at Roxboro Lane to O'Connell Street and the headquarters building came into view.

So did a clutch of overaged schoolgirls in tartan plaid skirts and knee socks and green cardigans, about to go into their mumbling act around a couple of Japanese tourists. I was halfway to rescuing the Japanese when I saw Brady up there on the headquarters steps, right by the door where he was supposed to be.

Brady saw me, too. And when he did, he pointed me out to the two beefy constables standing next to him.

Then the constables came running at me, guns in hand.

CHAPTER 37

CHANCELLOR PEADAR CAVANAUGH LEANED BACK IN HIS CHAIR AND
waited for his young interviewer to respond. He had time to
smoke one Rothman's, then nearly half another before Oliver Gunston managed to speak.

And then, he only stammered, "What you've told me here,
it's ... Well, the plan is surely extraordinary, but ..." Gunston
could not finish the thought. More to the core of him, he could
not begin such a thought. *The Nevermore Plan.* Inconceivable,
lunatic ...

Cavanaugh assumed as much. Of course. The most unbearable
thing about his old age, he had learned, was the weight of experience, which had rendered so many things of the few years remaining so utterly predictable. He would gladly suffer the loss of
yet another lifelong friend in exchange for a day with a single
surprise in it.

"Permit me to help you through this," Cavanaugh said. "The
scoop I've just handed you ... Oh, by the way, that is what you
call it in your business, is it not? A *scoop?*"

"Aye."

"Here you have a sensational story, and yet you know very

well it cannot be published. Certainly not in the *Irish Guardian*. Is that not your dilemma?"

"It is."

"And why?"

"Well, I ..."

"Come now, Gunston. I'm told you were a fine bright student here at the college not so very long ago. One of the eager types— on full scholarship were you? You haven't gone all cobwebby over there at that good gray lady of a paper, have you? Tell us now, why is your wonderful scoop of no value?"

Gunston wondered why Cavanaugh was taunting him. That crack about his scholarship status. He tucked the thought away. Then said, "I'd be daft if I brought it up to my editor?"

"Exactly so. I've long known the kind of men who rise to power in newspapers. Now even the women, too, God help us. Tell any of these cretins about Nevermore and they'd sic the doctors on you."

"They'd think me mad?"

"Positively barking. They haven't it in them to see that insanity is the rational adjustment to an insane world. Therefore, they refuse to publish madmen's thoughts, until they're dead. It's why the press is such a bore. By the way, Gunston, I find the stress of your sentences disturbing."

"The stress?"

"One more small sadness of our time. Men and women of your tender age no longer assert themselves in conversation. You say so little anymore that ends with nice, emphatic periods. It's all about question marks now. So early on in life. Pity."

"Speaking for myself, and nobody else my age, I'm up to stuffing with answers," Gunston said. "But I don't mind trying you for one. If you knew there was no way for me to publish, then why did you tell me?"

Now here it was the knowing Cavanaugh stroking his white beard, searching for the words to his thoughts. He brightened, finally, and said, "Why, Gunston—I thank you!"

"You're welcome?"

"I simply don't know why I told you. This surprises me. I am in your debt."

"Chancellor ... ?"

"Never mind." Cavanaugh took the silk from his breast pocket and wiped his lips. "It must have been all the lovely memories brought back to me by looking at your picture that intoxicated me, loosening my tongue like a jar of mist. My, just saying that makes me thirsty."

Cavanaugh twirled in his chair to a credenza behind his desk, on which was a small decanter. "Join me?" he asked Gunston.

"Thanks, no."

Cavanaugh poured himself three fingers of whiskey, then twirled around to face Gunston.

"May I see it again, the photograph?" he said. "And where did you say you came across it?"

Gunston went into the manila folder on his lap. He slid out the photograph of the Dublin Men's Society of Letters and propped it on the edge of Cavanaugh's desk, between a set of old-fashioned quill pens and a quite up-to-the-moment telephone console.

"As I told you," Gunston repeated, "the source is confidential."

"That you did say. And you still won't allow me actually to hold it in my own hands?"

"I think not." Gunston kept his own hand on the photograph, ready to snatch it away if Cavanaugh made a move on it.

"Only good sense, I suppose; although, as you realize, you'll have no need of it." Cavanaugh shrugged, then leaned forward and took in all the old faces once more.

"My, look at them all," he said, sipping his drink. "I do believe I hear us again—singing old Billy Yeats's unsingable songs, written to the tunes of 'O'Donnell Abu' and 'The Heather Glen.' God, it was lovely."

"And a lovely chorus of goose-steppers you were then," said Gunston.

"You don't approve."

"I surprised you again?"

"Not the way you think. The surprise to me is that you're not insisting I'm a wise man. Most young fools give me that awful respect as readily as a tip of the hat."

"There's nothing wise to your brand of cynicism."

"Bold and emphatic! Just see how you've come 'round to speaking your mind so well. Pray, tell us what more you think."

Gunston took a breath. "I think there are sociopaths on all sides of a war. I think your Nevermore Plan is only fostering a grotesque symbiosis. One terrorist outfit without the other, and you're all unemployed. You're not so much about battling the Brits as you are about maintaining some mutually agreeable level of deceit, destruction and murder."

"Now that is a fine flow of words, well chosen to indict," Cavanaugh said. "You will find it surprising, therefore, that I agree with all you've just said. Aye, 'tis the very genius of the Nevermore Plan—and our basic defense."

"The dirty business of a noble cause never ends? That's your rationale?"

"And see how we didn't even have to invent the notion? After all, it's a constant running through all man's fool history. People soon forget when the fighting dies down. So we make it our business to keep the pot boiling, no matter what."

"So you're saying . . ." Again, Gunston had trouble accepting his own line of thinking. "You're saying, you'd help the other side? The Royal Ulster Constabulary—that bunch of Prod fanatics up there? You'd help them against your own kind?"

"I'll say only that we'll do what we have to do to keep mistrust alive and well."

Gunston stood up. "I need air, you're making me sick," he said. "You sit here at this campus, you and your elites, and you—"

"You think we're elitists, boy?" Cavanaugh's voice rose, and his face reddened. He finished off the whiskey. "Think again. And then if you like, I'll tell you of the people where Aidan Hockaday and I come from."

"I was on scholarship, as you point out. I know what it is to come to this place the hard route. I don't need to be hearing your own biography."

"Perhaps you do, Gunston. Think of the famine time. No priest, no capitalist, no constable and no scholar died. Only the common people. We died! Now, look how we've done by that injustice—the Nevermore Plan. Look how we've planted ourselves amongst the privileged, and moved them to our own ends."

"It can be done without more killing of one's own, can't it?"

"Can it?"

"Look at your deceit," Gunston said, "your destruction, your murder—"

"Deceit, of course! But no murder and destruction like before, not like the days of only the English money and guns—and English deceit."

"Nevermore," Gunston said, sarcastically.

"Aye, nevermore! The English are not to be trusted. They've deceived us often enough. The best man of the race always has an ace up his sleeve that's not part of the acceptable pack."

"If you'll excuse me, I'll now go puke."

Gunston walked to the door, then turned before leaving, and said, "I swear, I'll find a way to tell this mad story of you murdering old bastards!"

"I believe you will," Cavanaugh said. He smiled, and Gunston stalked into the hallway. Yes, young Gunston has been sufficiently provoked; he'll fight for a way to tell the story. Cavanaugh said to the angry air, "In fact, I'll be obliging you now with a peg for the news . . ."

He waited a moment for the wild beating of his heart to subside. Then he wiped his hands with the silk again, and his brow as well. First he had surprised himself by telling of the Nevermore Plan. Now this, his sudden inspiration for the perfectly symmetrical end.

Cavanaugh reached down to the bottom drawer of his desk and pulled out a sheet of heavy ivory bond, the stationery he used for handwritten notes, along with an envelope. Then, from the top drawer, he took out the razor knife used for cutting newspaper articles.

He smoothed out the bond on the desktop, admiring the embossed seal of Trinity College, and his own name beneath, in deep purple: PEADAR CAVANAUGH, CHANCELLOR. He set the razor knife to one side of the stationery, the envelope to the other, then selected a quill.

How very, very fitting, he thought. He pulled back a sleeve, then a cuff. Then remembered the walnut box, in yet another drawer. He pulled this out and set it on his desk, then again pulled back sleeve and cuff.

But now his hands trembled. Was he quite ready?

He pressed a button on the telephone console.

"Yes sir?" came the secretary's voice.

"Come in here, Thelma, if you please."

"I'll be only a minute, sir."

He turned, and poured another drink. Then he rose and took it with him to the window.

The chancellor looked down over the campus he commanded; he, only a common lad from the poor, hard coast of Kilkenny. Down below his leaded pane window was where he had walked with them—Shaw, Behan, Joyce . . . and Yeats.

Could his sweet mother in heaven see him in this earthly realm? The Trinity greensward, the ancient stone walls, the vine-covered gates; there in the haze just beyond Trinity's walls, rising up the long hill that O'Connell Street made from the Liffey to the Post Office, the green, white and orange of the flag of Eire.

God, it was lovely.

Thelma entered, with her dictation pad. She said to the back of his black suit, "I'm here, sir."

Cavanaugh did not answer right away. He raised his glass, and slowly drank down the whiskey.

"I'll never touch my mother's face," he finally said.

"Sir—?"

"It's to be my worst punishment. Can you understand?"

"Sir, are you feeling—?"

He interrupted her again, now by reciting words unspoken since boyhood:

> "Th'anam chun Dhia! But there it is—
> The dawn on the hills of Ireland.
> God's angels lifting the night's black veil
> From the fair, sweet face of my sireland.
> O Ireland! isn't it grand you look—
> Like a bride in her rich adornin'?
> And with all the pent-up love of my heart
> I bid you, top o' the mornin'!"

"It's quite a lovely poem, sir."

Cavanaugh turned to her. "It's from John Locke, Kilkenny's very own. My mother would say it each morning at the breakfast board, like a regular grace. She believed it would cheer the day."

"Well, it is lovely," Thelma said again, uneasily.

Cavanaugh returned to his desk and sat down.

277

"I am writing a most important message, Thelma. It's to be hand-delivered when I'm through."

"Very well, sir. I'll attend to it myself."

"Perhaps you should know what the letter's about."

"Sir?"

"It's about the god of irony. At least, 'tis the god's hand guiding me in the writing. Do you believe in such a god, Thelma?"

"I am a Catholic . . ." Thelma's face went red. "And pious, sir."

"Wonderful. When you win your deliverance to heaven, please speak to the Holy Father on behalf of myself and my comrades. Explain to Him that we never wished to offend the martyrdom of His only begotten Son, which is why we committed a few violent sins."

"Blasphemy!" Thelma cried, clapping both hands to her hot face. The dictation pad fell to the floor.

Cavanaugh ignored the outburst, and told her, "Meanwhile, you may carry on. Come back here in fifteen minutes for the letter, and please close the door tightly as you leave."

Thelma picked up the pad, and fled.

God of irony.

He thought, Here am I now in the final minutes of my secretive life, an old man who has suddenly found the tongue for a boyhood verse. *Top o' the mornin'.* Indeed, how prescient. How very like *Peep o' day!* The god of irony had been early to work in the life of Peadar Cavanaugh.

He thought, too, of yesterday's encounter with Aidan's boy. How striking the resemblance between the two! Cavanaugh had felt time collapsing on itself just sitting with the boy.

For a moment, as the boy recited the words written on the back of Aidan's soldier picture, he considered telling him the truth of his father—and of the crucible of his time. He seemed to want it so. But he had told him, instead, to please go home to New York.

Did this spring from mercy, or cowardice? Or was it in respect for the ghost of dear Mairead? Was not ignorance for the boy her life's wish? And had he not done enough already to the boy's family?

His body shook, as if a sudden cold wind had swept in the window. Was it the Devil's breath?

Soon, he would be a ghost. But—one more thing!

Cavanaugh rose from his desk and crossed his office to a collection of photographs on a wall. All featured the humble lad from Kilkenny grown to become Trinity's chancellor, in dozens of hand-shaking poses with the dignitaries of the world. He took down the photograph of himself and Yeats, and returned to his desk.

He opened the frame, took out the old picture and examined the back of it. There, in blue ink applied by Yeats himself, were the words, *Hammer your thoughts into unity.* Cavanaugh folded the photograph into quarters and stuffed it into the envelope.

He rolled up his left coat sleeve, and turned back the cuff.

Then he picked up the razor knife and stabbed at his wrist until the skin broke and hot blood bubbled to the surface.

Cavanaugh put down the knife, and picked up his quill.

He dipped the quill into the now steady, thick spurts of blood, and addressed the envelope: *Oliver Gunston, c/o The Irish Guardian, Grafton Street, Dublin.*

He then began writing on the bond, dipping the quill into his slowly whitening arm:

My dear Oliver—
I am a madman of some stature—and, as you say, a murderer—now taken by my own hand and properly enroute to Hades, where I shall surely join my comrades in arms. Before going, I present you this manifesto, if you will. As I am thus at death's safe remove from readers of the Guardian, *perhaps here is your way of breaking print with our discussion this afternoon of the Nevermore Plan.*
A few remarks of preface:
—You will notice, of course, the copperish hue of my ink. I write in my own blood, for reasons of irony, further herein apparent;
—I pray you exercise perspective in the matter of William Butler Yeats, patriot, poet, playwright, politician, bitter foe of the Partition of Ireland, Nobel laureate, mystic—and, for a brief time, ardent admirer of the Irish fascist movement. Mr. Yeats owned great intellectual passion; he worried mightily that others, possessed merely of physical passions, might apply his ideas in fields of action, possibly endangering their own lives. He once mused in none other than the pages of the Guardian, *"Did that play of mine send out certain men the English shot?" The answer, of course, is a rousing yes. I confess that the erudite Mr. Yeats was a convenience to us, in the*

long tradition of aristocrats blind to manipulations by their lessers. His respect and eminence gave music to a cause even his fertile imagination never perceived.

Now then, to the Nevermore Plan.

Simply put, it assumes England will attempt violent overthrow of the Republic of Ireland at first available opportunity. Therefore, we must maintain a perpetual vigilence. And because the common people of the Irish nation have always born the brunt of English oppression, it has fallen to our class to invent a vigilent system. Again, simply put, "we" have created among ourselves a secret vanguard to ensure that England will nevermore put its boot to Irish necks.

We Irish are and always have been militarily impotent as a nation; and, as eight hundred years' oppressive history demonstrates, we may rely on no other nation of the world to rally to our defense against the rapacious evil of England's ever so genteel barbarians. Therefore, we logically conclude, there must be ceaseless guerrilla warfare waged upon our ancient enemy, with our warriors drawn all at once from every existing schism of political philosophy and from all classes of the Irish people.

This was our founding thesis. It remains so to this day. The cause will live into the next generation of Irishman, and the next, and the next, and the next—unto forever. No one may kill the hatred in our Irish heads. Nevermore!

Our beginnings came during the years of the Great Depression, and the gathering storm of the Second World War. There were a certain number of us in Dublin involved in regular political study. (Here I shall betray no one's identity beyond my own.) We became convinced that England's chance at recapturing Ireland lay near at hand, amidst the upheavals of the coming great war. Therefore, we cast our underground lot with those allied against Britain, using the stirring poetry of William Butler Yeats as our voice and unifying spirit. Today, we cast our lot with another force making war against Britain, the Irish Republican Army.

We are everywhere in Ireland, in the enslaved northern counties of Ulster and in the ever-threatened Republic of the south. And we are everywhere else throughout the Irish diaspora. We have used and will use for all time any means, any eminent personality, any public institution, any political organisation of any persuasion in

aid of our continuing holy cause. We are the despised and the privi-
leged, we are the poor and the rich, we are the weak and the power-
ful. England, beware—and forever be caught in careful wonder by
our strange unity!

I have now provided you the bare bones outline of the Nevermore
Plan. I shall go no further, providing no details of individual or
collective actions, save that contained in the next few paragraphs.

Why have I told you all this? Because I am an old dog of war,
dear Oliver, and because my commander has issued a final call,
which shall mean my death, one way or another. I choose my own
way out of this vale. And in parting, I wish by the foregoing to
justify the gravest of my own crimes of war, to wit:

In the dark of morning, 14th October of 1937, I, Peadar Cavan-
augh, did kill Lord Gavan Fitzgerald, the accurate particulars of
which were published contemporaneously in the Guardian. *I carried*
out this assassination against an Irishman who abandoned his own
kind to become a political enemy of the free people of Eire. This was
a warning to all the Fitzgerald ilk, the one-time local authorities
under British rule who itched to serve their overlords again, to retake
power under new British occupation.

It was, I, Peadar Cavanaugh, who dipped his hands into Lord
Fitzgerald's open chest and lettered his coup de grâce, this being
the sign hanged 'round his traitor's neck—the sentiments of Yeats,
"We wish to grow peaceful crops, but we must dig our furrows
with the sword."

I would do it again, may God have mercy on my black soul.
Nevermore!

> *Yrs in Xt,*
> *Peadar Cavanaugh*

There was little time now, maybe only seconds before Thelma
would return to his office. She was as punctual as she was pious.

Cavanaugh was near to fainting from the loss of blood, and so
weak he could no longer sit up straight. His head fell forward,
and he was helpless to prevent it. He was now slumped across
the desktop, arms to one side with his hands pressed together, as
if he were pretending to be a sea lion clapping for the amusement
of Sunday visitors to the zoo.

So very little time . . .

He managed to fold the blooded letter, and stuff it into the envelope with the photograph. Then he wrapped up his wounded wrist in the silk. And opened the walnut box.

Inside was a Mauser WTP .25 caliber automatic vest-pocket pistol.

He placed the barrel in his mouth, said "Nevermore!" and fired.

CHAPTER 38

THUS HAD I ARRIVED IN DUBLIN, AND THUS WOULD I NOW TAKE MY leave: again with a couple of gunmen tearing down the steps of a public building, holding me in their sightings. I had precious little time for such things of the spleen, but I made a dying wish that moment in Roxboro Lane.

I wished for the pleasure of throttling the treacherous Brady so completely that he would know his eventual journey to hell as a blessing. That decided, and the clock racing, I ran at an angle from the pursuing constables straight toward the Japanese tourists and the small mob of "schoolgirls."

They had completely surrounded the stunned Japanese now, like banners fluttering down a maypole, their quick thieving hands rippling under the cover of their cardigans. They mumbled, "Mister . . . Hey, mister . . . Hey, missy . . . Penny for the tinker's child, ma'am . . . ?" The mister of the two got the picture first.

"You . . . you wait minute!" the poor sap shouted at the girls, one of whom barreled up Roxboro toward me. "Thief! . . . You wait light here . . . !"

I grabbed the runner by her shoulders. She kicked my shins,

spat something thick and green in my face, and hissed, "Piss off, you filthy bugger, else I'll scream bloody rape."

"Listen—I'm not going to queer your play," I said to her, holding on as she continued kicking my legs. "I'm Mairead Fitzgerald's boy, and I'm in trouble. Understand?"

"Aye!"

"See back there?" I jerked my head toward the constables, now maybe a hundred yards off.

"The coppers, they're gunnin' for ye?" the tinker said, eyes wide. She stopped kicking. "Can y'run hard, man?"

"I don't know—"

"C'mon now, it's easier than bein' shot!"

She latched on to my coat sleeve, and we pounded up Roxboro through gathering crowds, the hard-faced girl in her flying tartan skirt and me stumbling along on my wounded shins. Behind me, I still heard the offended Japanese tourist shouting, "You wait light here!" And now the shrill police whistles blowing.

"Where are you headed—?"

"Hush—save the breath for your runnin', man!" The tinker girl turned, for a look back to the constables. "I'll be takin' you to Sister, it's all you need t'know."

I heard a shot.

"Gawd—oh!" the tinker girl shouted as we ran. "Fookin' saints preserve us!"

We dashed through a cobbled alley. I lost my footing when pain stabbed through my lower legs. The tinker held me up, and we kept running.

Another shot, this one ricocheting off a slate rooftop. At least they were firing in the air, I thought. The tinker's sentiments were not so grateful.

"Fook them coppers!" she shouted.

We ran past an old black van, stopped with the motor idling at the opposite end of the alley. And as we passed it, the tinker battered the passenger door with a well-placed foot. Then she reached below her cardigan with a free hand, emerging with a fat wallet. She held this over her head, and threw it high in the air, screaming, "Money, money, money, money . . . !"

There were now dozens of Irish pound notes, Japanese yen and traveler's checks spilling to the cobblestones. And women in head scarves battling one another to pick them up. I stole a look back. The van head leaped off the curb and now careered down the alley between the angry constables and us.

The girl made a turn at the end of the alley, into a short mall full of fruit and vegetable carts, fish mongers and scattered cafés. Cut off by this, the van that had shielded us from the constables kept straight on, bumping through the alley.

"I can't keep this up," I said, gasping, the pain drilling my legs.

"Y'got to, man—least 'til we double back t'the high street! C'mon ye, keep hold t'me!"

Another shot in the air, now a mall with screaming people. We charged wide around a café. I saw O'Connell Street again, between the tables.

A startled waiter lost the balance of a large round tray. Thick glass pints of ale crashed to the ground.

I slipped in a foamy stream of the ale and broken glass, and fell, my knee taking the worst punishment. I could see the growing bloodstain inside the pants leg, and sharp-edged stones of embedded glass. And as I looked at the gashing mess, I grew sick at myself for all my own drinking that day, and how it had weakened and slowed me.

"I can't—!"

"We're nearly there. Keep hold!"

The tinker pulled my arm up over her shoulder and kept running, like a hellbat. Now toward O'Connell Street, on our combined three legs.

"It's there now!" she shouted.

We ran toward the flock of her cohorts, all of them obediently standing near the raving Japanese tourist. At the curb was the black van, motor running. The constables were gaining on us.

Then something pierced my good leg, in the back thigh. The muffled sound of the shot came a half-second later.

I collapsed, striking my chin on the pavement. I heard people screaming, and I felt the tinker's two hands at my collar, yanking me along the ground. But this was all happening to someone else, not me.

The tinker's face glistened with sweat. I heard her voice, rough and loud over all the other sounds, "I've got Mairead's boy here ... he's shot ... get him to Sister's ...!"

Pain in my legs, from the tinker's assault and my fall and a constable's bullet, turned to warmth. My vision faded, colors turned to shadings of gray. O'Connell Street's fast sights and sounds belonged to other people, not to me.

The Japanese lady fainted, her husband screamed for help. The other tinker girls formed an insulating circle around me, covering me with their cardigans; hiding me, patting my back, and cooing over and over, "Mairead Fitzgerald's boy ..."

The side panel door of the van slid open.

Many quick, strong hands lifted me, shoving me into a make-shift ambulance.

"Careful of him, will ye? It's Mairead's boy ...!"

I imagined Ruby's face, and her voice. I imagined her telling me she was safe.

At midmorning of the next day, I came around. Two women were in the room with me. One wiped my head with a cold, wet cloth. The other sat at a table drinking coffee and smoking ciga-rettes. She wore a nun's habit.

Sister Sullivan's camp was set back in a scrub forest beyond the bogs and fen that line the North Road for miles beyond the slum-scapes of upper Dublin. It would be home for the next several days.

I lay recovering in a cot in the camp's only permanent structure, if it could be called such. This was a low mud hut abandoned by some nameless, starving farmer. Probably during the famine.

There was only the one square room to the hut, with the table and some chairs, the crumbled remains of a stone cooking hearth, a sleeping loft and a crucifix nailed to the wall over my cot. The doorway was small and airless, covered only by a sheet of canvas. Even the smaller children had to stoop to get through it. The ceiling beams were cracked, and the roof mostly gone. The tinker men had patched it with paper scraps and fallen timber, but rain leaked through anyway.

Outside the small window where I lay, I could see the tinker's painted wagons, with their rounded tin covers and chimney vents. There was also the collective property of the camp—pinto horses, dogs, a flock of chickens, three very old cars and the black van. The women wore shawls and kerchiefs and billowing skirts, some of the girls wore their working clothes—school uniforms. The men and older boys dressed with more variety, depending on how they wished to appear on trips into the city to scam the locals and tourists.

My own clothes lay neatly folded on a chair at the end of my cot. I lay beneath three blankets. My thigh was ripped by a bullet, my face and legs were a mass of scrapes and bone bruises. Also I was nursing the aftershocks of a concussion.

But I was alive, and free. And so was Ruby.

Ruby! I could only imagine my calling her name. My throat would not permit the cry.

"Easy, Hock," she said as I tried raising myself. Ruby put down the wet cloth, and called to Sister Sullivan, "He's back with us, Sister!"

Sister came to my side. "It's about time," she said, her lacy wrinkles turning up in a relieved smile. "Hush you, Hockaday. Save your strength. Feast your eyes on Ruby here whilst I check your signs."

She pulled up my eyelids, felt the pulse points of my neck and poked at my chest and stomach. "I'd say you'll heal all right, boy. Now, I expect you'd like to know how we've managed to reunite you two?"

I nodded, and took Ruby's hand.

"Like anybody with an interest in staying one step ahead of what passes for the law, we tinkers have our sources in the Dublin Garda, which costs us dear," Sister said. "Anyhow, it come to us that you and your lady was to be snatched by coppers what meant you no good. And so we come to pinch you first—our impersonators, that is."

"Only you'd already left the house when they came to take us," Ruby added.

"Aye, we had a hellish time catching up with you. You slipped by us at the depot." Sister shook her head. "This was a major miscalculation. We were looking for a fellow in a baseball cap, you see."

I managed finally to sit up. With a shot of water, I managed to speak.

"I had quite a day," I said. "I spoke to Francie Boylan's father, and got an earful there. And then another earful from a professor of political history at Trinity College who seems to think my father was a Nazi. And then after that, I telephoned Liam's house and found out that Moira had hanged herself and that the cops had you, Ruby."

Ruby took her hand away, stood up and moved to the table. She picked up a newspaper, the *Irish Guardian*, and came back to the cot with it.

I said to Sister Sullivan, "It's a damn good thing I saw some of your dippers working their number on O'Connell Street."

"Aye, they rescued you."

"I was just heading into Garda headquarters after Ruby with this lawyer I'd hired, who—"

Sister's face swelled with anger, and she cut in with, "The devil makes his Christmas pie with lawyers' tongues!"

"You're telling me," I said.

"We can sort it all out later, Hock," Ruby said, laying the folded *Guardian* across my chest. "Right now, I'd better fix you something to eat, you haven't had a bite in almost twenty-four hours. Meanwhile, here's some heavy reading."

Ruby kissed me. Then she and Sister left the hut. I picked up the newspaper and might have fallen down if I was not already flat on my back.

Unaccustomed as he was to being featured on page one, there was Oliver Gunston's big score, right where it should be. In fact, there was no other story to the front page of the *Irish Guardian* but Oliver's, which was emblazoned simply THE "NEVERMORE PLAN"—MURDER & MADNESS!

From the looks of it, Gunston had his editors by the short hairs. If they refused to run the ugly thing, they would only become another wrinkle to the story Gunston could publish anywhere else in a heartbeat. From Slattery, I know about a reporter's last resort for getting a controversial story into print: tell the boss you will gladly quit and take your story to the competition, along with the additional story about why you quit.

It embarrassed me to see the main photograph on page one—a blowup of the picture Professor Brennan had brought to our lunch, showing my father and Chancellor Cavanaugh, and a slightly bewildered William Butler Yeats. But I was glad for Gunston's success. He had broken the most important story in Ireland since independence, no less. And one more of the many untold tales of World War II.

Additionally, there were photographs of some of the lesser players in the horrible drama. Arty Finn's mug shot was a memento of some long-ago felony in County Kildare. Father Tim's ordination photograph had come by way of the intrepid Slattery, no doubt. Also the rooftop shot of Constable Dennis Farrelly's body at the bottom of a Hell's Kitchen air shaft. Chief Eamonn Keegan's last likeness was photographed by the Dublin Garda, his bulky body slumped across his desk, mouth spewing blood. I noticed the part of his desk where the Cuban cigars would have been if I had not swiped them.

Peadar Cavanaugh's final portrait was clearly the most lurid. Gunston and a photographer from the *Guardian* had clearly got to the scene ahead of the cops. Cavanaugh's head lay sideways on his desk, in a thick pool of brains and blood.

Under the subheadline MANIFESTO OF A DISTINGUISHED MADMAN was the full text of Chancellor Cavanaugh's incredible letter, the revelation of The Nevermore Plan, and his confession to the unsolved 1937 murder of my grandfather. Next to this text was a photographic reproduction of Cavanaugh's original letter, handwritten in his own blood.

There was even Gunston's thumbnail picture, minus the eyeshade, wedged into the body type of his main report:

As deadly historical backdrop for a shocking series of murders and suicides here in Dublin and New York comes the exposure of a wartime terrorist conspiracy that well may exist to this day, for the purpose of supporting a permanent state of guerrilla war between militant Irish republican forces in both Ulster and the Republic and British authorities.

"The Nevermore Plan," as the terror group is called, was revealed yesterday afternoon to this reporter by one of its principal founders—Peadar Cavanaugh, the chancellor of Trinity College, who shortly thereafter took his own tortured life by shooting himself in the head with a small-caliber pistol commonly issued to officers of the German Army during the time of the Third Reich.

The purpose of the Nevermore Plan, which appropriated

the more fervent patriotic writings of Nobel laureate William Butler Yeats as both its intellectual inspiration and call to violent action, is said to be ongoing vigilance against presumed British designs to forcefully reimpose London's rule over all Ireland. The organisation's roots are apparently set in the Irish fascist movement of the 1930s, which supported Nazi Germany during the Battle of Britain.

The other principal founder of Nevermore is believed to be Aidan Hockaday, a 1934 graduate, summa cum laude, of Trinity College and briefly a local writer, who emigrated to America, joined the United States Army and disappeared during the war. Mr. Hockaday, pictured on this page with his academic mentor Peadar Cavanaugh and the poet Mr. Yeats, was the son-in-law of the barrister Lord Gavan Fitzgerald—whom Mr. Cavanaugh claims to have murdered in 1937.

Lord Fitzgerald's disemboweled body was found hanged by its heels in the alley behind his fashionable Bloor Street home in mid-October of '37. That very day, his daughter Mairead and her affianced, Aidan Hockaday, set sail for New York.

Mr. Cavanaugh's confession to murdering the father-in-law of his protégé was included in his "manifesto", a letter written in his own blood (see accompanying document, this page). Lord Fitzgerald was killed as he slept, his chest hacked open and his heart removed, his blood used to letter a sign hanged 'round his neck meant as a terrorist warning to British sympathizers during wartime.

Linked by as yet officially undetermined ways to Mr. Cavanaugh's death are the following, in order of their event:

• The suicide last Sunday in New York of a retired Irish-American priest of that city's Catholic Church of the Holy Cross, Father Timothy Kelly. Father Kelly shot himself in the head while making confession at the church. Like Mr. Cavanaugh, Father Kelly used a Mauser WTP .25 automatic vest-pocket pistol.

• The death of Irish national Arty Finn, also in New York City, one day later. Mr. Finn, according to Lieut. Ray Ellis of the New York Police Department, was widely known in Irish emigrant communities of the city to be a fund-raiser for the

Irish Republican Army. Mr. Finn, himself an illegal immigrant in the United States and wanted by authorities in County Kildare, died in an explosion at the New York home of Police Captain Davy Mogaill. Mr. Mogaill's late wife, Brenda, was the sister of Arty Finn. She herself died twelve years ago in a Dublin bomb factory, said to be operated by the IRA.

• The death that same day of Francie Boylan in a hail of gunfire in O'Connell Street. Mr. Boylan, a chauffeur by trade and an IRA sympathizer, was driving two American visitors—New York Police Detective Neil Hockaday, son of Aidan Hockaday, and Ruby Flagg, the American actress and companion of Detective Hockaday.

• Constable Dennis Farrelly of the Dublin Garda, who died in a New York City slum after a suspicious fall from a tenement rooftop. Mr. Farrelly had been cashiered by the late Chief Eamonn Keegan on grounds of his association with the banned wartime-era "Hearts of Steel" political club, a right-wing tendency nonetheless classified by the government as a financial conduit for the left-wing IRA.

• Garda Chief Eamonn Keegan, who was stabbed to death in his Dublin office two days ago. His earlier dismissal of Constable Farrelly was accompanied by a controversial statement: "Let my action be clear warning to all others of the Dublin Garda that so long as I'm alive I shall not tolerate any manner of association with the IRA."

• Moira Catherine Bernadette Booley, a cook in the suburban Dún Laoghaire home of Liam Hockaday, retired banker and businessman—and brother of Aidan Hockaday. Miss Booley, according to the local Civic Guard, was found hanged in the cellar way of her employer's home in Ladbroke Street. Miss Booley's political sympathies are unknown.

That was essentially all there was to Gunston's story, save for a few paragraphs quoting Professor Dermot Brennan. Brennan's view, of course, served to buttress the major thrust of Gunston's story—that the Nevermore Plan was not merely some paranoid fantasy, that it warranted the immediate and critical attention of the police and the government.

Fat chance of that, I thought. Gunston might agree with that sentiment, and that might well be why he held back so much of what he knew. Gunston was obviously the type who prefers to leave a few questions begging, and thus his customers wanting more. Smart young man; that way, he always has a job.

I read over the text of Cavanaugh's letter once more. Sure enough, there it was again, the little matter that caught my eye on first reading:

... I am an old dog of war, dear Oliver ... my commander has issued a final call, which shall mean my death, one way or another. I choose my own way out of this vale ...

And the other questions floated back into mind as I let the newspaper slip out of my hands, as I shut my eyes.

Bullets meant for me?

Liam summoned me?

They were questions Oliver Gunston could not answer for me. Nor the ghost of my father, try as I might to summon him in sleep.

I tried moving my wounded leg, and quickly thought the better of that. The pain that shot up my back clear to the shoulders felt like somebody was peeling skin off me. My head still felt spongy from the concussion. Thinking about the things that Gunston had left out of his story—and why—was not helping that much.

I tried thinking of other things, faraway New York things. Opening day at Yankee Stadium, throwing a Frisbee to Ruby in Central Park, Szechuan takeout. I would hold these images in mind for a second, hoping for relief, but one by one they were crowded out by my Irish troubles.

There was no use in thinking of home. I could no more stop wondering about missing connections than I could stop breathing. I needed all the answers to the mystery of my makings, or I would never leave Ireland alive.

This realized, it finally hit me. There was a key that I had overlooked my entire life.

Ruby and Sister Sullivan returned. I soon had a fine plate of stew in front of me, with warm black bread and cider.

"Sister," I said, after I had filled myself, "tomorrow I'll need to get to a telephone. Today, I'll need you to tell me about my mother."

CHAPTER 39

"I BLOODY WELL KNOW WHERE THEY'RE HEADED, DON'T TRY STOPPING me!"

"You'll not get away with this."

"Nae! I have, and I will. Stay back off me now, fair warning!"

"Not this time you won't. You and your crowd, you're nothing but toothless old dogs."

"Who'd be the toothless ones? You don't read the newspapers, man? It's still just as he said, the cause will live into the next generation, and the next and the next—'til forever. Nevermore!"

"Crow while you can. The time for your side's running short as a leprechaun's legs. You don't think that reporter chap's telling all he knows, do you?"

"I said, stay back!"

"That peashooter don't frighten me. The wee pathetic thing's only been good for impotent rotters scared of getting it as they rightly deserve. Why don't you do as your fellow cowards done, turn it on yourself and be off to Satan?"

"Such fine advice coming from you."

"Here's more: you've got the boy to contend with, and he's a smarter one than what he appears."

"That may be—"

"And if he's not smart enough by his own, there's Ruby with him."

"They'll not stop me neither."

"Moira nearly did."

"The potty old cow, she'll talk now to *Gawd.*"

"You'd best not mock the Holy Father since you're so close to His final judgment now."

"Nae, you're the one close. All it take's a twitch of my finger."

"How'd you do it to her?"

"She done it herself."

"That's what your bought coppers might say, it don't make it true. And there's coppers even your gang can't buy, you know."

"Never did I meet the variety."

"The boy's one."

"He's the exception what only proves the rule. That makes him a fool."

"A fool like his own mother?"

"Mairead! Nobody needs die poor in America."

"Who's talking like the great fool he is now?"

"I had enough of this yap. Stand out of my way."

"Think hard what you must do to back that up."

"I'll do it, I swear. I told you fair."

"So much easier is it, the second time around?"

"You'd not be the second I killed, mate. Nor even the third nor fourth. You know better than most the blackness of my soul. But you don't know bloody all ..."

"What's this? How—? You coming at me now ...?"

"For the close range needed, aye."

One man died of a bullet to his stomach, fired by a Mauser vest-pocket pistol. The other man left the house on Ladbroke Street.

CHAPTER 40

"YOUR MOTHER MAIREAD WAS A RARE SWEET ANGEL, WHAT CAN I SAY?"

"It's not the way I knew her."

"The shame's on you then, ain't it, boy?"

"Yes, it is," I admitted.

Sister Sullivan was right. I hated myself for saying that.

"I don't mean she was hard on me as a boy," I said. "It wasn't exactly like that ..."

"Nae, it was the bad times she had is all. Haven't you the charity to see it? Her being a woman alone in a strange new country, with a child to raise up and a war come along and a husband gone left to fight? Cut the woman some slack, boy. She wasn't no better off than us tinkers."

Sister might as well have been a bona fide nun. She shamed me now, and I felt the poison of my own ingratitude deep in my bones.

I said, "I know, Sister, I know ..."

"Mama, I want you to look like this."

"That's only a magazine lady, Neil." Mama picked up the magazine and looked longingly at the woman in the swirling satin dress.

"No, no—I've seen the women like this ..."

The women with their hair done in shops, not in a tenement house kitchen reeking of Toni home permanent solution. The women wearing dresses bought by their husbands from Saks and Bergdorf Goodman, not dresses dispensed to widows from the dead table at Holy Cross Church. The happy women, not the tired ones.

"Not in this neighborhood you haven't."

"But close by, Mama. So close. Outside the theaters I've seen them. And where you work, too."

Mama cried. She always cried when he showed her a magazine lady.

"Well," she said, pulling herself straight again, laughing, running fingers through her brittling hair, *"we've got better things to do with the few little dollars in this house than tarting up your old mama now, haven't we?"*

"There was nothing to her fine upbringing to prepare Mairead for life as she found it. She was a rich girl once, only daughter of the high and mighty Lord Gavan Fitzgerald." Sister turned her head and spat on the floor. "That's in memory of Lord Fitz, making no apology of my ill regard for the bastard. I guess you heard about him?"

"I know of him."

"Your grandfather was a swine. Him and his daughter, they was like night to day. It wasn't any rebellion on her part. Mairead was just one of them rich folks that come 'round as often as January sun. She knew, she did."

"Knew—?"

"That the problem with being poor is poverty, and the problem with being rich is uselessness. Mairead would not tolerate herself being useless as all them rich girls she come up with, see. To her mind, this was a form of stupidity. She made no particular quarrel about it, but no effort neither to submit to the will of her tribe. Naturally, all her rich relations feared and hated her. That lace curtain bunch, they're every bit as intolerant of intellectual freedom as the bogsiders—doubly so when it comes to an Irish *woman* wanting to think for herself."

Sister poured herself more coffee, and lit a cigarette. Ruby took my plate and cup away. I caught her arm, and stroked it.

I said to Ruby, "We've got some hard things to talk about."

She said, "I know, baby."

Then Sister was laughing, blowing blue smoke in crazy circles. "You know what she used to say about money, your mother? Oh, it was the most delicious, subversive thing."

"What?"

"Mairead was always generous with her money, never spending on herself unless she bought the same for two or three more. I asked her once, I says, 'Mairead, dear, why do you get rid of your money so quick? Are you afraid your hands will get dirty?' And your mother, she says, 'When the purse is empty, the heart is full.' Now I ask you, ain't that beautiful?"

"To a fault," I said.

"I called her an angel, not a saint," Sister said. "All great ladies will have their faults."

"How did you come to know her so well?"

"It's her that troubled to know us is the way it was. She made it her business to learn how her father and the rest of the powerful poops was doing their best to dish us tinkers extra portions of the horror and misery during the Depression time."

"What happened to you then?"

"The mighty councils of privilege, sitting in their banks and their bailee courts and their brokerage shops, they put it out to the regular folk taught to respect them how it was us tinkers bringing down the whole house of cards. Imagine—*us*, who wasn't allowed into the house anyhow! The times, they were ripe for the big lie—and scapegoats."

"So I've read."

"I'll give you two short examples of a tall problem. First, there's the man in Cork who loses his carpentry job for the reason of his customers' life savings gone to the bank crash. The carpenter's got the need to strike out, I don't deny him that. Who's it easier for him to hit, I ask you? The nameless ones in their bowlers and suits, or the tinkers in the camp down the road—who are undercutting his price on what little carpentry jobs of work are left about?"

"I see what you mean."

"Now then, that same carpenter needs some money to feed himself and his family. So he goes down to the local bank that's been glad to hold his money for him during the good times, only to learn that since his times now ain't particularly good, there's no loan available to him. The poor sod, he won't do right and steal from them who've got too much anyhow. This is because he's been taught all his life by the priests and the coppers and the rich how it's a mortal sin to steal. So because of this lie about property being sacred, he goes instead and borrows off the gombeen man, which I regret to say is too often a tinker."

"Everybody resents paying high interest."

"Aye, resentment. Like a child's textbook, boy."

"What are you saying my grandfather had to do about this?"

"He exploited the situation, like any rich bastard will do to keep the focus off his own parasitic failings."

"How?"

"You first must understand how deeply us tinkers is hated. We're descended from the ones to first lose their land during the famine. Our ancestors lost their footing, and we never had a chance to get it back, you see. Tinkers, they call us, since the only work anybody's willing to give us is repairing their pots and pans. *Tink, tink, tink* we go at our work all the day long. *Tinkers* we become. People look at us, and they remember them times of famine hell from what the *shanachies* told them."

"And they're afraid."

"Aye, you catch on quick like your angel mother. The regular folk, they think if they touch us they'll lose the roofs overhead and the underfoot, and wind up like us, sleeping under the stars their whole lives."

"It's a short step from fear to hatred."

"Most times it's no step at all."

"You say Lord Fitz exploited the situation."

"Him and his cronies come up with the bright idea of herding all us tinkers from small camps like mine here into big flocks where the coppers can watch us close. Your grandfather, he had the jump on Hitler when it come to concentration camps."

"This happened here?"

"It would have, but for the angel Mairead come to be our savior."

"How—?"

"Lord Fitz maps a brilliant plan he bruits about the Dáil. He says anybody owing usury to the gombeen men should have the right to abolition of debt, with full protection by the government, in return for debtors testifying against tinkers in special courts set up to speed concentration. He's naturally hailed as a genius."

"I get the picture."

"Like your mum. She saw the injustice right off, unlike the useless rich girls she knew. So, she come out to the nearest camp of tinkers she knew, which happened to be one run by me own daddo, may God rest. Me and her, we got along just fine. She took what she knew back into the city, and went about speaking to any fine ladies' group with open minds. She'd tell them ladies how my people are human beings with rights, and we're about more than *tink, tink, tink*. And she'd tell them, too, that poverty is the greatest crime of all."

"Somebody told me my mother was political."

"Aye, she was. She and your daddo, they was quite the team. With her pushing one way at the ladies' clubs, and your dad pushing his fine friends at Trinity College, poor Lord Fitz never stood a chance of seeing his grand plan for exterminating us tinkers. It was the beginning of the end between your mum and her pa."

"My parents, they put the stop to concentration camps?"

"They did, and more. Your mother was famously quoted at the time, on the subject of the law. And this became the shame of the Fitzgeralds, old Lord Fitz being a right proper barrister and all."

"What did she say?"

"Mairead, she says, 'More people are hurt by law makers than law breakers.' This truth she'd say to her proper ladies' clubs. The ladies, bless them, they knew it. After all, it was their own husbands and brothers and fathers in the Dáil what didn't see fit to give them the basic right of voting back in them days."

"If you could have seen her in New York," I said, "you'd have trouble thinking of her as a radical."

"Radical she was, until they pounded it out of her."

"Who—the Fitzgeralds?"

"Them, but they weren't alone in taking her down. I don't like to say it, but your daddo had a part in it. Also that uncle of yours."

Sister stood up and stretched herself.

"You're not through talking to me, are you?" I asked her.

"Any more talk from me's going to require a drop of whiskey. What about you, boy?"

"Maybe later."

Sister reached under her habit and pulled out a flask. She colored another cup of coffee with whiskey, and went on.

"So far as I know, the first political types your mother hooked up with was the Hockaday boys—meaning your father and his brother."

"Uncle Liam?"

"Sure, there was quite the mix down at the pub they all went to way back then. I can't remember it's name . . ."

"The Ould Plaid Shawl?"

"That's it. Everybody of a certain type went there. Those caring about such things as voting, I suppose. Me, I say if voting made a difference they'd outlaw it."

"I think like you."

Sister smiled. "Well, it was fascinating times the young people had for themselves then. Wonderful nights of arguing politics into the purple dawn. Then the pairing-off part of it, if you know my meaning."

"Meaning my mother and father."

"Not at first."

It took plenty of time for the full meaning to sink in. My head, which had only just begun easing up on me, went spongy again. But Sister waited patiently as I thought out what she had intimated.

"There was someone else," I said. "Why shouldn't there be? She was young, beautiful . . ."

I knew what Sister meant. But I could not say it myself.

"Let's put it this way," Sister said, "if you had a brother, how would you like your Ruby straying over to him?"

Liam telling me, "Lose your darling and you're a bloody fool like myself. I lost a darling of my own, long ago, and now you know the great regret of my life."

Liam standing beside me at the open grave in St. John's Cemetery, Queens; me in my crisp rookie blues, him in his scuffed brown shoes and tobacco-reeked tweeds and black rain slicker, crossing himself, wet-nosed and weeping, dropping red roses into her final resting place . . .

* * *

"I'll have that drink now," I said.

Sister found a glass, and filled half of it with whiskey from her flask.

I drank a bit, and the fugitive thought of my grandmother Finola came to mind. I asked, "When she married my father, did that end it with Liam?"

"Aye, so far as *she* was concerned."

"But not him?"

"That takes a bit of explaining. Would you be wanting another drink?"

"I'm okay."

"Now, I don't know all the details, of course. But seeing them all together every so often as I would, I knew Aidan and Mairead was the proper combination. Your uncle, he was lacking in the high spirit your father had. He might have been the smart choice for Mairead of the two of them Hockadays, but she went with her heart . . . Sure you don't want a drink?"

"Thanks, no."

Sister fixed another for herself, this time without the bother of coffee to get in the way.

"Funny to think of it," she said, "but old Lord Fitz might have come to like Liam as a son-in-law, even coming from nowhere like he did. Liam done all right for himself, didn't he now?"

"I guess so."

"Fitz hated Aidan, though. And Aidan, being a high-spirited radical of his time—why, he hated Fitz and the poops something fearsome. I wouldn't be at all surprised if that was the major attraction for Mairead. I said she was an angel, I didn't say she was smart about her men, did I?"

"No."

"Mairead was crazy to get married. She wanted the whole big affair, with the church and all her family. I suppose she couldn't entirely abandon all that she'd come up with."

"I suppose not."

"Lord Fitz—well, you might imagine his reaction."

"Not good."

"He told Mairead, 'I'll break him, your Aidan—and I'll break you, too, if you don't leave him.' "

"And of course, she didn't."

"Didn't leave your dad, no. The two of them announced their engagement. Then Lord Fitz broke them, all right."

"What did he do?"

"He started by seeing to it no priest in Dublin would see fit to marry Aidan and Mairead. This just about killed your mother. Then the bastard Fitz went to work on your dad."

"I think I can guess. He kept my father from working?"

"He did. The bastard saw to it no magazine nor newspaper in the city would publish Aidan Hockaday. Then when your dad had to find himself a teaching job, this was closed to him, too. Aidan was desperate for work. Everywhere he turned, he found the doors closed. Never did he get the breaks. Everybody seemed to know Aidan Hockaday was on his way for a position, and they'd have their doors all ready to slam in his face. It was as if Lord Fitz was one step ahead of him, like he had a pipeline into Aidan's life . . ."

"Like an informer."

"Aye, and I wouldn't be surprised if the informer went by the name Liam. There was such a bitterness between the brothers."

"Did they ever get over it?"

"Not until your dad and mum had no choice but to leave for America."

"You make that sound like a terrible fate. I'm told my dad always wanted to go to New York. I even have a letter he once wrote to Liam, telling him how much he loved the city."

"All I can tell you is that at the time Mairead, at least, was devastated. Mostly because she wouldn't be making the journey as a proper bride. I said she was a fine radical, I never said she was entirely comfortable about it."

"Where did they finally get married?"

"Maybe this will upset you to know, but the two of them were married by my own daddo—in our tinker camp, by our own ceremony."

"You're telling me . . . ?"

"I'm saying so far as I know, they was never proper and legal about it, for what that's worth."

"And that's what you meant by it wasn't over between my mother and Liam so far as *he* was concerned?"

"Aye, it was my impression. I'm sorry to be telling you all this, boy. But Ruby, she explained to me how you come here to know it all." Sister turned to Ruby, and said, "Tell him that's right."

Ruby, who had sat so quietly at the table with Sister all this time, said to me, "You'll be okay with all that, won't you, Hock?"

"Do right by your bonny, and never lose her. You'll not wish to wind up in life lying helpless and lonesome on your back, listening to some faraway melody with lyrics that's stabbing your heart with the memory of old love."

There were two plums hanging on the tree, and he took one of them, therefore neither taking nor leaving plums . . .

CHAPTER 41

THE NEXT DAY, THE PAIN IN MY LEG SUBSIDED ENOUGH FOR ME TO STAND. I could even walk a bit without having to hang on to Ruby.

Oliver Gunston, meanwhile, was having a grand time of it. Once more he took page one by storm, this time by reporting the outraged reactions of government and Trinity College officials to the Nevermore Plan, as dramatically revealed by Peadar Cavanaugh's suicide manifesto.

He was still keeping our names out of the paper, and Gunston had to know by now the same thing that the tinkers had found from their own Garda sources: at least some of the cops were gunning for Ruby and me. He would also assume, since we were not in custody, that we were either dead or in hiding. And so leaving us out of the story for the time being was Gunston's demonstration of positive thinking.

Under the circumstances, I decided we should get on with the trip to County Carlow.

"What's there for you, Hock?" Ruby asked me.

"You'll think I'm nuts when I tell you."

"Like I don't already."

"I want to visit a dream."

304

"Of your father?"

"This dream is mostly a place. My father's in it, but so are some others, including Uncle Liam. The place is a sheepeen, and there's a wake going on."

"In a pub, how convenient."

"There's a big house up on a hill, and a stream . . ."

"Does any of it make sense, Hock?"

"Not until we get there."

"What if we don't?"

"Then nothing will ever make sense."

"We can't have that."

Sister Sullivan made us the loan of a twenty-year-old Volkswagen beetle and the gift of some travel advice.

"I don't need to be telling you to stay off the motorways," she said. "Stick to the little roads the sheep and the farmers use, and you're not likely to be troubled by coppers who might have the eye out for you still. If you leave by noon, you should make it over the Wicklows and into Carlow by five o'clock easy."

"We'll be back in a day or two," I promised bravely.

One of the other tinker women packed up a basket of roast beef sandwiches with mustard on black bread and gave it to us with a gold-toothed smile. Her husband wanted me to take his revolver along for the ride, but I declined the offer.

We were on our way.

An hour south of Dublin, one of the tires blew and there seemed to be a lot of steam gushing up from under the hood. Ruby can sew, she understands stereo components and she can actually set the clock on a VCR. But cars are out of her league. I myself am no good at any of it.

Fortunately, the breakdown occurred near a lakeside village called Pollaphuca, which had a roadside garage. We left the Volkswagen with a mechanic by the name of O'Malley, then followed his directions to an inn where we loitered over tea and biscuits. I used the telephone there and placed a call to Neglio.

"It's about goddamn time you called," the inspector said. As usual, our opening long-distance pleasantries were brief. "What's the matter? Somebody cut you a new place to sit down and all this time you couldn't drag your butt to a phone."

"Gee, it's lovely to hear your voice," I said. "And how's every little thing in New York?"

"There's harps all over town can't wait to see you again, Hock. Only I don't guarantee an entirely friendly reception line."

"What's that supposed to mean?"

"Slattery over at the *Post*, he's running a pickup from that Dublin rag that went and spilled it all about your Irish Nazis."

"The Nevermore Plan?"

"Whatever. That swell little club your old man started up back during the war. It's got the homefront harps rattled so bad you'd think Washington was going to enact Prohibition again."

"I don't get it."

"You ought to. You been to enough St. Paddy's Day parades in your time. For every shillelagh in the crowd there's about a dozen old glories, right? Nobody's quicker with that patriotic crap than your tribe."

"Unless it's your *paisanos.*"

"Now you're getting it, Hock. Old wops, they like to be one hundred percent American. That way, the WASPs don't get tense and start thinking Mafia and Mussolini and like that. You come from a house where the kitchen smells like ravioli, somehow you got to blend in with these people whose kitchens smell like ... I don't know, lettuce. This is just basic survival in the melting pot, okay?"

"Okay."

"Same with harps. Ask the old guys, they know because they're still sensitive. Just when you're comfortable and they're renting you rooms like a human being and hiring you for jobs and they aren't calling you mick so much anymore, along comes this war story about Irishmen and swastikas."

"Rattling stuff."

"Well—Davy Mogaill anyhow, he's pretty rattled."

"Mogaill? He's back?"

"Oh, yeah ..."

With the mention of Mogaill, there was now something strained in Neglio's voice. He sounded like the guest at somebody's house trying to be polite by not mentioning the smell of a dead mouse somewhere under the rug.

"Well—where was he?" I asked.

"Actually, we don't know. Lieutenant Ellis, he says your rabbi must have been dazed in the explosion at his house when Arty Finn got it and he just wandered off in the dark—for like a few days."

"Where is he now?"

"AWOL so far as I'm concerned."

"But he's all right? What happened?"

"I guess he's okay. Right now he's holed up someplace. Who knows? I got the feeling he's waiting for you to get back here before he surfaces."

"Waiting for me?"

"One night out of the blue, Mogaill calls up Ellis, and the two of them have a meet up in the Bronx. Your rabbi's got two things on the agenda. Number one, a tape recording he wants you to know about. Number two, he clears some of the dirty air by telling a story about his dead wife. Who it turns out was some kind of IRA bomb specialist—and also Arty Finn's little sister."

"Brenda was her name."

"That's her, and when she was among the living she was tunneling under Mogaill pretty good. Davy can tell you better than me. Anyhow, from the tape and from what Ellis figures, it looks like Finn got about what he deserves. Same with this Farrelly character."

"So, you're telling me—?"

"You figure it, Hock."

"Public service?"

Neglio said nothing, which was a good answer. A cop of Neglio's rank would not want to admit out loud that toe tags would pretty much be the extent of the homicide investigations of the unlamented Arty Finn and Dennis Farrelly. People have the strange idea that murderers are usually brought to justice. They do not keep score, and they watch entirely too much television.

"All right," I asked, "so what happens to Davy now?"

"He shows up for work sometime, or else I guess he becomes another Judge Crater. If it was me, I'd show. Who'd want to save the city all those years of pension checks?"

"You mentioned a tape recording."

"That's right. Actually, it's the audiocassette tape from that priest's answering machine."

307

"Father Tim."

"Timothy Kelly, that's right—the one who ate the gun. I had the tape transcribed. Your voice is on it, Hock. So is his—and so is this one very intriguing other caller, which makes sense now with those newspaper stories."

"What other caller?"

"Remember what you said about public service?"

"I remember."

"Keep that in mind when I tell you what happened. This guy calls your priest, long-distance it sounds like. He doesn't give a name, but he asks, 'What is a true patriot?' The machine's still on, like Father Kelly picked up in the middle of the call. So we've got him gasping on the line like maybe he's going to blow chunks, and then the padre just says, 'True patriots have guns in their hands and poems in their heads . . . Nevermore!' "

"Right, it makes sense," I agreed.

I did not have to guess the authorship of that poetically coded exchange. Or that Farrelly was the caller. Neglio had stopped guessing, too, by the sound of him.

I thought of poor Father Tim with his rosary in his red-knuckled hands, praying to St. Jude that day I last saw him and his troubled pale face and his puffy neck broken out in a rash. I felt in my pocket, and there was the medallion he gave me. And I thought about a line from Peadar Cavanaugh's letter: *I am an old dog of war . . . my commander has issued a final call, which shall mean my death, one way or another. I choose my own way out of this vale.*

"Hock . . . ?"

Neither one of us had said anything for several seconds.

"I'm here, yeah."

"You don't want to get any deeper in this shit, do you?"

"Not really." I rubbed the back of my thigh, where the dressed wound was still sore.

"Come on home where you belong, Hock. It's all over now."

"Maybe for you, and maybe in New York. But I don't belong there until it's over here."

"Don't be talking like a goddamn martyr."

"I won't die for anybody's opinion."

"You won't have any choice if you get caught in the crossfire of a couple of Irish hardasses having themselves a debate."

"I'll be seeing you, Inspector."

"You wish."

I hoped.

We drank tea, and I filled in Ruby on my talk with Neglio. When we grew weary of hanging around the inn, we hiked back to the garage. O'Malley had the VW patched up, and now was trying to figure exactly how much he could soak me.

"The tire, she'll run you only fifty quid since I happened to have a recap lying around and I wouldn't be wanting to cause undue hardship to a traveler," O'Malley said. He pulled the stub of a pencil from behind his ear, and wrote down this amount on a pad of paper spotted with grease.

"No, of course not," I said.

O'Malley looked up at me, then he screwed his face into pained concentration and said, "Then let's see now ... that radiator. The great leaky old thing, what a horror of a job that was ..."

Ruby kicked the new tire. It sounded like a beach ball bouncing along the Coney Island boardwalk. I saw that it had about as much tread, too. Fifty Irish pounds for a bald beach ball.

"How much for changing the water and adding a little radiator sealant?" I asked.

"Oh, 'tis far more craft to it than that—"

"How much?"

"Another fifty, I'm afraid."

"I'd be afraid to ask for that much, too."

"Shall we call it eighty-five quid in all, accounting for the wee break it's my pleasure giving to American passers-by?"

"Better sixty-five, and a fond memory of Pollaphuca."

"To that I would suggest seventy-five, sir, keeping in mind the sickness of my littlest child."

Ruby kicked the tire again, and said, "Pay it, Hock. It's another three hours to go, and in this thing we'd better get there before dark."

"*Hock*, that's an interesting name," said O'Malley as I peeled off some bills and put them into his hands.

"It's Gaelic for sucker."

*   *   *

309

Ruby drove for the next hour over a flat and lonesome and not particularly interesting terrain. I shut my eyes and tried lying back to sleep, but learned this is impossible in a VW.

There was the engine's high-pitched whine, air whistling through windows that would not shut tight, and the occasional *whump-whump* of wheels slamming over the road's many rough spots. Also the *scritch-scratch* of old windshield wipers beating back something between drizzle and a shower.

I finally gave up. When I opened my eyes, I found Ruby staring at me.

"Are you watching where you're going?" I asked her.

"I guess I can see as far as I need to," she said, glancing up the road for a second or two. Then she turned back. "So, you were dreaming about me?"

"What's to dream? You're here."

"Yes, I am. Cleft and all."

"What?"

"Back in New York, when I took you out to dinner for your birthday, you told me you loved the cleft in my chin."

"I remember."

"Do you remember proposing?"

"I wish you'd watch the road."

Ruby did not turn away. She said, "You made out like you were joking, but we both knew better. So, that was your first proposal. Remember your second?"

"You fell asleep."

"I said I'd get back to you."

"Yeah, you did. It's raining, for crying out loud. Will you look at the road once?"

"I know where we're headed. Do you?"

"We have to talk about this now? Bodies are falling down around us like maple leaves in October, with me being almost dropped myself. We're on the run from the cops in a VW that could break down any minute. And my old man is ... I don't know what, a Nazi."

"Life can be stormy."

"Gee, I guess it can."

"There's calm at the eye of a storm."

"Meaning you?"

Ruby smiled, looked at the road, then back at me. "I hate t
say it, but being calm is woman's work. Men aren't so good a
hard work like that."

"I see why you hate to say it."

"Tell me about my cleft again."

"First you tell me, what you think it would be like for you
you threw in with a cop."

"What's to know that I don't already know, Hock? I know yo
snore on your back with your mouth open."

"Look, I've been married before. I can't help thinking if I did
again I'd be like the crackpot who shows up at the station hous
confessing to some crime he read about in the newspaper."

"God, you're romantic for a guy who snores on his back."

"I don't get a break, do I?"

"O'Malley already gave you one."

"Some break. If you don't look out, we're going to run off th
road."

"Not if I hear what I want to hear."

"Okay, okay. Will you marry me, Ruby?"

"Maybe three's a charm," she said.

Then Ruby pulled the VW to a stop at the roadside. She opene
her door and stepped out, crossed around the front of the car an
pulled open my door.

"You drive now," she said.

"Don't tell me you're suddenly sleepy again."

"Shove over behind the wheel and just drive, Hock."

For the next thirty minutes, with the question hanging in preg
nant silence between us, I drove. Then as we began the long inclin
up into the green Wicklows, the rain let up and the sun appeare
as a fresh ball of orange in the white-washed sky of early after
noon. And stretching over the road we traveled, from the hillto
at our left to the one at our right, was a perfect Irish rainbow.

Ruby said, "They say there's gold at the end of a rainbow."

I said, "They never mentioned which end."

CHAPTER 42

TWICE I HAD SEEN THIS ANCIENT PLACE IN MY NEW DREAMS. ITS COLD, smooth walls and colored glass windows, atop a hill back up from the low sheepeen. I could wonder what lay inside, but I had seen its exterior, and only in the foggy moonlight.

Now it was near sundown. Now I was here for the third time. Now, inside the graystone manor house.

Ruby and I stepped through a slate-floored vestibule, then into a long and very dark entrance hall with a collection of different-size rugs laid end-to-end down the middle of the floor. The place smelled of tobacco, stale beer and ammonia. Back at the end of the hall, we could see a man's head and shoulders behind a desk with a lamp on it. As we walked toward the desk we saw eight rooms along the way, four to a side. Only two seemed in use. A group of old women with knitting in their laps sat in one, watching a blinking television set. The other occupied room was a bar, the quietest one I have ever seen, with a scattering of old men drinking pints.

The desk was a carved mahogany beauty that did not belong. It was massive enough to serve a major hotel in New York or London, and it spoiled the dramatic view of a grand staircase

behind it. There were a couple of Chinese garden pots at either end of the desk, inside of which were date palms dying from lack of oxygen and light.

"How might I help you?" the man at the desk inquired. He looked up from the newspaper he had been paging through. He was somewhere past sixty years of age, not by much, with a nimbus of silver curls around his head, a long sharp beak of a nose and hard brown eyes that darted quickly over Ruby and me, and our bags. "Would you be passin' through, or stayin' over in Tullow?"

"You're Mr. Roarty?" I asked.

"Aye, Ned Roarty." A middle-aged woman with gray streaks in her black hair appeared behind him. She was taller and younger than Roarty, and maybe thirty pounds bigger. Her features were mannish, and the same as his, the hard eyes, sharp nose and thin pursed lips, turned down at the corners as if she had just drunk vinegar. Roarty pointed an ink-stained thumb at her, and said, "This here's me daughter, Annie."

"The sign outside, it says you have rooms?" I asked.

"The sign don't lie," Roarty said. His eyes danced over our fingers. When he saw they were bare of rings, he asked sternly, "You'll be wantin' two rooms then?"

"Just one," I said.

"Maybe with a window looking out over that beautiful stream," Ruby said.

Ned Roarty muttered, "We'll see, ma'am, we'll see." He turned and scanned the wooden cabinet fixed to the wall behind his desk. The cabinet was a warren of mail slots, most of which were empty except for the kind of room keys sold nowadays in antique shops. Roarty hummed and contemplated the possibilities. His daughter stared at us with her sour face.

"Here now's the ticket," Roarty said, turning back to us with a big iron key in his hand. He shoved aside his newspaper. Beneath it was a pen and the cloth-bound registry, which he opened and tipped toward me to sign. He said to Ruby, "Number Six is a lovely suite with front bay and balcony, ma'am. All the way up top o' the stairs, so's you'll see down to where the water bends round and into the falls where they cast for salmon."

"That sounds very good," Ruby said.

"How much?" I asked.

"You're stayin' how many nights?"

"I don't know, it depends."

"Dependin' on what, might I ask?"

"On whether three's a charm."

"I don't follow you, sir."

"I never meant you should. I only asked the price of the room."

"Shall we say fifty quid, one night's advance?"

I nodded and signed our names in the registry. Ruby opened up her purse and paid him. Annie Roarty came around from behind the desk, not cheerfully, picked up our bags, and said, "Come, I'll take ye, long's you paid."

We followed Annie Roarty's steady trudge up four flights of wide and echoing stairs, until we reached our suite. I naturally considered the ironies at work. Here we were again, being led to our quarters in a great house by a large, sullen woman; here we were again, entering into a house that breathed mystery.

The suite had seen better days. The sitting room was plainly furnished, to put it charitably. There were two straight-backed chairs covered in torn silk, a small round table stacked with yellowed paperback novels, and a couch that dipped badly in the middle, as if a fat guy with a lap full of bricks had sat in the same spot every day for twenty years. The adjoining room contained a dresser and wardrobe, both of dented veneer, and a bed the fat guy had slept in. Plaster on the ceiling and most walls puckered with brown water stains.

As Roarty had promised, though, the balcony was very good. I stepped out and saw the stream below, down past the sheepeen at the bottom of the hill, winding crookedly into cascades around a bend of thick fir trees. The darkening Wicklows brooded on the horizon. There were rock ledges and boulders dotting the cold rushing water, covered in whitened grass like piano shawls, just as they were in the dreams. I almost expected to see Davy Mogaill smoking a pipe, calling to his Brenda in the evening mists, as in the dream.

"Like't all right then?" Annie was asking.

I turned from the view of the stream. Annie stood next to Ruby in the bedroom, just inside the French doors to the balcony. Ruby was looking at me, but speaking to Annie. "It will do us fine," she said.

"I'll be goin' then," Annie said. But she did not move.

I stepped back into the bedroom and gave Annie a pound note. Then I pulled another fiver from my wallet, and said, "This would be for your time in telling me something about this place."

"Such as what, sir?"

"The emptiness of the house, such as. I have the feeling we're the only guests."

"Well, that's so."

"How do you survive?"

"By sellin' the furnishin' around the place, year by year," Annie said, turning the fiver over in her hands, as if she had not seen one in a long while. "We're down t'bone now, as you see, sad and plain. And here's what I'm sellin' you now, my troubles."

"Where did your business go?"

"I don't know no better than anybody else in Tullow. I can only say we ain't got the rich hunters comin' in from Dublin like the old times, and there's precious little reason for anyone t'be here on any other account. Poor old Tullow's never seen fit to accommodate to new times of the outside world, so you see what you see, a peelin' old country inn without enough good payin' customers to keep proper standards."

"This was a hunting lodge once?"

"Aye, the last time it had any importance. Downstairs there was a fine big kitchen and master chef, and two refrigerated rooms for the wild game, and a wondrous dining hall. Oh, the grand dinners that was served here once." Annie slipped the money into a side pocket of her skirt, then placed hands on wide hips and surveyed the room, her eyes falling on a water stain snaking down from the ceiling to a baseboard along one wall. "Shameful how everything's tumblin' down, but what's there to be done? It's been a lovely place, though, before the world went all fast and vile."

"How long ago was this a hunting lodge?"

"Oh, five year it's been now, truly. We'd have the faithful ones up to a year ago, though. But only for the ghost of past comforts."

"And before it was a hunting lodge?"

"Goin' way back t'my girlish days, this here was a monastery.

The monks took it over when the English was all driven out from their fine country mansions, see."

"Of which, this was one?"

"Aye."

"You've been a great help to me, Annie."

"I have, sir?" Annie Roarty's face now filled with curiosity, as much question as I saw in Ruby's own face. Then something else in Annie, some dread that overtook the hardness in her eyes. She said hastily, "I'd best go now, you'll be wantin' privacy after your journey."

Ruby walked with her to the door. I returned to the balcony. When Annie was on her way down the steps, Ruby closed the door and locked it.

It was almost black now, and the air more chilled than it had been only a minute ago. I could no longer see the bend of the stream, nor many of the boulders. There was only a crescent moon in the sky, and the dark hills of the Wicklows that framed the valley of my forebears were felt, but invisible.

Ruby came to my side.

"This place badly creeps me," she said.

"I know," I said. "He's here."

CHAPTER 43

CAPTAIN DAVY MOGAILL, ROCKING ON HIS BARSTOOL WITH HIS HEAD IN his hands, said, "Well . . . I appreciate what you done."

"Skip the blubber. I saved your life is all. Want this?" Lieutenant Ray Ellis offered Mogaill a White Owl cigar wrapped in cellophane. Mogaill opened it, and lit up. Ellis asked, "What are you going to do now?"

"What would you recommend?"

"Climb out of your freaking grave."

"I'll consider that." Mogaill finished what was in his glass, then knocked it twice on the bar as the signal to Terry Two for another round. "But first, my friend, I'll be having myself a long, sweet drunk."

Terry Two approached, reluctantly. He and Ellis passed a look. Then Terry said to Mogaill, "It's enough now, Davy, isn't it?"

Mogaill laughed grimly, and said, "Can you not see I've two options? I can drink, or I can weep. Drinking's ever so much more subtle."

"Go ahead, I'll buy the hump one more blast," Ellis said, covering his own glass with his hand. Terry Two shook his head and poured another Scotch for Mogaill. Ellis said to Mogaill, "And then, Davy, it's time."

"Time? That awful place where everybody's lost?"

"I told Inspector Neglio you'd at least call him in the morning."

"And then what?"

"You do what you have to do."

"Resign?"

"Looks like it, Davy."

"I don't know how I'd live."

"You got your pension if you do the right thing now, and house insurance. That ought to be enough. It ain't like you got a kid in college. You want something to do during the day, you could maybe move down to Coconuts, Florida, or someplace. Get yourself a chief-of-police gig."

"Maybe."

"Come on now, Davy. Bottoms up. Then we go home."

"Where's home?"

"That you got to tell me."

"I'm staying in the Bronx with a bunch of old men, one to a window."

CHAPTER 44

WE TOOK DINNER DOWNSTAIRS IN THE TOMB THAT DOUBLES AS A BAR AND Tullow's only restaurant, so Ned Roarty informed us when we asked at the desk. So we had the leek soup, mutton, potatoes and bread, in contrasting shades of beige. There was no choice in the matter. It was Saturday night, which meant mutton and so forth on the only menu of the only restaurant in town. We had little choice of seating, either. Annie Roarty installed us at an unpopular table in the middle of the room, and she did not look much in the mood for an argument.

A few of the old folks we saw earlier were seated at tables along the wall, or against windows, ladies and gents together now and all in great seriousness. Ned or Annie would approach their tables and they would order their drinks, and the exchanges were so familiar it looked as if everyone was performing lines in a play. Anyone to the point of eating their beige dinner appeared to be asleep.

The bar itself did a slightly livelier business. There was muffled conversation and glasses clinking. A middle-aged couple argued softly; whatever the grievance, it was not difficult to see habit and regret at the root of it. A small group of suited men, business types, were drinking martinis and trying to impress one another. A bored prostitute drinking sherry gazed at a man in a black suit and hat sitting by himself.

"When you come in, you never told me your name was *Hockaday*," Ned Roarty said when he reached our table to take drink orders.

He did not say this loudly. Nonetheless, there was a stir. Everyone woke up and stared at us when my name was spoken. We were easy to see right there in the middle of the room.

"What if I had?" I asked him.

"It's surprisin' is all, the name's an old one hereabouts."

"So I understand." I looked over to the nearest table where there were old folks staring at me. One of the old girls took thick spectacles from a beaded purse and wiped them down with a napkin. I said, loud enough for the eavesdroppers, "I've come to Tullow looking for people who can tell me something about my father—Aidan Hockaday."

There was now a definite current circulating through the room. I had no way of knowing then whether it was good or bad. Certainly there was curiosity in the crowd, natural and innocent enough given the fact that few if any black women had ever visited the place. In the case of three geezers down at the end of the bar, I imagined the worst. They put on their caps and scowled at me as they left. Two walked out the door, the third came up and whispered something in Roarty's ear before leaving himself.

"Looks like I drove out the old boys somehow," I said to Roarty when he was back attending to us.

"Nae, they're only clearing out down to the sheepeen," he said. "Days up here on the hill, nights down below. It gives variety to life."

"Some life," Ruby said.

"I'll admit it ain't New York, but they like't here well enough, ma'am," Roarty said.

"The old guy whispered something to you, Mr. Roarty," I said. "What was it?"

"He said, sir, that you was to come down to the sheepeen yourself in one hour's time."

"Really."

"We'll be there," Ruby said.

"Oh—but no, ma'am!" Roarty was shaken. There was laughter rippling around tables within earshot. "It's the sheepeen, y'know. For the men folks only."

"Isn't that the wonderful thing about travel, though?" I said to Ruby. "No matter where you go, things have a way of staying the same. Like the sheepeen here, and that Park Avenue joint with the maître d' . . . What's his name?"

"Pierre," Ruby said, smiling.

"There's this place in New York," I said to Roarty, "where the men don't care for the women—" I was about to say more, but Ruby stopped me.

"Don't bother, Hock," Ruby warned. "I really don't mind staying in while you go on down to your smelly men's bar."

The old girls around us laughed. The old boys did not.

"Well now, Mr. Roarty, let's have a bottle of your best claret," Ruby said. "Then you may bring on the filth."

Ruby then turned on me. "As for you, Mr. Hockaday, let's have your answer. What do you mean, *he's here* . . . ?"

"I mean it all fits together now. I don't have a hollow place anymore."

"That's good?"

"It's a good question. So was the one I asked this afternoon for the third time. How about your answer?"

"Dear charming man, it can keep 'til the morning, can't it?"

One hour later, I was heavy with my dinner of mutton and I had run my case past Ruby. She walked me out to the veranda, and stood there watching as I made my way down the lane and off the hill toward the sheepeen.

I turned, and looked at her there in the moonlight. Her slim figure was softly backlit by the inn's open doorway. She waved, and I heard her voice floating down through the wet air. "Be careful, Hock . . ."

No, I would never lose her, I promised myself.

I then walked through a darkness so thick I could not see my feet sloshing through the grass, nor my hands swinging at my sides. But I heard the noise of the sheepeen, and even the rushing stream beyond. And from my dreams, I knew the way.

It was just as I knew it would be, the image planted in my

head as a boy by Uncle Liam's tales. The men of the village
sitting around tables, smoking and drinking and making supper
of fadge and stew. Dressed in their farmer's tweeds, all save a
priest in his suit and collar. All of them arguing about any
arguable subject.

But as I entered the door, all fell quiet. As if a funeral were
about to be held.

"Jaysus, Mary and Joseph—it's him!" someone shouted. "Young
Aidan himself come back from the past! Saints help us all!"

"Looks even a wee bit like his grampus," another man said.
There was much laughter at this. Then someone else shouted
"What d'you say about it, Father?"

The question was asked of the elderly priest seated at a table
in the middle of the cramped room, a pint of stout and a jigger
of whiskey in front of him. The priest did not answer directly.
Instead, he looked me up and down, then raised a cupped hand,
and said, "Come, son—let's see you close."

The men made way for me. When I reached the priest's table,
I held out my hand, and said, "Neil Hockaday, Father." The priest
was older than he looked from the doorway, maybe ninety or
more. The years had corrupted what was once a darkly handsome
face. His hair was still thick, combed straight back in steel gray
quills, and this is mainly what made him younger from a distance.
His eyes were bright and blue, sunk into his spotted face. His jaw
was still youthfully square, but full of an old man's shakes and
tics now.

A man to my left said, " 'Tis Father McGing you're addressin'."

"Father McGing," I said. The priest took my hand. It was large,
and surprisingly rough for a priest's hand.

"You do look strongly like Aidan," McGing said. "And
there's a touch of your grandmother Finola I can see in you,
too. And aye, I'll admit you're generally possessed of your
grampus's face."

Someone put a pint of stout in my hand. Someone else shouted
from the back of the room, "What about the prayer now, Father?"
And this request became a thumping demand, the men pounding
pints and glasses and fists on the tabletops, chanting, "The prayer,
the prayer, the prayer . . ."

Father McGing stood up and raised his hands high over his

head, silencing the smoky room. And when he had order, he said
what I had heard in Liam's house:

"Dear God, tonight as we partake of thy kindest bounty,
know that we'll be eating and drinking to the glorious, pious
and immortal memories of thy own Sainted Patrick and our
great good brother Brian Boru—who assisted, each in his respective way, in redeeming us Irish folk from toffee-snouted Englishmen and their ilk. We ask a blessing, if you please, on the
Holy Father of Rome—and a shit for the Bishop of Canterbury.
And to those at this table unwilling to drink to this, may he
have a dark night, a lee shore, a rank storm and a leaky vessel
to carry him over the River Styx. May the dog Cerberus make
a meal of his rump, and Pluto a snuffbox of his skull, and may
the Devil jump down his throat with a red hot harrow, and
with every pin tear out a gut and blow him with a clean carcass
to hell. Amen."

There was an explosion of laughter, followed by several seconds
of silence. Then Father McGing picked up his glass and solemnly
raised it, and said, *"Do schláinte, a chailleach!"* To which the men
replied in unison, with their own glasses raised, *"Sláinte na bhfear
agus go ndoiridh tú bean roimh oiche!"*

Father McGing held out his glass to me. I lifted my own, and
we clinked.

"What did the Gaelic mean?" I asked.

"It means a number of important things," Father McGing
said. "Good health to you. Welcome to the soil of great Irish
patriots ..."

Father McGing paused, and leaned forward to poke my chest
with a finger. I felt his hot breath in my face as he said, "And
may your good new blood replace the old."

Tears rolled from Father McGing's eyes, sudden and free. Then
he was surrounded by his table mates, who patted his shoulders,
pulling him gently away from me. I heard one of the men say,
"It's enough for now, Cor ... rest yourself."

Cor.

*... the randy priest who mum was carrying on with for all the years.
The priest's name was Cor ...*

"No!" said Father McGing. He broke free of his mates, stepping
back to me. He put his hands on my shoulders, pulling me into

an embrace. And he whispered, "Would you like seeing him now, boy?"

"I found my way, didn't I?"

His arm linked in mine for support and guidance in the dark, Father Cor McGing and I then walked back up the hill to Roarty's inn. And all he said to me was, "You found us, all right, you might as well know."

CHAPTER 45

"I HATE IT! PLEASE GOD, I HATE IT."

Having said this, he was at peace with all he had told me this night of treachery and war, murder and remorse. And a secret love I had already guessed . . .

"I was the perfect one to lead it, so Cor had me convinced. Me being in New York and all. So it's what I did for the cause. In those days, any Irishman active in politics was suspect. But it was nothing for an American soldier to be in London, see. It's how I managed to land there, after first getting myself detached in battle and presumed dead or captured.

"This next part, I give to you straight and quick, Neil. Time and war's made it quite incidental to the story, you might come to agree. It's just this: Liam and me, we're only brothers by half. Same mother, two different dads. You see? Myles Hockaday, he sired Liam, but that's all he done. Father Cor McGing, may God and the church forgive him for his love of a woman's flesh, he's my own real da.

"Anyway, there was waiting for me in London this true certificate of my Irish birth, with my true dad's name signed at the bottom—Cor McGing. And now I am no longer Aidan Hockaday, I am one Aidan

McGing, who has no past by his bastard name. Never would I know this—nor Liam, nor now you—if not for the needs of the cause. If not for the cause, old Cor would've taken the secret of his love to his grave, just as Myles and Finola done.

"Mine may well be one of a million tawdry tales. For one reason or the next, for one trouble or another, there was lots like me in that war—men with getting lost and forgotten uppermost in mind. All the wars of history have given troubled men such escape. Most had no cause, and led their secret lives until death. Others, like me, used this gift of anonymity as a tool for what we enjoyed believing was far greater good.

"My comrades and I in England, we done what we could by an ally in common, that being Germany. Some were saboteurs, some murderers, some inspiration to these actions. Some took jobs on the docks of London, and in the telephone exchange, and up in the mills of Birmingham and Coventry. All that was learned at such sensitive places was passed along to Berlin.

"I myself did all these things. And paid dear for it, too. I lost my sight to a blasting cap I once strung up to a London tram.

"This was my life, Neil. I had no other, save trusting for Liam's word through the years of the wife and baby son I had sacrificed.

"We done it for the German weapons we needed, and for German gold, and to bloody hell with England. And don't you look at me that way, boy! Listen!

"There is Ireland, and there is England. The histories we have built are the mirror opposites of each other. What the Englishman sees as glory, victory and the pursuit of happiness, as the Americans say, the Irishman knows as degradation, misery, ruin—and famine. England's freedom is Ireland's slavery. It was so for eight centuries before the republic, it is so today—in Ulster. And so it is we say, Nevermore.

"Long before I, there were Irishmen providing refuge and giving succor to England's enemies. The patriot's motto is, England's crisis is Ireland's opportunity. And in every moment of weakness, a patriot's duty is to stab his enemy in the back. As I did, one man in the long, mad history of my country.

"Well might you ask if I'm proud of what we done. I would admit to you first that I am not a good man. A good man commits no crime, nor does he fail to speak out against crimes he sees. Thus the good man lives without remorse. But I am bad, and have committed many crimes, and

*have not spoken out. Until now, boy, to you. To tell you that in order
to live, I have invented my own ultimate forgiveness.*

*"I have thought carefully on my life of crime. And it comes to me I
must atone, and that the only means of it is by heeding the spirit of a
verse written on a long-ago photograph of myself, written by a great
poet and patriot before he died—Yeats himself. That photograph I gave
to your mother, Neil.*

*" 'Drown all the dogs!' says the verse. It comes to me this means the
killing and the hating—the warring—has got to stop somewheres in the
line of history, and that it rightly falls to one who committed the most
crimes to drown it all. You see?*

*"I must drown the very dogs of war I made, the old and the new.
The whole bloody lot of them sleeping dogs—among the police and the
clergy and the counting houses, here in Ireland and everywhere else we
are. Drown them all! It's the only way. You see?*

*"There's not much time left to me now, Neil. I'm near my last, and
there's evil forces against me. My own brother, Liam, being most important among these ..."*

He turned his head toward the wall now, as if to feel a morning's warmth at the unseen window.

It was well past midnight, into black Sunday, but the time of
day had no meaning for him. A smile played carefully across his
face as he lay in his bed, a bed too big for him alone. I put my
hand on his. He let it lie there atop his paper skin.

I asked, "What is it you hate?"

He drew a deep breath and his blind blue eyes closed. Then he
quoted again, from what his mind still pictured of pages he used
to read, time and again: "Out of Ireland have we come; great
hatred, little room, maimed at the start ... I carry from my mother's womb a fanatic heart."

There was silence when I should have offered reaction, the kind
of embarrassed quietude that tells an old man he has not been
understood by a younger man. His useless eyes fluttered open
and he said, with some exasperation, "It's the root of this madness
I've grown to hate, it's old men at their windows I hate even
more." Then he lifted my hand away and said, "Now get you
off." That would be all for now, whether or not I understood. He
needed rest.

I walked to the door and opened it, but turned to look at him once more before leaving. He sensed this. His head rose slightly over the mound of blankets. He said, "When I'm gone, I want you to remember me."

I said, "Haven't I always?"

I stepped into the tiny hall outside my father's attic room, to where my grandfather, Cor McGing, stood waiting, a rosary in his hand.

From the bottom of the stairs came the pop of a small gun fired.

And the sound of a falling man.

Then someone crashing his way upstairs toward McGing and me.

A man in a black suit and hat, a pistol in his hand.

CHAPTER 46

"OUT OF THE WAY, BOY!"

He shoved past me, jamming the heated barrel of the pistol he had just fired into my ribs. This was not the most powerful force I have met in my time, but I fell, helpless in the shock of seeing my Uncle Liam on his feet.

It could have been worse. Down at the bottom of the stairs, there was Ned Roarty pinwheeling on the floor, roaring in pain, his hand masking a bullet hole in his shoulder, blood streaming through his tight fingers. I could hear Annie Roarty screaming for him now, "Da, I'm comin' . . . What's happened, da—?"

McGing grabbed at Liam's black coat as he pushed by him, too. But the old priest was no use in stopping a man with terrible intent. McGing staggered on his frail legs, then collapsed, striking his head on the floor. Liam flung open the door to Aidan's room, pulled back the hammer of his gun and stepped inside.

"Bastard!" he cried, bounding toward the bed. "I found you!"

I heard another shot, the same small-caliber pop as seconds before. Then a second shot, this one powerful. On my belly, I scrambled toward the door to my father's room.

Liam lay very still and very dead on his back, on the floor at

329

the side of my father's bed. His chest had a hole in it the size of a baseball. The blood-flecked black hat he wore rolled from his body, coming to a stop at a table leg. His black coat was now sopped with red, his startled face and open eyes streaked with blood. And still the blood flowed, making soft sucking sounds as it spurted from the gaping wound. He had been shot square in the heart.

I took a small German-made pistol from Liam's right hand. There were three slugs missing from the magazine.

In my father's hand was a double-barrel shotgun, sawed off at the front and back. He was sitting up in the bed, ugly and straight as his weapon, his blind blue eyes seeing nothing. There was a small bloody hole at the top of his chest, just under the collarbone.

Aidan dropped the shotgun, and covered the hole in his chest with his hand. "It's over?" he asked. He seemed so defenseless, yet he had just taken a gun from beneath his bedcovers and killed a man he could not see.

I pulled myself to my feet, and answered, "Yes."

"You there is it, Neil?"

I started toward him. "Yes."

"Come, there's not much time . . ."

I was now at his side. He was having difficulty breathing.

"I tried this a year ago," Aidan said, rushing himself, wanting me to understand. I smelled the sweetness of blood on his dying breath. "He come at my calling for a hunting trip in the Wicklows, which was when I shot him. He was to be the first dog drowned, see . . ."

"Only you missed."

"Aye, I dropped him, but it never finished him off. He went to the wheelchair, but the faking old fox never stood until he figured his moment of revenge was right."

"Meaning until he found you?"

"That's it."

"I know it's more than politics," I said. "I know about you and my mother and Liam—about the three of you, going back to your days at Trinity College."

"He loved her first. And said I stole her away, which I did, only to abandon her and you to the cause. And even though I was gone to the life of Aidan McGing, your mother stayed true.

This infuriated him, this above all else. To Liam, the idea of a lass so fair and fine as Mairead throwing away her womanhood like she done . . . well, by his lights it was unforgiveable."

God of irony. Liam with Moira in his house all those years, poor mooning Moira, the girl next door who threw away her womanhood; Moira, who knew how very deep and secret this all was, poor Moira, who died for what she knew. Did she hang herself, or did Liam kill her? Or Snoody? Who would ever know?

My father gasped, and pitched forward. I put a supporting arm around his thin shoulders, and my hand over his, covering the wound. Death would be quick. I had to put the questions to him now, to confirm the final bits of the puzzle.

"I don't understand about Patrick Snoody," I said.

"Patty was loyal to me, up to a point. After the hunting incident, I wanted him to take out Liam. He could do it clean and simple, no more than slipping a pillow over an old man's sleeping head. But Patty refused, and said he wouldn't see either of us brothers killed unless by old age. Or maybe Patty figured that drowning Liam would set the cycle in motion for his own end. Well, it was then I knew I had to go into hiding somewhere. I could trust nobody in Liam's house, see."

I saw only madness. And marching feet, and more marching feet. And like the man who gave my father and me the name of Hockaday, I now shed tears for all wronged Irishmen.

"Liam brought me here, to help him hunt you down," I said.

"I believe so, Neil. He was sick and vengeful, and wanted me bad enough to use even you in a dangerous game . . ."

Vengeful and sick the both of you!

"The way I'm figuring, he'd lure me out one of two ways no matter what happened to you. Liam could have you set up for killing. That'd enrage me, and force me to show myself. Or, he could rely on you as a detective to do your nosing about. Then he'd follow you straight here to me, which we see that he's done."

Aidan gasped again, and his head wobbled and fell to the side. He said one more thing before dying, "Now, boy, flee! Flee the rest of your Irish treachery! Go home, go home . . ."

I laid him back down in his bed and shut his blind eyes forever, ashamed of the only thing I could feel: contempt for my father, who cheated me out of his life. I left him, and walked through the door. Cor McGing still stood there in the hallway. But his presence now grew dark and strange, his voice an echo of my father's dying breath.

"I'll be sorrier than you know for doin' this," he said, reaching into his side pocket. He pulled out the same model of German pistol Liam had used on Roarty, still moaning away down at the bottom of the stairs. "I truly loved Aidan and Liam. But while they were survivin' one another all these many years, there was no way of servin' them both. Nae, they forced us all to choose between them, see, starting with your own mum."

"Give me the gun, Cor," I said, stepping forward. He refused me, raising the pistol instead, waving it wildly around. I retreated back into the doorway, my hands uplifted.

"Some say, it was a devil's bargain either way. Well, I chose to bargain with your da, though he was bent on destroyin' the cause these past few years. No matter, I stuck by him, a loyal soldier." McGing advanced, looking coldly past me to see the bloody waste of Liam and Aidan. "No need of choosin' sides now that we see both devils are gone."

"Cor, the gun," I said, trying again. "Give it to me. We'll end all of it, right here and now."

"Nae, I'm no longer bound by your da's wishes. And I did not serve Liam. So it's me and saying all on his own—Nevermore!" He stepped very close to me now, pistol flailing, as if he were hacking his way through tall fen grass. "I cannot let you be goin' to tell the outside world about this, boy—none of it, not a word."

McGing—my grandfather, my Grandmother Finola's dutiful priest and lover—pointed the pistol straight at my belly.

Flee the rest of your Irish treachery . . .

The pistol shook in his trembling hand.

He cocked the trigger.

And I thought back, one week to the day, of another desperate priest.

Always keep this in your pocket while you're on the other side, Neil. And for the sake of your life with Ruby Flagg, remember it's there when you need it.

I pulled Father Tim's medallion from my pocket.

"What's that you're doing?" McGing said.

"Take it." I handed him the medallion.

McGing dropped the gun, discharging a shot that cracked deep into the floorboards, harming no one but the mice. Though it well might have been the other way around, my grandfather looked at me now the way a mortally wounded man eyes his killer in that final, horrible twitch of life: eyes full of pity, resigned to the world's unending fool violence. No killer ever forgets this look.

A killer I surely was, for I had slain something that lay inside my Grandfather Cor McGing. Something dark, and worthy of death.

Of the medallion, he asked, "It's Tim's, is it?"

I picked up the warm gun. "It was."

McGing turned the medallion over and over, lips scarcely moving as he whispered an intemperate verse, stolen by dogs of war. *When nations are empty up there at the top . . . When order has weakened or faction is strong . . . Time for us all to pick out a good tune . . . Take to the roads and go marching along.* Obedience to the corrupted sentiment of an Irish poem had defined my grandfather's life, had turned his heart to steel. But now, with the passage of a fallen comrade's medallion, he wept.

"By honor mutually pledged among us brothers in the cause, I'm obliged to spare you, come what may." McGing stopped for a moment, as if the sound of his voice no longer made sense to him. He held up the medallion. "It's the meaning of the thing, see. On giving you this, Tim Kelly took his life. By his ultimate sacrifice, he insured your own safe passage among us."

It was not in me to be grateful for such twisted mercy. Again, I felt only contempt. "Some honor," I said.

CHAPTER 47

GO HOME. DARK AS IT WAS, WE DECIDED TO LEAVE THAT NIGHT.

I did not bother leaving money for the dinner bill I had signed.
Also I helped myself to a portable tank of gasoline I found in Ned
Roarty's garage. If Roarty wanted payment, I told him, he should
call out the local constabulary. Of course then he would have to
explain about the bodies upstairs. He saw things my way.

Anyhow, I considered my debt more than covered by medical
services rendered, in as much as I cleaned up the swollen mess
of his shoulder. Liam's bullet had landed in a soft spot between
meat and bone. Lucky for Roarty. Once the blood was sponged
away, I managed to calm down Annie, too. Then she and her old
man took a few drinks together, and she was off to fetch the
village doctor to extract the bullet and keep his mouth shut about
it, at least until Ruby and I reached Dublin.

On the road at last, with the scattered lights of Tullow growing
tiny behind us, Ruby said, "You seem so angry, Hock." She was
right. It was only anger that kept me from collapsing into grief,
like Cor McGing. For several minutes, I had nothing to say, and
I knew this worried Ruby. She placed a hand lightly on my arm
as I drove.

334

Finally, it came out of me. "I was looking for something here, and I hate what I've found. My father and my uncle took their vengeance, making everybody pay for the brutality of it; I've got a grandfather on one side who exploited the weak, and another who kept what he calls *honor*. None of these guys are honorable, they're cowards. This is my ancestral heritage, a string of cowardly bastards. So I'm showing my appreciation for my native land in the usual Irish way."

"Which is—?"

"I'm getting out of it as fast as I can."

"Don't be so hard on yourself. You're only a man, sadder but wiser."

"And still with my hollow places."

"Not anymore, Hock. There's your mother in you. You should know that, and think about her every day. She was glorious. I think you've been looking for a hero, now you've found one."

Ruby stretched herself. "I'm going to try to sleep now," she said, settling herself as comfortably as she could in her half of the tiny car. I thought about Mairead Fitzgerald Hockaday as I drove.

There would be no rainbow this time through the Wicklows. Only the musty dark outside, and the phosphorescent glow of the dashboard, and the high winds that kept us bouncing along in the Volkswagen.

On the other side of the mountains, daylight broke. Ruby took the wheel now while I slept. I did not dream. And knew that I would never dream of my father again.

When I woke, we had reached Sister Sullivan's camp at the north end of Dublin's countryside. My bones felt broken, and I vowed never to set foot in a VW ever again.

We washed ourselves in a spring, near where the horses were kept. I lay down in a green field, in the warmth of the morning sun, and shut my eyes. Ruby went off. For coffee, she said.

I dozed.

There was a stirring in the grass, and I woke. The tinkers were ringed around me, the men in suitcoats and hats, the women dressed in their most colorful skirts. Children with scrubbed faces held hands over laughing mouths.

Ruby wore flowers in her hair. Sister Sullivan held a Bible in her hands.

Ruby smiled, and said, "I'll marry you now, Neil Hockaday."

And so we were wed, as my own parents were.

Late that afternoon, we walked into the American Embassy in Dublin.

"We'll be seeing the ambassador now," I said to a fussy reception clerk.

"Oh, will we?"

"Tell him it's Mr. and Mrs. Neil Hockaday."

Ruby corrected me. "I said I'd take you, Hock. Not your name."

"Just whom shall I say is calling?" the clerk insisted.

"Tell the ambassador I'm the guy who'll see he's canned the hell out of here unless I get what I want. The name you already heard."

About five minutes later, I was using the ambassador's security line to ring up Inspector Neglio in New York.

"I'm coming home, boss. Only first, there's a wee bit of trouble here for me. Let's see how big a guy you are. Talk to the ambassador, and get us on the next flight out."

Neglio squawked, but he and the ambassador got us to the airport with no trouble from anybody.

Before we boarded for New York, I telephoned Oliver Gunston.

"Here's what I want you to do for me, Ollie. Find a decent lawyer and have him call me in New York. I'll be claiming the estate of my late Uncle Liam Hockaday of Dún Laoghaire. There's not much trouble to dividing the proceeds. The money goes in two directions. Enough for yourself to take a year off to write your book on all this, and the rest to a tinker woman called Sister Sullivan, to do with as she sees fit . . ."

"There'll be trouble about that, all right," Gunston said.

"Then I'd advise you to engage the firm of my maternal grandfather."

"Lord Fitzgerald's shop? Representing tinkers? I like it."

"Tell them they'll be handling the matter pro bono. Say that it's reparations for what old Fitzy did to a lot of poor folks. And if they don't like it, tell them I'll be back in Dublin to make things very embarrassing."

"I like it!"

"Now, about the house. It's a big place in Ladbroke Street out there in Dún Laoghaire. I want it to go to some people in Goff Street, Dublin. To Catherine Boylan, Catty for short, the widow of the late Francie Boylan. To her babies, and her father-in-law, Joe. Put the place in Catty's name. Joe took a swing at me once."

Epilogue

"SORRY I GAVE IT ALL AWAY, BABE. I NEVER EVEN THOUGHT. YOU COULD use some of that cash yourself, couldn't you?"

Ruby was thumbing her way through an impossible stack of bills, a risky combination of which threatened to close down her theater. Bills are not the nicest part about returning home to New York after a trip, which is why I was ignoring my own.

"Well, it might have been . . ." She stopped herself. "No! I can always go back to the ad agency."

"I thought you hated that."

"I said I hated the clients. You know what a client is?"

"Tell me again."

"Five guys who share a brain."

"How can you stand it?"

"The money. That part of the business I never hated."

"What would you do at the agency now?"

"Well, Jay called this morning. Jay Schuyler, my old boss. Elegant guy, you'd like him. He's everything you're not."

"What did he want?"

"He wondered if I was available."

"What's that mean?"

"I don't know. He said maybe he'd call me sometime, about being a consultant on some special project."

"Such as what?"

"I don't know. Maybe somebody will discover yet another part of the human body in need of deodorizing."

"This you want?"

"The money I want."

I shrugged.

"Mr. Hockaday, cheer up. I love you."

"What do you love most about me?"

"Like mother, like son. That's you."

"When the purse is empty, the heart is full?"

"Speaking of which, don't you have to be running uptown to see Davy Mogaill in that nasty bar of yours?"

Mogaill was chatting with Terry Two when I arrived at Nugent's. I expected to find him a drunken wreck, but instead he was a man transformed. There he was sipping something clear and bubbly in a glass with a red straw. It appeared to be plain seltzer.

"All part of the new Davy Mogaill," he explained when I asked what he was drinking, confirming my worst suspicion. "I'm now cultivating the cheerful mood. The less I drink the more cheerful I am."

"I'm happy for you," I said. I told Terry Two I would have a red label, and asked Mogaill, "Your new self won't mind?"

"Boozing's your pity now, 'tis no longer mine."

"On the other hand, I'd say leaving the department's a pitiful way for a cop to sober up."

"Say what you will. But I'm feeling I've got the weight of an old dead world off my back. I am clear-brained, for I am no longer the head of homicide in a homicidal town."

"That's nice for you, Captain." I was trying to be enthusiastic. I was not succeeding. "Real nice."

"Here now, you've got no cause for being a bloody dog in the manger. Not you, Neil, blessed as you are in coming back from Eire. There's hope in living to tell the story."

"Sorry. It was a hard trip. Some days it doesn't seem like it's over." I downed my drink and ordered another.

"There's hope, too, in the blessing of new marriage."

339

"Hope is fragile, Davy."

"Aye, heroes know this. It's why they protect hope, and all other fragile things of life."

You've been looking for a hero, now you've found one.

My head went cloudy, and I saw my mother. *Sleeping in the early morning when I'd get up for school at Holy Cross. She'd worked all night, pulling stick . . . I'd go up and say good-bye to her there in her bed, lying on her back with her hair stringing around her head and her closed eyes like they were ready for pennies. I'd kiss her on the cheek. I don't think she ever knew.* And Ruby. I saw my wife, too—lying on a beach with sand white as sugar; and in Ireland, in the green field of a tinker's camp, with flowers in her hair.

These were the hopes of my life. And so I, descended from only one hero among a string of cowardly bastards, would somehow have to become less fragile than hope. I wanted to say all this to Mogaill, but I could not. Booze had made pictures much easier than words.

Davy gave up waiting for me to say something.

"Did you know," he asked, "that I'm decorating a new apartment in the old neighborhood? Right around the corner from Nugent's here, up on Isham Street."

"*Sláinte.*"

"Thank you, Neil. And, speaking of fragile hope, I am also planning a business venture."

"Oh?"

"Sure, sure. Now I got the usual retirement advice: leave New York, go down to Coconuts, Florida, collect the pension. You know."

I groaned.

"My sentiments exactly. But me, I decide I'm staying here. So, I'm in the snoop dodge."

"PI?"

"Already have my license application pending."

I put back my drink, and ordered yet another. Mogaill was now watching me drink the way I have myself watched many other cops drink, him included.

"Look here, I see you're way down low," he said. "What can I say that'd restore the nip to you?"

Davy Mogaill, ever the rabbi. Had he not warned me in this

very bar the day before I left? *Sorry to say, Hock, there'll be no easy sleep under your Irish roof.* Now here was I returned, full of the predicted grief and regret, and drinking in this unattractive way.

"You're a right-born Irishman," I said. "Tell me, how much time did it take you?"

"Time for what, Neil?"

"To get over what it means being Irish."

"And what are you thinking that is?"

"I'm thinking, there's no sense to being Irish unless you know the world is going to break your heart."